SLEEPWALKING BACKWARDS

CATHERINE ZEBROWSKI

TouchPoint
Press

SLEEPWALKING BACKWARDS by Catherine Zebrowski
Published by TouchPoint Press
Jonesboro, AR 72401
www.touchpointpress.com

Copyright © 2017 Catherine Zebrowski
All rights reserved.

ISBN-10: 194692010X
ISBN-13: 978-1946920102

This is a work of fiction. Names, places, characters, and events are fictitious. Any similarities to actual events and persons, living or dead, are purely coincidental. Any trademarks, service marks, product names, or named features are assumed to be the property of their respective owners and are used only for reference. If any of these terms are used, no endorsement is implied. Except for review purposes, the reproduction of this book, in whole or part, electronically or mechanically, constitutes a copyright violation. Address permissions and review inquiries to media@touchpointpress.com.

Editor: Kimberly Coghlan
Top Front Cover Image: NGC7331 Galaxy Cluster, Kevin Boucher
Cover Design: Colbie Myles, colbiemyles.com
Author photo: Kate Del Rossi

Visit the author's website at
www.catherinezebrowskiwriter.wordpress.com

First Edition

Printed in the United States of America.

To my brothers
Fran and Roger

Part I

Prologue

I look to the sky, throw up my arms, catch flakes in my mouth. Eyelashes wet-blink my eyes, and I fall backwards, push myself into a white blanket, angel-flap my arms. Flapping my wings makes more fall from the big hill of snow next to me. I giggle. It tickles my nose. Snow is so much fun; I want it all around me. I fall backwards into the big pile and try to flap my angel-arms, but it's too thick. Snow falls into my mouth. I try to spit it out, but it falls all around, a cold breathless white.

At 7, Amanda brings her tea set out to the picnic table after school and pours tea for her three friends: Johannes Kepler, Sir Isaac Newton, and Albert Einstein. She has read about them in books at the children's library. She tells them about her day, and sometimes they help her with her homework. Her parents think it's cute at first, but then they begin to worry that she's too old to have imaginary friends. She tells them they are not really imaginary because they lived once. Amanda continues the tea parties even as she grows older, just her way of coping, perhaps, which is fine until they become something else, a force pulling her down a path to the unknown and onto the trail of a spirit.

At 5, Amanda wakes in mommy's arms being carried into the house—mommy's still in her nightgown, daddy walks beside them. "It's okay; it's okay, honey," he keeps repeating over and over. Amanda does not know if he is talking to her or her mommy. A sweet, sickening smell from purple flowers in the back yard fills her nostrils. Amanda is frightened by the look on Mommy's face.

Sleepwalking Backwards

In the house, mommy speaks in a calm voice, "What were you doing out there, silly bones?"

"I don't know. Looking at the stars," she says, thinking that that might make her mommy feel better. All she knows is that dreaming makes her feet move.

She's put on the couch and closes her eyes. She is pretending to sleep when she hears her daddy's footsteps leave the room. She smells coffee and then hears her daddy's footsteps come back into the room. Mommy is sobbing.

"Shhh," daddy says. "You'll wake her."

"I saw a shadow in the back yard," mommy whispers. "A shadow of our baby walking toward the pond."

She opens one eye and sees daddy holding mommy close, stroking her hair. Amanda closes both eyes but tries not to sleep. She knows she can't control it if her dreams make her feet move.

After that, her parents get a dead bolt for the door, but sometimes she wakes up and finds herself curled in a ball in front of the locked door.

At not yet one, she senses a voice lost in light then found again in darkness:

Hush little baby; don't say a word.

She leans her head, heavy with awakening out the tower window—beyond, stars spin out filaments of golden light. Threads connect ages, wordless, handed down without touching—unwinding through the millennia. Light filters outward diffusing into space—opening finally into eternity.

Who would not stand by the window and sigh?

Chapter One

March 1999
Kaleidoscope eyes

Turn away from the window, Amanda scolded herself then hefted her backpack onto her shoulders and sat down on the bed. She watched Peter take apart the telescope piece by piece placing each item into a blue plastic carrying case then sighed wishing she could be more like that. *Precise.* He stopped and looked at her.

"You act like you don't want to go back."

She shrugged and put on her glasses.

Her world became focused though still blurry around the edges. Tunnel vision returned. Sometimes it felt like she was seeing objects in bits and pieces like looking through a kaleidoscope. She'd tried so hard all her life to see like others. In college sketching classes, the more she tried to draw things exactly the way they were, the more they skewed out of proportion. The teachers had praised her work calling her a talented, primitive artist. Really? That's not what she was trying to do.

Now she watched Peter, all right angles and proficiency, and she wondered if that was just a mechanism he had for bringing order to the world. She hadn't wanted to be an artist, anyway; she'd wanted to be a scientist.

Someday there might be glasses that would normalize her peripheral vision. She had read somewhere recently that they were doing experiments and finding out that old people with dementia became less agitated when they were given dark glasses to wear.

The view out the window still beaconed. She continued to

scold herself. *Pull yourself away. He's going to think you're weird.*

She studied him differently now since they had come close this weekend to making a decision to spend the rest of their lives together. They had actually said the M word aloud. They'd definitely try living together first—which would definitely freak out her mom, even though she was a hypocrite because her mom and dad had lived up here in a commune in the seventies. Now it was just their summer home, which they never came to anymore. She wasn't even sure if her mom and dad were married when she was born, but now her mom didn't want her to make the same mistakes, didn't want her to be different, even though, once, they had always told her it was a good thing to be different. In the year they'd been together, Peter's inner chaos had only surfaced a few times, and when he was excited, he tended to talk with his hands. It was really cute. Sometimes he got angry, but it wasn't usually with her.

They carried the tube down together securing it in the back of the station wagon between pillows and blankets. She looked at the chalet, then back at Peter.

"Why can't we just stay up here, live *here*?"

"Yeah, right," he said and held her.

She snuggled her nose into his neck and the smell of Axe. He lifted her into the back of the station wagon, took off her glasses, and pushed her hair back into its spikes. Then picked her up and carried her toward the house. Her legs were around his waist, his hands holding up her butt. She felt the warmth of his neck, and her fingers played with the curls behind his ears. When they got to the door, she took one hand from behind his neck and turned the door handle. He kicked it open with his foot.

"Really, we should just move up here. My parents worry that this place is vacant so much of the year."

His hands went into the air. "Seriously? And we would work

where?"

She continued to hold on tight as her grip moved from his neck to his shoulders. She slid down and landed on the floor. Not quite the over the threshold she was expecting.

She shrugged. "I don't know"

"Are you all right? "He helped her up with one hand and pulled her toward the door.

"Let's just go."

"Wait I have to go to the bathroom," she lied. "Be out in a minute."

"Whatever."

She heard the door slam and found her way to a drawer where she kept an old pair of glasses. They weren't her current prescription but were better than nothing for finding her way up the spiral staircase that led to the loft. Again, she stood in front of the window watching a blurry Peter open the door and get into the driver's seat. He could be sullen, which was annoying.

She sighed and pressed her palms against the window. If she could just jump through the window and land on the lawn—no blood, no broken glass, just land on the lawn all in one piece—go back in time to when her mother Gloria lived here and her parents welcomed everyone into their home. It wasn't like wanting to fly; it was like wanting to meld through a membrane of some kind—a membrane no one saw except her. Of course, her three friends had to weigh in on this one.

Kepler said perhaps she could create a vapor that would make the glass malleable enough for the human body to slip through and invent some kind of a chair that would allow her to just float down to the ground.

"*She can't defy the laws of physics,*" Newton said. "*She'll break every bone in her body.*"

Einstein said if she just used her imagination, she could float outside her body at least for a moment. "*Just close your eyes,"* he said, *"and imagine."*

Newton shook his head. *"She can't do anything,"* he said, *"without experimenting, and that would kill her."*

"A thought experiment," Einstein said. *"I know; you don't get it. It was after your time."*

Amanda shook her head to dispel them. That stupid shrink would say she was afraid of commitment, but that wasn't it at all. There was a feeling she got up here actually scarier than the thought of spending her life with another person. If they spent more time up here, maybe Peter would have some understanding of it. Maybe she could explain it or share it somehow. The feeling of spaciousness but also suffocation, like she was being pulled and needed someone to be there, just be there, not even to pull her back, but just to be a witness to whatever she was compelled to remember from her early years before memories were really formed. It was like all her life she'd been unwrapping a gift she wasn't sure she wanted.

"Goodbye," she said aloud to nothing in particular. Then, she pulled her hands from the glass of the window, ran down the stairs, and went out the door. She locked the door with one hand and pressed hard on the wood feeling a push-pull as if it was transparent and her hand could go right through. It only lasted a millisecond, but it gave her a feeling of vertigo. It must be those stupid glasses she was wearing or too much coffee or not enough sleep. She looked over at Peter. He didn't seem to be alarmed. He gave her a look like *what the hell is taking you so long*. When she got into the car, she sighed, feeling the loss as they drove away.

"Don't be sulky," he said.

"Maybe we could scale down," she said. "Live like my parents did."

"It would be boring. That's why they took mind-altering drugs."

Boring for you, she thought.

Late March was a good time in Vermont. The skiers were nearly gone, and the sky was clear. She could remember, even as a child, when they came for the summer, she had wanted to stay here all year round.

Peter took a left turn onto 91 south—2 hours to Massachusetts and another 45 minutes to Holden, Jefferson—really, the tiny section of Holden. She looked out the window. Mist rose from the mountains like vapor after one of those experiments she used to do in high school chemistry class. White at first but with an almost bluish tinge, it rose in a thick, airy dance above the trees diffusing into the atmosphere like a fake magic trick—poof—one of those bombs thrown into a Halloween party before Dracula appears.

Out of the corner of her eye, she noticed something, the shape of a head, a thin finger of vapor curling around the mountains. She shivered and looked more closely; she squinted. Nothing. It was gone. She took off her glasses and inspected them; maybe Peter's leaving them on the car had somehow warped the glass. She held them right in front of her nose. Peter glanced over like she was weird, but she was used to that. She put them back on and looked at him.

"Maybe we could just move up here for the summer," she said.

Now Peter sighed

"Rent free," she grinned, desperately trying to add something Peter would consider practical.

He put his arm around her and pulled her to him. "You make me crazy, skinny girl," he said.

She put her hand on his knee. "You mean that in a good way, right?"

He hesitated for a long minute "Yeah," he said. "In a good way."

She was already starting to stress out thinking about the avalanche of meetings and chores back down at the apartment.

If only she could get Peter to move up here, even just for the summer, maybe he'd understand her daydreaming, her need to stare out windows when she couldn't be out with the telescope.

People were attracted to her because she was different and then seemed troubled that she wasn't like everyone else. Now Peter wanted to live together, maybe marry. She wanted that too, but she didn't want to be swept up and overtaken by someone else's reality. Wasn't hers good enough? She'd had it with overprotection from family. Her parents were actually worried at one point at her lack of rebellion, and when she finally did rebel, it wasn't the right kind. Not the kind her mother wanted.

Was she so different from them? They had once loved being here. She'd heard stories of how they'd lived in the seventies with dozens of people in a commune. Her father told her stories of when it was called The Rainbow House: flower children, transients, counter-culturists hanging onto a movement long after the summer of love.

Amanda had been born here, and she knew she lived up here at least a couple of years. Her mother insists she would have not been able to remember—but she does. Maybe it was just in the tactile nature of babies, but there is always a smell, a voice, something important, something left behind.

She looked at Peter. "Did you know that on the nuclear level nothing is predictable?"

He stroked her hair and rubbed his cheek against the top of her head.

"None of the laws apply. There are no rules."

"Interesting," he said. As if it wasn't.

She snuggled closer to him and closed her eyes, searching her memories of coming up here every summer as a child. Now all she could see of the house in Vermont was the one large room on the bottom and a bedroom loft, but when she had visited as a child, it had seemed the most spacious place in the world. You couldn't see it from the road so she always used to have a great fear that it would not be there as they drove the long path of a driveway overhung with top branches and the green fingers of maple leaves nearly touching like an arbor: the entrance to a new world. The lower leaves would tremble as they whooshed by, her father always driving too fast as she hung out the window grabbing at them.

"Sit down," her mother would yell from the front seat, always anxious at their approach although she was the one who said she wanted to go.

When the chalet came in sight, Amanda would tremble with excitement jumping up and down in the back seat.

"There it is," she yelled every year.

And every year her mother would laugh and say, "Of course. It hasn't gone anywhere."

Her parents always tried to get her to invite someone up to play with, but she wanted this all to herself. She'd run out of the car and stand at the door until her father came with the key and opened the door to the other world.

She remembered how the door seemed so big and had a sweet, burned odor. As soon as it opened, she would run in ahead of her father and make sure everything was still there. She'd look at the long, wooden table where she and her father would spread out wildflowers they found. It was the table where they'd arrange experiments they were doing to the point where there was hardly enough room for the three of them to eat.

She would touch each video game machine along the wall that her father had bought in the early eighties, look up at the high, cathedral ceiling, post, and beam. Then she'd run upstairs breathing in the smell of wood, emptiness, and nothing.

Her mother would come in complaining it was stuffy and close. It was always late July or August because they would go to Stellafane, a gathering of amateur astronomers, and see the telescopes while they were there.

"Don't run," her mother would say, but she would already have come to a dead stop in front of the large picture window making sure the mountains were still there. And she would stare out at them, relieved. Driving up the long path had been like being in a rocket, and she was afraid and exhilarated by the thought that there was no land around this house, only sky.

"Don't touch anything until we clean," her mother would yell, and something in her mother's voice at those times would make Amanda think that the house was special like a church or a shrine.

All this might have happened only once, but she remembers it as having happened every year.

The video games were not there anymore, or the long table. Why hadn't her parents rented it out? They never went up anymore. She used to worry they would sell it. It was one of the things she tried to tell them when she started having what they called 'her episodes' in high school. She had heard them talking once about selling it but didn't tell them about how troubling it was to her. The stupid shrink they had sent her to told them not to take her up there anymore when that was all she wanted—to be up there in the summer like when she was a little girl. Then they decided the problem was that she was bored with high school, so they had her apply to college early, and her mother, who had seemed so anxious to sell it at first, seemed relieved when they'd decided against it.

They were in Massachusetts heading down I-90 from route 2. It had snowed here over the weekend and they slid a little as Peter got off the Sterling Exit and picked up 122 into Holden. He stopped the car in front of her apartment, and she wondered where they would live. She kind of assumed he would want them to live at his place because it was larger and closer to the University since he always complained about her living so far out and how this road was the last one to get plowed in the winter. She would miss it here, though. There was less lighting and a hill nearby for observing. He helped her carry the scope up the narrow stairs and put it in a corner of her tiny living room.

Peter was over by the CD player looking through her collection. She sat on the couch and closed her eyes anticipating what he would choose. Techno, good. Low volume, good. Sometimes she liked to kind of lean into the sounds in order to hear them. She startled as he touched her shoulder but did not open her eyes when he pulled her down.

They lay on the couch kissing.

"Stay here," she said. "Don't leave me."

He outlined her chin, her bottom lip with his finger. "I won't have any clean clothes in the morning."

She sighed. "This sucks"

"Why don't you stay at my place?"

"I don't want to lug all my stuff over there. I have to give midterms tomorrow. I wish you would stay."

"I wish you would come over."

"I wish you would stay."

"I wish you would come over."

"Stay"

"Come over"

"Stay"

"Come over"

They pulled each other in different directions until she finally moved with him toward the door. "This doesn't mean I'm coming over."

They kissed at the door. He smoothed down her spiky hair.

"I love you," she said

"I love you, too. We won't have to put up with this bullshit much longer when you move in with me."

There it was said. She'd be the one moving. She went to the

window and watched him get into his car, put on the lights, and drive away. When he was gone, she walked around the tiny apartment, touching the walls, gazing out the windows. She hadn't realized what an attachment she had to these few rooms. She touched the walls and furniture like she was expecting something from them, like maybe they would touch her back. They were all hers. Her first apartment since she moved out of her parents' house three years ago. Her mother had hovered over her at first like she was going to have some kind of breakdown being on her own, but she had done it. When she knew he would be home, she called him just to say goodnight. And then, instead of organizing midterms, she walked to the hill with only her binoculars and lost her thoughts in a sky full of stars. She stayed out much later than she should have to face her students in the morning.

Chapter Two

June 1978
Gloria

"At least she sleeps." That's what she hears them saying all the time. When Thomas takes her hand and leads her to the bedroom in the loft, at least she sleeps. They don't understand how sleep disturbs her. The dreams of snowstorms, whiteouts, mounds of snow, tunnels dug through the mounds, falling away behind her, quickly disappearing covered in more mounds of white. Cascading flakes whirl at her like a hurricane funnel, making it hard for her to see, pulling her into a vortex. Her dreams disturb her. She wishes they'd give her something so she wouldn't sleep.

They won't give her pills. Her sister insists on vitamin supplements, E, D, C, such large doses Gloria feels like she's downing some kind of horse tranquilizers. Just give me a one-a-day, would you? she'd say, if her lips would do what her mouth wants them to. Her sister is still here. Her sister is her doctor giving her handfuls of pills each morning, but she calls them vitamins. She heard her sister yelling at her mother just the other day. "She doesn't need drugs. She's taken too many drugs; that is the problem. We need to get her system back in balance." Her sister seems to be in charge of pills and diet.

She brings Gloria her meals. The vegetables are always fresh. Gloria helps her sister make humus in the blender and likes how it makes the kitchen smell like lemon. She actually helps her sister. It's fuzzy, but she remembers helping her sister recently. She knows her legs and her hands were moving; her sister was giving directions. "I'll put the chickpeas in; you add the lemon juice." Suzanne talks down to her as if she were a little child, and Gloria is just starting to feel some resentment when she hears her sister's voice, but mostly she's relieved that someone is telling her what to do.

Her sister makes her stay busy. She has heard her sister tell Thomas it's better for her to move around, do something useful, not sit on this bench all day. But Gloria likes her time on the bench and seeks it out each time no one is paying attention to her for a few minutes.

Gloria still does not know why she needs to be taken care of, but they all seem to think she needs help, so she's going along with it. It has something to do with her dreams of snow, and she wishes she could remember. When she sits on the bench, flashes of her past start to create tunnels through her mind, loops of memory she hopes will lead her out of the fog. That's why she likes it here. She leans back, looks up at the sky, and remembers.

This is where they came, she and Thomas, one summer a long time ago just to get away. She's starting to remember, but not the present. Why are they up here? She, Thomas, and their baby Amanda live here. She looks down at her stomach, rubs it. Her baby. Why is her sister up here and her parents staying at a hotel or something? She adjusts herself on the bench, tries to concentrate and wrap her mind around what's going on. She remembers meeting Thomas, then remembers her first day of college in the fall of 1970 when going off to college was like going off to war. She remembers those days so clearly now like the shock when Kennedy was shot. Four students being shot dead at Kent State in the spring changed everything that year. Optimism and enthusiasm shifted to apprehension and fear as students headed to college that fall. At least that's how Gloria remembers it, and she was still living at home, had not even gone away to college.

She had been somewhat relieved that her parents had insisted on a school nearby even though they could afford Ivy

League. Her grades weren't that good, not like her sister who'd gone off to Brown three years earlier. She'd watched their faces as they watched the news every night—at first thinking they had escaped any personal tragedy because they didn't have sons. Now violence had come home to the colleges. She can't remember the last several months, but other incidents, from years ago, are coming to the surface clearly, if memory can really be trusted. She remembered reading somewhere that lack of short-term memory and clarity of long-term memory were symptoms of dementia. She was only in her twenties; what was wrong with her?

She calms herself down by breathing deeply, letting herself float into the memory of her college days. The first day of class rushing up the stairs because she wasn't sure of the room number, peeking in to the one she thought it was and then just walking in and sitting down. Everyone else seemed so confident; she could at least pretend to know what she was doing. It wasn't like high school—there were no bells. Thank god, there were no bells.

A woman came in with a pile of books and started handing them out only to the women. Granny glasses, hair down to her butt.

"What'll this cost me?" she asked, like her father, never trusting what was given out for free.

"Pay what you can if you have money."

She only had enough money for lunch and was flustered then. She tried to give it back, but the women wouldn't take it, acted almost angry. She hated these pushy military types—like her sister was turning into. They made her uncomfortable, but she smiled and accepted it just to be polite. She hadn't expected this at Worcester State. Berkeley, maybe, but not here. That was before she met Thomas; she changed after that.

She laughs inside now at how confused and anxious it had made her feel as that woman, all business-like, quickly went on to another student. How she hid the book from her parents because if they ever found it, they'd kill her. It had information about birth control and abortion. She'd eyed the woman suspiciously. It wasn't that Gloria hadn't wanted peace, but she'd stopped trusting the jargon after Kent State. So many people who wanted peace were getting too angry—and pushy. She waited until the woman left and looked down at the book—*Our Bodies Our Selves*.

Gloria didn't hear much of what the teacher said that day because the woman with the book had distracted her as had the book itself. She kept staring at it stuffed into a wire cage beneath her chair. Even back then, she wanted to believe that the world could change, but there was something deep in her gut about too much peace and sharing, some knowledge about how faith and love could turn cruel for no good reason. No reason at all. She should have listened to that feeling more back then, held on to her practical mistrust of the world. Instead, she had led the rest of her life leaning on some vague hope, and she is left now with this emptiness. Maybe if she knew why the snow dreams disturbed her so much she would be able to regain her speech and recent memory. She crosses her hands and waits for the day when she can speak, as well as, hear. So she can tell them to give her something so she won't sleep.

She hears voices through the window arguing. Her parents want to take her somewhere, to a hospital, an institution, maybe to a doctor they know back down in Boston. She jumps when her sister yells at them.

"You can't. They'll only load her up with drugs; those places *make* you psycho."

Her dad's voice comes back angry. "You think it's easy for me to set this all up. I'm sick of your bullshit screwball ideas. I won't let her drift anymore. Not see her lapse into a state of god knows what. We need to get her away from here."

"It takes time," her sister says, very slowly. "It just takes time," her sister says so slowly and calmly that Gloria feels better just hearing the words.

If Suzanne would only stop, Gloria thinks, *now that she's made her point*. But she doesn't stop; she keeps needling their father.

"It not your decision, anyway. It's Thomas' decision to make"

"I'm her father." He yells again and jolts Gloria out of her few minutes of calmness. She doesn't really want to go away. She hopes Suzanne will win the argument. She wishes she wasn't such a burden though she knows Suzanne and her father always argue.

"He's her husband," Suzanne says.

Then Gloria loses track of the voices because Thomas brings out their baby. All new and freshly washed, Gloria smells baby powder as she clutches her child to her. A few sobs break from inside as she snuggles her nose into the baby pink neck, and tears drip down. Thomas looks at her and seems to understand that these tears mean she is happy. She feels her facial muscles move upward. Thomas notices and smiles back. He takes their baby from her arms but does not take her away.

"Watch," he says. "She's trying to walk."

He settles Amanda up against the side of the bench and lets go. She stands up by herself holding onto it. Thomas sits a foot away. He holds out his hands to her, and she takes both hands off the bench, takes a step with her round little foot, falls to the ground, and laughs. She crawls to Thomas.

"Any day now," he says.

Gloria is beginning to notice things again. The baby's chubby legs, the way she scrunches up her fingers as if that would help her balance. It feels strange but good to notice again though over stimulating because she's been in a state of only sound for so long. She closes her eyes as the visual is getting too much. Thomas takes this as a sign that it is time to take the baby away, but that is not what she wants at all. She tries to tell him, but she cannot think of words. She thinks it might be a stroke, a physical illness. As he leaves, she feels emptiness filling in around her. Thomas carries Amanda back into the house; they turn at the last minute waving and smiling. They could be miles away, across a great river.

They are gone along with the voices from the window.

Chapter Three

1999
Lenses

Amanda held a cup of coffee with one hand and tried to scrape the windshield with the other. Then she jumped away when it spilled onto the front of the car. *Dammit*. At least she hadn't spilled any on her parka. She was in too much of a hurry. Maybe there was some advantage in living closer to work.

She stopped at Dunkin Donuts for more coffee; maybe it would jumpstart her brain. Her eyes ached as she drove through the college entrance, past the administrative offices, and navigated the car through loops of new buildings. Peter shouldn't be in yet because his classes didn't start until late morning, but he might come in early to socialize; he was so much better at that than her. Good. He could do the socializing for both of them. She passed several more buildings and pulled onto a narrow dirt drive that led to the oldest building on campus.

The parking lot had been plowed again, and dirt had been scraped up with the mounds of snow. She wondered if this was the same dirt that was around when Plato was walking along, rubbing his chin, and wrapping his mind around the puzzles of shadow and cave. Could that dust have blown to this part of the world?

The dark brick and massive pillars created a comfort zone for her with stone steps and windows so old some had the panes of glass that created ripples, a wobbly world from the inside out. It was always cold in these buildings except for July and August when the buzz of fans pushed stale air around. This is where she felt like herself, surrounded by anything that had been on the planet for a long time. Air so cold and close it might have been something handed down from another century—before air conditioning or central heating. It took her breath away. If her mother or Peter were around, they would hand her an inhaler.

She parked the car on frozen crab grass and stepped out gingerly taking another gulp of coffee. There were no other cars. Good. She would be alone to organize papers and stare through the distorted glass of windowpane. She bound up the stairs dropping papers from the briefcase she'd forgotten to close and, as she stooped to pick them up, the last of her coffee spilled. *Damn. Slow down*, she scolded herself and, taking her own advice, sat down to rest on the top step.

Hmm... She might like to teach a course just on the history of glass: Glass 101. That would be something she could really get into. How the very distortions allowed seeing in a different way. She made up an outline in her head:

Origins: sand, silica, tektites

Unique (weird) chemical make-up, considered a solid because of its amorphous structure but with the spatially disordered molecules of a liquid.

Course content: the makeup, grinding, and history of its uses

Theme of course: power of magnification.

She would give an assignment comparing naked eye viewing to looking through binoculars then telescopes. She imagined herself lecturing to wide-eyed enthralled students. After the very beginning, she would go on with the history:

The first men who discovered the powers of magnification were denied patents because the Dutch and the Spanish worried about the power it would give their enemies at sea. A spyglass capable of gazing so far was dangerous, but they could not stop the ideas by refusing to grant a patent.

The power of dirt, sand, glass—another course the administration would not consider useful much less the students.

She got up and fumbled with her keys then walked past the classroom to the creaky stairs that led up to her office. It was only on the second floor, but it seemed liked it was up in the clouds especially with the glass in that one section of the window with rippled distortions that made a leafless oak look like a cubist painting. She was always compelled to press her palm against it just as an experiment, to see if her hand would reach right through. She approached slowly and touched it now—nothing. Cold, hard, unmoving. Yet, well, maybe a pull, the pressure on her fingertips reaching beyond the solid to the more liquid molecules—hmm.

More cars pulled onto the crab grass. The students didn't look happy. Besides the exam today, they had to put up with the old building. She seemed to be the only one that liked it here: the only one willing to put up with the lack of heat and the distracting whistling and hissing when heat finally made it through. Over the winter, there were a few days when you could see your breath in the room.

While there was still a little time left, she pulled out her childhood tea set from a box behind her desk and poured tea (now coffee for her) for her three imaginary friends. There were only a few minutes for a chat. She had to get her complaints out right away.

The cold is okay if you dress for it. They nodded. *The clearest nights often occur in the middle of the winter after a day of gentle snowfall.* They agreed. *It keeps you awake; I've told them all semester, but they just roll their eyes and make no effort to even look like they're enjoying the course.* They shook their heads and tutt-tutted. *Of course, she said, this is a first semester required math and they just want to get it over with.* Very few students were interested in this class, but neither was she. Three nods again.

I get good evaluations so I must be a good teacher: fair to the students, approachable. However, she *was* getting a reputation for being a hard ass already, which was probably good. *Math is full of facts not full of opinions like literary criticism.* They all nodded, and one of them smirked. Students soon learned they couldn't bullshit their way through a math class. *I try to make it more interesting for myself, as well as the students, by throwing out some facts about you guys, but those lectures are not really relevant to what I am supposed to teach.*

Her friends had disappeared. She put the tea cups away, picked up the papers, and walked down the stairs. Most of the students were already in the classroom looking anxious and uncomfortable. This was not their only mid-term and not likely the one they had given the most prep time. The radiator was already spitting out warmth, which would be a comfort to some and a distraction for others. She silently handed out midterms.

The students looked so grim she wished she could offer them more—hot chocolate, a hot toddy, a beer. A real teacher would take them out on a winter night and show them what a few numbers and calculations could lead to—observing the moons of Jupiter, the rings of Saturn. It was either Aristotle or Socrates who said that a teacher only helps a student realize what they already know. All these students wanted her to do was dole out the information that they would regurgitate back to her enough to pass the test. They took in what they needed and sometimes not even that. No one came to her for extra help. She sat at a small desk in front of the class, a large chalkboard behind her, thinking how she never got past grammar school as she watched the students with heads bent down in concentration. Perfect attendance because of the exam, some never showed up at any other time.

Am I alone? Did she say that aloud? She looked around

alarmed, but no one had heard, no one had raised their head. She was beginning to feel alone quite often when there were people around. Like when she was a child and used to pretend she was a magician who could will the air to circulate around her, insulate herself from the harm her mother seemed to think lurked everywhere.

She got up and walked down the bank of windows touching the cold glass as she passed to bring back the present. When she stood at the back of the room, the concentration of the students was a low drone. A few sighs broke, knuckles cracked, pencils tapped the desk, scratched paper. She gazed out the back window where there were no screens. She'd like to take her students away from this dreary test. A field trip up to her office where they could gaze through the rippling windowpane, show them the impossibility of clear vision.

She heard stirring and turned around. They were leaving, a few nodded to her as they placed exams face down on the corner of her desk. Alone, finally, she stared out the window, put both hands on it, breathed onto the glass. Her world felt small and immediate; *without effort, one world moves into another*. A quote of wisdom from one of the yogi mystic books her mother had insisted that she read. It was either that or her mother would read it aloud to her. Breathing in, breathing out, her breath a vapor, a fog of condensation on the window, she pressed harder and breathed longer pushing to break a barrier; then she jumped when a face appeared. She looked away and blinked her eyes.

It was only Peter, and he laughed at her. Breathing close into the glass on the outside, he wrote something. OUY EVOL I; she read before it disappeared into a hint of letters, and she jumped when she heard his voice even though she knew he was coming.

"I brought lunch," he said, opening a small cooler pulling out a bottle of wine.

"I don't think so. This is a dry campus. You want to get us both fired?"

"This place is hardly even considered campus anymore."

"Well it's barely eleven, and a glass of wine would just put me to sleep." She snatched the pile of papers from the desk, and Peter followed her up to the office.

"There are sandwiches in here, too," he said.

"I'm really not hungry. I have another midterm to give in 30 minutes."

"30 minutes, hmm." He took her hand and brought her to the couch by the window.

She looked up into the endlessness of space. They made love on the couch beneath the distorted window. He breathed the present into her as she still reached for the past. They'd never done it between classes before. Isn't that something students were supposed to do?

When she had to go, she told him just go to the faculty lounge and she would meet him there when she was done. Instead, he stayed up there pouting waiting for her to give the second midterm; the students at this time of day finished more quickly, hungry for lunch, hardly able to concentrate. This semester, she was the only teacher holding classes in this building. The geology teacher was on sabbatical. Only the art teachers brought their students here on some afternoons, to set up easels and catch the light as it filtered through the old windows.

"How can you stand it here?" She knew he would start as soon as she opened the door. "NO computers, no heat." In the fall, he had thought it was kind of cute and mysterious that she hid over here all the time.

"I have my laptop."

"But you don't have the internet. You don't even have E-mail."

"I only need it for word processing. I can put my grades in

office and dump them in another computer with a stick." Peter shook his head. Why would she need E-Mail when he told her everything that was going on?

She took her coat from an old rack in the corner; Peter just sat. She looked at him. "I thought you wanted to go to the lounge?"

He opened the cooler and took out the wine and sandwiches. She had one glass of wine and a chicken salad sandwich with chips and homemade potato salad.

"This is heavenly," she said.

He smiled at her

"It's a good thing one of us can cook"

It wasn't that she couldn't cook, she wanted to say, she just never thought about it, or really about eating either until someone else brought it up. He reached over the side of the couch and brought up a thermos full of strong, hot coffee.

"Ohh, heaven," she said, and kissed him on the lips.

That evening they were supposed to stay at her apartment, but as soon as they were in the door, he tried to convince her to stay at his. He had papers to correct; it would be so much easier, so much more convenient for them to stay in Worcester.

"I want to observe tonight." She pulled a sad face.

"You can do that at my house"

"I want to go to the hill. It looks like it's going to be clear. You said you'd be busy with work tonight anyway."

"Not all night."

"Why don't we have dinner here; I'll go to the hill for a while and drive over later?"

"You Made dinner?"

"Frozen pizza."

"Oh."

After pizza, beer, and coffee he left; she put on her parka and walked to the hill wondering how late was too late to show up at his place.

She searched for planets and messier objects feeling exhilarated and yet lonely. Before she met Peter, she could go out and totally lose herself in these searches; now his absence was a presence. As if she was guilty of something. She had been as surprised as anyone when he started asking her out last spring. He was so sociable, and she hardly knew anyone. He was almost thirty and head of the English Department. She was the youngest teacher they'd ever hired since she'd been pushed up two years in high school and had her masters by the time she was twenty-one. They called her the campus monk because she stayed to herself in the old building. Her mother liked him, probably because he was older and grounded, way different from the other men she'd dated.

All her life, people tried to help her adapt, come out of her shell, but no one could understand how she craved solitude. Alone like this, with the sky, she teetered on some fine line, some indefinite point between past and present. A portal, maybe a point of departure, beyond which discoveries might be made. That little, lonely place inside, she could never quite balance was the place from which she could be an observer, as though all through life she was missing something she was right on the verge of, just beyond her sight. Would she lose it if she married Peter? She had her own grounding here as she gazed at the stars, her feet held by gravity to the green and blue planet.

Later she let herself quietly into Peter's apartment. . He was not sleeping but sitting in the darkness gazing into a green computer terminal playing one of those online games. She didn't mean to sneak up on him, but he jumped.

"I didn't think you were coming." In the darkness, she could hear his relief even through the accusatory tone. They went to bed and slept all night dreaming and breathing in each other's thoughts.

The next morning, they gazed over each other across a table

of cereal bowls, blueberries, strawberries, and milk. The healthiest breakfast she'd eaten in a long time. Her mother must have been talking to him. Peter said he had something special to tell her. Maybe it was a ring. How odd to be proposed to at breakfast in a bathrobe.

"Here's the thing," he said. "The University is sending me to teach at Cal Tech for 3 weeks in August."

"That's wonderful," she said, not sure if it was or not.

"I want you to come with me."

She stared at him blankly; in her mind, she began to recite the name of stars to calm herself—*Electra-the lost one, Insidia-the lurking one*. She couldn't leave, not in August—*Morope-mortal, wrapped in a nebulous haze*—Stellafane was in August, one of the best Astronomy gatherings. They had told her she could teach a class this summer, about Kepler, about his sci-fi story where he sends demons to the moon while the boy, Duracotus, watches with his witch mother. Of course, probably no one would sign up for it unless she really did get word out to the nerds on campus. She squinted; she couldn't see well without her glasses. Sometimes, to buy time, she pretended she couldn't see at all.

"I want to; I really do, but I'm teaching a class this summer, remember?"

"You can get out of that."

"I made a commitment."

He stared at her, wielded his breakfast spoon. "You never stick up for yourself. They pay you practically nothing and put you in that building where it's 105 degrees all summer."

I like it there, she wanted to say but didn't. "I wish I could go."

"You could if you really wanted to. You're not going to get five students to sign up for that stupid course anyway. They'll just end up cancelling it."

He left the table, and she could hear him getting dressed in the other room. She fought the urge to go after him and tell him yes. *Yes, of course, I'll go with you. I'll give up all my plans for the summer just to make you happy.* Instead, she went into the guest room and sat cross-legged on the bed.

Most of her summer clothes were still in the closet here from last year. Although she stayed with Peter in the master bedroom, she still considered this room to be hers. She tried to clear her mind, concentrate on breathing. She let out a long sigh and began to daydream. This happened every time she tried to meditate. Her mind would almost clear and then she would start to see images. Her mother would say she was doing it all wrong, but she could not stop the visions that took over her mind every time she tried to empty it. She pushed her three advice-giving friends aside. Maybe she was finally outgrowing that ritual.

Her mind wandered onto a road that turned to mud, and walking became very difficult. Her feet began to fall into quick sand, but she did not feel anxious or afraid that she would be pulled in. The soil was rich.

She came to a pool that was very still. It was evening and dark, but the pool glowed—*deep waters run still*—this phase kept running through her head. There were thin, high trees all around the pool, and stars reflected in its water. She dove in at first refreshed swimming calmly but then frightened that she was being pulled down and she would drown.

She shook her head and took another deep breath.

Now she stood on the hill looking through the telescope at the globular cluster M13, sparkling. She tried to look away, but her eye became a force that would not let her move. The more she struggled to break away, the more she was pulled, elongated, sucked in through the telescope into the cluster itself. She passed through a vortex of color, but inside, at the center, it was dark. She could not breathe; there was someone with her, standing beside her. Her heart pounded, her hands shook, and she felt like she was going to pass out. She opened her eyes, staring again at her summer clothes.

If she didn't go, they would be apart for almost a month. *If I wake in the night*, she thought, *who would hold me*? She would miss his night breathing. That was the problem with getting attached. She wanted to be with him, but she wanted to be able to be without him. It would be a test. It would make them see if they could live without each other.

She looked up because she thought she saw something at the window. A braid with a ribbon tied at the end? One of the neighbor kids? How long had she been watched? She hurried over to the window and looked out—nothing.

Chapter Four

1978

The sun is warm today, and Gloria looks at the bench she sits on, studying the mixture of metal and wood that seems to be the only surface capable of giving her comfort these days—like a child with a favorite toy. She rests her arm on its curving wrought iron arm, feels the steadiness of the heavy wooden seat, and intertwines her fingers into the latticework. It's the work of art she always wanted to walk into the middle of, functional and beautiful. She looks around trying to gauge the time. It must be late morning or early afternoon and she's been waiting and waiting for Thomas and Amanda to come

This is the same bench she sat on the first time she came up here with Thomas, and she remembers another bench, at the Cape, where she sat with Thomas when they had just begun to fall in love. She closes her eyes and pretends to be at the Cape, tries to pretend she can smell the ocean. It was the summer after her freshman year at Worcester State and she remembers how pissed she was when her parents told her she had to go with them to their cottage in Falmouth. She wouldn't have minded going down for a week or two, but they wanted her there for six weeks with her mother and sister and her father coming down on weekends.

She and her friends had been going to clubs every weekend. Every Saturday they saw bands at the Comic Strip, and all summer they had plans to go to the dances at SAC Park. It would be unbelievably boring to spend all summer at the Cape with her parents and her dorky sister. She'd begged them to let her stay at the house at least every other week, but her parent's wouldn't compromise. She thought they didn't trust her, wanted to get her away from her friends, and there was this boy she liked; she knew would be going to SAC all summer. She'd been waiting forever for him to ask her out and they'd finally been holding hands and making out in his car, and now her parents wanted to ruin her life! And that is what they did. Like all caring parents, they pulled her away from her summer of fun in Worcester and might as well have thrown her headfirst from the caboose of a rickety train.

That summer on a morning of ragged wind and scraggly seaweed, she sat on a rock writing a poem and spotted Thomas sleeping on the beach, unshaven, as if he had just been washed ashore. She kicked off her sandals as she walked over to take a closer look and cut her foot on a shell. Her small cry woke him, and he looked at her, blinked his eyes, got up, and came to her.

"Are you alright?"

She liked his voice. That was the first thing she'd liked about Thomas. She'd seen him before at school going into the coffeehouse.

She winced when he touched her foot although his hand felt very sexy and warm on her ankle. Then he picked her up and carried her over to the flat stone ledge where he could have a better look. He washed the cut with seaweed. The salt water stung.

"Sorry." His voice startled her again, her attraction to it, like his warm hand on her ankle. "Feel better now?"

"Yea, thanks," she said, looking at the ground

He yawned and stretched out on the beach. "I'm so hungry. Do you have anything to eat?"

"The stands open," she said and got on her feet, but the best she could do was hobble. He offered his hand and she leaned on his shoulder.

"I don't have any money, do you?"

Boys are supposed to pay, she thought, but since he'd

helped her with her foot, she decided she could get him something. First, they went to pick up her sandals, her notebook, and pen; then they headed for the concession stand.

"What are you writing?"

"A poem"

"Can I see it?"

"No!" Even then, she had been stingy with her thoughts, wary of being taken for a fool.

She put the small notebook in the back pocket of her culottes and hobbled over to the concession stand. They only had snacks, chips, candy, and soda. Thomas took some chips and gobbled them down like he hadn't eaten in days. Which she found out he hadn't. They sat on a bench by the concession stand, not as nice as the one she sat on now.

"Where are you staying?"

He shrugged

"In your car?" She knew some of the boys came down and slept in cars but usually they came in groups to party.

"If I had one," he said

"How'd you get here?"

He stuck out his thumb and smiled at her over the top of thick glasses. They both laughed even though what he said wasn't really funny. He stretched his hand over the bench behind where she sat. She wanted to lean into his shoulder but instead, hunched forward and drew letters with her toe in the sand. She could feel him staring at her, but she didn't look up.

"How's your foot?"

"Better," she said and smiled. "Thanks for rescuing me."

"Thanks for feeding me," he said, grinning back.

"I've seen you around school."

"Yeah."

Did she move closer or did he or did she only imagine the movement? She can't remember, but she remembers the weight of his hand on her shoulder that first day on the beach.

Then he was touching her hair; then they were kissing. She remembers his warm mouth and the smell of salt water. If she can remember this, why can't she remember the past few years, the birth of her daughter, missing all those hours, minutes? If she really had amnesia, she would not remember that Thomas was her husband, that Suzanne was her sister. There is something recent her mind won't let her remember.

She has not spoken for days, maybe weeks, maybe months. She can't remember how to speak, but she can remember falling in love with Thomas. She clings to that, that day at the Cape. If she follows it along, it may pull her into the present. She took him back to her parent's house; he had nowhere to stay.

"This is my friend from school," she said. "He was down the beach."

Her father had looked up from his paper, suspicious right away. She knew that look, and she had already grown to resent and ignore it at the same time. All the trouble they'd gone through getting her away from the SAC boys now she was bringing home some bum from the beach. That's what she had heard him say later.

"I cut my foot on a shell; he helped me."

Her father grunted and went back to reading his paper. She led Thomas into the kitchen.

"There's real food here," she said opening the fridge pulling out mayonnaise, cheese, slabs of ham and bologna. She laid them all out on the counter, and Thomas came up behind her.

"Rest your foot. I'll make lunch," he whispered into the back of her ear.

She did as he said. Put her foot up and watched him make lunch, watched Thomas, even that first day, taking care of her. She had studied him. The way his hair curled around his ears; the determined set of his jaw visible even beneath his two-day growth of beard. She remembers it so well. The smell of the ocean from the open windows, a breeze blowing around the light summer curtains, the stillness in the house and the click of the knife against the mayonnaise jar.

Suzanne has come out and sits beside her on the bench. She smells of cocoa butter sunscreen and strawberry shampoo. It makes Gloria want to gag. Suzanne has lived in California too long and now has to have everything on her skin all the time. Why is it the baby oil they used to put on their skin to sunbathe not good enough for her now and the Halo for her hair, the blue shampoo that Gloria still uses? She tries to listen. Her sister appears to be lecturing her again—blah, blah, blah—but then she says something that makes Gloria sit up straighter, something that makes her feel guilty.

"Your baby is learning to talk. Children need to hear words in order to learn speech. Amanda needs to hear you talking."

Gloria bites her lower lip feeling like a stubborn, contrite child. Suzanne's voice drones on like a sound recording of some expert psychologist, which she is, or some expert witness. Yes, Gloria's motherhood is on trial. But since she sits on the bench, shouldn't she be the judge? Her sister is mixed up and stupid; she's never had a baby, but still the voice comes to her through the fog, needling her, condemning.

"Conversation helps children learn. Your baby needs to hear her mother's voice; she needs to hear it often!"

Why is Suzanne shouting at her, accusing her of being a bad mother? What does she know? *I can't help it,* she wants to shout. My lips, tongue, and teeth don't know which way to go to form sounds, and my throat is so dry it chokes down the sound.

On the other hand, she's glad she can't say anything; she's so furious she wants to hit her sister, kick her, and accuse her of something. You never had a child; how would you know—how would you know what it's like? Is this what her sister wanted, to get her angry? How cruel when she knows Gloria cannot do anything with that anger. Her sister, still sitting, looms over her. Gloria wants to eradicate her, go back into the gray fog she's been living in, but she can't. She can hear again, smell again, see again, really see, as in notice, and there's no going back, but she can hold back speech. She tells herself she just can't figure out how to manipulate her tongue, lips, and teeth, but there's a stubborn part of her that doesn't want to remember.

"Give me a chance." She wants to tell her sister. "Give me time. What's wrong with you all?"

The last few nights she had not slept. At first, she savored the numbness that came from not sleeping, but now she feels everything too acutely. If she could speak, she would, just to get them off her back. She wants them to leave her alone. She knows if they hear one word, they will want it all. They're all so greedy for words. How do you feel? She won't have her head messed with. Her only power is in keeping silent or is it in not letting herself remember?

She lifts her arm, heavy as it is, determined to strike her sister, hard, but only punches her shoulder, a light punch on the arm like they used to give each other when they sat too close at church. Her sister then punches her back, pleased that Gloria has touched her, as if it were something done in comradeship. Will anybody ever understand her again?

Her sister gets up and leaves, pleased as though there had been some kind of breakthrough. Maybe there was. Gloria sits alone again, remembering how it was when her sister had decided to rebel, take their parents attention from her, making it easier for she and Thomas that summer.

Her dorky sister had dropped the bomb on her parents that summer , the perfect one who her father thought would have a great future as a corporate leader, announced she was dropping out of Brown and going to some new age alternative school in California. Their father refused to hear of it, forbade her to go, even crumbled the acceptance letter, his face red with shock and indignation. He had gone to Brown; he got her in there. He would not let her go off to some idiotic fanatical hippie-driven off the wall so-called school and waste his money and her talent. Gloria remembers how their father looked, incredulous and full of disappointment, but Suzanne had had it all worked out. She had received a full scholarship based on her 4.0 at Brown with an assurance that she would be accepted to grad school.

After the first battle, her father didn't talk about it anymore. He simply refused to believe it would really happen and buried himself back in the paper. Later, as he napped on the couch, Suzanne had placed a flower just above his ear.

Chapter Five

<small>VOICES NEAR</small>

"Amanda"
A voice pulled her up through layers of sleep.
"Amanda?"
Her mother's voice trying to reach her through a dream—wait, now she heard the pings and beeps of machines. Why was she waking in her parent's house? She and Peter had moved in together three weeks ago. She turned over, pushed the blanket off, tried to sit up, but just rolled over and put the covers over her head.
"Amanda!"
"What?" She sat up and rubbed her eyes. Why was in she in the basement of the "Fun room" as her mother had designated it many years ago? As a little girl, she had thought it was all one word like bathroom. Now it just freaked her out like the fun house at a carnival full of mirrors that warped your sized and reflected you back like dominoes into infinity. The only fun part was the video games that had been moved down from Vermont. When she was a child, she had sat on the steps and eavesdropped on the adult conversations at her parents' parties when they thought she was in bed. Sometimes she would actually have a friend over, and they would sit on the bar stools while her father would blend them chocolate and strawberry milkshakes. If it weren't for the fun room, she would probably have had no friends at all.

She sat up and felt around for her glasses on the coffee table. *Oh god, is it morning?* Peter would be frantic. She stayed up so late on the hill last night by the apartment that was no longer hers that she was been too tired to drive back to Peter's—well, her and Peter's home. He'd lecture her about how she needed to be more considerate; she was living with someone else now.

"Amanda."

She continued to ignore her mother's calls and looked around at the video games. She'd turned them all on last night and had been playing them with all the lights out. That's why she had stopped here, some compulsion to play these games. Her mother came down with a tray of fruit and cheese, put it down on the counter, and turned off all the machines.

"Peter was on the phone. I was trying to wake you. At least he knows you're safe."

"What time is it? " Amanda asked. "I thought I called him last night. I meant to."

She watched her mother unplug each machine as if these inanimate objects were the cause of her lapse in judgment. It was her father who loved these games. She was probably so good in math because in utero she had heard the bleeps and starts of video games more than the sound of the human voice. Even if it was only television pong back then. As a toddler, her father would lift her up to watch the green and black screen as Q-Bert missed his cubed block and went rolling down into a free fall: splat, annoying music, zero gravity.

Her mother gave her a look. Amanda brushed her hand over her spiked hair. It was easier in the summer when she didn't have to smooth down her hair and cover her tattoo with loose fitting blouses and vests or willowy skirts with navy blue blazers. She didn't have to look the conservative math teacher now. Her hair, dyed an orangey color, was smoothed down on the side she had slept on and spikier than ever on top. She wore baggy jeans and a flannel shirt of the night before. She had several earrings in one ear and a tattoo of the Pleiades on her upper arm. Everyone said she was too skinny. It wasn't on purpose. When she got involved in something, she just didn't remember to eat. She moved from the couch to a bar stool in front of the breakfast plate. Her mother went behind the bar and offered her kiwi-pineapple juice.

"I didn't know the fridge even worked down here anymore."

"It's a new one," her mother said. "Dad and I want to fix the place up a little. We might start entertaining here again."

Amanda took a drink, and her mouth puckered. She needed coffee, badly. "That's great," she said, not sure if it was. She didn't want this room to change. She wanted it to stay the same as when she was a child.

"I'm trying to convince your dad to get rid of these wretched video games."

"Why do you want to get rid of them? " She considered them the most important part of her inheritance. "I'll take them."

"To clutter up your apartment? You better ask Peter about that first."

"You could put them in storage. They're worth a lot of money."

"Selling them would help pay for a wedding."

Amanda's mouth went dry. Here it was again. They had just moved in together, and her mother was in a hurry to make it legal. She longed for strong, black coffee but her mother believed caffeine was an evil drug.

"Hold on to them," Amanda said. "They'll be worth more if you keep them longer. Why do you have to go redecorating all the time, anyway? You ruin everything."

"Remember we used to call this room the fun room? I just want to make it fun again."

"You mean open the bar again and have wild parties?"

"We could have a juice bar; maybe have a New Year's Party here for the year 2000, the beginning of a new century."

Amanda sighed. "The new century doesn't start until 2001."

"But all the good parties will be in 2000," her mother said, downing a glass of carrot juice.

Amanda wanted to gag. "Will you and daddy at least have a glass of champagne this year?"

"We no longer believe in mind altering substances."

Amanda thought some of the supplements she bought from the health food store were probably more mind-altering than a dime bag. She jumped down from the barstool and looked around for a brush.

"Peter sounded so worried when he called."

"Why didn't you wake me?" She smoothed her hair down but it stuck back up again.

"I tried. You were out. You should have gone back by dinner before you got so tired. What were you doing all night?"

"I told him I was going to observe if it was clear." She could hear the whine in her own voice, annoyed that she was regressing here, spending one night at her parent's house. She had to get out of here, stop explaining herself all the time.

"You and dad are the ones who gave me the middle name starry night."

Her mother bristled. "We changed that name to Rose," she said. "Your legal name is now Amanda Rose."

"Chill out," Amanda said. "I was only kidding." Her mother could be so weird sometimes.

"We were so immature back then, probably hoped you'd become an artist, probably your father's idea."

"And now you're afraid I'll cut off my ear?"

"Don't talk like that."

"So I like to stay out observing? Is that so awful?"

"No." Her mother had switched to a calm, reasonable shrink voice that really grated on her last nerve. "But, sometimes, you get, well, just a bit obsessive."

Why didn't her mother just come right out with it—she didn't always trust her sanity? She was still worried that her only child might have a breakdown like she had in her teens.

She heard her mother taking with her shrink aunt out in California back then saying maybe she was having seizures, her neurons were misfiring or something when she had 'run away' up to Vermont without telling anyone. Amanda had not considered that a breakdown; she'd considered it a "save my sanity by getting away from my parents for a while" stage. Still, her mother worried; she was always hovering. Her mother considered Peter a normalizing element. Good thing she didn't know about the lingering tea parties.

"Goodbye, mother," Amanda said, moving toward the stairs.

"You see, now; there you go pushing me away. You better not push Peter away."

"I'm not pushing anyone, anywhere."

"You're too thin," her mother complained. "I wish you would eat more, and only you could get away with that hair."

Amanda stared at her mother through thick horn-rimmed glasses. It was something she had practiced in the mirror as a child to freak her mother out when she noticed the lenses in her glasses made her green eyes look huge. She gave her mother a glassy, wondering stare, knowing it unhinged her. "That's right," she said. "Only me."

Then, she went up the stairs to wash her face and go back to the apartment. She knew her mother was imagining grandchildren, a boy and a girl running around the 'fun' room.

When she got to the apartment, Amanda opened the door to the smell of bacon and pancakes. She had been worried Peter would be off the wall about her not coming home last night, but he had cooked breakfast. She couldn't wait to run into his arms, but he wasn't in the kitchen or the living room, and no coffee had been brewed.

"Peter?"

Maybe he was out getting the paper. She poked her head into the bedroom. He was reading, and he didn't look up.

"Hey," she said, walking toward him.

He didn't look up.

"Smell's good."

He threw the book down

"What?"

"You leave me here alone on a Saturday night, one of our first weekends living together?"

She sat on the bed. He turned away.

"Sorry," she said. "I called at dinnertime and told you I was going to observe. You weren't even here. I left a message."

"You said you'd be home later. Did you come home? No." His hands sliced the air. "You were out all night looking at those goddamned stars."

"It was a new moon. You knew I was going."

"But you didn't come home." His palms were opened, fingers splayed.

"Sorry. I fell asleep at my parent's house. They don't have coffee there. If they had coffee there, I would have driven home."

Peter sighed. "I was worried, I guess, more than angry."

He was so different from her family, able to admit to emotions. It scared her a little.

"I'm sorry." She stuck out her lower lip and looked at him sideways. "Forgive me?"

He pinched her arm.

"Ouch."

He smiled. "I'll brew coffee, give you the energy you need skinny girl."

"I smell bacon, ummm"

He picked her up and carried her into the kitchen.

He made dropped eggs; Amanda made toast and heated up the bacon in the microwave. Finally they ate. Toast dripping with egg-yolk, maple syrup cured bacon washed down with strong coffee. Amanda stared out the window. Peter took her hand.

"Tired?"

"No"

"Good. I have something for you."

He took a small box out of his shirt pocket.

"Oh my God." She laughed as she opened the box. "Over breakfast?"

"Not my plan, your fault. If you were here last night, it would have been more romantic. Why do you think your mother wanted you back here?"

"My mother?"

"She helped me pick it out."

She looked at the ring on her finger then back up at Peter. "Yes, I will marry you." She hugged him and held him tight.

When Peter got up to pour himself more coffee, her eyes strayed back to the window, troubled that her mother knew Peter was going to ask her to marry him before she did.

Chapter Six

1978
Gloria

The air is getting warmer. Gloria sits on the bench wearing only cut-offs and a white flowered tunic, no sweater anymore. She looks down at her legs; she and her sister shaved their legs together this morning. Her sister says it's hip now, even if you are liberated, to be more hygienic that way. Hairy armpits and legs and facial hair left unplucked and unbleached are no longer signs of liberation. Gloria figures she should know since she lives in California. After they made hummus and ate fruit for breakfast, they sat side by side on the edge of the tub each with their own razor. She supposes she should be happy they trusted her to hold a razor. When she first started to come out of this fog, she had noticed the absence of all sharp objects.

She looks further up her body and notices why she is wearing a tunic. She hasn't lost all the weight she gained from her pregnancy. Her arms and legs are thin again, but this baby belly has been stubborn. Her breasts are still enlarged. The baby must have been weaned quickly when she fell into this fog—she just doesn't remember. Amanda doesn't need her milk anymore, but Gloria's body is slow to accept that. The fog is what she thinks of as the state she was in when all her senses were buried. When did it start? How long has she missed? She's sure she had time with her baby, months, at least part of the winter; that's why she has all these dreams, nightmares of snow. It's getting so warm now. She sits out here in this sleeveless tunic hoping it was just weeks, but it could have been months that she didn't feel or hear anything.

As a teenager, she would have been horrified even to have a

little fat on her stomach. Her sister had been the one who was tall and heavy, not at all concerned about fashion, as Gloria had been. It was funny that first summer she was with Thomas, she thought her sister was more the type he would be attracted to. In those days, Suzanne was the serious one, and Gloria the one who was into fashion like her mother, good at spending her father's money.

That's what everyone thought, anyway. That she was the one concerned with tangible things like clothes and status, getting ahead, but really, she had just acted like that so her father would notice. But he never did; he had always counted on Suzanne to be in the business.

When Gloria started her second year of college, it was like all the fierce battling and breaking convention had been a huge vortex of energy that suddenly became a kind of emptiness when kids returned to school. She had wanted to be a journalist, but somehow it had all become wrapped up in what Thomas wanted and her parents and even Suzanne.

When had she given up the search for material security? She had shown some of her writing to Thomas over the summer and he said it was good. As the summer ended, they had decided not to define their relationship, which she hated. The new rules were so confusing. She felt distant with her old friends: jealous when she saw Thomas talking to other women and panicked if she couldn't find him on campus. Her father had given her a hundred dollars to buy new school clothes. She went with her friends to the stores in Boston, but all she could think of was what she would buy Thomas. Unlike anyone before, he believed in her. She daydreamed about her future as a journalist as her friends picked out clothes, and she spent most of her money on a leather satchel and boots for Thomas, and, for herself, an expensive pen and pencil set and a journal.

The next day in the library Thomas snuck up on her and put his hand on her shoulder. She screamed, and they both laughed. He sat at the table beside her, and as he kissed her on the lips, she looked around to see if anyone was watching.

"Some of us are going up to Hubbardston. You want to come?"

"I have French at 2:30" It was only one.

"Skip it."

"I can't"

"Come on, I want us to hang out together."

"Just wait for me till 3:30?"

She hated how much she wanted to be with him, how much her happiness depended on him. At the very beginning of the relationship, it seemed she had the upper hand.

"I'm not sure. Let's get out of here anyway."

She remembers how warm the air was that day, how the clouds gathered as if a heavy rain were coming, the sound of his new boots as they crunched the leaves, and how it seemed like forever as they walked in silence towards the main building. She waited for him to say if he would wait for her. He took her hand, looked up at the sky.

"I suppose we can go a little later, but they're leaving now so we'll have to thumb."

She had never thumbed before but felt like it was okay as long as she was with Thomas. The summer had been like a fantasy, and now that they were back at school, nothing seemed to work in her old routine. They stopped at the coffeehouse and told his friends they would be up later. Gloria was apprehensive about thumbing. Her friends would think it was beneath her, or maybe they'd think it was exciting. Her parents certainly wouldn't approve.

That was another day her world had shifted. How could she have been so reckless? She knows now what it is to wonder and worry about your child. She had called home after French and said she was going out with friends and would get a ride home later, but she knew few of Thomas' friends had cars and they would all be getting stoned. She had no idea how she would get home.

So she went off with him, hesitant, as if the sidewalk they stood on were moving around them like the spastic movements of a compass pointing them in some inevitable direction. As if she were walking into someone else's life as they walked up route 122, away from her girlfriends and casual corner, their 'look but don't touch' attitude. Maybe doing something like this would gain her prestige because it was dangerous. They got a ride right away but only to the center of Paxton where they walked up route 56. There was so little traffic. Tired and hungry, she wondered if they would have to walk all the way.

She shivered and held her purse tighter. She'd only brought a light sweater, one that matched her skirt. Thomas took off his army jacket and put it around her shoulders. The leaves fell around them as afternoon light faded, and she breathed in the smell of fall, overripe apples, and a slight burning smell. She was so hungry she thought she might pass out when someone from the commune saw them and recognized Tom. She was grateful to be picked up and for the bag of apples everyone shared.

It could have been different. Other things might have happened that night. Her parents could have called the police, sent out a missing person's bulletin, but, as it was, that night did not end in any dramatic fashion. No police coming to find her, parent's forbidding her to leave the house. Someone was going back down to Worcester by seven and gave her a ride. Thomas was staying up there. After they kissed goodbye, as she got into the car, she saw the girls there looking at him and felt like she was the one being left behind.

Then, she remembers being up here, a year maybe a year and a half later, when Thomas wanted to stay up here and start a commune. They would do it right, he said. No religion, no politics, no bullshit. Just a community of people working together caring for each other. They'd been sitting right here on the bench looking out at the mountains.

She remembers all this but not the last few years. She knows she has a child but does not remember giving birth. Only in shadows and a puzzling sense of time. She hates this feeling that she is teetering on the edge of some knowledge and all the energy it takes to not remember.

Somewhere inside, Gloria is crying. Just when she feels some hope that she can grasp her status, there is a collapse of memory. There is something else, something urging her to stop digging, the weight of her own heart broken, like a branch sheared off in the wind of a thunderstorm. Like her mind is whirling in a vortex, and each time she tries to grip a small hand, she stands helpless on the outer rim with only one small branch of herself, small as the vein that pulses in her neck, yet significant enough to strip her of speech. She needs to keep sitting, remembering. Weaving herself and her memory back together until she knows what has brought her here.

She is drowning in voices and all the sounds around her: her parents angry and worried, her sister always solicitous, her baby laughing and crying. Thomas, especially Thomas, speaking to her, reaching for her. She wants to respond; she really does, but her throat is so dry, unable even to make a sound, much less to form a word. When Thomas comes out, she clings to the sleeve of his shirt like she did so many years ago. All the voices she can hear but cannot respond until Tom puts the baby on her lap, and she holds the baby and cries, not just feeling the tears dripping down but a sound, deep within her, a sound coming out of the silence tied up inside her. *It's a start,* she thinks then smiles, aware of the movement of her facial muscles as she holds her baby close.

Chapter Seven

Voices Far

"Night," he said. "I love you."

"Night," she said. "Love you, too." She hung up quickly not wanting to hear the click at the other end.

When they'd parted at the airport, she'd realized how much she would miss him. After only a few months of living together their lives were so entangled; he'd been gone for only a few days and she had trouble falling asleep. His sleep breathing, white noise, not quite a snore, just a quiet whistling as predictable as a heartbeat was like a sleeping potion for her. Since he'd left, she'd hardly slept at all. So here she was feeling all woe is me when he had actually begged her to go with him.

She hadn't quite told him that the class this summer wasn't really a required math. It was actually a class on a piece called *Kepler's Dream*. A fragment written in the 1600's where Kepler imagined a boy hearing a story of creatures transported in some magical way to the moon. Some considered it the first Sci-fi ever written. The strange thing was that some of the sensations he had described of these creatures hurtling through space were actually an accurate prediction of the elongation of the body. Descriptions very close to the spaghetti effect on the limbs that were mentioned as a problem of space travel to overcome in *The Physics of Star Trek*. Peter would think she was wacko if she told him about this so she hadn't exactly lied but just let him think what he assumed—that it was a basic math requirement and she was doing a few summer students a favor so they could get it out of the way.

Not many students had signed up, actually only two Physics students interested in sci-fi and some English Majors, but they let her teach it when she told them she would do it for free. She hoped it would be worth it now, as she lay awake and listened to Peter's voice in her head.

Arthur Koestler's *The Sleepwalkers*, a book she was rereading to prepare herself mentally for the course, lay on her bedside table. She picked it up and then put it down again. Her concentration was shot. She took up one of her sci-fi romances with the cover ripped off and finally fell asleep.

Startled out of sleep by the doorbell, for a moment, she thought it might be a visitor from some other century. A scientist to reassure her that the course she was teaching for free was worth it. She, of course, had a tea party and consulted with her three friends about the decision of teaching this course, and they had been supportive. She put on her slippers, peeked through the window, and saw her mother, standing perky and all business-like, at the front door. Her honey-colored hair, worn straight to the shoulders, caught a shine from the morning sun. Hoop earrings and a golden chain set off her powder blue silk blouse. Only a hint of color was painted on her nails and lips.

Amanda hurried out to the kitchen, put her glasses on the table, and opened the door. Her mother walked in handing her a basket. Whatever it was, they were still warm. Amanda sniffed.

"Gooseberry," her mother said. "Sorry I'm here so early, but I wanted to get these over. I have a house to show this morning."

Amanda had not combed her hair, and it had the wild look it always did before she smoothed it down. As she groped around the kitchen table, her mother handed her glasses.

"You have those beautiful big green eyes just like your father," she said." Too bad you can hardly see a thing out of them."

"I was just getting up," she said, knowing what her mother

was thinking. You're just like your father, a good brain, but no common sense. It might be hard for you to manage but that's okay. There are people around who are good managers.

"I'll make us some tea," her mother said.

"I'm having coffee," Amanda said, "but I'll make you tea."

Her mother looked hurt.

"We're at my place now," she said. "Let me play hostess. I'm practically a married woman."

Her mother's face brightened. The kettle boiled, and she poured herself instant coffee and morning glory tea she got just for her mother. A slant of light pierced the room as they drank and talked and ate muffins, Amanda eating around the gooseberries.

"Have you heard from Peter?"

Amanda smiled and smoothed her hair. "Every night he calls to say goodnight."

"It must be lonely to be that far away...all alone." Her mother sighed.

"Other people from work are there with him." She wasn't going to get into an argument or an explanation about why she didn't go. "He'll probably have the time of his life."

"But you could have been with him, like a honeymoon."

"I think that takes place after the marriage."

Her mother laughed. "Why do you want to be separated now, when you finally found someone?"

Could her mother even imagine how pathetic that made her sound? "He went away mother. Not me."

"But he wanted you to go with him; he told me. He was devastated that you chose to stay here."

Amanda finally just stopped listening like she always did. She watched her mother, pale lipstick coming off onto the teacup, eyebrows lifting and descending to make a point. She looked at the face, attentively, but did not hear a word. What was the use? She didn't want to explain that she wanted to teach this summer. She was looking forward to sharing *Kepler's Dream* with just a few students who hopefully would relish discussing how a scientist in the 17th century could be so imaginative as to project demons onto the moon in order to explain its terrestrial features. And she didn't want to miss Stellafane because she was going to give the Kepler talk there, too.

As her mother got up from her chair, Amanda brought herself back to the present. She watched her mother go to the sink, wash the cup, and put it upside down in the drainer. The sun caught some beads of water as they dribbled down the sink.

"What are you going to do today?" her mother asked.

"Organize a lesson plan. Errands. Get ready for Stellafane."

"What about shopping?" her mother asked, standing at the sink, facing Amanda down. "We could go look for a wedding dress?"

"We haven't even set a date yet."

"Amanda," her mother said, turning around to dry the few dishes and put them away. "I'm only trying to be helpful. Peter might like it if he comes back and you've found a dress. It would kind of make up for not going with him."

Amanda gave the unhinging stare to her mother's back.

They walked to the door, and Amanda leaned against the doorjamb still in her nightshirt with another cup of coffee. Her mother kissed her on the forehead.

"Listen to your mother, sweetie. Don't let this one get away. He loves you, and he's good for you."

"I know," Amanda said. "I know."

When her mother left, she went back to their room and began to put some clothes together for the long weekend in Vermont. The weather was going to be iffy so she packed rain gear. She could camp there at least one night, but if it got really bad, she could go to the chalet. It would be interesting to see if some real wackos showed up this year thinking the approaching year 2000 was the end of the millennium and some kind of spaceship would land on the hill of stars and take everyone there away. She shivered thinking of the cult several years ago all found dead in their Nike sneakers.

In the 1980's, when she used to go with her parents, only serious amateur astronomers went. Her mother was practically the only women there, and there weren't many children either. Her parents had gone every year from 1979 until the early 90's when that stupid shrink had told them to keep her away from everything up there. The year they said she had "run away," she had just gone up to get away from them. Her father might go with her if he were here, but he was never home lately, always away on business allowing her mother to write bigger and bigger checks to Greenpeace. They were tax deductible.

The apartment felt so empty without Peter, but she had kind of chosen Stellafane over being with him. Maybe she just wasn't ready to be married but really, that wasn't it. More like she was searching for an answer, but the funny thing was, she didn't even know the question. She packed faster, anxious to leave. Maybe spending some time alone at the house in Vermont would be good as long as she made it to Stellafane before nightfall to set up the tent.

She called Peter's hotel hoping he hadn't left for the day. It would have been about 8:30 there.

"Hello?"

"Morning, babe."

"Amanda?" He sounded surprised

"No, your other fiancé."

"It's just you sound so energetic. You're not a morning person."

"It's almost noon here."

"It's just that you sound so happy?"

The guilt begins

"Would it make you happy if I admit I'm miserable without

you?"

"Why don't you just fly out? It's not too late. "

The guilt continues.

"Peter, I'm not having this conversation with you over the phone. I just wanted to tell you I'm leaving early for Stellafane today and wanted to catch you before you left. Do you have to lecture today?"

"Not till next week, now. We're going up to San Francisco for the day."

"Sounds fun. I won't be able to call from Stellafane, but I'll be thinking of you."

"Why don't you stay up at the chalet at night?"

"Because if it's clear, I want to be able to look through all the telescopes in the middle of the night."

She didn't mention that she wanted to be there early in the morning for the swap tables that he thought were a lot of useless junk.

"Hold on. They're here with breakfast."

"Room service?" she asked.

"You could be sharing it with me."

Amanda listened to the silence on the other end of the phone. The buzz and static of the hotel phone line. She heard platters clank and tried to picture the room. It was surprising to her that he had breakfast sent up. She would have thought Mr. Sociable would have eaten downstairs with his colleagues. She thought she heard the receiver drop.

"You still there?" She panicked in the silence. "You still there?"

"Yeah."

"I guess I'll let you have breakfast. Call you from Vermont on Sunday. Have fun in San Francisco."

"Have fun at Stellafane, but don't spend too much on the junk at the swap tables."

Didn't he just have to get that in?

Chapter Eight

Her parents seem to have left. Her sister seems to be in charge of everything. She heard Suzanne telling Thomas he needed to take her for walks, get her off the bench. She needs exercise. It's good for stress reduction. Sometimes Suzanne tries to get her to meditate, but the funny sound of the 'ohms' only makes Gloria want to laugh. She feels bad because she knows her sister is trying to cure her, working so hard to make her better, but she can't help wanting to laugh when her sister meditates with her. They are all so earnest. She didn't mean to be ungrateful, but it just sounded so odd. She couldn't make the sound herself. She tried so hard, just to please Suzanne. Nothing came but a choking feeling then laughing on the inside as if she were mocking her sister.

Suzanne sat in the yogi position, hands on her knees, her eyes closed, showing Gloria, telling Gloria to sit just like this, and, though Gloria's body had felt all limp, she sat up as straight as she could, trying to please her sister. Good, Suzanne said, as if she was a little child. Then Suzanne sounded with the ohm again waiting for an answering sound. Gloria tried but couldn't do it.

"Ohm" Suzanne said, in an irritated way and snapped her eyes open, looking at Gloria, so Gloria tried again, but she could not make the sound. She knew Suzanne was getting frustrated by the tone of her ohms, but this only made her want to laugh more. She had to keep herself from laughing so Suzanne would not get mad. Suzanne's unique way of speech therapy was working but not in the way she had realized, not with the outcome she had expected. Gloria was laughing way down inside of herself, and for a long time, she couldn't stop laughing. It made Gloria feel good to laugh. She wanted to do something to make Suzanne angry again. After that, Suzanne did not try meditation therapy for a long time, and Gloria wished she could tell her it really had helped, but she couldn't get her throat to speak the words.

Gloria sits on the bench and wonders why they can't see that she only needs time. Time to sort everything out, time to remember. They beseech her for words with their eyes, with their silence. She can't give them words until she reaches around in a grab bag of darkness and finds something she is missing.

She thinks about how she and Thomas had sat on this same bench several years ago.

"We could have it all up here," he'd said, announcing his vision, his creed, almost a religion, so hopeful. She wishes that hopefulness would envelop her now like it did that day. She wishes she could steal hope back from the arms of harm and cradle it like a new baby. Let it spill from her, overflowing her arms like a lake of remembrance.

It must be four, five, may be six years since they first came up here. Maybe longer. They'd had no money, and the Chalet's ownership was being fought over by her parents and her sister who was supposed to have inherited it on her 22nd birthday, but she had let him dream, falling into his arms. Feeling the vibration of his energy had been all the security she needed.

It had been easy for them to come up here and spend a few days together without her parent's knowing. They were never home, and they weren't watching her so closely because they were having all that trouble with Suzanne. Gloria's father was beginning to favor Thomas because he got a job writing metric conversion tables for a company that did many contracts with the government. He made good money, and the company was going to pay his tuition at Worcester Polytech. Her father invited him to the family 4th of July picnic that year, and they talked of kilos, Decca, Pico's, hector. The politics of measurement had brought her father and her boyfriend closer even though their politics, in every other way, were so different. It's funny how things happen. Thomas became a math nerd who made money in metrics. Her father and boyfriend talked drams and hectometers—a vocabulary Gloria never understood. He could write manuals from home, wherever he happened to live—didn't have to go to an office at all. Suddenly her days were measured in micros and nanos when once her minutes ran in gallons, barrels, pecks.

Pecks, packs—she and Thomas used to run in packs; they and his friends searching each other out, living for the day. Even when it was supposed to be just she and Thomas, it was always she and Thomas and a lot of other people, and Thomas belonged to the world. By fall, he was at WPI, and she was still at Worcester State feeling left behind. On weekends, they saw each other. On Sundays, they'd go to the Clark Library to do some studying for a while then meet their friends.

Thomas clepped out of one year at WPI and took some classes in the summer so they let him in as a senior in 1972. For that whole summer, they came up here for part of the week. When he was wrapped up in studying and writing manuals, she took long walks by herself. On weekends, they went back down to Worcester and met their friends at the Blue Plate in Holden, dancing to the music of Zonkaraz with Tiny, the bouncer, dancing with everyone near the door. It was so much fun. It didn't matter if you had a partner. They all danced and sang to each other through the haze.

And Tiny stationed at the door just danced with everyone because nobody had to be kicked out. Nobody needed to feel unwelcome. Then Thomas would hold her tight as the lead singer crooned *Somewhere Over the Rainbow,* and he would say to her, "This is it; this is it, babe. We're going to bottle this and bring it up to Vermont. We'll call it the Rainbow House. You'll see. We can do it; nothing bad will happen."

It almost puts her in a swoon just thinking about it now, almost wants to make her sing. *Even though we have no money, we're in love and that's all that matters.* Just hearing the words in her mind makes her want to believe them, to sing them out loud and pretend she's at the blue plate with Thomas swinging her around on one arm and Tiny swinging her around on the other, then letting them go, spinning off like tops all the way up to Vermont and their new life.

Why didn't they just stay in Worcester? If they had stayed down in Worcester, something would not have happened to keep her from words. Breath, words, stories, all things she has to piece together now. *Breathe*, she tells herself inside herself, stretching out the word in her mind but still unable to open her vocal chords. Like her sister taught her with the weird ohms, she breathes deeply trying to bring in the healing air. And something smells strongly today; she's trying to guess what it is. She tilts her head deciding it is the blue flowers that come up by the pond every year on a bush of some kind. Such an overwhelming fragrance must be a bush. She sees the blossoms in her mind. White with reddish veins inside the petals. *No, it might be purple. What's the name of it?* She's forgetting words because she hasn't used them in so long. This is the last straw. She won't let this happen.

She says the word purple in her mind, and bunches of lush petals fall into her vision. *Just the word*, she tells herself, but her mind gets caught in the lush purple vision, and she can't remember how to make her lips move for the sound of the letter P. She tries and tries, but her lips only sputter, and now Thomas and her sister are nearby. They just look at each other probably thinking she is an idiot. They smile when she looks over. She hears her sister tell Thomas to take her for a walk. Thomas comes over and takes her hand, gently pulling her from the bench, and she doesn't resist. She sighs as if she doesn't care, but she does care. She wants him to know that she remembers the flowers.

She gently puts pressure on him, steering him toward the smell. An early summer bush growing in the back lawn, down the hill by the water. She wants to run from Tom to smell the flowers up close, throw them into the air and watch the lush petals fall, as they did in her mind, but he pulls her in another direction. They go down the long driveway and out to the street. Afterwards, they go into the house and eat lunch with her silence louder than anything in the room, louder than Amanda's chattering, fussing, and laughing.

Afterwards, she goes back out to the bench, sits, and tries to relax, but she can feel them watching her from the window. She gets a shiver in the heat as some memory of vigilance in watching from the window stirs a memory of knowledge she is not ready to find.

When Thomas brings Amanda out, Gloria listens to the sounds her baby makes. Thomas is trying to get their baby to walk. He sits on the grass just a few feet away from the bench where he has left her hanging on. Gloria not only notices her fat legs and squinching hands today but also the sounds. She's always making sounds.

"Amanda," Thomas calls to her with open arms "Walk."

"Auk," Amanda says

Gloria watches her mouth, how she makes the hard K sound by keeping her lips and teeth parted. She makes that sound and is pleased with herself, a hard sound coming from way down in her belly. She smiles and watches Thomas' mouth as he forms words trying to coax Amanda towards him, but he makes the sounds too easily, too fast.

Gloria watches Amanda trying to walk, and Thomas catches her as she falls. He lifts her up above his head and swings her around. She giggles.

Gloria's heart pounds. She wants to get up and yell, 'No! Stop! She might fall! You might drop her!'

"Gen, gen," Amanda says, each time he stops.

"Now to mama," He says as he flies her like a plane landing right onto Gloria's lap.

"Mama," Amanda says as she lands on Gloria. Gloria embraces her. *When did she start copying everything Thomas says?* Amanda stands on Gloria's lap, her energy unable to be contained. What happened to the infant that lay in a happy heap on Gloria's lap sucking breast milk? She falls into Gloria, laughing, her knees bent, and her head heavy against Gloria's neck. She lifts herself up again with the help of Gloria's hands, uses them for balance as she steps from Gloria's knees to her stomach.

"Mama," she says, falling into her again and plants a wet kiss on Gloria's ear.

Gloria holds her tight. Amanda pulls away, looks her in the face.

"Alk?" she says, determined but still questioning. She climbs down from Gloria, lifts herself up to the edge of the bench. Thomas gets into position.

Amanda lets go of the bench. Scrunching her hands opened and closed, opened and closed. Gloria watches as not only the feet, but Amanda's entire body lurches forward one side at a time then falls into Thomas' arms.

"Yea," Thomas shouts and claps. Amanda claps too encircled by Thomas' arms. "Yea" Thomas shouts again, and Gloria claps with them. Amanda lifts up her body this time holding onto Thomas' outstretched hands. She balances herself and let's go, lurching forward back to Gloria on the bench.

"Yea!" They all clap again, and this dance goes on over and over all afternoon—the lurching, the falling, the getting up, the Amanda Ballet.

Chapter Nine

Hill of Stars

Amanda chugged the station wagon up the steep, curvy road to Stellafane well before sunset. Signs on the way advertised lemonade, blueberries, pure Vermont maple syrup. When she got to the top, there was just a short line at the admission hut. She paid $10.00 and got a packet, a map of the site, a raffle ticket, and a red construction paper tag that said STELLAFANE 99 with a safety pin attached. She drove slowly through a jumble of narrow dirt lanes between parked cars and people walking in all directions. She found a place to park on the grass right beside Winnebago Alley. It was a good spot with an outhouse and water nearby.

On a sudden impulse, she had taken more than she needed for the weekend and had first gone to the chalet with boxes she had moved to Peter's and not yet opened. The apartment was just too small for all her stuff. Winter clothes, papers, books—it wasn't practical to keep it up here either. Still, she carried on. Her plan was to drop the boxes off and head right to Stellafane, but, once there, she'd walked around outside.

She had walked to the edge of the woods where her mother had once had a garden, picking flowers that had once been cultivated and now grew wild. She wandered around to the back and sat by the pond hugging her knees throwing flowers in one by one and watching them float away. There was something colorful beneath the surface. She reached in trying to pluck it from the mud and nearly fell in herself. She fished it out with a stick through the silt. A hair ribbon covered in mud that must have been hers when she was little. She rushed back to the house as if she had found some treasure and rinsed it in soapy water. Her parents had talked little about her childhood making any small token significant. She'd placed it on the window seat to dry in the sun and headed for Stellafane.

Now one side of the sky looked clear, but the other looked ominous, so she hurriedly pitched the tent to beat out the storm. Then she huddled into the sleeping bag all alone listening to the rainfall. A steady drip, drip lulled her as she pulled out several pillows and plumped them against the side of the tent. Safe in a cocoon of nylon and cotton, she picked up a paperback from the pile beside her, but instead of reading, her mind drifted into an evening nap.

She awoke sweating and chilled all at once, badly in need of coffee and a bathroom. Willing herself to get up, she would have to dig out toilet paper in case they were out and bring hand wipes. At least it wasn't raining anymore, but it wasn't exactly clear either. She hurried down a dirt path, stopped at the outhouse, and then hit the food tent. Weak coffee, lukewarm, but at least it was caffeine.

It was humid after the rain, the air thick as if the clouds had not yet released all their moisture. Observing would not be good. She looked around at the few people eating burgers under the awning. Water dripped from the sides of the tent where she was to give a talk the next day. There were worries that some nutcase with cult-like ideas might try to give a talk this year. So many people thought it was the beginning of a new millennium that this year people would wander in thinking it was an astrology conference. She scoped out the people sitting around her—the usual mix of bright tees, shirts and cut-offs. Some familiar faces but none she knew well enough to talk to. No one stood out—no one likely to go tent to tent trying to sell religion. She was hoping there might be a few Waco's here this year so her talk on *"Kepler's Dream"* wouldn't make *her* look marginal.

Climbing a few stairs to a table where mugs, tee shirts, and raffle tickets were being sold, she bought a tee for Peter and one for herself. On the way back to the tent, it started to drizzle. Only a few drops but the sky was covered with dark clouds. She took a coffeemaker, a fresh can of coffee, a can opener, and filters from the Station Wagon, wrapped them in a garbage bag, put on a baseball cap with the letter A, and went in search of friends.

She found a group of people she knew under an awning. A long table with an assortment of lawn furniture set up around it. The remains of supper, soda cans, beer cans, and snacks littered the table. They were talking, listening, reading, dozing off. Some nodded as she took the coffee maker out of the bag and put it on the table. The rain came down harder. Someone handed her a beer and took the coffee to a tent trailer. The bringer of good coffee, bearer of gifts, they had the means to brew it fresh here.

Someone nearby was cooking on a gas grill. The smell made Amanda nauseous. She put her beer down and closed her eyes wanting to cry for missing Peter. She'd like to be resting against him, her head in the crook of his arm. She pretended he was there.

Most of her Stellafane friends were either older or younger than her. Couples who used to come when she was a child, people her parents' age who still came. Very few children came when she was growing up, but now kids were everywhere. She sat back and only listened to words that drifted all around her until the sky crackled with electricity and thunder obliterated all other sounds. Everyone disappeared into tents and pull-trailers. She hurried back to her tent with nothing to do but fall asleep for the night.

When she awoke, the rain had completely stopped, but it was not morning. She opened an air vent on the side of the tent and looked out. It was clear. There were stars, many stars. Looking at them all made her feel disoriented and dizzy. A man with a long, pointy beard leaned over a portable table, a notebook and maps scattered in front of him. He looked over the papers with a tiny, red flashlight then up at the sky. She'd never seen him here before. She lay back down again and listened to the whispering voices setting up scopes. She heard someone talking with a German accent and picked up a few words. She'd taken a course in high school; maybe she could converse a little. It had been years. There were other voices too. She meant to get up and go outside, but she closed her eyes just for a minute, and when she awoke, light streamed through the air vent. *Damn.* She was mad for falling asleep.

It was well past sunrise. The light was strong, and people were up. A few dogs barked, and she could hear the footsteps and shouts of children running. It was early though, she thought, because she could hear the voices of adults crabby and half-asleep as they tried to put together breakfast.

Voices drifted in from all around. She couldn't hear the words clearly except for children shouting. A baby cried; she heard parents' soothing voices.

She grabbed a fresh tee and cut-offs, toilet paper, soap, and shampoo; she put them in a plastic bag and unzipped the tent. She made her way toward the port-o-potty and the shower, nodding to people, dodging children and dogs, hoping to see the man she heard last night with the German accent. Thankfully, there was no line at the bathroom. On the way back, she saw the man from last night. The table was still set up. She sat on the grass by her tent and listened as he talked with someone coming from a car, but he didn't speak in German and didn't have an accent. Maybe she had just been dreaming about the clear skies and the man with the accent last night, but it had seemed so real. It disturbed her a little because there was the table still set up.

She shook her head, picked herself up, and walked down the path past the shower and the outhouse to see how her friends were doing. The smell of coffee led her to the long table under the awning where she found Jason, a friend from childhood and an ex-boyfriend, making omelets on a hotplate. She poured herself coffee as he handed her a plate filled with vegetables covered with fluffy eggs smothered in cheese. Her stomach cringed, but she sat and picked at it to make him happy. She watched him. He looked different, thinner.

"When did you get here?" she asked as he folded cheese into another omelet.

"I don't know. About four, I think. It cleared last night."

"I know. I woke up, but I was too tired to get up. Where is everyone?"

"Sleeping, swap tables"

"Who's that for?"

"Whoever wants it."

Jason would not stop cooking even when everyone was done eating.

"I'm hiring you," Amanda said. "When I get married."

"Why not just marry me?"

"I'm betrothed to another," she said and showed him her ring.

"I'll be damned." He stopped cooking and sat down with Amanda to hear about her latest.

Amanda was glad everyone was at the swap tables; she wanted to be alone with Jason. She suspected that Jason was one of the reasons why Peter happened to have these plans in August and wanted her to go with him. He probably only came with her last summer because her mother told him she had an old boyfriend here, but Jason had not even shown up last year, and Amanda had been somewhat worried about him.

"Where is he?" Jason looked behind her and all around in a goofy way.

"In California, right now."

"Cool"

"He's at a conference, giving a talk." She hesitated. "He's a professor."

"So are you."

"Yeah, but he's really into it."

"And he has no tats or piercings, so mommy really loves him?

"Pretty much. He thinks I should have mine removed."

They both laughed.

"Your mom must be happy."

"Yes, mommy really loves him."

"Do you?" Jason moved closer to her; she resisted the urge to move away.

"Yeah, I do."

"You sound unsure."

She looked around. "I am, a little. I mean, I don't know, we're different. Everything has to be a compromise." Her voice cracked a little. Jason put his arm around her. His nose ring felt cold as he kissed her on the cheek. "I get so confused sometime." She took a sip of coffee.

Jason shook his head. "I can't believe you're still poisoning yourself with that stuff."

Amanda sighed. "You sound like my mother."

Jason laughed. "Ironically, we'd probably get along well now. I eat differently."

"I noticed."

It was after nine when she got to the swap tables. The good deals were gone, the sun was getting hot, and the day was getting muggy. Books, tee shirts, and gadgets were piled on tables. Eyepieces and old electronic equipment, mounted photographs were spread along blankets on the ground. The tables were set up in an L-shape with bigger telescopes and displays beyond in a shady area. Amanda walked around slowly picking up worthless instruments and tools that glittered in the sun, their prices stuck on masking tape with blurry ink.

She stopped at a table of books, mounted pictures of comets, colorful pictures of galaxies, and a pair of old binoculars. Looking through them in the distance, she focused on the top of an oak tree then moved down as she focused on a telescope tube beneath it. *Wow.* It was old but elegant looking. She'd never seen anything like it. Suddenly a pinwheel of colors appeared just above it, and for a second, it looked like a strand of golden hair let loose from the colors and took off into the sky. The sun beat down on her face even as a chill ran through her body. She put the binoculars down and stared at the tube with the naked eye, but there was nothing. Maybe it had just been a reflection. She moved beyond the tables toward the shade and leaned against the oak examining the tube more closely.

It was definitely one of a kind. Light blonde wood, fairly thick, with decorative markings around the top. An elegant pattern of squares and diamonds were carved and painted around the upper rim. A man sat beside it reading in a lawn chair. He had thick gray hair pulled back in a ponytail and a Fu-man-chu moustache that came down nearly to a beard at his chin.

"How old is this? She asked. "Where's it from?"

He looked up from his book. "One fifty," he said. At least that's what it sounded like. He had a thick accent. Russian? German. ? Dutch? He went back to his reading. Not much of a salesman.

She studied him. Could he have been the man she had seen last night, observing? He looked different. Of course, it had been dark.

"Did you make it?" she asked, in her best German, which was not very good.

"One fifty," he repeated.

A younger man came over from one of the tables loaded with moldy smelling overpriced books. "He'll take one twenty five," he said in just a slight German accent. He nodded toward the guy in the chair. "My uncle doesn't speak English. We're cleaning out his attic, practically giving stuff away."

"Did he make it?" she asked looking at the unusual carved design.

"It used to belong to my grandfather. I think he made it out of an old bureau, maybe brought over from Germany."

She touched the tube. Even one-twenty five was too much money. She'd have to haggle. She should be saving for the wedding. "Do you know what kind of mirror was in it?"

The man shook his head. "I don't know. There was some kind of glass with it, maybe a mirror. I don't know. It was no good all scratched. "

"You got rid of it?"

"Not yet. I have it in the trunk to go to the dump."

"Throw in the mirror, and I'll take it for a hundred."

He shrugged. "I guess, since you're saving me a trip to the dump."

As she wrote the check, she thought she saw the man in the chair smile, but mostly, he kept on reading. The younger man helped her carry it to the car.

Peter would be furious. She could never tell him how much she paid for it. He'd grumble about it being too big for the apartment. Maybe she would just leave it in Vermont. That way he wouldn't even know about it. He'd say it was a piece of junk, but to her, it was beautiful just to look at. She was sure that she could modify it to make the optics work at least fairly well.

She went to her friend's tents and found Jason. "I bought a telescope."

"Here?"

"At the tables." A silly smile glided across her face.

"You bought a telescope here? You do need a husband to watch over you." Jason thought as much of the swap tables as Peter.

"Want to see it?" she asked.

"I can't wait."

Jason tried to get her to eat a goat cheese and sprout sandwich before they left, but she only wanted coffee.

She opened the rear door of the wagon and looked at the tube and then at him.

He touched the blonde wood, examined the carvings. "Interesting piece. You know it isn't usable."

"It might be. It came with glass, but the guy was going to throw it away."

She opened a cardboard box and showed him the yellowed glass. "Can you imagine? He was taking this to the dump."

"And you're thinking you can make this work, aren't you?"

"Something like that."

"Good luck"

Was he speaking of the marriage or the new telescope?

Jason stood close to her, too close. She could smell the faint odor of Rosemary and thyme on his breath from the omelets he'd cooked earlier; the flavor of herbs and their sweet odor permeated his skin.

Her mother had been happy when they first started dating because she was twenty and finally had someone she called a boyfriend. Someone they knew: that nice boy she practically grew up with at Stellafane. They probably knew he came to visit when she went to Vermont alone occasionally, but her mother didn't get on her case about it for a glorious few months because she was so happy that Amanda was doing something normal like having a relationship. Then when she came home with her long, silky hair cut into short spikes, she saw the slight look of alarm on her mother's face.

"It's very short though, isn't it?" her mother had said. "A young face like yours, you can pull off anything."

When she started living in Jason's oversized flannel shirts, her mother had given her the L. L. Bean Catalog to pick out flannels that were more flattering for women. Then she wanted to move up to Vermont, and they begged her to stay down and finish grad school. Her father said she was almost a shoe-in for a job at the University once she graduated. So she compromised and got the apartment in Jefferson, and they freaked out again. She could just imagine how her mother and Aunt Suzanne were probably heating up the lines again about her neurons misfiring.

Then her former free-love parents tried to forbid her to move in with Jason if they were not married. She argued that Jason would never leave Vermont, and anyway, Jason and her were hardy an item anymore. They were just friends. Now he stood beside her, too close. It had been over two years since they'd seen each other. He had changed, but he hadn't. Now he was on a health kick. Now her mother would probably love him.

"I'm glad you're getting married," he said. "You need looking after." He clucked her chin and looked into her face. "I hope he cooks. You're too skinny."

Amanda sighed and rolled her eyes. She smelled again the herbs on his hands. "I have to get ready for my talk," she said

"You're giving a talk?"

She'd been hesitant to tell Jason about it, but then it slipped out. "*Kepler's Dream*. Didn't I tell you? It was only a fragment but really one of the first sci-fi scenes ever written down about a demon going to the moon."

"They're letting you give a talk about the Waco sci-fi stuff you always told me about?"

She shouldn't have told him. She hated when even he made fun of her. Somehow, betrayal was worse coming from him. "It's not Wacko, Jason. Kepler, you remember him, the man who wrote the laws of planetary motion? He wrote a fictional account of a boy watching a demon sent to the moon in order to explain Earth as seen from the moon."

"The millennium weirdos should love that one."

She was beginning to remember why she didn't date him anymore. *No imagination. Not that different from Peter, really.* Everything with him was so grounded, so physical, his tattoos, his obsession with food, even before this new health kick. He was thinner now, anyway. When they were dating, her parents had accused her of dating a biker even though he didn't own a motorcycle. But still, she was attracted to the smell of him, the scent of herbs. Even though he was joking, she could feel defenses kicking in. Star names and constellations filled her head: *Cancer, the crab, Capricornus, the horned goat Centaurus, the horseman's beast.*

"You really think no one looks at *you* and thinks you're a little strange?" she asked.

"I have a job now," Jason said.

"A real job?"

"A cook." He smiled.

"Oh, how would I have guessed? Brunch for Vermont tourists?"

"Maybe your parents would approve of me now. Not think I'm an axe murderer."

"They didn't think that."

"No they thought I was after your money and the house in Vermont."

He moved close to her again. She moved away. "I have to get ready for my talk."

"When is it?"

"Don't come. You'll make me nervous."

Jason gave her that 'huh' look. "You're a teacher. How could you be nervous speaking in front of a group? Could it be the topic is a little strange?"

"I see now that you've come into the mainstream with a 'real job' as an itinerant cook, you think my ideas are wacko."

"No. I always thought that."

"This talk is not about my ideas; it's about Kepler's ideas, idiot."

She went into the tent and zipped the flaps up even though it was sweltering inside.

Later it was muggy under the large tent where the talks were given. Very few people were around. Most people took this time to nap after staying up to observe all night. She watched the speaker who was finishing, fumbling with the slides. She hadn't brought slides because she didn't want it to be a lecture. When he was done, she set up chairs in a circle and handed out the dream fragment to the eight or ten people who were there and looked like they might stay. Jason had come to the tent and stood in the distance, but she shooed him away because he still made her nervous.

This was it. One reason she had risked Peter's anger by refusing to go to California with him, probably risked their engagement. She needed to find people who saw things the way she did, people who understood how imagination can become obsession and how that is not always a bad thing. Her parents, even Peter, would never quite understand, and that was okay as long as he accepted that her imagination sometimes took her away and was not a rival for him to compete with. They could love each other and still be apart sometimes.

Today she was not looking for someone to marry but people who were not afraid of their imaginations. This talk was different for Stellafane. It was not a demonstration of mirror grinding, not even a visual show with slides of an eclipse— beautiful and astonishing, mysterious. Everyone marveled at those pictures, but no one here ever discussed what was beyond the observed. The people who took those pictures were trying to capture something that couldn't be captured, like an artist trying to paint the way the sun shines through trees, but the light and shadow keep changing.

Astral photography, like the ways of observing before it, had created magicians. Once, people were convinced you could see canals on Mars if you looked through a telescope a certain way, but now they knew that was an aberration. Just like in Copernicus' time, too many brilliant people denied their imagination for fear of being laughed at. She would tell her group not to worry about ridicule.

Her group? Was she going over the edge? Getting some kind of ego complex? No. It wasn't for power. She just wanted to meet with others who did not leave their ideas up to pre-set rituals that made them more comfortable with what they didn't understand, or worse, believe in nothing. She had tried to start a group at the University called Physics and the Imagination, but the administration had been wary. She renamed it, and they did not realize it was the course she would teach this summer.

Her heart beat fast as she began the talk. People seemed only mildly interested. She kept the beginning brief, a little about Kepler's bio but figured most would be pretty familiar with it or would not have come. She focused on the time in his life when he finally went to meet Copernicus, which was the turn of another century, hoping that would bring more interest and relevance. It did. Then she asked them to read the fragment hoping at least one person had heard of it before, never mind read it, but there were no nods of recognition.

"Look particularly at the parts I've highlighted," she said. "A boy, Duracotus, watches as demons are taken to Latvania—the moon. He describes a violent pull of forces. Blank stares; she was bombing. "Let's compare his description from one taken form *The Physics of Star trek*.

A few faces perked up. Thank god, there were some trekkies here.

"Look here how he understands that acceleration would be the worst part, how it would cause a body to be thrown up like gunpowder and says they must be given opiates beforehand."

Sharing the ideas from Kepler's imagination gives her a thrill—even if no one is listening.

"He realizes their limbs must be protected or they will be pulled apart by the opposing forces of moon and Earth. What we call today the spaghetti effect. He has them stretching and propelling by their own force, as magnetic forces of the Earth and the moon hold the body in suspension."

She looked up at faces slightly more interested in either the work or her; she wasn't sure. They held one good discussion about whether the description of D. watching demons spinning through space on the way to the moon agreed or disagreed with the Physics of Star Trek and what was known, theoretically, about falling through a black hole. Other than that, the talk was pretty much a disaster. She tried to get a point across explaining how these early astronomers would give up their health, their lives, to discover the truth. She brought up how Newton nearly blinded himself with his experiments with sunlight and colors.

All she got was, "Dude, that was stupid. Didn't he know looking at direct sunlight would blind him?"

"No" she said patiently. "Not back then. No one knew then."

The whole talk was a disappointment. Most people just left the photocopies on their chair. She picked them up so Kepler's words wouldn't get blown in the wind and stomped on. Then she dragged herself back to the tent. Jason was sitting by the station wagon.

"How'd it go?"

She hurried past him into the tent. *Aires, the ram*, she said in her head. *Aquilla: the Eagle, Andromenda: the woman chained.*

Jason followed her into the tent. He looked worried. She must have had that blank look in her eyes she got when her mind went through these recitations.

"I am a wacko, a weirdo, whatever you said before," she

yelled, her concentration broken.

"Nooooo, you're not," he said holding the back of her head with both his hands.

"Yes, I am," she shouted. *I'll never be right for Peter or anyone else*, she thought. At that moment, Jason was a little too close again. She pulled away. "Sorry, I'm okay. Just a little disappointed."

She hurried out of the tent. Jason followed.

"Let's go to the hill," he said. "Check out the scopes"

"I can't. I have to go."

"Looks like it's going to be clear tonight."

"I know, but I really have to go and get down to Worcester."

He knew she was lying. Why would she come all the way up here and miss a clear night? He helped her take down the tent and pack up the station wagon.

"Nice to see you again. Take care of yourself." He kissed her on the forehead, and they held onto each other for a few minutes. Then she left, kicking up dust on the narrow dirt paths. She didn't head home but up north to the loft fantasizing that Peter would return early and surprise her there just before nightfall. But in the real world, she would be alone with the new telescope, the binoculars, and she hoped a clear sky. She remembered what her mother said to her about why she shouldn't be alone so much. She said the night air is a cold companion.

Alone in the loft with the night air, she did feel lonely. Was it solitude? That is what she had always told herself, but there was a burden to this silence since she'd met Peter. Still it was something she couldn't ignore—something he would have to accept. She knew she loved him now. She had no doubts as she looked through the long window to the mountains, and as darkness fell, she knelt at the window seat and picked up the ribbon, dry now, and she looped it around her fingers.

Even as a little girl, she had strange fantasies. Now she

wished she had the tea set up here so she could sit at the table downstairs pouring tea for Kepler, Newton, and Einstein. She'd have them all sit together with her defying the laws of space and time.

As darkness fell, she didn't set up the small scope or try to use the binoculars. She lay in bed with the drapes wide open staring at the stars, wishing she could dance among them, levitating her body, a gaseous form, frolicking and skipping and touching each star and planet as she did when she was a child trying to fall asleep.

She woke very early in the morning startled by an absence of sound, a deliberate quiet. She heard something. *Footsteps?* It could be Jason; she couldn't remember if she'd locked the door last night.

"Hello?" Nothing.

She pulled the covers over her head. *Could be squatters*, she thought. *Or the imaginary scientists helping themselves to morning tea.*

Chapter Ten

1978

All afternoon, Gloria helps her daughter discover the world step-by-step, plunking her feet onto the solid ground. Only one thing ruins it, her anxiety about Thomas' expectations. No, she wants to tell him. She wants to scream no about so many things. No, she did not want to kill herself by jumping into the water; no, she could not miraculously speak after weeks, maybe months of silence. No, she could not completely immerse herself with their beautiful baby daughter, and, no, she could not tell him why. Instead, after they leave, she swings her legs up, lies down, turns on her side, and stares at the sky. Studies the tops of the trees, goes over it again. *What could have happened to ruin paradise?*

She and Thomas had almost broken up the winter before they moved to Vermont. It was a strange time. Confusing, she remembers. She wanted to be more spontaneous, more open like Thomas' friends, but she was always too worried, always wanted Thomas all to herself. Freedom was too much, total freedom almost depressing. Thomas was on this ride without boundaries, and he wanted to take her with him, but if she didn't have his sleeve to cling onto, she would be lost.

Lost. That's how she feels now. So lost, she cannot grasp what has sent her into this state of numbness. Now she apparently had Thomas all to herself, and they have a daughter. They are not always surrounded by so many people, everyone expecting something of him. What is keeping her from paradise now? Something too hard to remember. Something has plunged her into this overwhelming state of gray, and she is trying to crawl out, trying to pull herself out. *People should pull themselves up by their bootstraps*, she remembers her father saying when she was a child. Anyone could succeed, he used to say, anyone with determination. They were all trying to help her, she supposed. That's why they were here, but when she thought too deeply, her thoughts became smothered in pain.

She remembers one night especially well. A night she and Thomas had almost broken up the winter before they moved up here. They had been at the Blue Plate, and she and Thomas got into a fight, probably about how possessive she was. It was November, a few weeks before his birthday. He had taken off in a car with some other people and left her there to find her own ride home.

"Don't worry about it. He'll get over it," Tiny, the bouncer had told her. "Everybody gets crazy in November."

She knew there were other people she could get a ride with, but when he just left like that, it had broken something inside her. Somehow she knew she could not be without him no matter what the compromises would be. She didn't want to need him so much, and maybe that was the same now—she didn't want to need anyone so much; that way no one could disappoint her or leave her.

Gloria, confused and heartbroken, had taken any ride she could get, found a ride with a group of kids going back to Worcester, his friends not hers. They stopped at the Wachusett Reservoir and walked around in a group, so stoned, all laughing, kissing each other, talking. How come women can't love women, men love men? She sat on a dam by the water. They were all making out with each other, loving each other, and she wondered why she couldn't be part of all that. It was a beautiful night, warm for November, full of stars falling from a meteor shower. She watched them fall around her, wondering why she couldn't be free like the other kids, open, not jealous, not tied down to conventions, but she just could not be like them. She didn't fit in anywhere.

One of the guys, a friend of Thomas', came over to her, sat down, stroked her hair, and kissed her lips. He lifted her into his lap, and they kissed again. Then, they both looked into the water. Shooting stars were coming down all around them, and they watched the reflection in the reservoir. She looked over at the others who were all watching the sky—girls kissing girls, boys kissing boys. All of them in a big huddle trying to break down everything, trying to open up new, purer codes of morality. She knew what they were doing was okay for them, but not for her. She wasn't cool with it. Her heart was empty for Thomas. She had to have that one person to hold onto who she knew would be there, but she envied them their freedom.

Thomas' friend and she walked to the car. They lay down across the back seat. He kissed her eyelids. He put his hand up her blouse then touched her breast, and she began to cry.

"I'm sorry," she said. "I can't. I want to but I can't."

"It's okay. It's cool," he said and held her while she cried.

She remembers pain and memories. Did she get into an accident? She thinks it was a long winter in New England but not as bad up here in Vermont as it was down in Worcester. She was sure they got a lot of snow. What else could they expect up here? But her mother had come up with a tee shirt for the baby that said I survived the Blizzard of '78. Her mother had thought it was so cute. She thinks she remembers some argument about it, looking at it saying, "But, ma, we didn't have a blizzard up here, not like you did." And it had become a big deal because her dad had started on how she could never accept a gift gracefully. She always had to have some kind of comment. It could not have been that long ago, and apparently, she was still functioning then, still able to talk.

She will look for that tee shirt, she decides, next time she goes into the house. Maybe it will spark a deeper remembrance. She tries to remember where she had put it. The chalet was not that large; storage space was minimal, so it shouldn't take long to find. It feels good to have some kind of purpose, some kind of clue. Maybe seeing the tee shirt, *I survived the blizzard of '78*, will somehow bring some realization some insight about the dreams of snow. Even now, she sees the drifts every time she closes her eyes, even though it's summer.

Thomas brings Amanda out, and this time, to her delight, they go for a family walk. Thomas holds one hand, Gloria the other, and Amanda waddles in between, her chubby legs skimming the ground. Thomas says "One, two, three, whee" and they lift her up, and she laughs and says "gen, gen." They walk through the back yard avoiding the fragrant bushes down by the pond where Gloria really wants to be, but she lets Thomas lead them feeling the pure joy of her hand in Amanda's. Though Amanda shouts "gen, gen," Thomas waits until their child has almost given up and suddenly breaks into a run. "One, two, three," and they both lift her into the air.

Thomas leaves again, and she is alone on the bench, and she is so happy with what happened today because she can feel her body a little tired, a little more alive. She even likes the soreness in her arms from lifting Amanda and bringing her down. She watches the sunset from the bench, feeling a little cool now with the cut-offs and sleeveless tunic. Her sister calls to her to come in, but she is watching the gray dusk begin to encroach on the pink wisps of sunset left behind as the earth turns away from the transparent blue of the daytime sky. She is glad that her sister stops calling and doesn't insist that she obey and follow whatever regimen has been designed this evening to make her get better.

They'll probably have a yoga session this evening, but Gloria feels like she has breathed deeper today than she has in a long time just walking with Amanda and Thomas. She has to remember when she goes in to look for the tee shirt. Her baby survived the blizzard of 78; the tee shirt says so. Why didn't she, Gloria, survive the winter? If she could find it, maybe she would remember. It must be somewhere. She'll look through the baby's drawers, the bassinette now too big to hold her. It might have tumbled between sweet powdery smelling blankets, stacks of white diapers, bibs, and pacifiers. What secrets do they hide?

When the sky is dark, every bit of color gone, she'll go in. She doesn't want to be pushed today. She'll join the others when she's ready. The baby may already be asleep, and Thomas may be playing pong on that snowy little TV her parents brought up here for them. Her sister is probably the only one who can't relax; she can feel her constant glance out the window. She's waiting for something more than the others. It makes Gloria nervous to think that when she does open her mouth, the sound she makes, the words she speaks, had better be something important.

Chapter Eleven

Hill of stars II

By Sunday morning, Amanda was down at the Worcester apartment reading the Telegram then the Boston Globe and thinking about Peter. She called him, but he was out. Next Sunday, the house would not be so empty; Peter would be back. Tomorrow was the first day of her summer course and she should have been putting together a syllabus, but she was restless. What kind of fun was he having without her? It was nearly too hot for movement.

The heat broke with a lightening show. The sky turned black and rain threw itself against the windows, washing over the thick panes of glass in the old Victorian. Amanda sat on a window seat surrounded by three panes of glass, putting her hands on the glass and feeling its coolness. Glass was always such a comfort to her, such a curiosity, and a boundary and a portal at once. Her glasses, the wavy glass in old windows, the optics in telescopes—a way of reaching beyond with your eyes, your mind, but not with your body. Not yet. She jumped when the phone rang. Peter. They spoke only a few words.

"Thunderstorm" she shouted through the phone above the static.

"It's beautiful here," he said and then the phone went dead.

She looked at the receiver for a few minutes.

"Bye," she said to dead air. "I love you."

After the storm, she walked to Dunkin Donuts with her briefcase, got a cup of coffee, and organized her notes for the class. Now she felt half-hearted about it, hardly knew why she'd insisted she had to stay here to teach it. It wouldn't go much better than the talk at Stellafane. She tried to forget what a disappointment that had been.

Instead of taking notes for the class, she kept thinking about Stellafane. She should have stayed and observed Saturday night, but instead, she had escaped to the chalet. Had Jason set her fleeing? Was she afraid of what Peter would think if he knew she ran into him? She didn't want to think like that. It was her mother's voice in her head telling her not to trust anyone, making her think all through her childhood that she was about to walk into the middle of a train wreck. No wonder she had slept-walked when she was young; it was the only time she could move her feet without her mother's warning signs blaring around her. But *something* had compelled her to leave Stellafane, go to the loft, and be completely alone as if she was running toward something, not running away.

The sky was completely clear when she walked home, the air refreshing. Tonight she would make up for the observing she had missed last night. The sun wouldn't completely set until after nine, and she had class tomorrow, but she didn't care. She would stay up half the night to witness a glimpse of whatever was happening in the sky.

The phone startled her as she was putting a scope together. She didn't know it was working again. Peter scolded her for not calling him back, said he was worried. He hadn't known the phone was dead. On his end, he'd hardly heard a crackle. She listened to him mesmerized by the solitude she had been in before he called. She didn't mention going to the hill tonight, feeling guilty as if it would take her away from him even though they were already apart.

The sound of his voice across the wires lulled her, sound always being more immediate to her than sight. They talked for a long time, and when she got off the phone, dusk had begun to fall. She started to bring the binoculars out to the car, and the phone rang again.

"Hello."

"Hi, honey." Her mother. "When did you get back?"

"Around noon."

"I was afraid you were stuck in that storm. I was worried to death."

Amanda sighed. "My phone was dead. That's why I couldn't call earlier."

"I called you a while ago and it rang. Then it was busy for a long time."

Amanda sighed again. "I was talking to Peter. I'm on my way out the door. I'll call you tomorrow. I'll come over after work."

She hung up the phone before her mother could ask her where she was going at this time of night when she had work tomorrow. She grabbed the binoculars and, at the last minute, decided to take just the optics that went to the new telescope then ran out the door before the phone could ring again.

Glad to be alone in the car, away from ringing phones, the disconnected voices over wire that always made her feel uneasy, she pulled out of the driveway and headed toward the hill near her old apartment. Funny how she never minded the bleeps and pings of her dad's video machines. She didn't have to answer to those sounds as she did to a ringing telephone or a clanging school bell; they didn't require her to explain herself or rush somewhere at a certain time. They were more like an invitation to her. Come join me; step right up little lady try your luck. See if you can toss these rings around the dowels, win something from the top shelf. The bings and bleeps pulled her in like the barker at the carnival offering a chance to find what she was seeking, to watch the man take down the biggest teddy bear and hand it to her, scowling, because she had won the prize.

He would have greedy eyes, this gatekeeper, so she would grab it and hug it tightly to her chest, dig her nose into its soft fur with the stale-sweet smell of cotton candy, rescue it from its carnival life. That prize that was so hard to win that it was compelled to sit on a shelf, season after season, and listen to the man yell. The sound of video games offered that chance. It always comforted her, made her lose track of time, swallowing her into a world of timelessness where at least there was a chance she would find what was missing. The beeps and pings droning on like a lullaby of hope.

She drove by her old apartment wondering who lived there now and pulled off the main road to a small dirt road leading to the hill. She stopped the car just before the path and realized her dilemma. Though the path to the hill wasn't a long one, in the rush to get out, she had forgotten to bring a flashlight. It was not completely dark but it would be on the way back. She walked up the hill through the long grass still damp with rain noticing all she could to orient herself later in the dark. The daises, buttercups, and Indian paintbrushes of June had been replaced with the purple flowers of late summer. She thought they were called swamp azaleas. There was water nearby. The low-bush blueberries already smelled like they were in over bloom.

At the top, she took out the binoculars. Mars was out, and if she stayed till midnight, she'd see Jupiter. As it got darker, she turned to the west searching for M13. A cluster of stars so far away, it looked like a fuzzy ball. Breathtaking. To see that far was even more amazing than the crackle of voices sent thousands of miles across wires. Maybe, in the future, Peter out in California could be projected at a god-awful speed in almost no time and be back at the apartment in Worcester. His molecules would come together and be dumped in front of her as she sat reading the Sunday paper on the couch. Hi, honey, I'm home.

Already, his voice could be transmitted from one end of the country to another. If it weren't for that damn ringing, she would almost like the telephone. She longed for this solitude, the deep connection to silence, and she wished a curtain could be pulled aside so she could see what the skies were like before light pollution and when sound waves that traveled were nothing more than human voices, water dripping, and footsteps crunching through deep snow.

The moon was only a sliver. She went back to the binoculars again searching for planets and star clusters, exhilarated and lonely, *almost* sure that marrying Peter was the right thing to do, yet still teetering on some invisible point between times, a boundary that frightened and compelled her, a need to step beyond solid ground like a child learning to walk, unaware of the laws of physics, ready to walk off the edge of a table if no one was there to stop her. She put the binoculars down and lifted up the cracked yellowed slab of a mirror she had bought at Stellafane. It was not that heavy.

She lifted it to her face and peered through, transfixed by a glow of overwhelming brightness. A light so bright it seemed to be falling toward her, (the full moon falling through the sky). She looked away, lost her grip, and felt herself falling backwards as the glass fell to the ground, but, strangely, she was still on her feet. The glass had not broken. The moon was still only a sliver. The glow was gone.

Okay, enough. She started to pack up. It would not be cool to fall asleep here under the stars, which she suddenly had the urge to do. Her mother and Peter would think she was crazy. She put her binoculars and mirror in the backpack, which seemed heavier than before, and walked down the hill. Somebody had probably just turned on some huge light, some beacon for a few seconds, or maybe it was late summer fireworks.

Her night vision was good; thank god for that. It was very dark. Occasionally, she bumped into a rock or a twig or felt an incline with a foot, but it seemed like solid ground beneath her. Then she put one foot into pure air but quickly brought it back again regaining her balance as she realized she was on the ledge that she usually avoided not far from where the field ended and the path to the road began. She knew the drop was not steep, but the rocks were slippery from the earlier storm. She stepped gingerly to the right where the path should be, concentrating on every rock, stump, and twig, but she lost her footing and fell sideways.

"Damn," she said, as she hit the ground. What was the use? What was she doing here anyway?

"Fuck, fuck, fuck." She lay on the ground for a while, knowing that when she got up again she would be in pain. She groped around for the binoculars. She pulled herself up, groaning, and she heard a rattle in her backpack. A small piece of the mirror had broken off. She put everything back and limped down the path to the car. It was late; there were no cars on the road. Her foot hurt but not too badly; it was the left ankle so driving wasn't a problem.

She limped into the house leaving everything in the car. She put ice on her foot, clicked on the TV, and fell asleep on the couch. She woke up at six am and checked the messages on her phone. One from Peter, three from her mother saying Peter had called to see if she knew where she was. She'd meant to call him, but it was late when she got in, and her ankle hurt, and she'd fallen asleep. Now she couldn't call because it was something like 3 am in California. It was hard enough for her to keep track of her own time zone. Weird how time was different in different places. Her class wasn't until ten thirty, and she should have organized, but instead she hobbled to bed, set the alarm for nine, and turned the ringer off in case her mother called while she was asleep.

Later, as she drove to campus, she chugged down coffee from Dunkin Donuts trying to ease the dizziness inside her head. She shouldn't have stayed out so late; her ankle ached, and she needed to get herself together. The first class was always the hardest. Trying to remember names, establish a pattern for the next few weeks, and to present herself as a professional, not some overtired science fiction obsessed mathematician.

When she got to the classroom, the fans were already on and the windows open. One student had come early, a girl so intent on what she was reading she didn't even look up when Amanda walked in. Amanda snapped open her briefcase trying to give the air of a teacher who knew what she was doing, pulled one desk over so it was next to the door, and placed several handouts on it. But when she turned around, a breeze lifted the papers, and they flew out of the room. The student looked up.

"That's what happens when a force besides gravity moves on a body," Amanda said, smiling at the girl.

The student, stone-faced, said nothing and went back to reading her book. Amanda gathered the papers and picked up a stone probably meant as a doorjamb and placed it on top of them.

"Gravity'" she said. "Wins out every time."

Other students began to come in. The room filled up quite well. She had not looked at the information the registrar had given her. She should have. The first class did not go well. She ran out of handouts. The grounds crew was working around the parking lot so she had to shout over the buzzing machines, and no one knew the answer to the first question she always asked a new class—what is a googol. She had a feeling the stone-faced girl knew but just wasn't saying. In fact, no one seemed very interested in physics at all.

There were a few English majors who had been interested in the sci-fi aspect of it but they were disappointed when they saw it was only a fragment. They were mostly students with other majors who wanted to get a science requirement over with in the summer. It was an all-day class held for only 2 weeks. No students inspired her to think they might be interested beyond a grade. They broke for lunch at 12:00 and were back at one. She went up to her office, took the tea set out, and whined to her imaginary friends.

I don't know what to do. I don't think I want to teach.

She poured more tea, coffee for her.

They'd all freak if I said I was going to quit my job: mom and my dad, especially Peter. So what am I supposed to do? Feel stuck forever?

They shook their heads.

Once my mother tried to push me into medicine. Remember that? She just wanted to be able to tell everyone her daughter was a doctor.

Her friends looked at each other skeptically.

Yes, she said. *These days, women can be doctors.*

They all looked at each other again. One raised an eyebrow.

And my father, she went on. *Once mentioned maybe I should look into accounting. Accounting! Imagine my father, who helped me do experiments, helped me with my science fair inventions, trying to get me to be an accountant.*

They didn't nod their heads at that indignity. One of them put his head to the side, pensively, as if he may have agreed with the idea.

They were not helping today. Nothing was helping.

She went back down to face her class for the afternoon, determined to make it interesting for herself and the students.

She stopped at her parent's house on the way home. No one was there. *Good.* She let herself in and went down to the basement. Her ankle ached, and her head ached; her throat was parched from the humidity and from talking all day. She'd kill for a cold beer but had to settle for papaya juice and gagged as it went down. At least it was wet. She plugged in her dad's video games; Ms. Packman was her favorite. She used to play with her dad so much they had made up Ms. Packman philosophies of life:

Ms. Packman says eat energy dots fast; Ms. Packman says grab all the strawberries; Ms. Packman says let them fill your tongue with flavor and life sustaining energy before the ghosts gobble you up.

She booted up an old Ben Franklin Computer and put in an ancient cartridge to start Jumpman then moved from machine to machine, drinking papaya juice, forgetting about eating supper and concentrating on the thoughts in her head.

Theories of time, how time traveled. She wanted to get at least one student excited about world lines, time cones closed time-like curves. Maybe some of them would get interested in folded space-time and wormholes. She debated with herself how much she should bring that up or if she would lose them or if they would even think *that* was boring. As long as they got by, as long as they graduated and got a good job, maybe a teaching job like hers, they didn't care. She didn't want to teach anymore. Not like this.

They'd all be on her back if she said she was going to quit her job. Peter, her parents. She pulled the knob back as far as she could; it sprung forward on its journey, sending six metal balls on a wild ride to hit 400, 600, 800 points. She shook her head thinking again of how he had tried to get her interested in accounting. What had happened to their life of discovery and experiments up in Vermont? The only part left of that life was the machines he refused to give up no matter how much her mother complained.

"They're antiques," she'd heard him say in an argument her parents had over and over again while she was growing up. "They'll be worth a lot of money someday. They're worth a lot now."

"Then why don't we sell them?"

"I'm keeping them as an investment."

Then her mother would lower her voice "They're not good

for Amanda. She spends too much time down here by herself. She's obsessed with them just like you were."

Amanda had lived in fear that her mother would win the argument and one day she would come home from school and they would all be gone. She'd liked having them on when she did her homework.

"They help me think," she would say to her mother.

And her mother would say, "How can you think with all that noise?"

She suspected they had helped her father think too until he had stopped thinking and become a businessman. She could live without a telephone, a cell phone, a television, a VCR, and an air conditioner, but somehow she could not live without the bleeps and pings of these games.

"They help me think," she said aloud as she lost track of time, her aching ankle, her empty stomach.

"Amanda?"

She jumped; she hadn't heard her mother come in the door or walk down the stairs. She turned around and stared back at her mother feeling guilty about something.

"What's wrong with you? You look awful."

Amanda hobbled to the couch.

"Have you eaten at all today? What's wrong with your foot?"

Her mother went to the refrigerator, spread peanut butter on celery sticks, and brought them to her on the couch.

"I'm alright. I turned my ankle."

"You don't look alright. You should go for an x-ray."

"It's... I've just been on it too long. It's not a big deal."

"I'll get some ice. You lie down."

Her mother turned off all the machines and turned the TV on over the bar.

Amanda sighed.

"Why don't you just stay here until Peter gets back?"

About now, Amanda wished she had gone with Peter. She

asked her mother for the mobile phone, and then her mother went upstairs saying she was going to fix her something more substantial. She rang the hotel. He picked up right away.

"Hello."

"Hi, it's me."

"I miss you, babe. How are you doing? You sound kind of ..."

"Disgusted? Well, I'm lying on the couch at my parents' house with an ice pack on my ankle, and my mom is driving me crazy."

"What happened?"

"I sprained it slightly last night."

"How was your class?"

"Disappointing. I should have gone with you. I wish I had."

She thought she could feel Peter's glee across the phone lines at this concession. Was it in his breathing or the slight pause, or the words he didn't say? He probably wouldn't be so gleeful when she told him she'd decided to give up teaching.

"I'm not doing much here either, going downstairs for dinner. Some of us might go out afterwards. "

"I hope you don't have any fun," she said.

"You could have come. I begged you to come."

"I know. I love you. Call me when you get in, no matter how late, okay?"

"Are you staying there tonight?"

"No, at the apartment. I told you my mother's driving me crazy."

"Love you."

"Call me to say goodnight."

"It will be late for you."

"Call me anyway."

"I will."

"Bye"

Amanda sat up. Her foot felt better, but she was dizzy from

not eating. What was her mother making upstairs? All she wanted was a burger.

Her mother came down with a tray of burgers, organic chips, salt-free mayo, and catsup; she poured two more glasses of juice. Amanda's mouth watered for real food. She picked a burger and took a bite.

"This is tofu isn't it?"

"You can't really tell the difference. Here, take these vitamin E pills to heal your ankle. I guess we won't be able to go shopping for the wedding dress tomorrow?"

"I guess not." Amanda shrugged.

Her mother went over to the fridge behind the bar probably seeking out some disgusting carob dessert.

"I saw Jason at Stellafane," Amanda said and looked at her mother whose face had frozen into a smile.

"Oh. How's he doing?"

"He actually has a job now." Her mother went to the couch with a plate of oatmeal carob cookies. Amanda went over to join her. "He's a cook. You'd like him better. He's into health food now."

"I never trusted that boy."

"Mother, you practically adopted him every year when I was little and we went to Stellafane. You liked him well enough then."

"I felt bad for him; his mother was sick." Her mouth puckered, her teeth stabbing at the carob cookies. "I never thought he was right for you."

Amanda sat forward. "I can't believe you still hold a grudge. You're convinced he was the one who got me to chop off my hair and get a tattoo when I wanted to do those things anyway."

Funny when they first started dating, Jason had told her she was so conservative that she was radical. She knew her mother had been afraid she would run away with Jason and move up to the loft and then she would see that weird haunted look in her mother's eyes. Then she would watch her mother's lips pucker and feel sorry for her, trying to comfort instead of confront. There was something her mother couldn't say in words, only in warnings.

Her mother looked around eyeing the pinball machines and games more suspiciously than ever.

"I'm going back to the apartment," Amanda said.

"I'll stop over before you go to work," her mother said. "In case you need anything."

Amanda escaped the house and drove back to the apartment only because her mother was worried if she stayed down on the couch she would end up getting up in the middle of the night in a zombie-like state, plug in all the machines, and play a subversive game of pinball while the rest of the world was asleep.

Chapter Twelve

1978

Last night Gloria forced herself to stay awake all night and think. As usual, her sister brought the calendar to her first thing this morning to make sure she knew what day it was. This is something that does not matter to her. How can she make her sister understand that she wants to be with her baby in the morning? She wants her baby to be brought to her while she's still in bed to drink from her swollen breasts, but Suzanne still does not trust her with the baby in the morning; besides the baby has been weaned and her breasts are no longer swollen. Gloria doesn't know when this happened. She has tried to piece everything together through what she hears, especially the arguments that Suzanne and their parents were having, but they're careful about how they talk when she's around. She's heard the words of concern drifting out the window, even when voices were not raised.

How long was it, at least a few days ago maybe a week, maybe two since they argued? Maybe it is worthwhile that her sister brings her to a calendar every day. Maybe she should pay more attention to what her sister tells her. Maybe her baby was weaned without her knowledge, abruptly, because she didn't pay enough attention to the passage of time. Maybe it was because she was taking medicine. There may have been reasons, but she will never forgive them for letting her baby's suck be taken from her so abruptly. The baby must have cried waiting to be put into her arms. She's getting angry thinking about it.

She looks down and notices she is wringing her hands. Silent tears fall down her face and onto her knees. They took away her morning time with her baby, just took her away; she is so angry. They should have just not given her the medicine for whatever reason she needed it, and brought the baby to feed every morning. This would have healed her. Now it's too late. They've severed her from her child. She thinks it's probably Suzanne's doing; she seems to be in charge right now. Her parents don't seem to be around anymore since the day Suzanne told them she shouldn't take medicine anymore. Drugs she called it, legal drugs. She guesses maybe she can't completely blame Suzanne because she never had a child and would not understand the deep need not to break apart the physical connection after you've given birth, the need for you and your baby to be connected at mouth and nipple, to keep giving that baby life from the fluids that are inside you.

Partly it's her own fault, she supposes; maybe if she could have uttered the words and told them, things would have gone more her way, but it's been so long since she talked now. The idea of making coherent sounds almost frightens her as if the words would really conjure whatever it is she can't or won't remember. So every morning now starts with her wordlessly helping Suzanne with breakfast, and then Suzanne takes her to the calendar as if it is of the utmost importance that she know the day of the week, the month, the year. Today was particularly annoying because she was so tired. Now that she's on the bench with the sun shining on her, she can think, maybe snooze for a while and wander through the thoughts that kept her up all night in spite of the sleepy time tea; her sister makes her drink so much tea to go to sleep, she's up half the night going to the bathroom.

She had gone looking for the tee shirt last night, the one her mother had bought for the baby during the winter. She had torn apart the bassinet and the drawers with Thomas staring at her like she was a lunatic and Suzanne holding him back saying, "Let her be." Gloria had actually been somewhat amused because they had no idea what she was looking for but also frustrated and angry with herself knowing they could help her find it if she could only ask. Help her get to the bottom of her mind's need for that tee shirt and how the mounds of snow from last winter made her forget how to be alive, how to talk. She wants to remember now, doesn't care how the remembering might rip through her heart. She wants to finally break the sound barrier even if it begins a howl, a scream so deep and enduring it would rend them all apart.

    She wishes she could jump up and scream, but instead, she just watches her hands as she wrings them. She feels the silent tears drip and notices a small stirring in her feet, a movement of pent up agitation, something you'd see people doing in a classroom or at a meeting when they wanted to get up and leave but they couldn't because it would be impolite. Her feet move faster, and she wants to get up and run. Why can't she? She can't move the way she wants to because something is keeping her back. Fear. She must control this restless agitation right now just as she must control her vocal chords. She hasn't felt this kind of energy for a long time. She's afraid of her energy—afraid of her own feet. The need to move is so intense it might propel her right off the Earth. Her feet might run to the pond in the back yard, to the overwhelming sweet smell of the flowering bush, the smell of death, of funerals, too many flowers in one room. Cut flowers, their stems dumped into water that will only keep them alive so long.

    Besides, if she got up and began to run around the house, which she wants to do right now, they would only think she was crazier; it would reinforce their beliefs about her and only keep her from her baby longer. They have taken her baby away, broken that bond, and that is the cruelest thing of all. How could they claim to love her? They all want her to get better, so they say. They all want her to talk. But they would have to deal with the consequences of her broken silence too. Did they realize that? Were they strong enough?

Last night, when she was tearing through everything in the house, especially the baby things, they had looked at her in alarm. Even though Suzanne had tried to keep her "professional face," she could see that her sister was getting concerned. If it wasn't for their faces, faces that seemed to warn caution, she may have broken the barrier last night. She may have started the scream deep in her stomach and have begun to throw everything around because she was disappointed at not finding the tee shirt. Something inside her had begun to make her very angry as she lifted the blankets and diapers and toys, had begun this anger she was still feeling this morning.

She had wanted to throw everything in the air, throw it against the wall. And had they not held her back with their looks of concern, she might have hurled it all through the large picture window at the top of the loft just for the relief of hearing the glass shatter as she got rid of these things that were causing her grief beyond all understanding. But she had managed to grit her teeth and squelch the scream. They were watching, her family was watching, and she was mostly afraid they would never trust her to be a mother, never trust her with the baby again. She had stopped her search when Suzanne called her to the table for supper; then after they were asleep, she began a quiet search again. Calmly, methodically she had continued the search.

So she's very tired sitting here today, and she just wants to cry, but also she wants to run. She is no closer to finding the tee shirt that she is now convinced is the key to something that happened, and she wonders if Thomas will still bring her child to her considering the way she acted last night. She cries quietly making a sound that nobody hears but herself. If her sister is glancing at her from the window, will she notice her body shaking even in the June heat? It would be so simple just to tell them what she wants to find, but when Thomas had asked her, with all his patience, "Honey, what is it you're looking for?," she had only stared at him, still struck mute and gone back to bed.

She tries to remember if she has ever felt this restlessness before. She had felt restless when she was in college and had to sit through boring classes. That restlessness had become more intense when Thomas transferred to WPI and she was still at Worcester State. She knew he still loved her, hadn't left her behind, knew he would still pick her up in the brightly painted "garden van" when she was done her classes for the day, but she still felt left behind. As it was, she had been missing something she wanted to be part of, and, though Thomas had been so thoroughly involved, she remained on the outskirts, an observer.

It wasn't his fault. She herself had been unwilling to completely commit to the freedom. A commitment to freedom—that's what he'd wanted from her, not a commitment of a life together. The chaos of it all had confused her though her adolescent spirit wanted to accept his ideals. Thomas had just gone right on believing that he could change the world, even after all those rock stars OD'd in '69, even after Kent State in '70. He just went right on believing that we could change the world when all the others were dropping out, burnt from years of drugs, saying "fuck it," and letting society roll along and simply leaving it, giving up, not even trying any longer to bring about change.

After the community in Hubbardston started falling apart, Thomas and a few others were trying to start something up on Highland Street at the Garden of earthly delights, but no one seemed to be as enthusiastic as him anymore. She remembers one night when they were at the Struck of Loke, a storefront restaurant a couple of their friends had started with loans from their parents—the only place in Worcester besides the Garden where she and Thomas would go. It lifted his spirits to be in a place that had been created with a vision. Two of their friends, Denny and Freddie had started it first selling their wholegrain bread to students at Worcester State and then serving the loaves at the storefront café with bowls of soup. They were the first vegetarians she'd ever known.

That day, she and Thomas were seated at a table by the window with a huge papier-mâché character seated next to them. All around the restaurant were these characters an artist friend had created, characters who sat forever in their seats where the smell of bread lingered and the smell of every meal clung to their paper skin. It was a long narrow restaurant and had always made Gloria feel a little claustrophobic, with characters looming and a huge blackboard between two long rows of tables advertising the day's menu. The candle was lit on their table, and they'd sat in silence for a while sharing a basket of bread.

Gloria could see Thomas was discouraged. He rested one elbow on the table. She remembers his hand behind his ear fidgeting with his black curls that were growing all tangled around it. He took off his glasses and leaned into Gloria speaking softly.

"I don't know, babe, there so much tension even at the Garden now." He shook his head. "I thought we could get something going around here, but I'm not sure if we can. We might have to leave Worcester, this whole area."

He'd rubbed his eyes, looked at Gloria in a kind of pleading way, as if she had some answers. At this time, she didn't know what he was getting at, not yet, but she'd liked the way he was looking at her in a kind of conspiratorial way. Truthfully, she remembers she was hoping it meant they would have some time alone together as a couple. Hoping it meant they would have a break from the changing world, but, though everyone else seemed to be running for cover after the great wave of energy, recovering from all the changes in the 60's, Thomas had never seemed anywhere near giving up. If anything, he was dreaming bigger than ever before.

Her ruminating stops suddenly as she hears the giggles of Amanda being swung like an airplane by her father toward her mother.

"Gen, Gen" she cries. Thomas swings her right into Gloria's lap. God bless Thomas—St. Thomas the kind, for bringing her their baby again. Gloria puts her arms around Amanda and holds her very tightly; at first, she squirms but then stops and puts her head on Gloria's shoulder. Thomas sits next to them, pulls Gloria toward him, and kisses her on the head. Thomas rubs Gloria's shoulder. Gloria strokes the baby's back with the fingertips of one hand, and they all hang onto each other for dear life.

Later in the day, Gloria gets up from the bench and goes inside. She goes to the small fridge at the top of the loft and gets Papaya juice. This is mostly what it is stocked with now that her sister is here. Apparently, it is some kind of breakthrough because her sister approaches her beaming, elated that Gloria has left the bench without any prompting and that she has helped herself to something. Apparently, according to her sister's hyperactive chatter, she hasn't taken anything to eat or drink for quite some time unless it's put in front of her. Strange then, Gloria thinks that she hasn't lost her baby tummy. The Papaya Juice is tart but refreshing. She licks her lips.

At evening yoga, she makes an extra effort to breathe the way her sister instructs her. Deeply, hold it; let it out slowly. A storm has come up; she can hear the thunder. She peeks out when she is supposed to be in deep relaxation to see sheets of rain flowing down the picture window. She hopes it ends by tomorrow; she doesn't know what she will do if she can't go outside and sit on the bench.

Chapter Thirteen

THE LETTER

When Amanda got home that night, she hobbled to the back yard, took out her briefcase, and stuffed it under a workbench after taking out a pair of binoculars. She had sat on the bench observing and thought about her day. It wasn't that she didn't want to teach. She just wanted to teach differently—more like Socrates did sitting under a tree or here in her back yard. Maybe she could be a tutor—homeschool kids in science. Maria Mitchel was a teacher. She had actually been younger than Amanda when she opened a school in her home.

She looked over at the sawhorses Peter had set up, his sawed planks by the side of the house covered with tarps. He had been busy with some project when he left but wouldn't tell her what it was. She heard a car door slam, hard. *It must be a neighbor.* There were a bunch of kids in the neighborhood, and with school starting soon, maybe she could start some kind of after school program that would combine science with childcare. On Friday nights, they could all clamor around her telescope. They could go on field trips to the hill by her old apartment. Kids might be more interested at a younger age.

"Mom?" Amanda couldn't believe the person scurrying into the back yard was her mother. "What's the matter? Did something happen to daddy?" She always worried about her father; he was away so much of the time.

"What are you doing out here? Where's the portable? You shouldn't be on that foot. Peter's been trying to call you for hours."

"He has? What time is it?"

"He's frantic. I said I'd call when I found you."

"When you found me? Was I lost? Mother, what did you tell him?"

"I told him you left our house hours ago to rest your sprained ankle. He'd been calling you and there was no answer so he called me."

"I just decided to observe for a while. I can't believe how clear it is. Look. You can see all seven sisters."

"Amanda, call Peter. He's worried sick."

"Thanks to you."

Her mother went into the house and turned every light on. She had already dialed when Amanda took the receiver from her.

"Hi, it's me."

"Where were you?"

"In the back yard." Amanda glared at her mother who went into the other room. "What did my mother tell you?"

"That your foot was worse. That no one could find you."

Amanda shook her head. "She's pathetic. If she doesn't know where I am for one second, she panics."

"So you're all right. There's nothing wrong with you?"

"I'm fine."

"I was worried. Why didn't you call?"

"I called earlier, remember?" She was tired of being scolded.

"It's nine here, so it's midnight there. Why do you have to be goddamn observing in the middle of the night?"

"That's when the stars are out?"

"When are you going to sleep?"

"As soon as my mother leaves."

"Well, I'm glad you're okay. I miss you."

"Me too."

She hung up and went in to the kitchen where her mother was waiting. She put some water on to boil.

"I have some sleepy time," she said. "Just for you."

Her mother sighed. "I'm going to be exhausted at work tomorrow now anyway."

"Why don't you stay here?"

"No, you're father might try to call. My body is already unbalanced. I'll take extra ginseng root in the morning."

"You talked to dad?"

"I put in a call to him. It's hard to get a hold of him when he's in Japan. The time difference." She shook her head, hurried to the door.

"When's he coming home?"

"I'm not sure. They keep changing his schedule."

Amanda dragged her briefcase into the house, iced her foot, thinking about her mother. How her mother must have missed her father when he went on so many business trips across the world in the last few years.

Amanda stayed focused on her family for the rest of the week—calling Peter, calling her mother, taking care of her ankle—missing Peter in California and her father in Japan. She had a few more tea parties in the office to get her through. She wondered aloud to them about how families coped in other centuries without phones when they needed to be apart. What worries families had when they needed to be away on business in the 17th century. How hard were the comings and goings? At least now, we could have the illusion that we were living without such uncertainty.

Peter came home on Sunday. Amanda hadn't realized how much she missed him until she saw him rushing over to her. He lifted her up and twirled her around right in the airport. Embarrassed, confused, and overjoyed she took his hand, wrapping herself in his solid arms for the long walk to baggage claim. They didn't leave the apartment all that day—not even to get the paper. They didn't answer the doorbell when they knew it was her mother. It had been good that he had gone away; the separation had made their love stronger than ever.

Amanda still had one more week of teaching, and on Monday, she came home exhausted from the heat and trying to teach students that had no interest in learning. Mercifully, Peter didn't say I told you so and go into what a drain it was to teach in the summer. Four days to go, then who knows. They had a glass of wine and some cheese and lay together on the bed only half listening to the sound of another car in the driveway. Her mother was coming over so they could go shopping for the wedding dress.

Amanda thought her mother was acting a little peculiar about the shopping. Like she was really all into it, but it was also kind of a chore, something unpleasant. She'd never seen a picture of her parent's wedding. They wore rings so they must have been married, but her mother never talked about it. It was in that time, that hippie time that her mother wanted to forget. Maybe it wasn't a legal wedding or maybe it had been one of those giant weddings in central park where some maharaja performed the ceremony for hundreds of couples at once. Whatever it was, she knew enough not to bring it up, and she supposed she could handle all the traditional crap if it would make her mother happy, if it was something she had missed.

Her mother had come in with a pile of mail that had come to the house in her name. Some flyers, a magazine, and a few envelopes she plunked down on the counter and stood in front of it.

"Amanda still gets mail at the house." She looked at Peter when she said this with one of those stuck smiles on her face and pushed her handbag up higher on her shoulder. "I won't keep her out too long, I promise."

Amanda poured herself a strong, dark coffee to fortify herself for a long afternoon.

"I won't keep her too long," her mother said again, smiling at Peter in the same phony way.

Amanda gave her mother a look, and she actually had to

pull her from the counter to get her outside. Maybe her ginseng intake was out of balance. Once in the bug, the AC brought back her drained energy. Maybe Peter was right. She shouldn't be putting herself through torture in that old building in the summer time. Their time apart had made her feel closer to him, and now she felt ready to go shopping for the dress. She felt closer to her mother too—who, strangely, was sitting next to her not saying one word. *Everything will work out,* she told herself. *I will get the dress I want and not the one my mother wants.*

They sweated as they walked from the car to the mall, and once inside, a blast of AC hit them so coldly, it nearly knocked Amanda over. They trudged toward Filenes. Her mother stayed upstairs; she headed down to the basement.

"I thought we were shopping together." Her mother called out, but Amanda just kept walking. Her mother came down in a few minutes telling her about a lovely cream-colored dress: lace arms, lace neckline, very Victorian, very traditional. "It would look so cute on you," she said. "Give a feminine touch to that short hair."

Amanda only half listened; she was heading toward the dressing room with an armful of dresses. "Come with me," she said to her mother. "Tell me what you think."

Looking for a dress was more fun than she thought it would be. Her mother seemed quiet, not nagging, or bossy. She tried on one after another, but nothing seemed right. One bunched too much at the waist and actually made her look too fat. Another had fitted lace arms that were too loose. Her mother made faces each time she came out in one. Amanda had to agree.

"We'll go to a bridal shop," her mother said." You may be hard to fit."

Accused again of being too skinny as if it were a crime, she didn't want to get involved in alterations and waiting periods and all the scrutiny and expense of a bridal shop. She sighed and looked at her mother.

"Let's go look at the one upstairs."

Amanda tried the dress on, and it did fit her. Maybe a little extra material here and there for a dress that was supposed to be fitted, but she liked flowing clothes. Her mother, of course, thought it was perfect because she had picked it out. As they paid for it, Amanda was relieved that this was over but also felt closer to her mother. As pathetic as it sounded, she and her mother had bonded over a dress. It was something. She realized in all the years she was growing up, although she was always in close proximity to her mother, there was something that wrangled at their ability to feel comfortable together. She always supposed it was just mother-daughter stuff. Today it seemed to her they had enjoyed each other's company. Her mother had picked the dress, but she did not feel it was forced on her. Back in the heat, they put the dress in the trunk and looked for a place to eat. This would have to be a compromise.

They went to a café inside a bookstore. Amanda ordered coffee and a BLT; her mother had red zinger and a cucumber and sprout sandwich.

"How was Stellafane?' Her mother asked

"Pretty good" she said, surprised her mother was bringing it up again. "I gave a talk this year. Not too many people showed up, but it was alright."

"A lot of people we know still go?"

"A lot of people looked familiar. The Burkes still go. They asked how you were doing. You and daddy should go up again sometime."

There was a pause. Her mother was acting weird again. Her hand trembled as she lifted the tea to her lips. "A letter came to the house from Jason. Were you up there with him?"

"Yes, I mean, no. What do you mean by with him?" There was that intensity, a restrained questioning in her mother's voice that she had recoiled from all her life. Still, she felt close to her mother today, so she touched her trembling hand. "Actually, you'd probably like him now. He's on a health kick."

Her mother looked away.

"How can you still be mad at him? You and daddy loved him when he was a boy at Stellafane."

"That only makes it worse. If anyone could ruin everything, it would be him."

"What are you talking about?" Amanda's heart began to race in panic. Confused, she remembered the way her father always seemed to be protecting her mother from any emotion. Be careful around your mother. He never really said the words, only with his eyes,

"He wrote you a letter."

"And...did you bring it?"

"It's in the pile of mail at Peter's apartment. Okay—your apartment." Her mother seemed to be calming down as her own panic was escalating. "I left it in the pile of mail so it wouldn't look suspicious. Whatever you do, make sure Peter doesn't know it's from your old boyfriend—the one you just happened to run into at Stellafane after you turned down the opportunity to go with him to California."

"What are you saying?"

"It doesn't look good."

Amanda gulped down the rest of her coffee and nearly burned her throat.

"Don't drink so fast," her mother said. "It's not good for your digestion."

"I'm done," she said, getting up. Her mother paid the bill and then followed her out to the car where Amanda was sitting with her arms crossed in the front seat. "Ever heard the word trust?" Amanda asked. "Peter and I trust each other."

They drove to the apartment in silence. Amanda gave her mother a kiss on the cheek before leaving the car. She had actually been enjoying herself until her mother brought up Jason. Was there no part of her life that could still be free from her mother's scrutiny?

She carried the bag containing the wedding dress into the house and found Peter sitting at the kitchen table staring at sketches for some mysterious building he was working on. "You survived shopping with your mother and actually found something?"

"Barely survived."

"You got in a fight."

"Not until we tried to have a meal together."

Peter got up and began to open the bag. Amanda closed it on his fingers.

"You can't see it before the wedding. It's bad luck."

"You both agreed on the dress?"

"Yes, that we agreed on."

Amanda folded the edges of the bag and put it down on the kitchen table. She looked at the drawing of blueprints spread out across the table from end to end. Peter was looking at her like he had something to tell her, some surprise, something her mother, no doubt, already knew.

"It's the shed I'm building," he said "I'm designing it myself."

He was in such a good mood she tried to act enthusiastic, but she couldn't make herself ask any more questions.

"It's so draining being with my mother for hours."

Peter took her hand and led her through the archway into the living room. "Your mother really is nice, you know. She wants the best for you."

"Ugh. You sound sappy. How many beers did you have while I was gone?"

He pulled her down on the couch, and they snuggled together watching a movie. When Amanda went into the kitchen to make popcorn, she noticed the letter from Jason on the counter. She looked at it curiously, maybe even a little excited. It wasn't Jason so much she missed as that year they spent together, especially that summer; they had spent so much time in Vermont. Now she was falling into this boring life that maybe she wasn't ready for. That's why she was trying to get Peter to move up there with her just for one year, or maybe just one summer. There was something magical about that chalet, something her parent's had searched out and found and now denied. She ripped open the letter while the microwave hummed.

Dear Manda,

Good to see you again. Glad you're doing well. Don't worry about your talk not going well (picture of a sad face). You're so far ahead in your theories you leave us all in the dust. Enjoyed cooking for you (picture of a pot boiling over) and just talking. You were going on some pretty strange head-trips that year we were together, and I just want you to know you can always talk to me. Say "HI" to your parents, I know how much they loved me (Ha Ha). I still had the urge to take you in the bushes, but I know you have a fiancé now, so I'll just leave it with call me if you want to talk (#). Maybe I'll see you next year. I've decided to go back to Stellafane every year because it's good for my soul.

Peace

Jason

The microwave beeped, and she put the letter back in its envelope and tucked it into the pocket of her flannel shirt. While they snuggled, Peter took it out of her pocket.

"Who's J Miller?"

Chapter Fourteen

1978

This morning it is raining, raining, raining hard, and Suzanne tells her she can't go outside. Are they afraid she will melt? She decides to stay in bed longer than usual, and apparently, they've decided to let her. Amanda came up this morning before Peter took her off to a playgroup that meets in a church every Wednesday morning. Wednesday, middle of the week—it doesn't matter to Gloria. To her, it's like an eternal weekend, which, when she was younger, would have been a dream come true. She sighs and watches masses of water slide down the huge picture window. She can hear her sister rattling around, perhaps dusting, in the bottom part of the chalet.

Maybe it was good this morning that she couldn't go outside because Thomas brought the baby up right from her crib and Amanda flopped around the bed pretending to be a bear or a fish or something. Thomas would "catch" her and then throw her back into the pillows, which seemed to be the water or the forest. Gloria had rested at the edge of the bed watching them happy when Amanda flip-flopped over to her for protection. She sighs. *It is something*—Amanda still relating to her as a mommy protector.

Still, the change in the flow of the day is making Gloria anxious. She almost wishes her sister had made her get out of bed and look at the calendar today, instead of sending Thomas up here to say the day was Wednesday, the day of Amanda's playgroup. Now she sits alone watching rain pour down the heavily paned window, so restless she wants to get up and scream, pace the floor. The rain is denying her the bench and her memories. She hopes Suzanne is dusting downstairs because she is starting to notice dust in the corners. This morning, when she'd gone to the bathroom, she'd noticed soap scum on the sink and smears on the mirror. Thomas had never been much of a housekeeper, but neither had Suzanne. It's starting to bother her more now as she sits and looks around. The place needs to be cleaned. It needs wax, polish, a new smell. Everything needs to be scrubbed.

Suzanne comes up after a while intending that they do some morning yoga. She brings their mats—two thick beach towels. She lays them across the floor, but Gloria knows she is too restless to do anything so calm. When her sister coaxes her out of bed, she walks right over the towels and down the stairs to where she knows the cleaning rags and bottles and cans of cleaners are kept. She starts with Thomas' pinball machines. She has been noticing dust on them for a while, every time she moves past them to go outside to her bench.

She sprays and scrubs every inch of every machine. They will be brilliantly shining when Thomas plays them. She pushes into the screen with the duster almost breaking the glass. With all her energy, she pushes the dust from the indented corners. She thinks ear Q-tips might work better. A little alcohol with Q-tips along the indented corners of the screen would pull out every bit of grime and leave a new smell. She glances over at Thomas' desk. She will do that later. Right now, she does not want to rifle the papers; that makes her think again of the tee shirt she had not yet found, and she scrubs more furiously.

After what seems like hours, she is satisfied at how clean this machine is so she goes onto another, polishing the outside surface and scrubbing all the ridges of the screen. Thomas and Amanda come home, but she hardly notices. She is sure all of them now, even Amanda, see her as a lunatic, scrubbing every available surface still in her nightgown, hair uncombed, unbraided, falling into her face. It feels so good, she doesn't care. It's good to somehow get rid of a smell that has been bothering her—a presence in the house not unlike the sweet smell of pot being smoked or wisps of baby powder, long unused, still clinging to wood, glass, and metal. Hadn't anyone done spring-cleaning this year? When she finally exhausts herself, she retreats to the bed again. Neither Suzanne nor Thomas can convince her to get dressed. They bring food to her.

In the afternoon, it still does not stop raining; there is thunder and lightning, Amanda is put down for a nap. She can hear the hum of the games Thomas is playing, even in an electrical storm, and Suzanne is in a corner downstairs reading. Gloria can just see her from where she lies on the bed. Suzanne has been keeping an eye on her so long she enjoys invading her sister's privacy for a change, spying on her private moments. Her sister goes on reading, unaware.

Gloria watches another flood of rain wash over the window. It's hard for her to think on this day without the bench. She's aware that something in her wants to change. The break from routine, the storm that has kept her away from her precious bench, perhaps is a good thing, though she hopes the routine will start again tomorrow. She hopes tomorrow her sister will take her to the calendar, and then she will walk to the bench. This routine is her grounding as she pushes herself out of the haze. Everything is all mixed up today—all her movements, and it makes her heart beat fast and her feet restless, but she does not want to leave the bed again.

She dozes off and wakes up to the smell of simmering vegetables, garlic, and humus with fresh bread. Rain still drips down the window although it looks like the worst of it has stopped. The sky has brightened some though she knows it is evening. Daylight goes on forever in this time of the summer solstice.

She remembers now that Suzanne told her she might have a few people over for a solstice party. She hopes it isn't tonight.

Though, at least, she thinks, the house is clean, and it makes her feel good thinking that she has contributed something. Thomas comes stomping up the stairs like a monkey swinging Amanda on his arm. When they reach the top, Thomas whispers something into Amanda's ear.

"Din," she says to Gloria. "Din, Din." And she rips the covers off Gloria grabbing at her arm.

Thomas and Suzanne have found their secret weapon to motivate her. She gets up and lifts Amanda to her shoulder, her full baby weight a welcome heft, a burden of joy she is reluctantly willing to accept.

This day, unlike the other, with no opportunity for remembering, is closing. It doesn't look as if guests are coming tonight. The table is set for only a few. She wonders if tonight is the actual solstice. Maybe it would say on the calendar. She puts Amanda down gently in the high chair and goes to the calendar trying to remember what day of the week it is. *Wednesday*, she thinks. *Isn't it Wednesday?* She sees Suzanne and Thomas exchange a look.

It's probably not exactly the solstice or Suzanne would have made a bigger deal out of it this morning. She walks back in her zombie way and sits down. Thomas and Suzanne are already eating; Amanda is dipping her fingers into a bowl of humus and sucking it off all the fingers while she holds her spoon in the other hand.

The storm seems to have mellowed everyone out; the silence at the table makes Gloria hyper aware of sounds—the chewing, the clicking of forks and spoons against bowls and plates, Amanda's chubby foot hitting the edge of the table. Suzanne gets up and mixes lemonade. Gloria starts at the sound of the clack the ice makes against the glass of the pitcher, the swish of the wooden spoon as the sugar is mixed around. She watches as Suzanne pours a thick lemony-sweet waterfall into each glass. Watches sugar and bits of lemon swirl around and then settle. She picks up a long silver spoon that has been placed by her and mixes it again before drinking.

Even Amanda seems quiet except for the kicking. It is like the house is full of a dead silence that Gloria has longed for, and now it makes her uneasy. She almost makes herself speak just to break the silence and because she is curious. It seems like a long time since she wondered about something besides her own condition, and suddenly she wants to know when they are going to have company just so she can get used to the idea early in the day, even if only to give her a chance to withdraw if she wants, feign illness, go to bed early. Curiosity. She sighs, annoyed at her lack of even the most mundane details of the near future. Knowledge is power, as well as the withholding of words. She's glad when Suzanne finally gets up and begins to clear the table. Thomas wipes Amanda's face, lifts her out of the high chair, and flies her across the room in circles, dancing probably just to see her toothy grin. Suzanne yells at him saying he shouldn't spin her like that after eating—she'll throw up. It's such a relief to Gloria that the others are acting like they are alive again.

After Amanda is put to bed, they do their evening yoga and meditation. Thomas plays pinball. Gloria breathes deeply, lets out the breath—listens to the voice telling her what to do, telling her to grasp the moment. She hears her own voice saying to reach inward, into the gray area. Within the cocoon of forgetfulness, she continues to breathe, to search out a memory, a spec, an eye, a peephole through the door.

Chapter Fifteen

The Green Monster

Amanda was surprised to see her mother's yellow bug turning the corner as she pulled onto her road and into the driveway after work. She honked, but her mother didn't seem to notice. Exhausted from the heat, she was actually glad for the papaya juice her mother had left in their fridge. She took a swig from the bottle and put it back calling for Peter. No answer. His car was out front. She found him in the study staring at the green screen of the computer terminal. Resting her head on top of his, she massaged his neck.

"It's too hot," he said, pushing her away.

"Grumpy." She went to the kitchen, peered into the fridge. "What should we do for supper? Should I try to make one of my mother's health food specials?"

He didn't answer. She brought him a cold beer. He took it and continued to stare at the screen. That was enough. She left the room and withdrew into the back yard with a plate of cheese and crackers.

The shed was partly assembled, but something must have gone wrong. He should have bought some kind of design, not tried to do it himself. She'd leave him alone and he'd get over it. At least it looked like I t would be clear tonight. She'd pack up and go to the hill later. So what if he didn't want her company? She sat in a lawn chair and read.

She heard him in the kitchen a few minutes later; felt him staring out at her. She was tempted to look up and stick her tongue out, but she didn't, just continued reading. He came out holding the letter from Jason.

"Who is *this* guy?" He threw the envelope at her.

"A friend I knew from Stellafane when I was a kid."

"The guy you went out with?"

"We dated for a while. I thought I told you about that like last summer. Is that what this is all about?"

He didn't answer, just flung a beer bottle against the side of the shed. It shattered into pieces, and dark liquid dribbled down the side. He walked over to the sides of the shed and pounded on it. Amanda went over and touched his arm. He pushed her away. He'd been drinking way too much. She could see that now. It's the only thing that would put him in such a nasty mood.

"I hate that damn tattoo on your arm," he said. "I wish you'd get rid of it."

"And you wish I would grow my hair out and not stare at the stars at night. You wish I was someone else, someone just like you," Amanda yelled, frightened that she could be the cause of such anger.

"What about me? What about this Jason guy? You just happened to run into him at Stellafane?"

"Yes," she said, walking toward the house. "He's a friend and I just happened to run into him." *Cetus the sea monster, Hydra the water snake, Septra the hand of justice.*

"Where are you going?" he demanded.

"To the hill."

He came toward her. "I want us to be together tonight."

Amanda hesitated. She hugged him. She could feel his heart pounding. He kissed her hard and carried her into the living room. He touched her eyebrows, brushed his thumb across her lips while they lay on the couch. He fell asleep, and Amanda got up and to gather her scope and binoculars.

"Where are you going?"

"To observe for a little while."

"I want you to be with me tonight."

Amanda turned toward him almost deciding not to go just to keep him from getting mad again, but it was too much of a demand. "I'm just going for a little while. You're sleeping anyway."

He sat up on the couch. She could feel him watch her put things together. Her hands trembled.

"Come with me," she pleaded. When they had first started dating, he used to go observing with her sometimes.

"If you walk out that door and leave me tonight, that's it. Don't bother coming back." His face was red; he pointed his finger at her. Bullying again.

She packed everything up sweating and stumbling and drove off full of angry determination. She heard Peter slam the front door as she drove away. Once at the hill, she cried into the steering wheel, loud noisy sobs. She cried out of anger, confusion, and just the beginning of sadness. She would not go back to the apartment. It was his place—always had been, always would be. She didn't want to become him.

When she was done crying, she trudged up the hill wondering still if he might come after her. The wildflowers on the hill had given way to overgrown grass. Even the yellow ragweed and wild azaleas were beginning to look worn. Fall in New England was painting its chilling handprints on the landscape barely before the end of August. Someone, probably her mother, had told her that Native Americans used to boil the swamp Azaleas as a cure for arthritis, but there was no cure against the coming of winter. She set the telescope up and looked through the lens to a view of Mars, then the globular cluster M13.

For a while, she did not think of Peter or her mother or Jason. Instead, she thought of dead scientists. How they would have marveled to be able to see this far into the sky, how they would have stayed up all night, every night until they went mad with exhaustion. She thought of Maria Mitchell standing on the roof of her home in Nantucket, still a child, scanning the sky over the ocean, searching years until one October night, she left a family party early, climbed up to the rooftop, and discovered a comet. She was only twenty-nine.

How had they managed to push the world away? Kepler, Newton, all of them, touching like the blind examining the nose and eyes and face of the universe, greedy to discover a world beyond. They stumbled on secrets barely realizing what they had discovered. How had they managed to persevere in their uncompromising beliefs that looked to others like madness? Thank you, she would say to them if she could. If she could send a thank you note through time, she would thank them for experimenting, inventing, imagining.

"I don't have the patience or the attentiveness or the dedication for discovery," she would say to them. Or maybe, "My fiancé and my mother keep getting in the way."

That night she made a decision. She would not go back to the apartment from which she had been banished. She went to her parent's house. It was late, but she let herself in with a key, quietly so her mother wouldn't hear. Her mother was not up. *Good*. That meant Peter had not called here. She went downstairs, turned on all the machines, and fell asleep to the humming and beeping—the lullaby of her childhood.

The next morning, her mother left early to show a house. Amanda called Peter when she hadn't heard from him by ten.

"You didn't come home last night," he accused her.

"You told me not to."

"I don't think this is going to work."

She had never heard him so sad and hurt. It was too much that she could stir up these emotions in someone. She only made him miserable. She didn't know what to say. "Okay," she said, tears dripping onto the receiver.

"I love you, Amanda, but you know."

"I know."

"Oh, and, that project I've been working on for the last few weeks? It's not a shed. I was building a goddamn observatory for you!"

"That's so sweet," she said, ready to run over to the apartment.

"Yea, maybe you and Jason can live in it."

He sounded mean again, angry. *Was he drinking already?*

"I'll be over," she said, "to pick up my things."

"Fine," he said. "I'll try not to be home."

She went back to Peter's in the afternoon, and he wasn't there. She packed her suitcase and left her key on the table. She took off her ring and placed it in the box with her wedding dress. Somehow, she could not take that out of the apartment, so she hid it under shoes and winter clothes at the bottom of the guestroom closet.

Chapter Sixteen

1978

The rain stopped overnight, but everything is drenched, and there is no sun yet—just clouds as far as she can see above the trees, across the sky. After the morning orientation in front of the calendar, her sister had tried to get her to do something different. She had suggested they go shopping. The nearest store is a long ride from here, and Gloria knows she is not ready for that yet. The thought had made her shudder: the claustrophobia in the car, the stimulation of being around crowds. She couldn't go, and Suzanne just kept smiling and pushing her toward the car. It was almost enough to make her shout, *No. Leave me alone,* but her vocal chords were still unable to respond to any messages from her brain.

As Suzanne opened the car door, Gloria had shaken her head, might have even put up her hand like a stop sign. It wasn't much, no sound, but this silent communication seemed to have made Suzanne brighten, Gloria noticed, as if it were some kind of breakthrough.

Then Gloria had walked to the bench, controlling herself because she actually wanted to run. She had sat down here with her arms folded like a petulant child. The bench was still a little wet, but she didn't care. She sat still with her arms folded, her heart beating fast from the energy of going against her sister and making some form of communication all in one moment. Her mouth was closed in a defiant pucker. *I'm being a child*, she thought, suddenly amused, relaxing her mouth. She didn't know if her sister was still by the car, if her sister would go without her. She knew she didn't need some damn field trip to a shopping center; even she knew enough to know that that wouldn't help her.

She had never liked crowded places or even public places even though she'd liked to shop around for stylish clothes when she was younger. Her mother had taken her to Denholm's from the time she was about five years old to try on clothes. She thought Denholm's might not even be in Worcester anymore, neither was Eddy's on Park Avenue—the other place her mother considered one of the better places in Worcester. At first, her mother would make her try on so much stuff she would always end up crying, but afterwards, she would take her to Kreskie's for an ice cream soda. When she was a little older, it got to be a bore, a big day in the city with her mother that Gloria could live without, although she always liked how the other girls admired the clothes she wore to school for several days afterward.

Suzanne would never come with them; nothing her mother did could ever convince her sister to be stylish. Suzanne spent more time with their father, going to work with him sometimes and even to the golf course. Funny that her father had picked Suzanne to learn about the business. She was smart but never concerned about money or material things.

Thomas had always been so nonchalant about money. The first year, he was getting paid for his metric conversion brochures, and she sometimes used to find checks months old tucked into books or hidden behind dim lamps in the basement of the Garden of Delights. It was funny that they had even been attracted to each other. They were so different. But she remembered the ache she felt each day in her heart after she was 'left behind' to finish her year at Worcester State and how she worried that one day he would not show up to pick her up after classes. She worried that he would just have disappeared with a bunch of his friends driving away to Canada or California in the Garden Van.

It wasn't that she hadn't trusted him, but she had never

really trusted fate. And now, here they were all by themselves with a beautiful baby daughter, living her dream. And then something had happened to her—if she could just remember what it was.

She sighs and looks over at the car. It's still there, and her sister is not in it, so she must have decided not to go after all. She must have gone back into the house. Gloria yawns and stretches her body out. She would like to lie down on the bench and fall asleep like a bum, but something inside her keeps her from relaxation. Something keeps her vigilant, even up here, even just sitting on the bench.

If she lets her mind wander, she worries about where it would go, and suddenly she has a thought that makes her feel dizzy—a horrifying thought that makes her lurch forward and makes her feel like she is going to vomit, but her body just gives up a kind of dry inward heave. It is something about her baby; something bad had happened. She knows, just knows that she could not have tried to hurt her baby.

She has heard that sometimes women get very depressed after they give birth. But the funny thing is, she doesn't remember Amanda's birth. She kind of remembers the ease of breastfeeding and bonding—at least she thinks she does, but not in the way she can pull up images from her mind. It's more of a sensory thing, but no, she's sure she never hurt Amanda. That couldn't be why they are keeping her away. Now she really wants to speak and ask. She wants to yell and accuse them. *What have I done for you to keep me from my baby?*

Could it have been something to do with drugs? There were still some drugs around, but Thomas and his friends had always done so many more drugs than she had. She'd smoked weed occasionally but never when she was pregnant. And she absolutely refused when Thomas' friends tried to get her to take orange sunshine or coke. She thought of how, when they were still down in Worcester, friends sometimes would make her feel so uncool because she didn't want to get into a group high. Thomas hadn't really done too many drugs either. Although people thought he did, he stayed relatively straight and mostly took care of anyone who OD'd. He mostly stayed high on some natural overflow of optimism that he seemed to be able to sustain even in the dreariest situations. But he did have his dark side, a slow anger that only she saw. It usually caused him to withdraw, and she would try desperately to pull him out, see him shine again.

  Strange now how she was the one caught in a deep and total withdrawal of her own, and though she loved him and he loved her, it didn't help. He could not rescue her. She could only hear his voice slicing through the air, revolving on the periphery of her own sullen world. Pulling him in would only bring them both down, she thought. She could only stand to give her care and comfort to the child they had between them.

  Thomas was a kind man. He would not bring their child to see her on the bench every day just to rip her away. There had to be another reason. Gloria was tired of mulling over the possibilities.

  No, she had never been as optimistic or as brave as Thomas. In fact, she remembers the first time he had mentioned that they should move up to Vermont and start their commune. They were at the Blue Plate and he had been swinging her around to a *Zonkaraz* dance tune. Then, when the song ended and the clapping and hooting afterwards ended, everything became silent as the lead singer began her haunting cover of *Over the Rainbow*. Thomas had taken her in his arms, high, but not on drugs, and he said he had something important to talk to her about. Gloria had thought maybe he was going to ask her to marry him but knew probably not because he didn't really believe in marriage. He had taken her by the hand and led her outside after the song because with the noise, you couldn't hear anything without someone shouting the words to you. They walked toward the pizza place that was in the same parking lot as the Blue Plate, and he lifted her onto a low, stone wall.

"I have a really good idea, babe. We can name it the Rainbow House."

He looked up to her for a reaction, and she tried to cover because she was not sure what he was talking about.

"Up in Vermont," he said. "The commune? We'll call it the Rainbow House, and we'll run it differently than all the others. In fact, we won't run it at all. No one in charge—everyone in charge. We'll just honor people for what they can do; it's amazing what people can contribute when they're given a chance. I know it can work."

Gloria had not been so sure that it could work but had been pulled in by his enthusiasm. She knew her sister had been involved with their parents in ownership of it when she turned 22, and her sister had won the battle. She was living in California then but had complete control of the chalet and would be more than happy if Gloria and Thomas turned it into a home for displaced hippies and back to the landers.

Gloria had followed Thomas into what seemed was a new world, a world without boundaries, a confusing world, never speaking her doubts or the grayish worry that always hovered by her heart when Thomas sounded too optimistic. This time she had wanted to believe him, maybe because she was afraid of losing him.

Now he stands around the edges of her sorrow trying to pull her out of her silent world, and she prays he will not give up, not lose faith in her.

After what seems like forever, he comes out with Amanda in his arms, her chubby fingers clasped tightly around the handle of a picnic basket. Her daughter grins at her, and she tries to smile back, but the sight of the basket reminds her of Easter, and for some reason, it sends a throbbing pain to her stomach.

Something about jellybeans and colored eggs makes her heart beat faster, makes her sick. Was it Easter when something happened? She can't believe she has been living in this shadowy world all that time. She knows it's well into June. Easter would have been back in April. Even the word April gives her a bad feeling.

Thomas plunks Amanda down on the ground rather than bringing her over to the bench. He must have noticed the look of puzzlement in her face. He shows Amanda how to help him spread out the red-checkered picnic blanket, and then she squeals in delight as they pull out the food. Grapes, apples, thick sandwiches on whole wheat bread stuffed with tomatoes, sprouts, and lettuce are all in baggies wrapped as if they were going on some long journey instead of just out the door to Gloria's bench.

"For our picnic," Thomas says. "We're having a family picnic."

"Nic," Amanda says pulling out bottles of juice and blue Mexican chips as if determined to empty the contents completely. She rips open the chips before Thomas can stop her, and they scatter onto the grass. Amanda looks at him and begins to cry.

"It's okay," he says. "The ants need some, too."

Amanda smiles and waddles over to Gloria offering her a chip. Gloria has almost forgotten the confusion she felt about the basket and Easter. She smiles at Amanda and takes the chip though something still gnaws at the edges of her remembrance.

"Nic," Amanda says pointing to the food spread on the lawn. She takes her mother's hand and pulls her onto the lawn. Gloria has no choice now but to pull herself away from something she may be remembering. Thomas just sits waiting to see what will happen. He munches on a piece of celery spread with cream cheese.

This is Suzanne's doing, she thinks. She must have told

Thomas not to bring Amanda right to her but to have her come to them. She feels somewhat like she is being bullied and manipulated, but she looks at Amanda, who has no hidden agenda, just wants her mommy, and Gloria wants to cry and say "Oh, honey, mommy wants you too." But she doesn't want to scare Amanda with an overflow of emotion after all these months or weeks of nothing. Zombie Mommy. How she wishes she could find somewhere in between, some balanced state.

Amanda is tugging at Gloria's sundress now as she leads her over to the food. She sits down, and it feels okay. The food spread, the checkered throw, it's all fine as long as she doesn't look at that damn basket that seems to remind her of something. She positions herself to where the basket is not in view, and she's all right. Amanda rests next to her knee, and Thomas comes over next to her with a bunch of grapes dangling them over her nose.

"Lean your head back," he says, but she doesn't. She feels she's been compliant enough for the day.

So he plucks them by the stems one by one and brings them to her mouth. She eats each one slowly chewing the refreshing pulp and feeling the juice slide down her throat. She never stopped eating, but she has not enjoyed eating like this for a while. Her lips curl over the rim of each grape as he puts it into her mouth, and she tastes the salt at the tip of his fingers. He smells good.

Amanda giggles watching her daddy feed her mommy grapes.

"Me, Me," she yells, and Thomas drops a grape into her open mouth.

Gloria is overwhelmed with happiness by the food and Thomas and their daughter but doesn't want to show it. Somehow, she feels guilty that this simple family gathering can bring her so much joy. She stares down at the grass; she slides her hand across it. She hardly notices that Amanda has taken off her shoes and is squashing grapes into the bottom of her feet. When she does notice, she wants to say something—to be a mother. She is about to reach out and say "no," but Thomas is too quick. He picks her up and cleans her feet with a napkin. Gloria is jealous at the ease of his parenting. *It's probably just as well,* she thinks; her 'no' probably would have scared them all, and she doesn't want that to be her first word uttered to her daughter after all this time. She has decided now that she wants to talk. She feels ready to talk, but she doesn't know how to begin. Thomas hands her a sandwich and Amanda a cut, peeled apple. Just like any family, they have their picnic.

Chapter Seventeen

Departure

Amanda's mother held her in a death grip until she pulled herself free. She supposed it was her own fault for crying in front of her mother. They sat on the couch in the 'fun room.'

"Our poor baby is heart-broken," Amanda's mother said to her father who had just come down the stairs.

"Daddy," Amanda ran to her father and held him.

She looked up at him. She hadn't seen him for months. His hair was greyer than she remembered, and his face a little sunken. He never had much of an appetite when he went to the Far East, she remembered him saying so to mom. He always came back thinner and with a scent of strange lemony spices. His glasses, as usual, were falling off his nose. He picked her right up into the air and twirled her around then put her down on the couch next to her mother. Her mother's tone changed.

"She does bring it on herself sometimes," she said as she spooned tofu ice cream into papaya juice as a special treat for her heartbroken daughter. "She can be quite stubborn, and I don't know what possessed her to hang out with Jason again."

"Hello," Amanda said. "Your daughter is in the room." She rolled her eyes and covered her head with both hands. She looked at her father. "I ran into him. We conversed; end of story."

"He wrote you a letter. That letter is why you and Peter are no longer together."

Amanda pounded a small couch pillow into her forehead.

"Amanda," her mother said. "Are you okay?"

"Who writes letters anymore?" her father simply added.

Amanda put the pillow down, smiled, gave up, and accepted

the tofu treat. She put her head against her father's shoulder and closed her eyes. She felt a little better, knowing he was home. Her parents talked above her head. They hadn't seen each other for months. You would think they would somehow be closer. Maybe it was just that she had inserted herself in between them. Maybe it was just that when love got old, it wasn't as exciting as it once had been, but it seemed to Amanda, as she listened to their voices, there was something else. A hesitancy, pauses, fits, and starts. It seemed to her, after knowing someone for decades, they would be a little less guarded. She almost felt like they wanted her to be in between them. The guilt and burden of the only child, did they ever really want her to grow up? Why hadn't they had another child?

Her father put his arm up on the couch behind her, and she peeked out to see that her father's hand gently stroked her mother's shoulder. Maybe they were closer than she thought.

She stayed down on the couch after her parents had gone up to bed thinking about the last few weeks. Thomas never talked much about his family. She'd never met even one of them. She knew he grew up in the Midwest and had several siblings. Maybe she was selfish because she had never had to share her parents' attention. She did not unpack her suitcase—it just didn't feel right. She had given up her old apartment so there was no way she could go back there. She was not going back to Peter's, but there was her suitcase, still packed, on the floor beside the couch in the basement where she slept. She even left her toothbrush in there, moping through the next week, teaching her course without interest.

She talked to Peter a few times. Some days it seemed like they might get back together; sometimes it seemed like they were on the verge of holding onto each other again.

They did not see each other—only spoke on the phone. Conversations that always started out making a connection but always ended badly. Then Peter hinted he might be dating someone. Just to hurt her, she thought, or save his pride. It didn't matter, they were over. She had made a decision that night on the hill. All she needed was the courage to go through with it. A few weeks before classes started in the fall, she went to see the department head and handed in her resignation.

The first hurdle of guilt was laid on. Did she realize what a difficult situation she was putting them in with little time to find a replacement? She apologized, left the office, went into the ladies room, and cried. She cried with relief and sadness and shame because she had failed again, had let everybody down. She drove to the old part of campus intending to clean out her office except for a few things, but she couldn't—she stood immobilized, overwhelmed by the thought of what she had just done, unable to carry away the mundane objects of her life as a teacher. She stared down pens, binders, pencils, old syllabi, and class lists, and then she gazed through the warped glass of her favorite window. She didn't even take the tea set—something she might regret. She'd leave everything here, she decided, probably no one else would want an office here anyway. She'd leave her dust and molecules behind.

When she got home, she called Peter and left a message on his new answering service explaining what she had done but did not tell him of her plans to move to Vermont. There was nothing to keep her here. Maybe she'd be a cook, like Jason, but she wasn't very good at cooking. She'd probably just find a job as a housekeeper at one of the ski resorts and spend nights observing. She should have anticipated her parents' total failure to understand.

"You're running away," her mother said. "You can't just leave your job and run off."

"I not running away" she said, unsure if she was telling the truth. "I can get a job up there."

Her mom glared at her dad who was just coming down the stairs. "Now she's quit work, and she wants to move up to

Vermont."

Amanda sat on a bar stool trying to hold her own. Her father came down and took over where her mother had been sitting next to her. Her mother retreated to the couch taking a ginseng pill from her purse and swallowing it down dry.

"Daddy," Amanda said, taking off her glasses, which were way too big for her small face.

"That's better," he said. "Why does my baby need such big glasses for her little face?"

Amanda was almost ready to give him the look, although it probably wouldn't work on him. "Why do you wear those tiny half-glasses when Lennon died almost twenty years ago? Wire rims aren't even retro cool anymore."

Her father laughed.

Her mother spoiled the fun. "Don't try to change the subject. She wants to quit her job. Run off up to Vermont."

"I can work up there. I can get a job. Tell her."

"But there aren't very many colleges up there, honey." His voice was deep and comforting.

"I know. But there *are* jobs. I'm tired of teaching."

"You'll be lonely up there," her mother said. "With nothing to do."

"I won't be lonely. I'll have solitude."

"Dark of night is a lonely companion," her mother said

Amanda sighed. "Daddy, I know what I'm doing. I want to live up there. Just for one year. I'll work. I'll get a job at one of the hotels."

"Do you hear her?" her mother yelled from the couch. "We put our daughter through school so she could be a chambermaid."

"It's just a way to make money.'" She looked at her father. "Just for one year."

He wasn't taking sides.

Amanda looked at her parents, followed their gaze back and

forth. Her mother's eyes were dark with a pleading, haunted look that was always her last desperate attempt to get her way. Her father acknowledged it, slightly lifting his hand toward her, and then he looked away.

"I don't think we can stop her if she wants to go."

"Thank you, Daddy," she said and kissed him on the cheek. Then she hurried up the stairs. She didn't completely close the door and listened to her parent's talk.

"Don't you understand?" her mother asked, crying now. "She's having another breakdown."

"She seems pretty calm for all she's been through."

"She's running away, Thomas, running to the past. She's not acting like an adult."

"She's only 23; maybe it's her way of getting over Peter."

"You're not here enough. You just don't know. Since she was a teen, I've been parenting her alone. And I told you, I told you so many times you should get rid of those damn, old pinball machines."

"What do the machines have to do with it?"

"They're some kind of trigger. They spark something in her. When she gets upset, she puts them all on and goes from one machine to another."

"Fine," her father said shouting instead of whispering. "We'll get rid of them all. How about by the weekend? Would that be soon enough?"

"That sounds reasonable," her mother said, back to whispering. "I know you're attached to them, but it would be best for Amanda."

"I'll put them in storage," Thomas said. Amanda breathed a sigh of relief.

Later she heard her father make the call to Acme trucking to haul the machines away to storage on Saturday. So she decided that would be the day she would move to Vermont. She was already packed, so all she had to do was go to the bank and get some cashiers' checks to open a new account on Monday. She had been saving up money for the wedding, and that would be useful now.

On Saturday, she said her goodbyes to her parents early in the morning. Her mother cried.

"It's not like I'm moving to Siberia," she said, but mother had packed her enough sunshine cupcakes as if she were, and she told her father he didn't have to stick around—that she would be here until the machines were hauled away.

Her mother was showing a house, so Amanda made sure she stayed around until the truck drivers came. She intercepted the truck driver and said there was a change of plans. The machines were to be brought up to Vermont. They called their boss.

"We can do it," they said. "But it will cost another $150." She handed them the money in cash along with the delivery address.

"I'll be up to meet you. You may have to wait just a very short time, but I'll get there."

They nodded, Seemed happy with that. She supposed they were getting more money and could stop and have a snack or lunch on Company time.

She hadn't heard from Peter in a few days and had resisted the urge to pick up the phone and say goodbye. She wanted nothing to break her resolve; besides the truckers would be waiting on the other end.

She worried a little about what she was doing with the machines, but she figured they wouldn't notice that they weren't getting bills from the storage facility for a few months. Then, she got in the car feeling guilty, wondering how long it would take them to figure out where they were. It could be weeks or months before they visited her. Maybe her mother was so disgusted she wouldn't come up at all.

"Maybe I'll start a commune up there like you did," she had

teased her mother in the last few days.

"Don't even think about it," her mother had said. "We were so young. It wasn't all love and happiness, you know. It's not easy living with no money."

"I heard you took drugs instead of eating," She had said it to be a tease, but her mother had teared up.

"I'm sorry. I didn't mean to make you sad."

Her mother pulled herself together quickly, as always when Amanda tried to comfort her.

"Don't worry" she said. "I promise not to start a millennium cult, and you can visit whenever you want."

Now she was hoping she wouldn't regret those words. She suddenly feared her mother might be the one up in Vermont when she got there, intercepting the truck drivers outside the loft, the sun catching her blonde highlights, standing irresolutely as she pointed south, directing the truck drivers right back down to Massachusetts.

Part II

Searching

"LET'S PRETEND THERE'S A WAY OF GETTING THROUGH INTO IT, SOMEHOW, KITTY. LET'S PRETEND THE GLASS HAS GOT ALL SOFT LIKE GAUZE, SO THAT WE CAN GET THROUGH." —LEWIS CARROLL

When Amanda was sixteen, she ran away from home; at least, that's what her parents called it. One morning she got up, grabbed some money stashed in a drawer, and told her parents she was going to stay at a friend's house. Her friend gave her a ride up to the chalet in Vermont, and that's where she stayed. All alone for one glorious weekend, she read the *Star Names* by Richard Hinkley Allen over and over until the names of stars and constellations took over some deep, empty spot inside her and would not leave. She whispered them to fall asleep:

Andromeda, the woman chained

Apus in China, a curious sparrow

In other lands, the bird of Paradise

Aquarius, the waterman, pouring water from a bucket or urn

Aquilla, the eagle flying toward the east and across the Milky Way

Messium, the harvest keeper, gathering a harvest of comets

In Chaucer's time, Corvis was the Raven; now it is known as the crow. Crater is now known as a cup; in Ancient Greece, it was a Goblet.

Ancient word names were given to star formations, different names, different times, in different countries. China, Greece, Native America. She learned star names from everywhere finding one constellation, like Sagittarius, could have many names: *The archer, the bow-stretcher, drawer of the arrow, the herdsman, the quiver.*

Sometimes the dipper was called a ladle, and Aquarius the water-carrier poured the flowing water not into a bucket, but an urn. She liked the ancient sound of the words as they rolled on her tongue—*Quiver, nectar urn*—as if the act of recitation validated the importance of words, of names. That had been when she decided she needed to study the stars her whole life. It might not bring her money, might not be a career, but just the act of reciting gave her strength and courage and purpose.

Greek, Latin, Chinese, Middle English, modern. She imagined all those people looking up into the sky and using their own words to express what they saw. It was like her imagination could merge with all those people looking up into the sky at different times in history, and when she read the word out loud, it was like a chant, and her breath gave strength to the world's imagination validating some search that had been going on forever.

When she got back, or when they found her, at odd times, the names seemed to burst from her brain when she was supposed to be thinking of something else. Sometimes she even said them aloud, and everyone stared at her. It wasn't until she decided to buy a telescope and started to observe that she could maintain control over the vocalizations. Still, when she was stressed, star names and constellations seemed to calm her, astronomy her drug. They filled her mind and blocked out some strange, unnamable fear.

Chapter One

ALL HALLOWS EVE, 1999

Amanda had been in Vermont almost two months working as a housekeeper in the hotel where Jason was a cook when she began to have trouble sleeping. It snuck up on her. Everyone had left her alone for the first week. Peter, who had not called her parent's house on purpose, had not even known she had left for over a week until he finally called. Her mother had probably told him she had moved to Vermont by herself to get over him. Then he called her cell every day.

"I want us to be together." How his story had changed.

"I don't know," she said. "Come up here, and we'll talk about it."

"So you want me to drive three hours to get to work every day?" Silence, a bang in her ear; he'd dropped the phone. Then, more calmly, he said, "They want you back at work. You could get your job back."

"This is where I am going to live, "she said. "For at least a year—if you want to be with me, it will have to be up here. You could take a sabbatical."

"And do what? Build snowmen?" She braced herself for the phone to drop again.

Whenever he called, they argued. Still, he persisted, though the calls were less often. Sometimes she wanted to call him, but she kept herself from calling though she did miss him and admonished herself for the indecision. If she started calling him, he would only think she was ready to go back down.

Jason came over after work on Halloween, and she sat in the rocking chair trying to keep her eyelids popped open. She knew once she actually tried to sleep, it probably wouldn't happen. He sat on the bed. They had become close again but not lovers. It was nice to have Jason around. There was still some attraction between them, but he was into a Zen celibacy thing right now, which was good, because the last thing she needed was the complication of romance.

Sometimes she imagined the place when it was a commune. She felt spirits here from the past like someone else's memories. All alone, she thought she heard breathing in other rooms, energy from another time that lingered on dusty, neglected surfaces, which had been stirred up when she had 'run away' and had her 'breakdown.' They had all been afraid that she was going to hurt herself when all she had done was come up here to be alone and spend time reading and memorizing star names.

The presences seemed particularly intense lately probably because of her lack of sleep. She tried taking walks during the day so she would be tired at night. She thought about asking Jason for some herb for sleeplessness, but she didn't want to draw attention to it and have him worrying, and she wasn't ready to give in to her mother and the natural cures.

When she had been an adolescent and they were all concerned about her sanity, she wished they had given her a pill to help. A psychologist suggested it, but her mother had freaked out and insisted on no pills. It was clear, anyway, so if she had insomnia again, she could stay up and observe.

"I'm proud of you Manda," Jason said, spinning a plate around on his index finger. He was always fidgeting, juggling, whatever, a man in perpetual motion; just watching him made her tired. Even though he didn't live here, he did most of the cooking in the small kitchenette. She liked when he called her Manda, a habit from when they were kids together at Stellafane. "I didn't think you'd stay here this long. I thought Miss Math Professor would be back to her cushy old life again by now."

"I'll probably be up late tonight observing if you want to stay," she told Jason, who had finally put the plate down. She didn't quite know why she was trying to keep him here. Maybe it was just that it was Halloween and she couldn't imagine another night wandering through the loft too hyper for sleep and too exhausted to concentrate on keeping her log. She had been tracking the movement of a few of the same stars since moving up here.

"Love to join, ya, darlin," he said "but this cook has a very early gig. They're serving a special brunch tomorrow at nine. I have to start everything before six. Come down. I'll sneak you free food."

"Maybe, but If I'm up all night, I may sleep through the morning."

When he got up and put his coat on, Amanda wanted to stall him.

"Brunch goes till two. I hope you're up by then."

She began to speak, but hesitated and walked him to the door.

"See you tomorrow." He kissed her on the cheek and was gone.

She wandered around. Ugh. It was only eight and it felt like midnight. She had only been able to pick at the veggie lasagna that Jason made; eating made her nauseated. She was glad he didn't notice or hadn't bugged her about it anyway.

She wanted to observe, but this morning, her coffee cup trembled in her hand because she was so tired. She promised herself, as soon as it was dark, she would take a nap just to get the edge off. She lay on top of the bed and tried to trick herself to sleep reciting star names, but just as she was about to nod off, her head would feel too heavy on the pillow. She had to keep turning over to get comfortable; almost asleep, her arm or leg would go into a spasm and wake her up. Every time she closed her eyes, she saw faces. Finally, she opened her eyes and stared at the ceiling. Tomorrow she'd ask Jason for one of his herbs.

She sighed and made her way down the stairs, sat on the floor, and tried to do some breathing exercises and yoga. *Clear your mind*, she admonished herself, but she couldn't stop thinking.

Didn't Jason used to come over more often? For a while, every morning he would come over before work, and they would do the salutation to the sun. He said it would help to stretch their bones and wake up their blood. Then they would meditate and breathe together. Sometimes he would get mad because she would finish with coffee.

It wasn't working now because it wasn't morning and he wasn't here. Nothing was working. She shook her head to try to clear it. Maybe she had a fever or something. No, she was just tired. Jason would have noticed if she were sick. Maybe staring into the sky for a while would help.

She rifled through a box in the corner where she kept telescopes and binoculars and found the old cracked mirror for the telescope. She'd put a piece that had broken off that day on the hill into a locket, and sometimes she wore it on a chain around her neck like a sixties medallion. It felt heavier than it looked, heavier than she remembered. It weighed her down as she walked up the stairs. Maybe it would be a magic charm, the talisman that would finally bring her sleep.

Leaning into the picture window, one of her knees pressed against a small knob to a draw she had forgotten was built into the window seat. It had always fascinated her as a little girl. She always wanted to see what was inside it, but it was always locked. She pulled on the knob now, and it opened. Some notebooks, paper, crayons, and other supplies she supposed were there to entertain her when she was a child. Pushing all that aside, she found a bottle of pills. *A little draw with a bottle of pills*, she thought, how Alice. She unfolded a piece of paper

and read:
> *CRaZy LadY AliCe*
> *The trees breathe*
> *I feel like Alice*
> *In relation and proportion*
> *To the center of the universe…*

She refolded the paper quickly, not wanting to read on, not tonight. Some tripped out hippie poet who lived up here when it was a commune must have written it. *Oh, god, this is too weird.* She opened the bottle of pills she had found.

Odd. She knew how her parents, especially her mother, felt about pills of any kind. She looked closer and saw they were over the counter sleeping pills. No way, her parents would have kept these up here. She pushed the draw shut again with her leg and gazed out the window at stars and galaxies.

Climbing on top of the seat to get nearer to the sky, she leaned into the window, took the broken glass out of the locket, and peered through it holding it up like a monocle to one eye. The tiny piece of glass weighed a ton. She looked down with it, and suddenly it was daylight.

Her dad was on the ground waving at her like he used to do when she was a schoolgirl coming up here for the summer. It felt like when they just arrived—when she used to check from this window to make sure that the land and the sky had not become one, her mother in the background yelling that it was not clean yet, yelling not to touch anything until she cleaned.

She looked back up to the sky and shivered with an eerie feeling that was strangely comforting. The light of the universe shimmered. She closed her eyes and heard a loud bang. A swish of wind had blown the door open downstairs, and it was opening and closing, banging against the wall. Relieved to realize the noise was coming from something so ordinary, she remembered it was windy out and remembered feeling the pressure of the door when she tried to close it after Jason left.

The phone rang, and she tried to pull herself away from the glass, but she could not pull away, could not move. Helpless to answer the ringing phone and close the banging door, her nerve endings would not listen to her brain. She looked through the glass, her face against it, until it seemed as though every light source in the galaxy was headed her way. The skin on her face, like rubber, would not pull away from the cold surface. A gust of wind came through the door and traveled up the stairs to the loft, knocking over the bed stand and blowing the telephone off the table and onto the floor. Amanda heard the funny beep of the phone when it's left off the hook as she was blown through the glass of the window.

Chapter Two

Gloria sits on the bench biting her nails thinking that one day away from the bench has done something to her momentum, a setback of sorts. The break in the rhythm and routine has made it all not work again. She moves around to different areas of the bench trying to get comfortable. She tries lying down but quickly sits up again. This morning when Suzanne had brought her to the calendar, she had looked at the date and all those around it, but the solstice was not written down. She had been hoping, even if it was not marked on the calendar itself, Suzanne would have made her own notation to remind herself there were people coming over. Today is June 20th, and that might be it, but Gloria is not sure; it could be the 21st or even the 22nd. She stares at the clouds as if they might give her some indication. The entire landscape from this bench seems to have changed just by her missing one day.

Something irretrievable, irreversible has occurred. Her heart, frozen solid all this time, has reopened with one fast chop down the middle, and she has discovered that it's soft inside. It hurts, this exposure, but she can still breathe. It's not like she is having a heart attack. She swallows the desire to wail because she's afraid they would take her away from the bench. She needs to stay here, somehow adjust herself to it all over again.

She looks up and around realizing there hasn't been such a big jolt in surroundings after all, not like she'd fallen asleep and woken up on another planet. The changes are subtle. A new smell or a sound. Maybe the leaves on the trees are a darker green as spring gives way to summer. Maybe some flowering shrub has died away in the storm a few days ago, lost all its leaves, and another flower, inspired by the heavy rain and the sunlight, has blossomed for the first time this season. Something is different, off kilter, but she can cope. She tries to settle down—descend into her memories. She takes some yoga breaths, opens her eyes, and looks down into her hands, which are balled up, little fists of energy. She wills them to open, places them on her knees, thinks of what a relief wailing would be, but knows she can't risk it. She's a little cold and wishes there was a blanket she could wrap around her knees like her old aunts used to do on Holidays when her mother drove them home in the car. *I can't turn into them, not yet*, she thinks, *when I'm not yet thirty.* Then she relaxes remembering something funny about her 25th birthday, and she tries to hold onto the memory, retrieve others from it, but it disappears quickly.

A thought comes to her. *They might not know*, she thinks. Thomas and Suzanne and her parents might not know about her amnesia. They might think she remembers everything and that's why she doesn't speak. They may have no idea she is sitting here trying to piece everything together. How would they know when she couldn't talk? All her pondering here day after day may be totally misunderstood by them. They may think she's trying to forget—not trying to remember. They may think this is just simple withdrawal, her way of coping with whatever has occurred. They might think she has passed the milestone of remembering. This scares her. How can they help her if they don't know? They'll have it all wrong, just like when they were giving her drugs to sleep and she did not want to. It will disappoint them somehow, too, if she speaks and they realize she just doesn't know—doesn't remember what she did or what someone did to her.

There used to be a lot of people around here, she faintly remembers. Or does she just surmise this, remembering what Thomas wanted and what he had dreamed? The dream he had spoken to her about that night at the Blue Plate.

She had gone home that night feeling off kilter too. It was the spring of her junior year. Thomas had officially dropped out of WPI, much to her father's disappointment but had impressed her father again by landing that lucrative job helping our country with metric conversion. It was the beginning of that controversy about whether we should join the rest of the world and how presumptuous was it for us to keep our own separate system. It was very political, so naturally Thomas had been happy to get involved. At the time, she thought the whole thing was just boring. She didn't understand what the big deal was about, but she was happy that Thomas had found something lucrative to put his ideals into because it was the only way they would have any independence. And truthfully, though she would have done anything to be with Thomas, she had not cherished the thought of some flea-infested farmhouse being their first home.

She saw the importance of it now. Years living with Thomas had made her see the importance of numbers, mathematics as communication. At one time, she had only been enthralled by words—whether written or spoken, but now she understood how numbers connected people too. When there were so many different languages in the world, she saw how measurements and graphs could be a communication across nations, though one she could never quite understand. She remembers how she had ambitions of being a writer for a newspaper or even for TV. She had been a creative writer keeping journals full of poems and images she remembered from her dreams. She smiles thinking of that. Retrieving something of herself, she supposed, piecing together the parts of her crazy quilt of a soul.

There used to be people around all the time, dozens of people. That's how Thomas had liked it. Now why was it only her family, only some of her family, even her parents banished? Had too many people pushed her over the edge? Had they done something to her, all those people coming and going, those kids, the bikers she began to fear? She sort of remembers talking to Thomas about being a mother who was fearful for her child among these strangers, but that seems like years ago, and Amanda is not even a year old. She remembers being frustrated because it took a long time for Thomas to admit it wasn't all love and peace anymore—that there was a new element, one they could not control. Free love twisting into greed in some individuals, and when you were parents, you couldn't risk these dangers as you could when there was just the two of you.

So now she is remembering some things that happened or, at least, conversations that may have occurred in the not too distant past, but there is a big chunk missing. How did they get up here? Her mind went back to Thomas sharing space in the basement of the Garden of Delights on Highland St. in Worcester with Tinker and the 'garden bus' he picked her up in every day after classes at Worcester State. She was nearly done with her junior year and really feeling like she wanted to be free like Thomas. She was jealous that he could sit around all day talking, smoking dope, perhaps making plans without her while she had to sit through her boring classes. She was so restless by that summer that she would have taken off anywhere in the garden bus.

That entire spring, Thomas and his friends were just getting stoned and making plans to go across the county in the bus once summer arrived. They were anxious to get going by the beginning of May, but there were others, like her, who were students and had exams. She knows that trip never occurred, but she cannot remember why. The magic bus never got on the road; the journey of joy and freedom never happened. She remembers being relieved and disappointed, and she and Thomas had ended up here in Vermont instead.

Thomas brings Amanda out now. Actually, she comes out of her own accord holding Thomas' hand. She's walking, trying to run now, just a few steps then falling into a crawl. It's such a joy to see her. Thomas lets go of her hand, and she runs to Gloria, hugging Gloria's legs, and Gloria lifts her high into the sky like she has seen Thomas do. She feels more strength in her arms today. They are no longer limp, so she can hold up her daughter. Mother and daughter look at each other, smile. They try to sit, the three of them on the bench. Thomas with his arm around Gloria, they cradle their daughter between them. Amanda seems to like being squished between mommy and daddy at first, but she is too full of energy to stay there for long. She wiggles down and uses her mobility to crawl away from them.

"Amanda, stop," Thomas shouts when she gets too far away. She does not listen. She darts down to the back yard toward the pond. He runs after her, picks her up, and swings her around, and they don't get a minute of peace in the whole time she is out here now because her new game is to run and crawl off in whichever direction they don't want her to.

Gloria feels drained after they leave. There was something in Thomas' voice. She had heard it before, but it was more pronounced today as he was giving Amanda parenting directives to protect her safety. Something about the intensity in his voice, perhaps fear, when he cut her freedom short, something overprotective. *It's because of me*, she thinks. *He has to be more vigilant because he is trying to parent all on his own.*

When she goes in this evening, she decides, she is going to try to write in a journal. She doesn't want the others to know, so she'll wait until they are asleep. When she was looking for the blizzard T-shirt, she had found a drawer in the window seat, kind of a hidden drawer. Inside were crayons, paper, pens, and a shoebox. Inside that was a copy of *The Little Prince* and some of her old journals.

Later, as Gloria and Suzanne do their evening yoga, she keeps staring at the drawer with the journals in it. She tries to concentrate and stop obsessing about it, but her need to put words on paper is now like a horse she has fallen from dragging her along. *Get back on the horse,* her mind keeps saying, but she can't do anything about it until later when they are not watching. She's afraid she won't be able to do it. Not that she won't have the words but that her hand will tremble and the words she puts on paper will be scratches that nobody can read. As long as nobody knows about it, as long as it's something she does in secret, she thinks there's a chance that her hand will flow, unlike her frozen vocal chords, allowing her to finally communicate.

When everyone is asleep, she gets up trying to be quiet, but the excitement of what she is doing makes her rush, feeling greedy as she pushes the paper around in the drawer and looks for something to write with. She pulls out a crayon and opens her journal to the last empty page. At the top of the page, she writes as much of the date as she remembers: June 1978.

Chapter Three

"Most endearing Lunacy"
Arthur Koestler, *The Sleepwalkers*, pg. 49

When Amanda opened her eyes, she expected to be covered in blood, but no, there was nothing. Her molecules must have passed through the dispersed molecules of glass with its amorphous chemical makeup. She didn't even feel any pain, only a kind of numbness as if she were sitting in a dentist chair and her whole body had been anesthetized. Actually, she was sitting in a huge wooden chair with a long table in front of it scattered with thick parchment and antique maps. She couldn't move. *Empty your mind*, she said to herself, remembering Jason's lessons in meditation, but her mind was not clouded. It seemed very clear.

Okay, she thought. *I am in the rocking chair at the top of the loft. Jason has slipped some kind of drug into the food. He saw that I was exhausted and wanted to help. Hypnotics. I'm only dreaming.* She shook her hands, opened, and closed them. The numbness was wearing off.

There were diagrams and letters written in longhand with black, blotchy ink. She touched the course, rough paper. A bottle of ink, several styluses, and sealing wax were stuffed into a box in the corner. She managed to get up from the chair, a little dizzy at first, and leaned over the desk trying to put everything together in her mind and make sense of the different pages. She'd seen it before, Kepler's notes, the first piece of sci-fi, Kepler's dream. She jumped away. Not daring to touch the papers now in case she created a paradox by moving things around, changing his notes, changing history.

Things couldn't be stranger if she'd fallen off the edge of the

Earth. Jason had brought her some sunshine muffins. Maybe he had added to her mother's recipe, but Jason would never drug her and leave her alone, would he? She pushed herself up. This had to be some kind of an illusion. Moving around might change her perspective, trigger some wake-up call from her brain cells.

When she stood, her legs were steady. *Good*, she thought, *gravity is still intact*. She tiptoed over to a window almost afraid to breathe, afraid that her molecules, the energy from her body from the future would somehow mingle with the past and change history. When she touched the thick glass of the window, it was cold and unyielding' still, she worried that the surface would pick up her fingerprints, her saliva—leave DNA. She remembered the melting sensation when her fingers had gone through the glass just as she landed here. Perhaps this had been her place of entry, but now it was closed.

She touched all around the edges of the glass in a panic. No softening, no melting. She started to pound lightly on the glass, and then harder. She began to cry. It couldn't be a dream, for she could even taste her salty tears. Here she was in the very room in the very year Kepler had started putting together his dream visions , the work she had admired so long, the work she had tried to make her students read and study, and it was a prison.

"I want to go back," she said, pounding on the window again. "I don't belong here."

The glass did not break, did not yield with her pounding. After a while, she just stopped and looked out the window at a strange world of peaked rooftops and stars. So many stars in a sky void of light pollution made her dizzy, and she held onto the window ledge. If she just relaxed, maybe the glass would open again when it was ready to take her back.

"When I come back you will be gone," a voice shouted sternly.

Amanda froze until curiosity overcame fear again, and she turned around slowly. She glimpsed a thin man with a pointy black beard disappearing behind a massive wooden door, and she heard a board sliding across it. There was a peephole, and she thought she saw an eye staring through. She hurried back to the table and stretched out both hands to meditate and chant herself back to reality, but her throat was too dry to make a sound.

She heard the wooden board being dragged again across the door. *Has gunpowder been invented yet?* Somehow, she doubted Kepler had the means to use it. She hoped she wouldn't be arrested, hanged, or burned as a witch. Like her, his curiosity seemed to be outweighing fear. He entered the room again, and as he walked toward her, the musty heavy smell was taken over by a strong, offensive odor. He didn't carry gunpowder for safety but strands of garlic around his neck.

"Humph," he said as he looked at her face. He circled the table rubbing his beard into more of a point, shaking his head. "Humph" He said again, and then he pinched himself. "Ouch. It appears that I am awake."

I hope I'm not, she thought, but she hardly moved an eyelash. He continued to circle.

"Perhaps this is my moon-boy come alive, a vision of Duracotus from my story." He shuffled through the papers on his desk. "Perhaps I should not have pushed my methods over into such imaginative realms, but it was needed," he argued with himself. "It's necessary for me to do that in order to understand and explain the Earth's relation to the moon."

He looked at her again and scratched his chin. "Perhaps I need sleep," he said to himself. I've never gone this long without it before, but this has been my only chance without the distraction of teaching. Perhaps I'm just too overexcited because tomorrow I leave to meet Tyco Brae."

He walked a little closer to Amanda, touched her shoulder, and then jumped back with a little yell. She tried not to move. "That's strange," he said. "I was sure my hand would fall right through. Now I hallucinate with a sense of touch? Maybe I will try to get some sleep. This will only distract me from my projects."

Unable to resist, he touched her again. This time, he pinched her arm, hard.

"Ouch," she screamed.

"Humph," he said. "This is certainly an aberration. I don't need this tonight. I need some rest before starting my journey."

Then, looking closely at her face, he whispered, "My moon boy has been crying. There, there." He patted her back. She tried not to gag at the smell of so much garlic. "I feel responsible," he said. "I'm the one who conjured you."

Wait, she wanted to say, *I'm the one who conjured you,* but when she turned around to confront him, he was gone.

Alone in the room, she went again to the window. It was a clear night, and she thought she would love to get out of this room and gaze up at the sky. She heard the bar being pulled across the door again, and he came in carrying a candle.

"I see you can't sleep either, my moon boy," he said. "I have so many questions, but now I can't ask them because I must go away. I suppose you're not a talking hallucination anyway or you'd have spoken anon."

He went to the desk and put his head down, and at first, she thought he might have fallen asleep, but he lifted his head and went on talking to the air, to her, to himself.

"Finally I got a letter from Brae. He agrees we should meet. The Barron's carriage is coming here on the way to Prague this morning. I've arranged to go with him. I don't know why he wants to travel on the first day of the year, the first day of a new century!" He shook his head. "I hope the driver has not spent the night imbibing." He stroked his beard. "But I must leave today before he changes his mind."

He seemed to notice her again and spoke the next words to her.

"I don't know why it has taken so long to get a formal invitation from him. I can't think of why he wouldn't want to share his observations with me. What have I ever done to make anyone doubt my honorable purposes?"

Amanda shrugged. She wasn't going to get into that conversation.

"We're alike," he went on. "We both have the same burning desire and interest to find the truth behind the universe."

Amanda nodded.

"I fear I have to leave you and you'll be gone when I come back. What am I saying? You are not real, anyway. The correspondence I received from him was like a dream in itself, and I must leave right away."

She nodded again.

"I don't know what the world is coming to. Sometimes it seems all this toil and travail is for nothing. Sometimes I think we will all blow ourselves up with gun powder before we get very far into this century." He shook his head. "They claim I am not a man of faith, but this letter has given me hope. Speak up, boy, if there is anything I can do for you before I go down to meet my coach."

Amanda swallowed. Her throat was dry, and she didn't know if he would understand her language even if she could manage words. "There's one thing, sir. Could you please let me out of here just once before dawn to see the night sky?"

"Humph." He cupped his elbow with one hand and stroked his beard with the other. "It's something I had not considered. Should I let my own lunacy follow me outside? What would I be unleashing into the world? Could you exist outside this room? What kinds of things might happen if I led you out? Would you blow up in a poof as you walked out the door? What effect would the outside air have on you? Humph." He looked at her. "It was clear, but now a storm is brewing." He shook his head. "I hope this won't hamper our travel."

Amanda looked to the window, and sure enough, large flakes were swirling. Still, she wanted to try. She wanted a glance of the skies that Kepler saw. Maybe there would be a pause, just before dawn.

"People might think you look peculiar." He considered again. "Ah, I know what I can do."

He left the room and was back soon with a long, woolen cape.

"Here, put this on." He helped her into it. It was nearly down to the ground and had a hood. He himself wore a topcoat now and a hat. He led her out and down a dark stairway until they stood in an entry with a high ceiling.

"You must not talk to anyone out there," he warned "Not even me. Keep your face hidden beneath the hood."

The cape was heavy and didn't smell good, but Amanda felt bolder in her disguise. As they stepped out, she felt dizzy like too much air was getting into her lungs. The air was cold and more bracing, and she couldn't breathe. When she looked up at the sky, she saw stars *and* snowflakes rushing toward her. Then she heard a giggle, and whirl of snow enclosed her like a cyclone. She reached for a hair ribbon that went sweeping by just before the Snow completely engulfed her. She had to close her eyes from the impact of the soft flakes coming at her from all sides. Like an embrace, it swept her higher. Then suddenly, it was like she was falling upward experiencing vertigo and a feeling of numbness all at once. The snow cleared, and the stars were bright.

Did it look like a poof to him? That's kind of what it felt like only she was still at someplace in between. She saw him look down at the cobblestone street only seeing a cape on the ground. He scratched his beard.

"I'm going mad," she heard him mumble. "Escorting an empty cape, full of hallucinations, all the way down here with me. I hope the letter from Brae was not some hallucination. No, here I see the carriage coming now."

She was in his quarters again standing by the window, watching as a carriage picked up Kepler just at dawn on January 1st, 1600 and took him off to meet Tyco Brae. This time, she didn't try to pull away as her hands then her entire body melted though glass. She just closed her eyes and let it happen. She was thinking it was too bad she didn't have time to make it to the Thomas fort Fair, but at least she got a glimpse of the night sky without light pollution.

When she opened her eyes, she was lying on the floor by the window seat in the loft, and Jason was above her waving something that smelled like vanilla over her nose.

"How do you feel?" he asked. "Does anything hurt?"

"No, What?"

"Does anything hurt?" he repeated, louder.

"No, I think I just finally fell asleep."

"I didn't want to move you. It looks like you might have fallen. Are you sure nothing hurts?" He looked at her with such an expression of concern she wanted to laugh. He had on a muscle shirt in the middle of winter, and the tattoo of Gemini, his favorite constellation, on his right arm made her feel romantic. He'd always taken care of her, good in any medical crisis. She supposed it was because his mother had been sick when he was young.

"I feel fine," she said, sitting up. "I think I fell asleep in the rocker and maybe fell off, what a klutz."

"I don't know. I think I should take you to the ER. It seemed more like you were passed out. Do you have a headache? You probably bumped your head."

Over at the kitchenette making tea, he said, "It's a good thing I forgot my key. What if you had passed out and nobody was here? You didn't answer when I called. Do you remember hearing the phone?"

"I might have," she said. "But I didn't wake up enough to answer it."

"You were passed out then," he said. "Not just sleeping. I'm taking you to the hospital."

Maybe the psych ward would help, she thought. "No, please, I'm okay. I just want to stay here."

Jason brought her tea, and she looked at him suspiciously before she began to sip.

Chapter Four

Gloria sits on the bench pleased with herself this morning. The sun is already warm making her think of when she was a child and how she used to walk through a meadow near her house on those first few days that school was out for the summer. Just walk, all alone, looking at the wildflowers. There was a large, flat rock in the corner near the edge of the meadow that she would walk to and sit on, scanning and surveying the land like it was her own private paradise. She liked those late June days when the sun was hot but it wasn't muggy yet. Like a blanket of color, the meadow would be filled with Indian paintbrushes, daises, and wild, light blue forget-me-nots. She knew that just beyond the edge of the woods she would find lady slippers, almost in over-bloom already and jack in the pulpit. It was so calming to just be alone and sit after the long year of classrooms and noise every day. It was even nicer when a slight breeze came along, and the grass and flowers swayed. There were bugs, too. Ants that she used to watch; at least by June, they were done with the black flies. There wasn't much water nearby so she seldom had to worry about mosquitos.

Her wrist aches today. Last night she stayed up for hours writing, had switched from crayon to pen and filled up several pages in a journal. She wrote poems, the beginnings of stories, memories—she doesn't even remember what already, but she remembers the feeling, a big breakthrough, a great relief. She doesn't want to share this milestone with anyone yet. Not until she's ready. She's afraid their knowing might somehow stop her hand. Afraid it might cripple her newfound freedom to communicate.

The solstice is today, and she found out the party consisted of Suzanne and her friends going out at sunrise to a structure that was built to catch some kind of energy from the first light as they peeked through a hole on a certain side. They had tried to get her out of bed, but she refused to move, pulling the covers over her head; she had just fallen asleep after her night of writing. She had missed breakfast with Suzanne and the calendar check this morning, which made her feel a little unhinged.

She looks at the trees, the wildflowers, and the grass almost as if they could give her absolution—as if they could make her feel like she did when she was schoolgirl. Absolve her of the guilt that abided from whatever she had done or whatever someone had done to her. The wildflowers here were different, even the bushes. She missed the landscape of lower New England—hilly but not mountainous, not as rocky, with the meadows from her childhood that seemed to stretch forever.

She swallows self-consciously and clears her throat. Had she made a sound out loud? She wasn't sure. She sits cross-legged in a yoga position on the bench, hands on her knees, breathing deeply. She feels a certain freedom because Suzanne is still with her friends and not keeping her usual vigil by the window. Thomas is probably busy with the baby. With no one watching, she sits up with her back straight, a strong position, and breathes. She makes a sound when she exhales. She's quite sure it wasn't just in her head. She looks around and doesn't see anyone by the window; she might try chanting and see how loud she can get with that. Chanting a long Ohm, she is aware of the sound of her voice, and the energy of it all makes her whole body tremble. She has broken her own sound barrier and doesn't even realize she is crying until she feels the wetness of tears dripping down her face and onto her thighs. She crouches over, puts her head down, exhausted, crying aloud with happiness and relief and confusion.

Thomas comes running out with Amanda. He sits down on the bench holding Amanda with one arm and Gloria with the other as she weeps loudly. He is probably angry that she is upsetting their daughter, but she can't help it. If she could talk, she would have told Thomas to take Amanda away although she wanted them with her. She was a good mother, she thought and didn't want her daughter to be upset. When she is almost totally exhausted, she looks up at the baby and sees that she does not seem frightened but more concerned, curious. She had not seen her mommy show any emotion in a long, long time. Zombie-mommy was cracking. Maybe it was a good thing, cathartic even for a child. She smiles at the baby, and Amanda smiles back. Gloria begins to laugh, and Amanda laughs too. Thomas looks concerned, which makes Gloria laugh even more, a secret language between just the two of them.

When the laughing and crying stops, she feels the exhaustion once again and rests her head against Thomas. He holds her tightly, and she starts to fall asleep on his shoulder. She can feel the energy of the connection, of him wanting to be there and her wanting him near, but Amanda is bored by now and pulls herself away from Thomas running down across the lawn toward the back yard.

"Amanda," Thomas yells, but he can't keep her still and he goes after her down the hill to the back yard. It would have been nice to just rest her head for a while longer on Thomas' shoulder like when it was just the two of them, but at least she had felt a few minutes of connection. She savors it thinking of the smell and feel of Thomas as she puts her head back on the bench and closes her eyes. Hearing Amanda's squeals and Thomas' voice guiding her, she thinks of the summer meadow when she was a schoolgirl, and she must have fallen asleep because she's sure she had a dream of a little girl, older than Amanda, screeching and squealing down the hill then running to her bench. She offered her a bouquet of wildflowers picked from their own back yard, and when she opens her eyes, she is lying down on the bench, and someone has put a pillow under her head and covered her with a beach towel.

She lifts her body, still groggy, and looks around trying to tell what time it is by instinct. She is getting rather good at that. How long has she been sleeping? By the empty feeling in her stomach, it's past noon; by the look of the trees and the sounds of the birds, it is not yet evening. She has found that without words, you listen more acutely and has found herself now like some animal relying on instinct, hyper aware of what time of day certain birds might be in trees, the variations in the sounds of their chatter.

Creatures seemed to rustle in the bushes at the edge of the woods in a more or less predictable pattern. *Deer*, she supposes, *following a prescribed route*. She knew about the time Thomas and Amanda would come out every day by the sound of the ducks leaving. Their splashing and honking interrupting her reverie of thought would cause her to look up knowing in a few seconds she would see them flap across the sky gliding together in an aerodynamic ballet.

She listens now but is having a hard time gauging except knowing by her hunger it is afternoon. Would she lose this ability of acute hearing if she started her verbal communication again? Is she losing something and gaining something else already? She has slept well on the bench, she realizes—better than she has in a long time. And her writing has been a major accomplishment. Suzanne's car is back in the driveway. Was it she who had covered Gloria? *Probably Thomas*, she thinks. Suanne would have covered her with some kind of quilt instead of a beach towel.

She wants to go inside. Seek food and company. This confuses her because she usually does not go inside until a family of deer make their daily trek across the lawn in the back yard. Sometimes they stop and drink from the pond. She always watches intently sure that Thomas and Suzanne don't know there is actually some organization to her day, that she has her own cues for start and finish of her movements no matter how circumscribed her life seems. The disturbing thing about this long nap is that it has taken away the time she usually spends trying to remember. Now she can't focus on remembering because her body is telling her, perhaps prematurely or perhaps because they made their daily jaunt while she was sleeping, to go inside and join the others. If she goes in earlier, they might make a bigger deal out of it than if she goes in late. If she goes in earlier than usual, it might be disturbing for them also. Maybe they are into a routine that they don't want interrupted. Maybe her entrance into the house would make them feel there is something wrong. Maybe they have also grown so used to her routine that breaking it will make them anxious.

She laughs to herself thinking that her mere presence makes them anxious. She doesn't know how to change this. She decides to make herself sit just a little longer and listen and watch for the usual cues.

Suzanne comes out carrying a tray with two glasses of what looks like iced tea and sandwiches on thick slabs of bread, another break from the usual routine. It must be nearly suppertime after all. She puts the tray down on the bench, but doesn't sit with Gloria; instead, she pulls a lawn chair up close to the tray.

"We're having company tonight," Suzanne says, looking at Gloria.

Gloria stares into the sky, can't even handle a nod to her sister, some reassurance to Suzanne that she has been heard. There is something in Suzanne's voice that is disturbing, an over-cheerfulness, but also an insinuation that she should try to act normal. She feels guilty about this anger and inability to respond to Suzanne, of all people, who is trying to take such good care of her.

"Our Solstice Party, remember?" These words come out in a

more neutral tone—one that does not make Gloria feel defensive. She makes herself at least look at Suzanne now. They haven't had company in a long time. What are Suzanne's expectations of her, her expectations of herself? Gloria picks up a sandwich and begins eating; Suzanne leans back in her chair and eats too. It seems like they are eating and drinking for a long time without words.

The deer have not come across the back yard; it must be later than she thought. When they are done, she helps Suzanne carry the plates and the tray into the house. Gloria wants to ask her sister, *"Aren't you glad I cleaned the house so well?"* She wishes she could illicit some reassurance. See, look what I did. I scrubbed the house a few days ago so I helped prepare for guests, too. I did my part. She is feeling somewhat excited.

When Suzanne's friends come, it is a letdown. They sit on pillows talking, doing yoga, drinking some kind of orange drink from the health food store. Gloria rocks Amanda to sleep then sits with her in the rocking chair for a long time. It's different for her to have so much time with Amanda at night. They are still doling out her time with her own child—these people who claim she needs healing, those who claim to love her. She listens to Amanda's breathing in starts and fits. She kisses her head feeling joy in the weight of her sleeping child, rocking and rocking for a long time.

Thomas sits with the others, but she can tell he doesn't want to be. He looks at her anxiously. She smiles at him, holds the baby more firmly with one arm around her back, fingers splayed, and one arm holding the back of her head as if she were a tiny infant. Thomas smiles back. Reassurance. He seems more relaxed after that, but still, she notices him eyeing the game machines whenever he doesn't have to make direct eye contact. She marvels at her sister, who used to be so shy and withdrawn and awkward in high school, socializing with ease, running this gathering of friends as if she were facilitating a group of her psychotic patients or a group of burnt-out executives on a 'we all love each other' retreat. People look up to Suzanne now as they had never done before, and Gloria thinks of how their father had seen this in her, had hoped at one time that Suzanne would bring this all into a boardroom and become the president of his company. How ironic it was that Suzanne had taken all those expectations and just put them to another use—one that didn't make her rich as their father had been hoping for.

"You'll never disappoint me, little pumpkin," she whispers very softly. Then she looks up suddenly fearful that someone has seen or heard, and her body trembles. When she sees no one is watching, she kisses Amanda's head. *Any way you want to be is alright with me*—she only thinks these words, says them in her head. She goes on rocking thinking she has again broken her own sound barrier in a whisper to her daughter. The thought of it makes her breathing come fast. Maybe she can start slowly, like this, in whispers to her daughter. She sighs, and Amanda moans in her sleep. Thomas looks over at them again. He comes over and offers to take Amanda to bed. Gloria lets him lift their daughter from her and feels lightheaded.

She goes over and sits on the cushion that Thomas has vacated. Suzanne's friends smile at her no doubt all aware of her muteness. She smiles back to make them more comfortable with her presence. She can be generous now; she has another secret, one she only shares with Amanda. It's such a relief that she can decide the moment that she gets her voice back again, that the whisper came out without prompting from them. It's like she's someone in a wheelchair now that no one knows can really walk.

Later, when everyone is asleep, she writes some poems on stray pieces of paper. Then, she writes in her journal:

June 21, 1978

Sleepwalking Backwards

Today is the Summer Solstice.
I whispered today.

Chapter Five

THANKSGIVING

Amanda looked at herself in the mirror as she leaned over and sprayed Windex into the glass. Her shift dragged on. Her parents were coming for Thanksgiving, and all she could think of was all that would have to be done the next day. It was clear, anyway. Even with the hotel lights, she could see the big dipper and at least five of the seven sisters. She was glad she' d been up here for the Leonid Meteor Shower a couple of weeks ago. She and Jason had stayed up all night watching the shooting stars. Down in Massachusetts, it was always overcast in November.

Had she changed in the last few months? She felt like she had. She was getting older. She hadn't grown her hair out or anything and she didn't look quite as conservative because she didn't have to teach every day. Was her mother right that she couldn't wear her hair short and punk forever? She was looking forward to seeing her parent's again but was hoping they wouldn't try to pressure her to change her mind and go back down. Was she was being foolish to just stay up here, with her life on hold? She did feel disappointed and lonely sometimes. She was changing inside and didn't know if anyone would like her new self, much less truly love her. There were all these things she was still trying to understand. It seemed so easy for other people to make decisions about their lives. She always wanted to go completely in one direction, and then the other. *If I do this with my life, what am I missing?*

She thought of Kepler, although since the episode on Halloween, it gave her an eerie feeling. At one point, he had had eleven prospective wives to choose from and had actually written in detail about this dilemma in his notebooks. It was his second marriage after his first wife died. His indecision went on for two years as friends tried to tell him what he should do and whom he should marry. There was a widower, but she wanted to marry off one of her two daughters instead. He thought they were too young. Another prospective bride had bad breath, and another was too heavy—they wouldn't make a good match because he was small and skinny. Over the two years, he kept going back to choice #5 who was a woman who had kept house for him and his first wife. He really wanted to be with her, and she was good with his children, but everyone warned him against marrying her because being in service, she was beneath him. In the end, she supposed, he did what many people couldn't do in those days. He followed his heart and chose bride #5. She guessed it had always been hard for a person who couldn't make decisions because friends and family would always be giving them advice.

Peter would be coming up for Thanksgiving. She had told her mother to invite him. Would he be bringing anyone? She had said that would be okay. He had said he was coming and had left it at that, so she would set up a sixth place—just in case.

Jason had done most of the shopping and helped her with the organizing. They had rented a table and chairs, which they had set up in the lower part of the chalet next to the machines.

It was almost eleven when she got back. Jason was sleeping on the cot. He lay face up with his arms dangling over the side and a book on his lap, snoring. She tiptoed over and took the reading glasses, which were cockeyed, off his nose. He made some snorting sounds, blinked his eyelids as if he were swimming back to consciousness, but then she turned off the reading lamp, and he fell back into the even quiet breathing of the truly exhausted.

He'd already begun the cooking, and she let her nose follow

the smells of oregano, garlic and chestnuts to a crockpot set up on the counter. It was a very dark night with no moon and only the light of stars through the big window. After a few steps, she bumped into the table, hard.

"Damn," she said and then looked back to where Jason was sleeping.

He did not stir. He did not change his breathing.

She felt her way around the table and walked carefully up the stairs feeling exhausted but too wound up to go to bed. She brought a pillow and blanket to the rocking chair where she eventually fell asleep staring out at the stars. Early, a bright, harsh sunrise awoke her—the red golden sun rising like a communion wafer. Jason, downstairs, slept through the whole thing. She peeked at it only a few seconds caught unaware between waking and sleeping then covered her face with her hands and hopped into bed pulling the covers over her face. When she closed her eyes, she saw circles and colors coming at her, yellows and reds from the sunrise searing into her brain.

Neither she nor Jason woke until the doorbell rang. She bolted for the bathroom still dressed from the night before.

"Be right there," she shouted so unbelievably loud to her own ears that they probably did hear it all the way through the door downstairs. She could see Jason get up, stumbling around, probably unsure of where he was. He was breaking down the cot and putting it away when Amanda flew down the stairs, now in jeans and a sweater. She tried to catch her breath before opening the door.

Her mother, father, and Peter were all dressed up and ready for turkey. She looked down the driveway and saw only one car. *He must have come with them.* What time was it, six am? She looked at the clock; it was almost ten. The bright sunshine gleaned off her mother's sunglasses and her silver blonde hair. Amanda squinted and blinked her eyes.

"Did we get the wrong day?" her father asked, dryly.

"Oh, daddy," she said and kissed him on the cheek, feeling the stubble of a day or two of growth, remembering he never shaved on holidays.

"We thought we'd start out early and miss the traffic," her mother said.

"Don't apologize. I'm glad you're here early." She hugged her mother and whisked her in. "It's my fault. I feel asleep in the chair after work last night."

"I told you this would be too much," her mother said.

Peter stood back holding an apple pie. Their eyes met, and she smiled. It was awkward with Jason upstairs warming up the hors d'oeuvres. Her mother took the pie from Peter, placed it on the table, and went up to help Jason. Her father had already turned on the pinball machines

"Is she sleeping better?" she heard her mother ask Jason.

Amanda took both Peter's hands in hers feeling giddy and uncomfortable, almost like they were starting something all over again. "I'm glad you came," she said.

"Me, too."

They held onto each other, and he brushed his lips across her forehead.

"I miss you," she said

"You can come back."

"I thought you had a girlfriend. You said it was over."

"I don't know."

"We'll talk later," she said and led him by the hand to the table where Jason had just brought down slices of cheese, crackers, and strawberries with cream.

Her mother placed a tray of broccoli and cauliflower on the table beside a bowl of onion dip. "Why is there an extra place setting?" she asked, staring at Amanda.

Amanda looked at Jason. They had forgotten to take the extra setting away that could have been for Peter's date, but Amanda didn't want to bring that up right now.

"It's a tradition," Jason lied. "Kind of a Vermont thing. You always set an extra place at Thanksgiving in case an unexpected guest drops in—maybe someone lost in the mountains, stuck in a blizzard."

Amanda's mother looked troubled. There was a long, uncomfortable silence as her mother dropped the bowl of dip onto the table and stared off in that haunted way. Her father glanced over worriedly from the pinball machines. It was a strong déjà vu from when she was young and something would set her mother off as they all sat at the table up here. Peter held Amanda's hand.

"I like it," her mother finally said. "I like that custom."

Her dad's attention went back to the machines.

"Everyone sit," Jason said. "Enjoy. This is just to open up your taste buds. I put the turkey in a little late, but the first course is almost ready."

"Sit down with us," Amanda urged.

"No, you guys talk and relax. I want to get back to my vegetable barley soup."

Her mother didn't follow him up the stairs this time. She grabbed the snow shovel and went out the door. Even though the driveway had been cleared, and all the necessary paths had been shoveled, she began shoveling her paths to nowhere just as she had done when Amanda was a child.

It had always been her mother who shoveled the snow and not her father. At first, she would shovel paths to the cars and the propane tank and the mailbox like all the other neighbors, but then she would make these other mazes—paths to nowhere Amanda used to call them.

Amanda spent hours as a child walking these zigzag paths pretending they were roads to take her anywhere she wanted to go. She thought it was something her mother did just for her, creating places for her to play. She knew her mother didn't like to talk when she was pushing the snow away with such energy, so she would watch from the window until her mother would come in exhausted. Her mother had never allowed her to make a snow fort or even a snowman, but she let her play in these paths that ended abruptly, leaving Amanda no choice but to walk or run back the way she had come. She would wave to her mother sometimes—her mother always watching from the window. Other than those paths, she would not let Amanda play in the snow. Her father never went out when there was a snowstorm. He just stayed in bed late, read the paper, watched TV, and made her mother do all the work.

Peter came up behind her and brushed his chin against the spikes of her hair. "Why is she shoveling?"

Amanda shrugged.

Jason came down with the soup and a plate of seven-grain bread. Her mother's sunshine muffins sat lost in the middle of the table. Amanda took one with a shot of black coffee. Her father took some veggies on a plate and went back to the machines. Jason went back up to prepare the main course.

Her mother came in looking tired. She leaned over the table. "You should go up and help him," she said to Amanda who was just getting ready to enjoy the soup.

"He doesn't want my help. Trust me, he likes doing this."

"Well, *I* will help him then."

Amanda rolled her eyes as her mother clomped up the stairs, snow falling from her heels. Amanda was afraid she would just annoy him, but soon she heard them exchanging recipes and talking about the value of different herbs. Her father had a few glasses of wine and went back to playing the pinball machines leaving Peter and her alone at the table. He poured her a glass of wine. They moved to the end of the table that was not visible from upstairs; Peter glanced at her father who was completely engrossed in Ms. Pac-Man. He fed her a strawberry and she pursed her lips over the tips of his fingers. He kissed her lips.

"He's gay, isn't he?" Peter whispered in her ear. "All this time I was jealous of someone who was gay."

"He's a friend," she said. Her mother must have told him that. Let him think what he wanted.

"We're going for a walk," Amanda shouted up to the loft. Peter looked puzzled.

"It's freezing out," her mother yelled.

This from a woman who just came in from clearing paths in the cold for no reason. Amanda took Peter's hand and led him out the door. The glare of the sun on the snow reminded her of the early morning sunrise, and she put her scarf over her eyes, thinking of Newton almost blinding himself.

"Are you turning into a vampire?"

"I don't like the sun," she said, "You lead."

"Don't like the sun since when? You've been up here too long."

He led her only a far as the backseat of her car. There was plenty of room because she was storing her telescopes in the closet of the loft. They lay down together, and he took the scarf from her eyes. The glint of the sun through the windows was still too much so she buried her face in the crook of his shoulder. He held her close, touched the back of her neck, kissed her ear, and pulled her body into his to protect her from the sun.

"I miss you," he said.

"Me too."

"I think we still have a chance"

"Me too." She had been worried that she had changed and he wouldn't like her now. "We better go back in."

"In a while," he said. "In a while."

When they got back into the house, her father was still at the machines and her mother still in the kitchenette with Jason. Salads and condiments had been added to the table, and soon bowls of potatoes and vegetables were brought down. The smells and the food brought them all back together, and the meal went on in the long, slow contented way that holidays should. Amanda had been worried about the awkwardness, but everything seemed to be going smoothly. She felt guilty leaving Jason doing all the work, but he seemed to be enjoying being the host. She got up and cleared the table, washed some dishes, and checked on the pies.

Peter came up behind her and kissed her neck. "I think it was good, you going away like this," he said.

"Sorry I left so suddenly. I just had to do it. I didn't want you and mom to talk me out of it."

"At least you didn't lose your job at the university. That's the main thing. You didn't just walk away from your job."

Amanda moved away. "I did walk away. I quit my job."

They faced each other now. "Well, yea, I mean you did walk away, but now they're calling it a sabbatical. You can come back for second semester."

Amanda turned to the sink. Her head down. "You don't get it. I don't know if I want to go back or not."

"But in the car, you said..."

She could tell he was trying not to raise his voice. Her mother and father and Jason had gone quiet at the table.

He lowered his voice and spoke more slowly enunciating each word as if it would make them louder. "In the car, you said we still had a chance. You said you were ready to come back."

"I didn't say that," Amanda whispered.

The conversation had resumed at the table below. The whirs and buzzes of the machines were back again, drowning out the world. Jason and her mother were exchanging herbal remedies for indigestion.

"Well, you didn't think I was going to move up here," Peter whispered.

"I don't know," Amanda said. "I don't know what I meant. I'm not coming down in January or February. I'm staying up here till June."

Peter shook his head; his hands sliced the air. "Can you please explain to me what the attraction is?" He spoke softly and moved closer to her. "I really thought it was him. Now I know he's gay. What is it? Why else would you stay up here putting up with ice and snow probably well into April and working as a maid? You don't ski like everyone else up here. Not even cross county."

He stood in front of her inconsolable, her behavior so incomprehensible to him, it made her sad.

"What is it?" he asked, grinding his teeth. "Tell me."

"I don't know." She wished she could explain, but his intimidation wasn't helping. With him, everything had to be a confrontation.

"Then you're not coming down at the holidays?"

"I'll be down for Christmas and New Year's, but I'm coming back afterwards."

"Then you're not going back to your job in February."

"No."

Since he was backing her into a corner, she would make the decision now. She checked the pies. They were done. She called down to Jason.

"You are the most stubborn woman I have ever known," Peter said. Amanda handed him some plates to bring down, and he walked toward the stairs.

Jason and Amanda served tea and coffee. Peter sat in the corner sulking; Amanda ignored him. She knew if he had taken his own car, he would have stormed out by now. After pie, whipped cream, tea, and coffee, everyone was falling asleep at the table except Amanda's mother.

"It the tryptophan," she said. "That's why I don't eat meat." Jason had eaten some turkey because he said it was from a free-range farm.

"Why don't you stay here tonight?" Amanda asked. "You

and dad can have the bed, and I have the cot and a couple of sleeping bags."

They looked at her dad.

"I wouldn't mind waiting till tomorrow to drive," he said.

Peter looked crabby. Would he volunteer to drive? She knew her dad didn't like other people to drive his car, and Peter would probably act polite no matter how he really felt. They all looked at him.

"I guess I don't need to be home first thing in the morning, but I have plans later in the day."

He looked at Amanda. Was she supposed to care about his plans? *Let him have plans*, she thought; she didn't care. Although, she was a little relieved they were all staying the night considering what had happened on Halloween.

By ten, everyone was asleep but Amanda and her mom. Amanda wanted to go to sleep too, but her mother sat in the rocking chair drinking sleepy time tea, all wound up and in a weird mood. Amanda watched her closely.

"I remember when we first lived here," she said. "It was amazing the amount of kids who used to fit in this place overnight." Amanda perked up. "Outside, we would set up tents for the overflow like the circus was always in town."

Her sudden laughter startled Amanda. It was frightening, almost manic. She was used to seeing her mother smile a lot, but she never laughed. Amanda thought her mother was on the edge and maybe she should wake her dad or something, but she listened, mystified, not wanting to break some kind of spell that had seemed to fall over them. Her mother had become the speaker of things that mattered. She listened as her mother told stories as if they had fallen and been trapped in some kind of web, a cocoon, just the two of them, wound together in silky threads.

She'd heard most of the stories from her father, so she was barely listening to the words, more the treble in her mother's voice. She only picked up bits like dozens and dozens of young people would bring friends and friends and friends. Everyone worked; everyone shared. She heard the words Utopia, Emerson, Alcott. Younger kids were showing up later, runaways, some dangerous people, bikers. She thinks they decided to close the Rainbow House around the time she became pregnant. For a while, Amanda felt like a child leaning into her mother's stories for answers until she realized her mother had wandered into her own quiet reminiscence as if Amanda were not there.

Her mother talked into the night until a loud snore from Jason down on the cot seemed to pull her out of her reverie. Then her mother got up, kissed her, and dressed for bed leaving Amanda in the middle of a spell that wasn't broken. She went to the bottom floor and stretched out in a sleeping bag next to Peter.

They left early the next morning, and by afternoon, it began to snow. Even Jason, after giving her instructions about the leftovers, had taken a flight down to Florida to visit his dad and step mom. She called her mother late in the afternoon to make sure they made it home safely. Her mother's voice sounded far, far away.

"It went pretty well with Peter, I thought," her mother said. It was more a question than a statement. She obviously wanted information. "He was quiet, though, on the way home. At least he didn't bring a date. I told you he wanted to work things out."

"Yeah, it went pretty well, I guess."

"Don't leave him waiting too long."

"Mom, it's not a game I'm playing."

"I'm sorry. I was just trying to say something positive. It's so cozy up there in the mountains. It was really a lovely Thanksgiving, but you are coming down here for Christmas and New Year's, right?"

"Yes, mother."

"You would not believe all the people we have coming to the millennium party. We'll be entertaining downstairs just like when you were a kid."

Amanda stared at the snow coming down. "No two flakes are alike," she said.

"What's that?"

She tried to listen to the voice on the other end of the line, but her mind felt so insulated.

"It stopped here," her mother said. "Not coming down at all. Are you okay alone?"

"Mother, I have enough food left over to eat for two weeks."

"With some of the storms up there, you might need it. I hate to admit it, but I'm glad Jason is nearby." She hadn't mentioned to her mother that he was going away. "When do you have to work again?"

"Not until Sunday."

"Good. Just sit tight and enjoy the storm."

Amanda, as usual, hung up first. The disconnection of voice made her feel even more insulated. She didn't like a storm like this when darkness descended so early. Thick flakes swirled around the window, disorienting to watch, and it was so quiet. She couldn't see the mountains and she couldn't see the sky, only large thick flakes swirling around the outside of the window. She walked downstairs and turned on all the pinball machines then sat at the long table all by herself eating warmed over turkey and drinking a beer listening to the music that calmed her, the music she is convinced she had heard in utero, the hum and ping of pinball machines.

The tryptophan and beer must have put her to sleep; when she awoke, everything was dark and silent. She felt her way up the staircase and fished around for a flashlight on the nightstand but found only matches. Someone had been in the secret draw. They had found the medallion she had made out of the broken optics and hung it like a sun catcher on the side of the window tied with the ribbon she had fished out of the pond last summer.

Chapter Six

Gloria sits on the bench feeling more disoriented than the day before. She thought the solstice or her secret whispering would open some kind of valve in her memory, which would allow her to be herself again and she would just have to get used to her old self, remember how to act as her old self, before letting the others in on her breakthroughs, but she feels only anxiety. She sits on the bench trying to ground herself as Suzanne had taught her to do in yoga. She tries to fall into the length of the bench, let herself go and let the bench support her. She wants more of a grip, to pull her real self, her former self out from within; breathing, trying to force calmness, she nearly passes out. They are not watching her as closely. They think she's getting better, but now she's feeling worse. So undone. *But, at least,* she tells herself, *I whispered.*

She assesses the morning light coming through the trees at the edge of the woods. Was there a half-minute of extra darkness this morning or will that be tonight? Did the birds adjust their song? She hears them now and sees them, mostly blue jays and mourning doves, hopping around grubbing worms from the rich soil beneath the grass. She should be gardening, she thinks. It seems like in other years here, there had always been a garden. She has a vague memory of one; maybe it will string along others. She tries to remember more; her entire life has become one long déjà vu.

She knows there's a woodpecker nearby. She can't see him but hears him drilling into a tree wishing she could batter slowly and patiently at her memory like that until she opened up a hole of entry. Restless, she moves to the other side of the bench. Adjusting herself for comfort. Still, she feels awkward.

She gets up and pads to the edge of the woods hoping to spot the woodpecker, the exact tree he is working on; the jays and doves fly at her approach. Her ear bends in the direction of the woodpecker. *Which tree is it he batters for nourishment?* Maybe a garden is something she and Thomas can work on together. *Although, it is late to start planting*, she thinks, as she tries to narrow down the exact clump of trees by sound and then the exact location of the bird by any movement in the leaves or changes in lighting. She still hears but can't see as if a blur covers her eyes. She'll look for a garden. There must be one around. Suddenly the thought of their little girl digging in dirt and filling pails with water frightens her. Overcome by panic, she retreats to the bench once again.

The sun is hotter, burning into her face and upper arms. She welcomes the pain somehow feeling she deserves punishment. *It will be sore tomorrow*, she thinks, and finally picks up the straw hat she always leaves here for the glare and covers her face. It is a relief not to have the blazing so directly on her forehead, but she can feel the sweat now accumulating around the front of the hat brim until it runs down in beads. She catches some on her lips and tongue, tastes the salt, wonders why she feels the need to do this penance. Like hell or purgatory are just like having nothing to do, no direction, no memory of recent past, little thought of the future. Some people might be envious, might think it was heaven just to sit in the hot sun.

What does she need to repent? If she could have spied that woodpecker, working so hard for his nourishment, she feels she could have remembered something of what used to make her want to be in the world. She feels shame along with everything else. Hoping Amanda is too young to resent her inability to motivate even her mother. *You are the first one I whispered to*, she says to Amanda in her mind, to assuage some of the guilt. *You are the only one who could break the sound barrier. You are my motivation to get up, wash my face, help Aunt Suzanne with the breakfast—it's all you. You are the reason I have to sit day after day and squeeze reasoning into my hollow spirit and try to remember why I am here.* Not being with Amanda is like a penance she can't remember the reason for.

The thought of a garden makes her excited; the image of her little girl hauling pails of water to help with watering makes her shudder. She tries to ignore that creeping anxiety. Tries to think of the joy she may feel again digging in the dirt, Thomas and Amanda working beside her. Her daughter seeing her mommy doing something useful, she thinks she would sleep better if her muscles were just a little sore.

She remembers when Thomas was living at the Garden of Delights how a group of them tilled and tended what they called an 'urban garden,' which was kind of a joke because no one really thought of Worcester as a city even though it officially was one. Unlike Boston, there were many places to eke out gardens even in the most built up areas. She supposed the importance was that it was a community garden, the effort of a group. Just so Worcester wouldn't have its inferiority complex, there had to be a few crops and herbs grown in the middle of the city surrounded by barbed wire. Theirs was located in main south, a run-down section of Worcester. Maybe they thought growing crops in that area would make the prostitutes more wholesome and the fights less violent.

For whatever reason, Thomas' pot smoking friends had decided to start it, and she remembers being grateful. It had pulled her deeper into his world, a world that she still couldn't fit completely into but circled around the edges as she had circled around the edges of groups her entire life. She never fit in during junior high, high school, or even in college, her own fault. She had always been an observer more than a doer, and it was fine that way; in fact, she preferred it, though it was hard to always feel that you weren't quite accepted. That's why she was so glad when they had started the community garden. Something she could do and feel good about, digging for hours, losing track of time, getting the acceptance she resented and needed, her contribution to harmony and world peace.

Thomas had been proud of her involvement. The others, perhaps with the lethargy of being stoned half the time, didn't do that much when they showed up. They talked more than they worked. The rule was you couldn't go there alone. It had to be a community effort. Gloria had snuck there sometimes alone enjoying the effort in silence and solitude. Her father had thought it was a joke. They had a couple of acres around their house with good soil to grow a garden, hoses, and a sprinkler system, yet she went into the city to a scraggly fourth of an acre, scratching into the ground, hauling buckets of water. Her parents had both worried that it was a dangerous area; she told them of the rule that no one went to tend it alone.

Thomas comes out carrying a tray of ice tea, Amanda walking beside him. Gloria accepts it eagerly, the coldness of the glass both a shock and a relief to her sweating hands. Before taking a sip, she takes off her straw hat and swipes the cold glass across her forehead, smiling with relief, smiling at her family who has come to rescue her from her own thoughts. She drinks too quickly and begins to choke on the cool liquid. Thomas pats her back. She is too hot, too cold, too overexcited. How will she communicate her wish to start a garden when the words still choke before leaving her throat? She takes a deep breath, drinks more tea. She will have to whisper her need to her child in the evening, whisper to Amanda her dreams about the garden and how it will heal them all. Thomas is done patting her back, and she stops choking, and he holds her to him. Thomas and she are just beginning to have some of that closeness from long ago when Amanda runs from the bench ready for a game of catch-me. Thomas runs after her and picks her up, twirls her around, takes her hand, and they run back to

Sleepwalking Backwards

the bench.

"Take mommy's hand," he says. "Time for a walk."

"Auk," Amanda says and hops down.

Gloria smiles at her daughter, kisses her sweaty hair, takes her hand, and they are off.

"One, two, three...whee," Thomas says as he and Gloria lift Amanda, and her legs dangle joyously in space, kicking the air. They walk quickly toward the back of the house, Gloria taking her cues from Thomas as he speeds up into a run and counts the one, two, three, and Amanda shouts whee as they pull her up, legs dangling free, lifted from the force of gravity. Gloria doesn't understand why children like this feeling so much. It must be wonderful to be new enough to the world to be comfortable not being grounded. She's been in a free fall with nothing joyous about it. She wishes she could be like a child again not struggling so hard to find something solid, able to take things as they come without worrying about destination, no worry about the pain if you should fall. Maybe her daughter will be an astronaut, Gloria thinks, as she and Thomas swing her higher into the air.

She does wish they would slow down though. She is getting tired and hot and keeps looking around for where a garden might have been planted. There has to be a grassless, mulched patch of soil somewhere around here. She was sure they once grew vegetables. Why was no one tending a garden this summer? She would search later, when they were not with her. For now, she decides just to enjoy being with her husband and daughter.

When they are back at the bench again, Gloria sits, and Amanda climbs up on her lap. Thomas sits and puts his arm around them. Gloria is content, but Amanda begins to squirm. She gets down, running around in front of them. Thomas Doesn't mind sitting, and Gloria feels grateful. Again, she feels the renewed energy between them. *Safe*. For a while, when she was deep in the fog, even Thomas' presence had not given her solace.

Amanda runs to the edge of the woods.

"Stop," Thomas yells.

Amanda turns, grins, and runs into the woods.

Gloria almost yells, but her scream to Amanda is swallowed into a silent panic. Thomas runs to the woods.

"Amanda, stop, now."

Gloria gets up and runs too, feeling helpless as she sees the edges of Amanda's little pink dress disappear into the trees. As she runs, there is a voice in the back of her head. *The woods will gobble up your child.* Then everything turns black for a second, and she thinks she will pass out, but Thomas is by her side steadying her and holding Amanda who is laughing, delighted with the new game of hide and seek she can play with her parents.

Thomas helps Gloria to the bench and makes her drink a glass of iced tea.

"I'm afraid we wore mommy out, today," he says to Amanda, picking her up. He leans down and kisses Gloria on the forehead.

Amanda wants to give a kiss too and scrambles onto Gloria's lap. Her hot pink cheeks press against Gloria's neck as Gloria embraces her daughter, kisses Amanda's head, and Thomas lifts her again, pulls her away.

"We have to go in now. Leave mama to rest."

Gloria doesn't really want to rest. She wants to follow her family into the house and do whatever it is they are going to do next, but she doesn't know how to do that, and she is still afraid her presence will make Thomas and Suzanne uncomfortable, trying to adjust their schedules to Gloria's new need to be a part of it all. It might even disturb Amanda to have her mother in the house, off the bench, at this time of day. So she remains seated as Thomas and Amanda enter the house.

No one is watching from the window, so Gloria decides to take her own walk and look around, figure out where to put a garden. She walks all the way around the house then down the double row of trees that borders the long driveway. Trees planted by her father when he was a young man. Her parents had bought the chalet and kept it probably as a tax write-off. Her parents didn't even like it here, she thinks. They had seldom come up here when she was child. She sighs, thinking of how hard they had tried to wrestle it legally from Suzanne when she wigged out of their father's good graces. They had lost that battle. Suzanne was over 25 now. She owned it clear and free.

She walks down the lane for a while thinking how strange it is that her own illness or crisis or whatever it is has seemed to precipitate some kind of reconciliation between Suzanne and her parents. She remembers they were up here for a while. Although they didn't agree on the approach to her healing, at least they had spoken, spent some time in a common cause. She wonders where they are now. As she walks down the long drive, it becomes more than a palisade; the trees on the side become the edge of the forest. At this point, she heads back, intent on making her walk purposeful, intent on finding a spot for the garden. She cuts through the line of trees and heads to the opposite side of the chalet from the bench, looking up at the sky as a hawk circles just over the pond and flies out of sight into the thick trees.

She makes herself focus; she looks at the ground. Will the soil be richer near the planted trees or in back near the pond? She looks across the sloping grass, grown too long. These grounds are being left neglected. But how could Thomas do all the jobs around here when he has to do hers too? It's pretty in a way. The lawn that used to be manicured when her father owned it stood now as a wild meadow. Daises, violets, and buttercups kept company with the weeds. She scans the area wondering where she should put a garden. She thinks, though the soil might be richer near the pond, she should plant by the edge of the forest near the shade. There's a flat area with a few apple trees just at the line where the back yard begins.

She runs over to it digging with a stick then her nails. The soil is soft, richer than what is around it. She can plant tomatoes here and lettuce. This will be her task. She thinks she can see an outline of a garden about three by five feet, where the grass had not quite overtaken and the soil will be easier to till. The first things she will need are gloves and a shovel.

She goes to the shed built into the foundation at the back of the house, and as she opens it, she feels a welcome dampness, a smell of coldness, earth, a hiding place. The floor is dirt, the walls cement. *An old structure*, she thinks, *much older than the chalet itself.* She thinks of closing the door and just sitting inside for a while. She could sit on a brick in the corner, make it her new bench; maybe the dankness could cut through her memories as the sun never could. Instead, she stays her purpose, takes gloves from a bucket, and grabs a shovel that rests against the wall.

She is halfway back to her new garden spot when she hears Suzanne screaming her name. Suzanne races around the side of the house until she stands right in front of her, panting.

"Thank god, you're okay."

She wants to say she is sorry for frightening her. But really, where did she think she would go anyways? But words still fail her. She does touch Suzanne's elbow, though, to calm her down, somehow realizing the significance of Suzanne's vigils at windows of the house ending. In a matter of seconds, Suzanne regains her calmness.

"It's the solstice," she says. "It makes us all a little uneasy."

Suzanne takes the shovel and gloves from Gloria. She leaves them on the ground and leads Gloria into the house for supper. Gloria obeys for now but what she wants is to be digging. She helps Suzanne prepare a salad, watches her cut fresh bread into thick slabs and mix herbs and mayo and tuna. She listens to the spatula hitting the sides of the bowl. Her hearing is still acute; she is glad of that. After dinner, Suzanne and Gloria clean up, and they fall into their routines. Suzanne bathes Amanda while Thomas plays video games. Gloria quietly lets herself out of the house, picks up the shovel that has been left on the ground, goes to her plot, and begins to dig.

    She kicks down the edge of the shovel, pushing it into the soil as deeply as she can, turning over large chunks of dirt and grass. This soil had been tilled fairly recently. She runs into few stones and roots. It's good to watch it pile up on the side, a measure of her labor. The bugs fly around her straw hat, and sweat pours down her face from under the brim, dripping down her nose even as the evening turns cooler. She stops and looks up at the sunset, a pink arc descending like a cloak beyond the trees. She looks toward the house and sees Suzanne and Thomas by the window, staring at her, sadly, as if she is digging a grave.

Chapter Seven

Reflections, Refractions, Inflections & Colours of Light

Amanda peered through the sun catcher, which oddly picked up light even in the blizzard. Was it the sunrise? She moved her gaze to the periphery. As much as she wanted to know the source of light, she couldn't look at the sun full on. An intensity of heat and light drove toward her, forming a roiling ball swirling right into the glass of the window. It made her want to vomit. *I am dying*, she thought, *going toward the light. All those wacky books my mother gave me to read—they were all true.* Pulled into the vortex, her body floated; her skin tingled. Then she noticed an eye peeking back at her.

There was a tiny hole poked into a shutter where a beam of light shone into a dark room. She moved her eye away then looked again. The other eye had disappeared. It was warm. The air smelled like spring, and she was standing in front of one of those old-fashioned windows with wooden shutters.

It didn't look or feel like Kepler's Germany. There were roses growing abundantly in front of the brick building. Everything was green, grey, and a dark, muted red. She smelled manure and a dank river smell, as well as, the flowers. After a feint knock, she decided it would be better for her to just enter, confidently. She walked in and saw a young man, possibly younger than her, trying to jot something in a notebook. *Would this be considered heaven or hell? Walking in on Sir Isaac Newton when he was only nineteen and nearly blinded himself with experiments concerning the nature of light?*

He had probably not seen her eye staring back, had probably been doing these experiments for a while now and could barely see her as she walked into the room. He didn't look up from the notebook and missed the inkwell when he tried to dip the nib of the pen.

"Wickens," he said in a loud voice as if he had been startled. "I didn't know you would return so soon." He sighed. His voice was loud, excited. "I think I may have gone too far. I fear I may not be able to see. But my finding s *are* interesting. Maybe you can jot them down for me."

She wondered how to respond. How much could he see? She looked at the small hole he had made in the shutter where the sunshine was coming through. There was a prism on a high table in the middle of the room that picked up the light in a rainbow of colors. He was doing the experiments that would be written in the *Optica*. She felt like she should say something, but he would know she was not Wickens. She cleared her throat and walked slowly to his desk.

He thrust a pen into her hands and got up so she could sit, and she clumsily dipped the nub into the inkwell, hunched over the notebook, and tried to write. Great globs of ink fell from the pen. She would need practice. Her hand trembled. Is that why she was here—to be Newton's secretary? Any minute now, he would start to dictate important theories, and she would be unable to transcribe them. But Sir Isaac was in his own panic.

"I can't see, Wickens. I'm glad you returned early. Maybe I can tell you how to make a salve for my eyes. There is something funny about you; you smell odd. Not a bad odor—just one I'm not familiar with. Maybe it's just the blindness making everything seem strange. I must stay in the dark. I think if I stay in the dark for a few days, any damage will repair itself. But first, I must dictate my findings."

He covered up the hole in the window.

"I can't see to write now," she said, in a husky voice. "Sir. I mean Isaac, ah, Newton."

"Of course you can't. I'm all in a flurry like the chickens. I'll just bury my head in the pillow here. I'll cover my eyes with it only so you can still hear what comes out of my mouth. What have I done to myself now, Wickens? I always seem to go too far. I pray this blindness will pass."

She wanted to say something to comfort him—tell him he was not going to go blind—that he was going to live into his eighties, sight thankfully intact, to observe and calculate the foundations of mathematics.

"I pray it will, too," she whispered.

"But I found from my experiments that light cannot be merely a pressure. It must be made up of particles. How else could white light split into so many colors? It seems to bounce, actually bounce off objects. It must be that light is corpuscular, so the color of an object depends on which part of the spectrum is absorbed by it and which reflected. It's surely made up of particles."

Amanda was blobbing up the ink too much and not doing very well at all. She was thankful when he abruptly stopped speaking. She had hardly been able to manage the word particles.

"I just can't go on right now," he shouted. "This blindness is too distracting. What have I done to myself, Wickens? What kind of future will I have if I can't see?"

She went over and put her hand on his shoulder, cleared her throat, and made her voice as low as possible. "You only need rest. I fear you have been up too many nights and suffer from exhaustion."

Newton sighed. "When I close my eyes, I see nothing but colors. I may lose my thoughts if I don't get them down."

She convinced him to lie down on the bed. "I'll procure a woman in town to nurse you," she said but he probably didn't hear because he appeared to be asleep already.

Amanda put her head down on the desk hardly moving for what seemed like a long time. She tried to feel how Sir Newton must have felt. She looked into the darkness of her eyelids, the darkness of her inner self and thought about where she was. This room, this time should be charged with knowledge, but here she sat, and it was like any other day in history. She lifted her head and looked around. All the windows were shuttered, but light shone through a crack at the bottom of the door, and she could smell spring outside like any other spring. Maybe there was more of a chance she could go outside, walk through the paths of Cambridge in the 17th century. This time, she had landed outside.

When she was sure he was asleep, she took a hooded cape off a hook in the corner. It draped along the floor somewhat, but she could walk in it if she took her time. Maybe it belonged to Wickens. He was apparently much shorter than Sir Isaac. She picked up a black leather bag next to the door and peered inside. There were Newton's salves and medicines. She opened the door and stepped outside. Sir Isaac turned over and sighed but didn't wake.

She hurried down a dirt path between hedges to a cobbled lane. *I'm like little black riding hood*, she thought, as she walked along hidden in the black cape carrying the black bag. The lane opened wider, and she walked along with the clomp of horses, children running, and people shouting to each other. If she was tripping from fumes of her gas stove, it was a pleasant experience and she could see why her parents and others had gathered in the loft for drug parties and 'happenings.' It was even kind of fun trying to avoid the horse poop.

Then she felt a shiver in her body even through the spring warmth. Hadn't Newton had to leave Cambridge for a year because the plague came to London? Suddenly the smells and sounds took on a dreary aspect. Voices that had sounded so quaint now sounded like garish echoes of voices. She noticed children sharing cups and wanted to tell them to stop. The water of the Thames was yellowish green. She saw a rat run under a bridge.

It was the next spring, she thought, but she wasn't sure. *About a year after Newton's experiments with light the plague descended on London and he left for the countryside*? After that, the fire of London had actually helped to end the plague. *Could it have been this year?* She turned around, walking quickly, feeling dismal in her black cape. A harbinger of death, is that what she was? Could she tell them what was going to happen? Who would she go to? Who would listen? How could she explain?

They would think she was a witch. It was the 1600's, and she knew what was going on in Salem, Mass. Maybe she could leave some kind of note for Newton about the rats, but she knew he was never infected with the plague so she better not do anything to interfere. It might change everything for the worse. She hurried back to his lodgings and opened the door just enough to squeeze through. He turned over and squinted at her.

"You must be the nurse Wickens procured for me?"

She nodded then remembered he couldn't see. "I am, sir."

"I just need rest," he said.

He yawned long and deeply, turned over, and went back to sleep. Amanda walked over and covered him with a blanket that was neatly folded at the end of the cot. Then she sat down in a spindly rocking chair and took off the cape. At least now he knew she was a woman, but what about the way she was dressed? What did a woman nursing someone wear in the 16th century? When his breathing was regular and deep, she got up and began to look around the room. There was a trunk in the corner. She opened it slowly, but the hinges still creaked. She looked over at the bed, but he was deep in sleep now and did not awaken. There were clothes in the chest, another blanket, and some papers. At the bottom was a piece of cloth, neatly folded; she opened it. It was a few yards wide and smelled a little moldy but other than that seemed clean. No stains. She shook it out a little and tied it around her waist, kept her jeans on underneath, and just rolled them up. Not perfect, but it would do. His eyesight wouldn't be perfect yet even after he awoke. Except for a small piece of cloth she tied around her hair, she put everything else back in the trunk and carefully closed the lid.

She looked around for food, but there was nothing but wooden shelves with a few bowls, a pot, and some wooden spoons. She wondered how long Newton had gone without eating or sleeping. The room was getting dark, but she hesitated to light even a small candle since Newton's eyes were at risk. It had been a clear day so maybe she would get to see the stars over 17th century London. How clear would it be? How much would pollution interfere? After what seemed like forever, Newton woke up.

"Wickens, is that you?" he asked.

"No, Wickens has gone off," she said. "I am the nurse he procured."

Newton went to the desk and lit a small candle. "How many days have I been sleeping?"

"Just a few hours, sir."

"I'm ravenous. Could you make me a stew?"

"A stew, sir?"

"Did he not procure food for us?"

"Wickens, I'm afraid, sir, did not leave anything." Damn, she should have thought to buy something when she was out. But how? She had no coins they would recognize.

"Well, make me something," he said. "Make some porridge, anything. The oats and honey are in the cupboard, and there is a small basin of water in the back garden." She nodded. "And don't use too much honey; it's too dear. I don't like it sweet. Molasses will do for thickening." He mumbled to himself, shaking his head. "Procures a nurse who can hardly make porridge. I hope he's not paying her too dearly."

He sat down at the desk, gathered his papers together, and then seemed to forget about her completely as he wrote furiously in his notebook. He dipped the pen and scratched out his new theories of light's refraction. She had her own role and stayed out of his way.

She lit a fire, and, finding a large pan beside the hearth, went to the back yard to fill it with water. It didn't look as clean as she would have liked, but she would boil it extra-long. She didn't mind when he had posted her as his secretary and had felt honored, though she wasn't capable of the job. Now she had been degraded to kitchen scullion and hoped she had the wherewithal to make a decent porridge. It couldn't be that different from brewing a strong pot of coffee.

It seemed to take forever for the water to boil and then she had a hard time controlling the bubbling. It wasn't like a stove you could just adjust with a knob. Now she wished she'd been carrying the microwave when she went spiraling through space and time. But there would have been no electricity except during a thunderstorm. She threw in the oats, then molasses, and a little honey and stirred continuously to keep the bottom of the pot from burning.

She wanted to be outside. When she fetched the water, she got a glimpse of a clear star-filled sky, but now she was stuck inside making porridge. She stirred it with a big wooden spoon, her face turning red from the flames, and sweat dripping from beneath the kerchief—all to make sure Newton's porridge did not burn.

How would she know when it was done? She took a clump on her spoon and tasted. It was bitter; she would have preferred more honey, but he probably liked it this way. Besides, honey was *so dear*. She filled a bowl and brought to him at the desk, and he carried it to a small table. She went back to the fire and watched. At least he was eating it.

"A bit lumpy" he said. "Not so bad."

She had failed as his secretary but apparently passed the test as scullion.

When Newton fell asleep, Amanda went outside, stretched herself out on a bench in the back garden, and stared at the sky. It was hard to pick out familiar clusters so many stars were visible. What did she know that he didn't? What had been learned in 300 years? *Not that much*, she thought. He seemed so like people in her own time, unaware of his genius, fretting about his health. *Hungry, tired, obsessive.* Certainly more obsessive than anyone she knew in her own time but not so different.

She smelled burning. The fire was still going, and he was asleep. She tried to get up, but she was drifting. Her eyes closed until she felt something strange. She opened them to find a little girl staring down at her. An image of her mother hovered in the background. *You can't be too careful*, her mother's disembodied mouth was saying. *Wait till I clean before you touch anything.* The child threw water in Amanda's face from a dirty cup and ran off giggling.

"Sir Isaac," she shouted, not even remembering it would be decades before he would be knighted. "Sir Isaac, get up; the fire is out of control."

She was saying the words or just thinking them when she finally pushed herself up, but she had the sense of falling backwards, her head spinning, her stomach lurching, dizzy with vertigo. Was it the porridge, the Black Death?

"Sir Isaac!" She seemed to be screaming inside her head. Then a thump as if she'd fallen off the bench and she looked around to find that she was in the loft of the chalet. The gas heater's flame had risen high and caught the edge of a cloth covering the bed stand. She pulled the cloth off in a panic overturning a lamp; books and whatever else had accumulated there, and she stomped on the edge of the cloth, snuffing out the flame.

Tired and bewildered, she walked down the stairs. The electricity was back, and all the machines were whizzing and beeping. She would have killed for electricity just a few minutes ago, just long enough to nuke something in a microwave to make Newton happy while he finished transcribing his notes. Through the whirs and buzzes, she thought of the people she had walked by in 17th century London, unaware of the coming plague.

She grasped the joystick more determined than ever to erase all the dots and evade the monster mouth waiting to snap her up.

Chapter Eight

After breakfast and the calendar, Gloria seeks her usual place on the bench. Last evening, as she was turning over dirt, she decided she would sit on the bench in the morning trying to remember, and then, in the afternoon, she would work on the garden. Now she is too restless to sit. She tries to calm her breathing, tries to listen for the sound of the wind and the birds and the unknown rustlings that have taken place each day beyond her range of vision in the woods. All these things that have lulled her for the last few days or weeks, the routine that has provided her reflection, cannot convince her muscles to rest while her memory takes over. She cannot sit.

She gets up and walks around the back of the bench sweeping her hand lightly across the wood, fingering the curlicue wrought iron arms. She tries to sit again, gets up, and circles around. She thinks of the bench almost as a person, or at least an entity, something that has held her and given her solace when no one and nothing else could. Did these thoughts mean she was mentally ill? She walks around one more time already missing the reflectiveness that she knows the bench can no longer provide. It is time to move on.

Hurrying to the shed in the back, her muscles still sore from the night before, her arms tremble to reach the garden , to move dirt, to dig and dig a hole until she gets to somewhere solid where she can start to build a foundation for her broken life.

As she opens the shed door, a damp smell hits her and the coolness. She grabs the pick and shovel deciding that morning is the best time to dig before the sun is too hot and trusting that she will know when to stop before her body collapses from dehydration and heat stroke. It feels good to begin to trust herself again even if the others don't. She surveys the work she did yesterday, the patch of overturned soil, tries to decide how much more to dig, what should be the boundaries of the garden.

She decides it should be large; she wants to grow root as well as above ground vegetables. She also wants to turn over an area for some flowers and may be some fruit trees. If she plants flowers all along the edge of the woods and creates a boundary, it will help Amanda understand her boundaries when she toddles around the yard. It will be easier for them to watch Amanda when she is outside if Thomas can just say to her stop. Stop when you get to mommy's flowers.

She heaves the pick into the earth. She stands on top of it to send it deeper into the layers of twined roots. She picks up a clump of rocky soil and grass and shakes it out. What will they do when they come out today? What will Thomas and Amanda think when they don't see her at her usual spot? She hopes they will help her, working together like any family to make a garden. Amanda likes to play in dirt. She hopes Thomas will dress her in old bib overalls and not a sundress today, so she can sit and make mud pies out of dirt while mommy and daddy dig and turn over soil. She is on her knees shaking out the good dirt from clumps of old grass and weeds. She has stopped digging because she has started to sweat. She feels thirsty and thinks of retreating to the coolness of the shed. They must have noticed by now that she wasn't on her bench. She thinks she can feel Suzanne's eyes on her from the window, but doesn't look up.

She is getting tired; her sore back muscles about to cause her to topple over when, somehow, Thomas and Amanda manage to sneak up on her. They come with lemonade and cookies. Gloria takes off one glove, accepts the thick glass, although it trembles in her hand, and drinks it down. Thomas offers her one of Suzanne's Hermit cookies. She waves it away and lifts her glass for a refill. She hadn't realized how dehydrated she must have been. She'll have to drink this one more slowly so she won't throw up. Another half glass and she feels better.

She takes Amanda's hand and leads her to the shed; it feels good finally directing her child in some way. When they enter the shed, she hands Amanda a small watering can and she helps her fill it up from the spigot on the side of the house. She feels Thomas watching as he sits by the garden. She is glad he has not risen in concern and followed them like Suzanne would have done. He is beginning to trust her, too.

He must be wondering why she is having Amanda lug water when there is nothing planted yet, but he just sits and watches as they trample back to him, Amanda looking proud that she is helping. Gloria looks at Thomas thinking he would be happy to see her interacting so normally with their child, but instead, when Thomas' eyes meet hers, there is a haunted look, an overwhelming sadness that jars her and makes her look away quickly.

Thomas has dressed the baby in shorts that are very light and will stain, but still, once they are back, she sits Amanda down in the dirt. She gives her a trowel and shows her how to dig, how to build a small mound, shake out the dirt, then add a little water, and finally slap it down with the palm of her hand. With Thomas' approval or not, she will teach her daughter to make mud pies.

She avoids looking at Thomas, angry and confused about the look he has given her, spoiling the most normal family day she had been able to create in a long time. Doesn't he know what it took for her to act this normal, to interact outside the dark gray area her mind has wandered in for so long? She slaps down the mud pies, and Amanda laughs and slaps hers down harder. Mommy is playing with her; mommy hasn't done that in a long time, possibly, never. Maybe Thomas is angry because he is being shut out. This was about her and Amanda, and he is not used to sharing their daughter anymore. She is thinking this when she feels his hands grasp both of her shoulders at once, snuck up on again.

The touch does not feel angry or controlling. It feels comforting as he sits down right next to her, turns her toward him, and brushes her cheek. Amanda slaps the mud and squeals. Her chubby little fingers spread wide apart, and bits of mud shoot up into her face. She begins to howl. Thomas picks her up and calms her down, searches her eyes for bits of sand. When he puts her down, Gloria takes one little muddy hand in hers and brings Amanda to the spigot, washes the mud off her hands, takes a tissue from her pocket, wets it and cleans around Amanda's face. She swallows hard, the joy of caring for her baby making it hard to breathe. The feeling of déjà vu so strong that it takes all she can do to breathe and look over at Thomas, who sits by the abandoned mud pies, looking sad and unsure of what to do next. She remembers this mood of Thomas', an intense concentration; it usually means an important decision will follow. It used to mean he would say something unexpected to her.

As she walks back, Thomas begins to pick up the glasses and tray. Amanda breaks from Gloria's hand running over to help him. Gloria thinks again today she might want to go into the house with them and waits for Thomas to say something. Is that what she is waiting for? To be invited back into her own life? He assumes she will be staying out here as she has been every day and gives her a kiss on the cheek. Amanda gives her a wet kiss and a hug before they go inside. Not knowing what to do, Gloria walks back to the bench, stretches herself out, and covers her face with the straw hat. She doesn't feel that she will sleep. Though she feels tired, it is more like her mind wandering. She thinks about Thomas' sadness, revisits the feeling of déjà vu, and thinks about it all in a detached sort of way. Isn't it all déjà vu for her now? She will rest on the bench for a while and think and remember. *Make* herself remember.

She wants to remember something good, something else like the communal garden, something that will bring her hope. What had they been trying to create when they started coming up here?

She remembers a day in May, exam time, the academic stress had always made her feel anxious, and it was worse this particular year because Thomas had dropped out of WPI and had this plan to take the garden bus cross country. Gloria didn't want to commit to an entire summer away, but she knew Thomas would go and did not want to be left behind. She had tried to stay focused on her studies, but the summer stretched in front of her so open with plans to leave that had no end. It was warm, not quite mid-day and she'd just finished an exam in Victorian Lit, and she was sitting on the grass musing about what she would do for lunch.

She sat alone. Most of her friends were now Thomas' friends; the kids that she used to hang out with had become mere acquaintances. She didn't have another exam for a few hours and intended to sit and study, maybe get a candy bar from the vending machine, but she got restless. Instead of studying, she walked down Chandler Street to Friendly's. The idea of total freedom made her head spin or maybe it was just hunger or the smell of the lilacs from the bushes that had recently bloomed. It made her happy but scared thinking of the life she and Thomas were about to plunge into together. There were twenty or more kids planning to take to the garden bus by the end of May, planning to make it their home for the summer. There were some kids practically living there already; kids who had nowhere else to be or just preferred the freedom of the bus to their parent's homes. She had always thought that she would be making a commitment to marriage around this age, but instead, she found herself making a commitment to a band of travelers with the idea of hope that Thomas had brought to life in her, and it felt every bit as hopeful and doomed as every new phase of her life ever had.

She doesn't have a memory of ever going off on that bus for the summer. Something happened to change all the plans. She tries to remember what it was.

Thomas and Amanda come out again with lunch. Thomas puts a tray of sandwiches and juice down and actually walks away leaving Gloria alone with Amanda. She doesn't know what to do, taken by surprise like this. Thomas says something to her as he walks around the side of the house, but she doesn't hear him. Is it safe for him to leave her all alone with Amanda? He seems to think so, but she's in a panic. She holds Amanda too close and she pulls away. She runs toward the woods, and Gloria runs after her scooping her up and whirling her around as she has seen Thomas do. Thomas comes around to the front with a small, plastic pool and a bicycle pump. He calls Amanda over to help daddy with the pump. Then he goes away again leaving her and Amanda to finish the pumping saying he will get the long hose because the spigot is on the other side of the house. Gloria wants to tell him it's okay—that they can move lunch to the other side of the house, but the words still will not leave her throat, and he is already gone.

It is a good idea to fill the wading pool. Thomas throws in several of her toys, and it keeps Amanda occupied so he and Gloria can actually sit and eat together. He puts his arm around her, and she leans against his chest taking small bites of her sandwich watching their daughter splash and squeal. She wants to ask Thomas why they hadn't gone off in the garden bus that summer, gone cross-country like they had planned, but she tries to forget about it for now and just listen to Amanda and watch as she immerses herself in the properties of water.

Gloria watches as sunlight hits an arc of water that Amanda throws into the air. She watches Amanda patiently scoop water into a pail and dump it onto the grass, or sometimes half of it back in with the other water and half of it onto the grass. So engrossed in watching the water fall and what happens, her little physicist not yet a year old. She and Thomas sit very still as Amanda's play becomes more and more spirited. She hopes that Thomas, like her, is feeling the closeness and hesitancy to get up. As Thomas turns toward her and she towards him, their warm breath mingles as they kiss on the lips, but Amanda is done with playing alone and is jumping up and down in the middle of the pool so that almost all the water is gone. Thomas smiles at Gloria, and they rub noses. She wipes her tears as Thomas goes to pick their child out of the water and bring her to mama.

Thomas plops their wet daughter down on her lap, and immediately Amanda stands up and rests her head on her mother's shoulder. Water dripping from her hair tickles as it goes down Gloria's neck and back. Amanda puts her lips onto hers in a big wet kiss then pushes herself off with one great heave and starts running toward the woods. Thomas follows slowly pretending to be a monster then scoops her up and brings her back to the water. He sits right down in the pool, his long legs dangling over the side, and Amanda sits on his stomach filling buckets of water and pouring them over his shoulders until suddenly she throws the water right into his face. He pushes his head back toward the sun laughing and shakes out his long hair that dangles onto the grass, pushing away her hand when she tries to do it again. When he sits up, she tumbles down his side into the water and they splash each other back and forth.

Gloria feels detached suddenly as if she is watching a movie of someone else's life. She wants them to be inside all of a sudden and away from her. Thomas' kiss that made her feel so happy—she knew it came with expectations. Love suddenly felt like a burden, their laughter a sound that could throw her over the edge. She tries to keep her face neutral; she doesn't want to be like this, really. She wants to join the happy family, but something falls over her, keeps her from sharing this joy of a summer day, something unspeakable, the shadow of guilt and loss that has taken away her speech and fragmented her memories.

Thomas looks at her, but she cannot meet his gaze. He scoops Amanda up, and they go toward the house without the usual goodbyes. *He is angry*, Gloria thinks. That kiss on the lips had surprised them both, only opened more of a wedge into the confusion of her neurosis. Maybe he had been hoping it would open a dialogue or something, that it was the beginning of something she couldn't handle just yet.

He must be getting tired, losing patience with her. Before they enter the house, Thomas lets Amanda down, and she runs back to the bench, hugs her legs as Gloria sits stiffly on the bench. She has let Thomas down again today and that makes her very sad. She strokes Amanda's head and pats her on the back. How does a child know that love is there even when it can't be expressed?

"I love you, honey," she whispers so quietly, really just a slight movement of the lips; the air currents take the sound away before Amanda could have heard let alone Thomas.

She sees the deer that afternoon as they scamper out of the woods and into the back yard trailing along the pond in back then she goes in for supper. The days are still long, June pushing into July.

After supper, Suzanne reads, Thomas plays video games, and Gloria stretches out on the floor with Amanda. She raises towers of building blocks, and Amanda pushes them down, over and over and over again, fascinated as she was with the properties of the water in the pool. *Her father's daughter*, Gloria thinks, *destined to be a math and science nerd*.

As evening wears on, with Suzanne and Thomas engrossed

in their own activities, Gloria decides it is time she bathed Amanda and put her to bed. She fills the bathtub with just a few inches of water as she had seen Suzanne do, and she peels off Amanda's dirty clothes. Suzanne comes in, and she is afraid she will take over, but she just circles her fingers in the water to test the temperature and then stands at the door as Gloria bathes her child.

First, she wipes around Amanda's face with the wet washcloth and then puts the baby soap over Amanda's fat belly and legs, rinsing them off with a cup of water. She lets Amanda splash as she lifts one hand at a time and washes under the arm, in the crook of the elbow and then into the webbing between each finger. She washes Amanda's neck and under her chin, then her lower body down to the baby toes. She reaches for baby shampoo and rubs it into Amanda's delicate scalp, and then rinses, trailing her fingers through the wispy curls making sure all the soap is gone. She does this in silence and concentration.

When she lifts Amanda out, Suzanne hands her a towel and smiles at her. She is still being watched, guarded. She swaddles her baby as if she were a newborn gently drying off each part of her, between her fingers, her toes, rubbing the towel through her hair and then rubbing her soft clean belly with powder before slipping her into summer pajamas. Suzanne is still smiling; she must have passed the mothering test. She carries Amanda down the stairs, kisses her cheek, and gives her to Thomas, relinquishing their child to him for the night although she would have liked to put her to sleep, sing her a lullaby. She's sure Suzanne and Thomas would have let her, but she feels exhausted from the joy of holding Amanda swaddled in her arms. She is not yet ready for that ritual of songs and stories before bedtime. While powdering her belly and drying between her toes, Gloria had almost caught a memory that had pushed her back to an edge of the gray fog. It had taken all her strength to stay focused, to show Suzanne she would not walk away, she could be a good mother.

Chapter Nine

Holiday Cheer

The week before Christmas Amanda was waffling on the promise to her parents that she would stay with them for two weeks during the holiday. What could she give for an excuse? She had to work? They wouldn't buy it. She could pretend to be sick but then they would only come up to take care of her. Her mother had even invited Jason down so he could be bartender for the 'party of the century' on New Year's, but she knew he was working on Christmas. At least it would have been more bearable with him there. Something about leaving was upsetting her, so she reconsidered, and then, the day before Christmas Eve, she called her mother.

"I have to work on Christmas Eve," she said. "Just until three-thirty, but you know how it gets dark so early now, so I might drive down Christmas morning."

"But, Amanda, I thought you said you took the time off."

"I asked for the time off." She could hear the whine in her own voice. "But one of the housekeepers is sick."

She hated the disappointment in her mother's voice, but if she left too early on Christmas Eve she feared something would happen while she was gone, that she would miss some opportunity, something that had to do with time, had to do with her understanding, something that had to do with acceptance. She needed a little part of the Holiday up here. Right now she did not want to be pulled away by her mother's disappointment, but there was sadness—a tremble in her voice. She could hear it even over the phone line. When her mother said, "come down," sometimes she heard "stay, please stay," and it wasn't as if she felt her mother did not want her near.

When she hung up, she felt so guilty that she began to sob, a heavy kind of grieving that shook her body. She sat in the rocking chair till she was all cried out, made some of her mom's sleepy time tea, and finally, around midnight, began to nod off. Strong coffee got her through the next day at work, and when she got home, Jason was there sitting in his car outside the chalet.

"I was hoping I would see you at work today," she said. "So I could wish you a Merry Christmas."

"Well, lucky you," he said. "You get to see me all evening and all night."

"My mother called you, didn't she?"

"Yep. I'm here to make sure you get down there tonight."

He insisted they needed to leave right away giving her no time to argue or get a feeling for the disconnection of what she may be doing.

"I thought you were working on Christmas," she said as she filled a duffle bag with jeans and sweaters.

"I was, but they didn't need me." Jason plugged in one of the arcade games and pushed buttons randomly watching Amanda up in the loft.

"They didn't need you on Christmas?"

"Someone else wanted it."

"On Christmas?"

"He's probably Jewish."

Jason didn't look at her now but had his eyes peeled on the screen.

"A Jewish cook for a Christian feast," she said. "Will the food be kosher?"

Jason just stared at the screen, probably eating a line of blue dots. Maybe it was someone like her trying to get out of spending the Holidays with family. She zipped up the duffle bag and snapped it onto her shoulder, pulling herself away. *This is my cocoon*, she thought as she closed the door, *where I lived when I was in my mother's belly, my tunnel to the unknown, my first home.*

Jason started up both cars while Amanda locked the front door. They brushed each other's face with a kiss and drove out of the driveway with Amanda in the lead as Jason had insisted. By six, they were there. Jason sat in the car listening to the end of a song. Amanda let herself into the house undetected by her mother and stood at the door of the kitchen.

"Thomas, where the hell are you?" her mother yelled. "I told you not to let the dog in the house. I told you at least seven times—don't let the dog in"

She said the last four words very loudly. The trash had been ripped to pieces, and there were paw prints on the glass door that led to the deck. She put three bags of groceries down and yelled again.

"Thomas, where the hell are you?"

She opened the door to the basement and mumbled something about him hiding down there.

"I'm down here," he yelled as the dog came bounding up, and when he got to the kitchen, her mother was lashing the dog with a broom. Amanda hid behind the doorframe wondering if she should go out and make another entrance.

"I thought you were taking an herbal extract that was supposed to make you calmer," her father said.

At that, her mother almost swatted her father with the broom, but he moved out of the way, grabbed the dogs leash from a hook on the wall, and dragged him out onto the snow-covered back deck.

"Don't let him in here again," her mother yelled as he slid the door closed.

Amanda couldn't resist. She snuck up right behind her mother. "Boo!"

Her mother turned around, almost dropping a bag of groceries. "Amanda, you're here, thank God."

As she held her mother, she knew coming down tonight was the right decision. Jason walked in and shook his head.

They cleaned up the kitchen, unpacked the bags, and began preparations for the evening. Her mother boiled eggs for deviling, the only concession to an otherwise vegetarian diet, and mixed a dip of sour cream and tofu. Her father and the mutt started to ascend the steps of the deck, but her mother gave them a murderous look so they didn't even attempt to enter the house through that door.

The timer rang for the eggs. Her mother whipped the yokes, placed them into the whites, and sprinkled them with paprika. Her father came in with the dog that bolted for the kitchen, but Jason and Amanda intercepted him and herded him into the basement.

Amanda went downstairs with Jason to show him the couch in the basement where he would be crashing later. He loved the mutt instantly and ran around with him as if they were outside. Amanda just looked around. It looked empty without the arcade games, even with all the decorations and the tree.

"I'll tend bar for the night," Jason yelled up to her mom, who was at the top of the stairs closing the door quickly before the dog escaped. Jason was lining up the juice selections, and Amanda noticed he had changed his usual nose ring for a diamond chip, which must have been his special way of dressing up for the occasion.

You're a guest tonight," her mother argued. "We're not putting you to work."

"I have to earn my keep."

"You've done that by getting my little girl down here."

"Mother!"

"Well, you were hedging on the phone… yesterday, making your poor mother worry."

"You knew I would come."

"I wasn't so sure."

Jason looked from one to the other; he offered them both a glass of tomato juice with a celery stick.

"I'd rather be bar tender than referee."

Gloria took the juice, and Jason drank the other one. Amanda looked in the refrigerator for something more interesting and saw they had at least bought beer and wine.

"Let him tend bar," she said. "He likes to wait on people."

"Okay, but I want to pay you whatever you would get working at the hotel on Christmas."

"Sweet," he said and gave her mother a high five.

Amanda went up to her room and unpacked her jeans and sweaters. Would she have come if Jason had not brought her? She wasn't sure. She was glad she was here now. She didn't mean to make her mother worry, but since she was a child, she had received so many conflicting messages about what was expected of her. She opened her childhood closet full of flowery skirts and blazers and touched them all. When she was growing up, everyone said she was too quiet and withdrawn. Then her mother had totally freaked out when Jason helped her come out of her shell. Now she was someone; she had her own style.

She touched all the books in her bookcase, gliding her hands over them, reading each title, considering all the thoughts and imaginings other people had put into her mind. *My dresses? My books? Is that who I was or who I am now?* In a bizarre kind of way, everything seemed clearer when she was in the loft at the chalet. Comforting, somehow, that need to be alone. *What is wrong with being quiet and introspective?* Would she ever marry or did she need to be alone forever? She had heard or read that Piaget had lived half the year traveling and meeting with people and the other half in almost complete isolation. She supposed he'd had enough money to do something like that.

What about street people who had died and they would be found to actually have thousands and thousands of dollars?

She'd heard of the balloon man who used to sit on a folding chair at the corner of a park in Worcester. He sat day after day in dark glasses, coat sleeves too big for his thin wrists, holding bunches of painted balloons floating at the end of spindly sticks. It was found he painted and sold them to buy art supplies to paint landscapes. She thought of the balloon man, an obsessed character living in her own lifetime.

She heard the doorbell ring and thought about going down instead of lying on the bed full of inertia and mild contentedness. She kind of wished she hadn't left the tea set at her office; right now she could use a little advice from those obsessed scientists. Although it would be awkward now since she'd had those visions or journeys or whatever they were. Maybe there was some truth to what they were saying when she was a teenager. Maybe she had some kind of weird epilepsy, and under duress, her neurons could misfire and cause hallucinations. Anyway she could never be what her mother wanted, whatever it was, or Peter. They would have to accept her. She would breeze though her parent's party as if she were sleepwalking, dodging questions carefully, like she used to do when she was a young girl.

She forced herself to move but went only as far as the window. No stars. She looked more carefully. It was snowing lightly. Christmas Eve. Had her mother invited Peter? Of course. Would he come? She wondered.

She put on one of her flowery skirts and went downstairs, hiding for a while in the kitchen.

"Amanda" she surprised her mother who had come in on the run, her face bright from too many herbs and juice drinks. "I thought you had fallen asleep."

Her mother turned around from the refrigerator and handed her a tray of dip and veggies. She took the tray of deviled eggs.

"I have to warn you," she whispered. "Peter is here."

"I'm not surprised," she said.

"He has a girl with him, but he seems to be avoiding introducing her. He probably just felt like he had to bring someone since Jason was going to be here."

Amanda sighed. "Maybe it's his cousin," she said, sarcastically.

"Maybe it is," her mother said.

Amanda descended the staircase, and the full impact of the room hit her senses. *You're only sleepwalking,* she told herself. Another couch had been moved downstairs and more chairs than she ever thought could fit down here. She put the dip down and leaned on the bar feeling dizzy and overstimulated from so many conversations and the lights blinking on the Christmas tree.

Her mother took her arm and introduced her to old friends. Amanda smiled at them all, shook hands, and pretended to remember who they were. Her mother had not had a party like this since she was small. How old were these friends? All she wanted to do is ask them if they had lived up in Vermont and tell them she lived there now, but she knew that talk of Vermont would ruin the party for her mother. Pulled from one area to another, she shook hands and nodded until finally, a crisis in the kitchen sent her mother away and gave Amanda the opportunity to escape.

She made her way to the bar and watched Jason in action. He was lucky. He had his role of bartending. She hadn't seen Peter yet. Maybe he'd just made an obligatory appearance and left. Jason was busy mixing special juices and herbs for her mother's crowd. All tripping on Hopi medicine now, just as they had done up in Vermont on pills.

She stared at the Christmas tree. It hadn't seemed very impressive when she first got here, but now, in the darkened room, the lights glimmered and shone, lighting up trinkets and baubles she hadn't seen since she was a kid. Sir Isaac Newton had been born on Christmas Day.

"What can I get for ya, Manda?" She jumped as if Jason had snuck up on her, but he only stood solidly on the other side of the bar, just where he should be.

"Do my parents have any champagne?" She cocked her head to the side.

"Hmm" he said, opening the refrigerator. "Nothing on ice. There's beer," he said. "Wine?"

She scrunched up her face.

"A glass of wine."

She drank one glass quickly and asked for another. A group of people got up from the couch and went upstairs. Amanda took her glass and moved to a comfortable spot at the end of the couch thinking she would just park herself there, safe for the evening. Then Peter appeared descending the stairs with a woman.

Amanda froze then took a quick slug of wine. She was taller than Amanda and even younger than her. *Just a baby. There ya go, Peter, robbing the cradle.* She sipped her wine, took a handful of tofu delights, and pretended to be interested in the Christmas tree. The tofu turned her stomach. She could feel them move toward her. Peter led the way.

"Amanda," she heard Peter's voice say, strong and loud then more quietly. "This is Michelle."

He seemed intense more than tense, Amanda thought, as he sat Michelle right down next to her on the couch, and he himself sat right down on the table, his butt inches from the tofu. He was cutting off most of her view of the Christmas tree.

"Michelle" he said. "This is my friend, Amanda."

He got up, clumsily, almost spilling the tofu treats. "I'm going to get a beer," he said. "You want anything?"

Michelle shook her head, no.

"How about you?"

"I'll have another wine," Amanda said. She leaned down,

and they both sighed as he took her empty glass. Amanda looked sideways at Michelle. She was staring out into the roomful of people seeming oblivious.

Amanda tried not to watch Peter as he walked to the bar. She looked to see if Michelle was watching. A Christmas Eve date, that was pretty meaningful. Only instead of taking her to his parents, he took her to his ex-fiancé's parents. Poor thing. What had Peter told her? She was probably a student. Did they have a date on New Year's Eve? She wouldn't let herself feel anything. So Peter would ring in the New Year with some bimbo student. She'd rather be up in Vermont. The silence was getting too long. Should she say she was his cousin?

"I know you and Peter used to go out," the woman said. "I've seen you together at the university."

Amanda felt herself shrink down on the couch. The woman towered over her. She remembered her now. She had seen her in the teacher's lounge. She was a TA grad student.

"Peter says you left your job and live in Vermont now."

Amanda nodded.

"That's Awesome."

The woman was looking at her, bright-eyed, apparently not bothered at all that she had been taken to a Christmas bash at her boyfriend's ex-girlfriend's.

Amanda stared past her at the Christmas tree and listened nodding once in a while and looking into her eager bright eyes. Listened to what she had in mind to do with her life after she graduated in June... she wanted to be a teacher... she heard there was an opening at the University... bla, bla, bla. Was she coked up or something? Amanda looked around for Peter. He was trapped by her mother, her smiling, radiant mother. Her father had disappeared altogether from the party to who knew where. He would come down every once in a while just to show them all he hadn't fallen asleep. Wherever he was, he was probably having more fun than her.

Amanda excused herself saying she had to go to the bathroom. She walked by Peter with barely a nod and took her glass of wine upstairs in search of her father. She found him in the den watching A Christmas Carol… the 1930's version. She drank her wine and rested her head on his shoulder.

"Do you really like it all alone up there in Vermont?" he asked.

"Yeah, daddy," she said. "I really do."

****

Christmas Day was sunny. Amanda had a slight hangover, and it hurt her eyes to see Jason go off with the sun beating down on the snow.

"You're deserting me," Amanda said when she discovered him sneaking out with his suitcase. "You're leaving me here alone with my scheming mother." He hadn't told her when they came down that he had to work second shift on Christmas.

She wasn't even dressed yet but had thrown on a parka and boots and followed him out to the driveway.

"Check the loft every day," she said as if it would burn down or simply disappear if she was not in it.

He kissed her on the cheek and got in the car.

"Merry Christmas," she yelled as he pulled out of the driveway.

No turkey dinner awaited, she was sure of that—not with her mother, lots of vegetables, potatoes, and sauces, but no meat, not even on Christmas. The pies would all be chewy and healthy, nothing gooey and luscious. Only the bread smelled good, baking in the oven, Jason had put it in before he left. She followed the smell into the kitchen and brewed strong coffee. She sat at the kitchen table and began peeling carrots and yams. Her mother walked in.

"Is it just us today?"

"Just the three of us."

Her mother sat down and began peeling.

"We won't need too much then," Amanda said.

"Sometimes people show up later, unexpectedly."

Amanda wondered who her mother expected to show up unexpectedly. Certainly not Peter after last night. She got another bag of veggies from the fridge and started peeling, their hands almost touching, her mother still in her bathrobe, barely out of her own dreams, as they created a mound of discarded organic material.

"Is Jason gone?" her mother asked.

"He just left."

Her mother sighed, and then yawned. "He's a nice boy."

"Didn't you think I'd make it down here on my own? Didn't I promise?"

"I didn't know," she said. "I wasn't sure."

"Please stop worrying about me."

"What else can I do? After all these years, what else can I do?"

"Worry about dad."

"He's another one." Amanda's mother laughed a little.

"Why did you leave Vermont?" she asked her mother. "Didn't daddy want to stay?"

"I don't know. I guess so. It was a long time ago."

Amanda sighed. Couldn't her mother remember how anything felt? "Merry Christmas, Mom." She got up and kissed the top of her mother's head, poured a glass of black coffee, and munched on a celery stick. "Ugh" she said. "Is McDonald's open on Christmas?"

The day was quiet; a few people did stop by in the evening. Amanda watched A Child's Christmas in Wales with her father, but he was in bed most of the day not feeling well. She had the chore of walking the hyperactive dog. She moved her overnight bag downstairs now that Jason was gone, her new preferred center of operations, even if she did have to share it with the mutt.

The week between Christmas and New Year's, her mother dragged her to "sales of the century," and all the broadcasters shouted from the TV the impending problems with technology in the coming year Y2K. Grocery shopping was almost impossible. Everyone was stocking up on canned goods like she'd heard people had done in the fifties to avert being uncomfortable and hungry in the case of nuclear war. Baby clothes, toys, toilet paper—everything had a Y2K theme. The week dragged on until finally, it was New Year's Eve, and Jason came back down.

Her mother was cleaning again for the big party. She kept talking about how Amanda looked so much better after just a week down here. In the kitchen, her mother stirred root powder into a glass of water, something she only did when she had a headache. Jason was putting a soufflé into the refrigerator.

"I know I shouldn't be doing this."

Her mother nodded at him, smiled absentmindedly.

"These should really be eaten immediately, but when you're making so much for so many people it's not possible."

He took mushrooms out of the fridge and began to de-stem them.

"Let me help," her mother said, and Jason handed her a vegetable brush.

Amanda stood at the door. They seemed unaware of her presence.

Her father came into the kitchen looking pale. They offered him gingko root.

"Just a cup of tea," he said. "Black tea."

The mutt heard his voice and bounded up the cellar stairs. She heard him thump his head against the closed door.

"What are we going to do with him tonight?" her mother asked her father who looked like he was about to retch. He shrugged and went into the living room. Her mother finally noticed her. "We're having a party here tonight. I could use some help."

"What's there to do? The house has been spotless since Tuesday, and Jason doesn't really like anyone in the kitchen when he's cooking."

"You could take the dog out."

"Oh, yeah, I forgot about the mutt."

She went upstairs to her room for a warmer sweater and opened the shades in her room. It was snowing. Maybe no one would show tonight. No need to voice that thought and panic her mother. She had called Peter earlier; he sounded better than he had on Christmas Eve. She had woken him up, and he sounded kind of sexy. She found herself looking forward to seeing him.

Her mother appeared, frazzled. "Take the dog out," she said. "Now."

"Sure he wants to go out in all this?" she asked walking toward the door. "I got a hold of Peter, and I think he's coming, and I don't think he's bringing a date."

She left her mother standing there to mull that over.

Amanda wanted to get the dog out and back as quickly as possible. It was turning colder. Too cold, it seemed, even to be snowing. They were the big flakes not the sideways kind that usually come when it's windy. Thank God it wasn't windy, yet. These were the snowflakes that drifted right into your face and stuck fast, making it feel like you were in an alternate universe. The whirling tornado of flakes that would make it difficult to drive. Tomorrow they would be stepping into another thousand years.

Well, not exactly, it would take a whole year for one millennium to end and another to begin. It would start tomorrow though, a whole year of in-between time like walking through a tunnel connecting millenniums. Anything could happen. It was taking the mutt forever to do his business. Fine for him, he had fur. When he finally was finished, she whooped and whistled for him, and he ran toward the front door. Her mother met them. As she spoke to Amanda from behind the storm door, the mutt's paws were already scratching it.

"I don't know if we should let him in," she said. "I'm cleaning down there right now."

"At least let me in," Amanda shouted through the glass.

Chapter Ten

This morning Gloria feels a real change in herself as she walks out of the house, not to the bench, but to the garden, the plot of grass that she's turned over. She feels a quickening, an urgency that she had been quelling since last night. She had wanted to come out after Amanda was asleep last night. She wanted to come out and dig through the sunset, but she had held herself back, decided it would look better for her sanity if she stayed in, tried to appear as normal as possible, and not let Suzanne know how emotional she felt about her time with Amanda last night. Now she hurried to the shed, almost tripping over her own feet, so ready to get the pitchfork in her hand and stab it into the rooted ground.

In the shed, the usual feeling of calmness then dread overtakes her, the dampness a relief. Possibly, she could be happy just sitting here all day, hidden, wrapped in the security of an earthen cave, but she knows they would never let her have more time with Amanda—they would consider it a setback if she sat in this dug-out all day. They will accept her digging. Somehow Gloria digging is saner to them than Gloria on the bench. At least when she's turning over earth, she looks like she's doing something constructive. She grabs the gloves, the bucket, the pitchfork and stares at the stool in the corner, still thinking about sitting. No, she'd gone past the bench sitting. It's time for her to make herself useful; too much reflection is indeed driving her batty.

She surveys what was done the day before. It's getting to be a large plot; she thinks that today she will begin to turn over soil at the edge of the woods for the flowerbeds. At the end of the lawn, the soil is more stubborn. She pushes the pitchfork in as far as she can but runs into more rocks and heavier roots from the forest plants.

Her mind goes back to Worcester again and the communal garden. She had some anxiety that summer in Worcester as she worked so hard while the others socialized. She tries to remember if there was an actual day or incident when it was decided the Garden Bus would not, as planned, go cross country for the summer because she remembers, distinctly now, that they never did take the bus to California that summer. Something did happen, and she tries to remember more as she shakes the dirt off clumps of grass and dumps the grass and roots into the bucket.

At first, she hadn't known anything was up. Her exams were over by the second week in May and she was still living at home but spending most of her time with Thomas in the basement of the Garden on Highland Street. She remembers the first thing she noticed was that the kids that gathered there were suddenly not talking about going away so much. For some reason, it was always like she was the last one to know when plans had changed. At the time, she had blamed Thomas, annoyed that he didn't keep her informed; she had been paranoid that he held information back from her on purpose, still unsure of his love, still afraid that he would just be up and gone someday taken off on the bus without her. Now she realizes she was the one who was holding back, not sure if she wanted to get involved. Loving Thomas was so complicated, perhaps not the loving but having a future with him. At that time, Thomas still belonged to the world.

At the communal garden, sometimes she'd heard voices raised. It was not as organized as it once had been. As late spring went on, the soil was turned over, and it was time to plant. She often moved away from the others, planting rows by herself, not wanting to hear the jabber of Thomas' friends. Maybe it was simply arguments about needing someone to stay behind and tend the garden. Sometimes she was happy when they argued; they could be so smug about being perfect and changing the world.

She tries to remember when it was decided they would not go—how she felt about it, how Thomas took it. It must have been such a blow to him, all his plans. She thinks she was probably disappointed but also relieved. She remembers something. The sullen way that Thomas had acted, how she tried to pull him out of the glum. His resentment toward her because he knew on some level she was happy and she had not wanted to go.

All that late spring and early summer, plans were falling apart at the Garden of Delights. People were acting lazy and probably smoking so much pot they didn't really care. It had been a nice adventure to dream about all winter for everyone else, but for Thomas, it was a reality. He had really thought it would happen. He had people lined up, some kids who were actually living in the bus at that point, kids that were too young, she thought. Some of the others even said the same thing. At one point, she tried to tell him it might look like something not good, a kidnapping maybe, some kind of cult. They all might get in legal trouble, but Thomas thought even sixteen-year-olds should be able to do what they wanted. Now, as a parent, he probably thought differently. How much freedom would he give their daughter, she wondered?

She flops down on the grass beside the trench she has dug and stares up into the sky. Her muscles are already sore and tired; her stomach is growling. She finds herself awaiting a morning visit from her family, lemonade to cool her. She closes her eyes, feels the sun on her face, and covers it with the straw hat.

She *had* been relieved when Thomas and his friends had decided not to take the bus cross-country that summer. It must have been about '73. Thomas was in a dark mood. He had dropped out of WPI and was making more and more money with the metric conversions. He would sometimes go to WPI and use their monster computers, huge contraptions that took up half a room to do the calculations. He would use their electronic typewriters to put together brochures, pamphlets, and all the work he had to do for the companies. Sometimes she would go with him, sit for hours in the stuffy room just because he liked her to be near. He was trying to get a lot of work done that spring so he could take off for the summer of freedom. Then plans got put on hold, and kids started going back with their families, and the hanger-outers at the garden started to think about summer jobs. Thomas said they weren't dependable; Gloria could have told him that. *No one* had his commitment.

She sits up and sees Thomas at the window. She waves. He smiles and waves back. She makes a motion with her hands as if holding a glass and throws her head back—a communication, a mime. It was something. But when he comes out with Amanda and the tray, why can't she just do it? Utter the syllables, say the words, any words, but her throat is constricted even after the lemonade. She makes words in her mind. Tries to ask him why. Why they didn't go across the country that summer, but the sound will not come, not the syllables, not the words.

She can only use sign language, as if the electricity had failed and they were entertaining themselves with a game of charades. Her body and her mind loosening up with all the work she was doing perhaps helped her to communicate with her husband on this other level, one step beyond silence, waiting to break out of an invisible box, but the vowels and consonants still would not come. Her spirit was stingy with words; maybe protective was a better word, as if the slightest utterance would scare away her sanity. How could the long silence be broken with anything but a scream?

Then she remembers the whisperings to Amanda, and the

corners of her mouth turn up in a conspiratorial smile. Who is she conspiring with in this silence? That, she doesn't even know, but she knows if she tries to talk to her husband, ask him a simple question like why had they not gone cross country, her throat would again constrict, not ready for her utterance or maybe not ready for the utterances of others. There was something that couldn't be laid out in words because, once the words were out, that would make it so. Gloria shudders in the warm sun glad that Thomas and Amanda have brought her a snack, but now, suddenly, she wants them gone. She feels exhausted and wants to sleep on the bench, but Amanda is grabbing her arm, making her be part of the family. It takes all of her strength, but she pretends to want to be with her family.

Amanda pulls her by the hand and picks up the watering can anxious to get to the business of making mud pies. Gloria pretends interest, follows Amanda to the spigot, helps her turn it on, placing her hand over Amanda's anxious chubby fingers. When the water sprays out sideways, Gloria jumps to the side and listens to Amanda's delighted squeals as she jumps up and down, her sun suit drenched within minutes.

Thomas comes over. "Must need a new washer," he says.

All this enthusiasm with life is too much for Gloria today. She watches Amanda doing a little dance in her wet sandals. Thomas has reined in the spray by hooking up the hose and is now squirting it toward Amanda holding on with his thumb to create an arc of water that falls onto the grass just in front of her. She jumps into the waterfall and out again immersed in the properties of water. Gloria can imagine a physics lesson for Amanda, Thomas explaining to her how droplets evaporate, some sink into the ground. The sunlight creates a rainbow, and seeing it makes Gloria sad when she had just started to feel a little better and part of a family moment. She remembers jumping through the sprinkler with her sister, and that makes her even sadder. She sits on the grass and begins to cry.

She hasn't cried in front of her daughter in a while. Amanda comes over, and Gloria feels her flop her wet body over her neck and back. Gloria shivers and tries to make herself turn around and embrace her daughter; she gives her arms a minute to hang sullenly. Then she turns quickly and grabs Amanda making it a game, pulling her into her lap and tickling her belly, but her child can see she is crying not laughing. Thomas comes over, not offering her comfort. *He's pissed*, she thinks, that she is not making faster progress, that she has exposed their daughter once again to her grieving. He must have thought she was beyond that.

"Let's go bring the tray in," Thomas says.

He picks up Amanda, and she feels like her child is being ripped away.

After they leave, she cries into the emptiness of no child in her lap. She gets up finally and drags herself to the bench wondering if they are watching from the windows to make sure she isn't going in the direction of the pond.

She flops down on the bench but finds she cannot keep her head up. She lies down, her face toward the back of the bench, her eyes open staring through the warm wooden slats just in front of her eyes. The warm wood across her cheek is starting to relax her some and she wonders why she hasn't been told to take therapeutic walks with Thomas and Amanda lately. Maybe Suzanne has decided that garden digging is therapy enough. She is starting to get her mind and her will back, she thinks, and she knew they wouldn't like it. Even though they love her, they want the control. She's resisting their suggestions as she gets better, and that makes her unpredictable to them again. She shouldn't have cried in front of her daughter. *Thomas was right to be pissed*. No matter what it takes, she must pull herself out of this fog and not pull their daughter into it. She is angry with herself but too exhausted to even think about it. She wonders if they will trust her to bathe Amanda again tonight as

Sleepwalking Backwards

her eyes close and she falls into an exhausted sleep.

She wakes up slowly, a sound first breaking through layers of consciousness, the loud chorus of crickets in the pond. She feels sweat around her forehead, and her mouth and chin are wet with drool. Someone has put a blanket over her. She sits up feeling hungry and dizzy and tries to find her center point, as Suzanne has taught her to do in yoga. She pushes her head back, and her eyes are confronted with the sunset, ribbons of pink across a sky of powder blue, an assault of beauty upon her eyes, and, though she does not want to see anything so life-affirming mocking her gray mood, she cannot look away. She finds it not quite as difficult to observe as the rainbow through water had been.

When she enters the house, Suzanne offers her salad and cold soup. She takes what is offered wanting something more substantial. She wants lamb stew, barbecued burgers, and hot dogs, maybe fries, but of course, Suzanne is vegetarian. Part of her healing program is to stay away from meat. She remembers bits of a conversation when she was deep in the gray fog. She remembers her father arguing with Suzanne that they should take her out and feed her steak and baked potatoes, something to get her strength back. Suzanne had been horrified and lectured him on what was wrong in the world, including he and mom's carnivorous diet.

She wishes they were here now, wishes for her mom and dad, wishes to be a child again just for a day or two as she chews on crunchy sprouts and realizes she hasn't gnawed on anything for a long time. The thought strikes her as funny and makes her laugh. She looks around to see if this random laugh has registered with Suzanne. She feels like she was always in the middle, the middle of Suzanne and her parents' fights.

First, it had been this place. Suzanne getting control of it, letting her and Thomas live here. Now, in her darkness, she is being pulled in between them again. Suzanne always seeming to win as her parents recede farther away. She wants them now, wants them here. Maybe she will call them, she thinks, call her dad and ask him to meet her for a steak.

She really doesn't want to rock the boat. Maybe it was just the way Amanda was playing in the water this morning that reminded her of she and Suzanne playing in the sprinkler. It had begun to unravel another thread of memory, something about an older sister, something about the joy of sharing those kind of moments with another child. Maybe it was just that Gloria thought it was not fair that Suzanne was keeping Amanda from her grandparents. *She needs her grandparents*, Gloria thinks, and suddenly remembers if she wanted to telephone them, she would actually have to speak. She could call to hear their voices and then just hang up.

She looks around. Suzanne is gone; she is upstairs bathing Amanda. Gloria walks to the door of the bathroom, and Suzanne hands her the baby all clean, pj'd, and wrapped in a blanket. Gloria carries her down to the rocking chair, kisses her head, and rocks her, as her eyelids flutter shut. She wonders if Suzanne has any idea how angry she is that their parents have been sent away. As Amanda's breathing evens out, Gloria begins to plan for the next day.

It occurs to her that if she wants to plant a garden, now that the soil is turned over, she needs something to put into it, and she wants to make choices of what is planted. In order to do that, she will have to leave the loft and somehow let Suzanne know that she wants to go to the store to pick up vegetables and flower seeds.

Chapter Eleven

Y2K—Let's party!

Amanda sat on the couch, miserable, pouting, while everyone around her was having a good time. Her father was nowhere in sight. Jason was behind the bar, serving, his eyes so bright he almost looked psychotic. High on nothing. She knew he didn't drink anymore or take anything that wasn't organic so why was he so GD happy? Her mother shot her a glance. Could she help it if she was not a party animal? All the conversation and cheerfulness only made her lonely.

In less than two hours, it would be the year two thousand, and she didn't know what she had expected, but somehow it was just more. Weren't there supposed to be some kind of spiritual overtones or something, especially with her mother's crowd? Peter wasn't here. She had been expecting Peter.

The universe does not care, she thought, as she sat on the couch. *The universe is not ruled by numbers and dates. Time only flows. Floes. Like ice moving through water.* She heard a dozen conversations at once, smiled only if someone looked at her, patted the mutt who lay sleeping and drooling on her new dress, and felt millions of light years away and very, very alone.

At 10:53, the phone rang, and Jason picked up the portable behind the bar. Amanda watched the lines of Jason's face go downward then upward again. He smiled and nodded as if the person on the other end could see him and walked toward Amanda with the phone. Leaning down very close to her ear, he spoke loudly.

"It's Peter. He's in the hospital, but he's okay."

She grabbed the phone. "Peter," she shouted into the telephone.

He was talking on the other end, but she could barely hear him with the noise. She swung the dog off her knee and pushed her way through the crowd to the stairs. Her mother was aghast and began to follow her, but Jason pulled her aside. Amanda closed the door at the top of the stairs behind her.

"Where are you? What happened?" The phone trembled in her hand. She'd had a funny feeling all day—knew something was going to happen. "Are you all right?"

"My car hit some ice. I guess I'm okay. I think the car's totaled."

"I don't care about the car." She sounded like her mother, yelling at him. Oh God, he sounded strong anyway. "I'll be down as soon as I can," she said, glad now that she hadn't started on the champagne.

"You don't need to come down."

"I want to." Did he have somebody with him? Is that why he didn't want her there?

"They're keeping me overnight. I got a little banged up. I'm in the ER waiting for a bed."

"I'm coming down."

"No! The roads are bad."

"I have blizzacks. I live in Vermont, remember?"

"Amanda, you don't have to."

"See you before midnight," she said. "I love you."

"Love you too."

She hung up reluctant to cut off the far away voice coming through the receiver and stared at the telephone.

Jason was behind her. She hadn't even noticed. His eyes were shining again, hyped on the cooking, the party, the people. She handed him the phone back.

"I'm going," she said.

"I'm taking you."

"No, I don't want to pull you away."

"You think I'd let you go alone on the streets tonight?"

They went downstairs to tell her mother they were leaving. They found her in a corner surrounded by guests.

"Is he okay?"

"I think so. They're keeping him overnight."

"Sorry I have to leave my post."

"You just go," her mother said. "Take care my baby doesn't get in an accident too. Someone will take over the bar."

"Happy New Year, mom, the big one." She kissed her mother and headed for the door.

"Yeah, Happy New Year, mom," Jason said, chuckling and following Amanda up the stairs.

And there they were in the Jason-mobile. The clocked ticked down towards the big one, but the streets were eerily empty. Was this really a ploy and they were being whisked off to god-knows-what planet? She was almost expecting him to detour off to the top of some sacred mountain. It was 11:29 on December 31st, 1999. Why were the streets so empty? Where were the usual drunks and stragglers trying to hail cabs on New Year's Eve? *Spooky.* They passed the University, and there seemed to be some activity there. Lights were on in all the residences. The snow was slowing down, but the roads were still icy. She didn't want Jason to go any faster, but she still wanted to get there. She kept thinking, *Please, we've got to get there before midnight.*

They turned on the road to the hospital at twenty to midnight. At least it was sanded. Amanda closed her eyes. *Noctua, the night owl, nebecula minor-the lesser cloud, lesser was different than smaller.* Jason was hardly parked when Amanda flew out the door into the emergency room. The waiting room was empty, not even a night clerk. Where was everyone? She looked at Jason in a panic. He pointed to the sign on the desk—"Please ring for assistance."

She pressed down so hard on the buzzer that a woman came running out, crumbs flying from her mouth, a piece of cake with candy confetti frosting inside a napkin in her hand. She looked from one to the other as if they were aliens and gave them papers to fill out.

"We're here to see someone," Amanda said, leaning over the desk. "Peter Bennet. He's supposed to be here waiting for a bed."

The woman looked into her computer and nodded. "In the green room" she said. "I'll take you there."

"I thought this place would be packed," Amanda said to Jason.

"Shhh!" The woman said. "Don't even think it. Usually it is packed on this shift New Year's Eve. Drunks, fights, accidents, crazies. Tonight your friend's been the only one in. It's eerie. I hate when it's this quiet at the beginning of shift; you know anytime all hell will break loose. When I heard the bell ring, I thought you were the beginning of it all."

They were at the end of a hallway. She opened the door to the green room.

"Go ahead. You can stay there with him. He's only waiting for a bed upstairs, might be here most of the night," she said.

Amanda wasn't sure if she wanted to look. He was hooked up to an IV, and his face was bruised.

Her lips began to tremble.

"Do I look that bad?"

"No, you don't look bad."

He knew she was lying, and she knew he knew it. She kissed his mouth. His face smelled like dried blood and antiseptic.

"My head hit the windshield lightly so they scheduled CT scans and all that." He rolled his eyes. "I feel fine." He laughed. "Except for the pain. They're going to keep waking me up all night in case I have a concussion."

She looked at the IV.

"Just a precaution in case I'm bleeding inside, and they don't know it, which I'm sure I'm not or they'd know by now."

Jason hung back at the door until Peter waved him in. "Thanks for getting her here, bud."

Jason nodded. Amanda couldn't remember if they'd ever spoken to each other before.

"Sorry," was all Jason said as he approached the bed.

Amanda had never seen him so uncomfortable. She thought he would be comfortable in a hospital. He seemed like such a natural caregiver. He looked like he might pass out at the sight of blood.

Peter sat up, perked up a little. "Sorry I ruined the party."

She wondered if Peter was on his way to the party when he crashed. There was no one else around—no sign he had been on a date or anything.

"How long have you been here?" Amanda asked.

"Since about eight, I guess"

"Why didn't you call earlier?"

"I was hoping they'd let me out and I wouldn't miss the party. It wasn't until they put this thing in that I knew they wouldn't let me go."

"You should have called earlier," she said. "I wanted to be with you."

Jason walked over to the door. Amanda looked over at him. She knew how he felt. *Three's a crowd.*

"I think I'll go scrounge up a bottle of champagne or something," he said as he left. "I hear there's a party in the staff lounge behind the nurse's station and they have confetti cake."

Amanda looked at Peter again. The bruised face, the IV—he looked so hurt. He had closed his eyes and fallen asleep and she looked at the clock on the wall. Four to midnight. Was it accurate? She'd forgotten her watch so she really didn't know. As the minute hand stepped into the year 2000, she would probably be unaware, and Peter would be sleeping. This was it, big party at mom and dads. She sighed then jumped when she heard whoops and hollers from the nurse's station. Peter woke up. He kissed her with his swollen lips. She got beside him in his hospital bed and put her head on his chest and they both faded into sleep.

Chapter Twelve

Gloria doesn't sleep well. Why would she when they let her sleep all day? She roams around the house, writes in her journal for a while, even plays a video game with the sound turned off. She wants to go outside and dig now that her energy is back, but she realizes what that would look like to Thomas and Suzanne if they woke up and saw her out there. She didn't want to lose the trust they have begun to put in her sanity, her ability to take care of her child. She sits at the table, ringing her hands wondering what to do with her energy.

She goes to a small desk where Thomas puts together pamphlets for metric conversion. The government is still trying to get the country to step in line with the rest of the world since Carter's been elected. She can't believe it's still so lucrative. It's their only income besides Suzanne who takes on a few private clients in therapy and teaches yoga once a week. Her method of psychoanalysis is not as popular in New England as in Southern California, but they get by. Suzanne has never charged them rent on the loft because she considers them caretakers; Thomas is good at fixing whatever needs repair. Gloria and Thomas are used to living with next to nothing, but she wonders about Suzanne. How much of a step down is this for her? She appreciates her sister's help as much as she resents it.

She grabs some pieces of paper and pencils from the desk and takes them to the table, begins planning out the garden and flowerbeds so immersing herself in carrots and peas, potatoes and green beans, that she hardly notices the ribbons of color beginning to envelop the large picture window at the top of the stairs. She pictures rows of tomatoes and peppers, vines wrapping around wooden stakes, and then she pictures the flowers she will plant at the edge of the woods: pansies, daisies, gladiola, bushes of roses. She has heard there are certain flowers that keep the bugs away from the vegetables. She'll have to get some books when she goes out today, as well as the seeds and plants and some money from Thomas.

When she finally looks up, the sun has almost risen. She walks up the stairs toward the hot, red globe, too intense for her to look at except for a glance and shades her face against the brightness. Has she never recognized how big this window is before? How can the baby and Thomas sleep through this? She crawls in next to Thomas and puts the covers over her head, the magnificence of the sunrise still pushing its intensity into the loft more assaultive to her senses than the sunset had been last evening. No wonder it upsets the birds so much every morning they scream in confused chatter.

She wakes up late. It's hot and stuffy in the loft. She turns over and stares at the sky that is now a blank blue slate, a gaseous expanse that matches her neutral state and lies in bed listening to Amanda's chatter downstairs. It could even be past noon, the first morning she has not been either on the bench or digging in the garden that she can remember, since she has come out of the fog. She may have been sleeping all the time when she was immersed in whatever she was immersed in that had sent her sister scurrying here from the west coast to take care of her.

She feels no urge to move, so she just closes her eyes and pictures her garden. Won't they be surprised when she takes an interest in going beyond this chalet, the garden, the bench? She thinks about how she will do it, maybe just take the keys from Thomas or Suzanne and drive herself to the store. She's not sure if she remembers where it is, but something like that would usually come back as you're driving. Eventually, she would run into one of the Vermont everything stores where she was sure she could find plants and seeds and books and tools.

Then she realized she better have Suzanne with her in case she does get confused or overwhelmed. There would be a lot of tourists at this time of year, though not as many as in the fall. Maybe Thomas and Amanda would come too, and they could be like a regular family, walking around the common, getting soft serve ice cream.

She stretches and sits up gazing again at the blank sky. She must be getting better, she thinks, to plan a day away from the house. Weeks ago, they had been trying to get her to go somewhere, nagging her about barely having left the loft since last winter except for some kind of therapy. They seem to have given up recently, and now she wants to go on her own.

Amanda spies her awake and begins to climb the stairs. Gloria jumps out of bed hurrying to pick her up before she falls. Why hadn't they been watching her? She picks Amanda up and carries her down. Thomas is at his desk; Suzanne is on the telephone.

"Mama," Amanda shouts as they reach the bottom stair announcing her presence as if she were a contestant in Miss America. Thomas and Suzanne look up and meet her eyes for the first time she can remember without that deep worry that has been reflected in them for so long. Perhaps it is right that Amanda has announced her so enthusiastically. Perhaps she sensed, before the adults did, that she was announcing the return of mommy, bigfoot emerging from the gray swamp.

Thomas goes back to his work at the desk, and Suzanne resumes her phone conversation.

She puts Amanda down among some toys scattered in the corner of the room and puts on water for tea, relieved that no one rushes to assist her or lead her around to calendars. Then she sits at the table sipping tea and munching on one of Suzanne's day-old muffins. She looks around the one large room at the bottom of the chalet with a beaded curtain divider hanging from the ceiling set up to make a separate bedroom for

Suzanne. Amanda is always going for it, and they have put a gate to keep her out. Gloria sits with her head to the side remembering when it wasn't there.

She has a memory, somewhat foggy, of several kids sleeping on the floor down here. There was no curtain dividing off a room then. It must have been put up recently for Suzanne's privacy. Gloria shakes her head amazed; she's hardly noticed it before. Of course, she has stared at it, seen it for the past several weeks or months, but never really registered that it was not there before, before whatever had happened.

She remembers now all these people, when this room was all open, lots of kids in sleeping bags on the floor. Outside there were tents in the summer strewn across the lawn, tents with even more kids. She remembers walking over sleeping bags in the morning and begins to remember why they had not gone cross-country in that summer. Somehow, they had ended up here.

She leans her head on the table, looks through the small window that faces out into the back yard, and stares at the garden area where she has been working so hard to turn the earth over. She remembers her mission for the day. She feels a curious lightness with no urge to sit on the bench, no manic need to dig into the earth today. Today, she will leave the loft for the first time since she can remember. She will leave the loft to buy plants and seeds for the garden.

When she gets up, she cannot resist going over to the beaded divider that she has somehow managed not to notice for so long and feels the pressure on her hand and the clicking of the beads as she pushes it aside.

Amanda runs over to her. "No, No!" she yells with her baby voice as if she were the mother and Gloria, the child. She must have been told on a daily basis not to go in there, to leave Auntie Suzanne's things alone. Gloria turns around, and they are all three staring at her. *It was only because I didn't remember it being here before,* she wants to tell them. She lets the bead drop and shrugs her shoulders, showing them she is fine, trying to explain herself without words. They no doubt wonder what they are going to do with her now.

Suzanne is off the phone, and Thomas is playing with Amanda, so Gloria goes upstairs and gets dressed. She takes out ten dollars from Thomas' wallet on the nightstand and his keys. She will leave alone if she has to, she decides, just drive to the nearest store. She knows that will get them all upset, although she feels quite capable of getting into the car and driving to the nearest town. It is *her* car too. She is better; she can feel it, and the words will come soon.

As she walks down the stairs, she panics at the thought of leaving alone but summons the most in-charge posture she can and walks over to Thomas jangling the keys in front of his face. Amanda tries to grab them, wanting to play. Thomas just takes them not getting it.

Suzanne jumps up from the table where she had been reading the paper. "She wants to go somewhere!"

They are making it easy for her not to talk now. She felt the silence in the house today. It is not her inability to talk, but it seems everyone else is talking less. Suzanne losing herself in her papers; Thomas sitting at his desk. The lack of noise in the house today is eerie. It is incredible how they have enabled her, especially Suzanne being a shrink. Now suddenly everyone in the house is excited. The power she has scares her—Suzanne's enthusiasm almost frightening her into not wanting to go.

"We'll go out for ice cream," Thomas says. Something in his cheeriness makes Gloria shrink back.

What are the expectations? She sees Suzanne give him a look. They have a conference by the window. It is decided that she and Suzanne will go out and bring back ice cream. Her shrink sister doesn't trust her yet. Maybe it's better; she doesn't want to traumatize the baby any more than she already has.

At first, Gloria feels claustrophobic as they enter the car, as she's not used to such confinement. Suzanne leaves the driveway telling Gloria they will just go to the general store, acting like there is nothing unusual for the two sisters to be riding along together. Gloria begins to breathe deeply, gets dizzy, and considers putting her hand on Suzanne's arm, signaling for her to stop the car. But she doesn't; she just breathes through the dizziness, and Suzanne looks at her.

"You'll be okay. It's okay," she says. "Just slow down your breathing the way I taught you in yoga."

Gloria feels a little better. As she watches the landscape slide by, she turns on the radio then turns it off quickly. An old Stones song made her anxious. She clings to the silence once again and the hum of the motor. They are going to the general store. Gloria knows she can get seeds and plants there. Suzanne pulls into a parking space at the edge of the common. Gloria holds her breath. Across from the common, there are a series of stores bigger than she imagined. Lots of tourists everywhere.

One foot in front of the other, she tells herself. As she is getting out of the car, Suzanne comes around and takes her hand. They cross the street arm in arm as if they were any other tourists. Gloria follows Suzanne's step, quick and steady as they walk under the flag and up a few steps into the store. Gloria jumps as a bell rings above the door and the screen door slams behind them. Inside, it is dark, cavernous. For some reason, this makes Gloria feel calmer.

There are people everywhere, and she hears the hum of dozens of conversations. Sounds but not words, she can't quite grasp what anyone is saying. She gazes around, disoriented, not sure who is speaking to whom. She follows Suzanne's lead, does her yoga breathing, looking around for an area of the store that might be unoccupied. She is starting to recognize the set-up, has probably been here many times. Suzanne is telling her something, steering her toward the back section of the store.

It is one of those stores that has everything. The front section set up like a traditional country store with a long counter and behind it are shelves cluttered with all practical needs from socks to matches. There are barrels everywhere full of candy and pickles. There is an area of fishing poles and tackle, wellingtons and cable knit sweaters. There is a ben franklin wood stove in the middle that is being used as a table for complementary coffee and tea, cheese and crackers.

Suzanne takes a sample as they walk by and leads her down a few stairs to the back of the store that looks like another land altogether full of clothes and cards and pictures of Vermont winter scenes. She steers them toward the pottery while Gloria stares at rows and rows of tee shirts.

This area is even more crowded, making Gloria feel an urge to bolt. She looks around for a back door. There is only one other door in this room, and that is probably a bathroom. She tugs Suzanne's arm and points to it. Suzanne follows her to the door. Thank God she can't follow her inside. Gloria wants to be alone, totally alone. She sits on the toilet with her head down. This hasn't been as bad as she thought. If it wasn't so crowded, she would probably be fine. She knows she only has so much time until Suzanne will get worried and try to barge in, so she stands up and gazes out a small, high window and quiets her breathing. Really, she feels it is going to be okay now that she has had these few minutes alone to think, to formulate a plan.

What she wants is the gardening section with tools and seeds; she had seen a few plants in the front but had been too distracted to really look at them. She hadn't seen a gardening display in the front room so it must be in this one. Now that she has adjusted to being in this rush of people, she will look around in a more focused way; she is ready to walk out, to let Suzanne know she is fine now. No need to lead her around—she is not blind except in certain parts of her recent past; it is her voice that has withdrawn inside her. In a place like this, where the outside world was so noisy, she had a new respect for her inner silence.

She composes herself and opens the door; Suzanne is right there ready to take her hand. Gloria brushes Suzanne's arm and points toward the tee shirts. To her chagrin, Suzanne follows her instead of going back to the pottery. Beyond the row of tee shirts is a large window. Next to that, Gloria sees a rack of books and seeds. There is a window seat with a few plants and a stack of wire baskets for shoppers; on a hook by the window are canvas totes. Gloria forgets her claustrophobia in the excitement of finding what she has come for and rushes to pick a tote and a basket then hurries to the rack of seeds. Suzanne finally seems to understand what she is doing and goes back to the pottery.

There are mostly flower seeds. The vegetables must have been out in the front, and she missed them. She'll get tomato and pepper plants on the way out. She piles her basket high with Chrysanthemums, phlox, and sunflower seeds feeling Suzanne's eyes on her even from a distance. She mustn't get too greedy. She can't remember how much money she had taken, and she needs money for the vegetable plants she knows are outside. The early bloomers, snowdrops, daffodils, are on sale so she takes even more of those. She will plant them in the fall for the spring. She'll get some tubers on the way out; they must have been outside too in the barrels in front of the door. Potatoes, carrots, food that actually grows under the ground so she can dig deeper. She needs spinach also and maybe some herbs for a special garden. She picks out a few brochures about planting and throws them into the basket. The books look interesting, but she knows she does not have enough money for them.

When she got all that she could afford from the gardening area, she goes back to the tee shirts. She must buy something for Amanda and maybe for Thomas on her first trip out in she doesn't know how long. She's sure Suzanne has some money. Walking through the rows of tee shirts, it is as if everything is normal. Forgetting the core of silence inside her, she observes and wonders what her husband would like. There were some with deer that they both would think were too touristy. She considers a plain hunter green that just says Vermont on it, but why would he need that when they lived in Vermont-duh. Finally, she just picks a plain light blue tee shirt with nothing on it and stuffs it into the tote bag. Then she goes back to the rack of children's sizes.

This is a huge step, being among people again. She practices quiet breathing each time her heart begins to race and looks toward the window by the bathroom if she starts feeling claustrophobic. It isn't as crowded in this room as it had been. The flow of traffic seems to be moving into the front room and probably spilling out the door. The thought of that calms her. When she breathes out, she thinks of crowds of people pushing their way out the door giving her more oxygen, more peace. For some reason, her anxiety is increasing as she fingers the children's tees.

She touches the materials trying to decide if she should get something light that Amanda could wear now or something thicker for the fall. How much would Amanda grow by the fall? She'd probably be at least up one more size. It was such a relief to think about her daughter and Thomas and not about her memory problems, to think about the future instead of trying to regain the past.

She pushes her way through the racks of tees with Vermont flowers and deer. She sees one that says Vermont grown and has a picture of a child sitting in a garden, flowers in her hair. She puts that one in her basket and looks around a little more. Then she sees a rack of sweatshirts with snowflakes winter scenes. *I survived the blizzard of '78?* The one she sees does not have writing on it, buts she rushes over to see if she can find one. Maybe this is where her parents had bought it last winter. She's excited and getting angry as she paws through the over-stuffed racks. Some fall to the floor as she searches out what she wants, what she needs. *Nobody up here*, she says in her mind, *had to survive the blizzard of 78. That was down in Massachusetts.* It was stupid, she thought for such a shirt to be on sale up here. It had just been a regular Vermont winter hadn't it? She couldn't remember. But still, she wants that tee shirt. She scours the rack, pushes entire colors aside, looking for the one, the one that would say, I survived.

She drops the basket. All her treasures for the garden scatter on the floor. Someone is picking them up for her as she is tearing into the tee shirts, ripping them off the hangers. Suzanne is with her trying to unhinge her from the glut of tee shirts she is clutching, a handful she is holding so tightly to her chest it makes her fingers ache. She only wants to bury her face in the shirts and weep until she can weep no more. She hears Suzanne's voice authoritative and calm.

"Put the tee shirts down."

She hears Suzanne thank a woman who has picked up Gloria's basket and refilled it with all the merchandise.

"Put the tee shirts down," Suzanne says. "We're going now."

Gloria obeys.

Suzanne takes her arm and holds it tightly, leading her to the front of the store. Gloria stares back at the window, wanting to break it, get herself out of this cave of people and objects as soon as possible, but she walks next to Suzanne arm in arm and is glad to notice as they walk through the door that Suzanne has retrieved the basket and all its contents from the other woman. She manages to take money out and hand it to Suzanne, though a feeling of rage deep down is trying to pull itself up through her stomach, then her lungs, and finally her throat. She swallows it down, constricts her windpipe, and tries to keep her body from shaking as Suzanne pays at the long counter in the front.

Why had Suzanne pulled her away? Didn't she know that Gloria was starting to remember something? She'd just wanted to be surrounded by the children's tee shirts burying her face in them, smelling them, washing them with her tears. She is angry with Suzanne for not understanding but manages to keep her body calm as Suzanne orders the ice cream promised to Thomas and Amanda.

After the incident at the store, Gloria has no real desire to go anywhere. She has her seeds to plant, and she has her remembering bench to sit on when she is tired. Suzanne does not even tell Thomas of the incident when they get back. She is glad of that. No conference by the window.

When they get home, Amanda gives Gloria and Thomas their presents, and they eat ice cream like other families. Amanda wears her new tee shirt all day, somehow knowing it is an accomplishment for mommy, the simple act of purchasing a gift.

Chapter Thirteen

"Why is it nobody understands me but everybody likes me?" —Einstien

Amanda delayed the trip back to Vermont for a week so she could help Peter recuperate at home. She went to his house every day but did not stay the night. They had not redefined their relationship. They hadn't talked about the future. It was funny, almost like they were married. She'd never been a caregiver, so the role felt odd. Her mother urged her to stay and not go back up. At Peter's, she looked for hairs in the sink, a different coffee cup, any traces of someone else. She found nothing. Why now did he seem so detached? Maybe when he bumped his head on the windshield he got a concussion. It was just strange. She was taking care of everything. He was letting her. She even made most of the calls to get a rental car. The day before she was leaving to go back up, they sat on the couch, arms around each other, until it was so late, it made sense for her to stay.

"I better go," she said, "Before the snow," hoping he would ask her to stay.

"What time will you be leaving?"

"Not sure"

"Call me before you leave."

"Okay."

Amanda slept late the next morning, and it was almost noontime before she started packing. She was putting jeans and sweaters into a backpack when her mother came into the room.

"What are you doing? There's a storm just starting."

"Mom, there's always a storm in Vermont in January."

"This is going to be a bad one. You can't drive in this."

"That's why I want to leave in daylight."

"Then have daddy drive you up. He can stay the night and come down tomorrow."

"Mom, I have to go. Really, I love you, but I have to go."

"You are so stubborn." Her mother stomped out of the room like an angry adolescent.

Why had everybody been regressing down here while she was gone? Her dad was still sick, three weeks with the flu, Peter needed taking care of, and her mother was acting younger than she was. What happened to everybody taking care of and worrying about Amanda? She went to the kitchen and poured herself a cup of strong coffee and took it downstairs to the bar where her mother was sulking with an herb-laced drink.

"I thought you and Peter might get back together after the accident. You're over there every day. I thought you might be over this Vermont thing."

"Guess not," she said.

She watched her mother touch the rim of her glass with her index finger and look down into the steaming liquid. Why did her mother always have to be so intense about everything? She was just going back to her life—the life she wanted for now.

"What do you want from me?" Amanda's voice was louder than she had intended.

"What's best for you." Her mother's voice broke. "A normal life?"

Amanda closed her eyes: *Capricorn, the centaur archer, god of war, the star of the bow.*

"Mom," she heard herself whine, which was even worse. "I just have to go back"

"Why?"

"I don't know. I just.... don't know." Amanda put her head down.

"Peter loves you."

"Maybe"

"He's a good man."

"I know." She was speaking loudly again, letting her mother get to her. This is why she had to get away from here.

"Why are you letting him go?"

She wanted to scream. *This is exactly why I'm leaving.* Instead, she got up and walked away spilling hot coffee on her arm. Her mother followed her to the couch. She had stopped acting needy but was making Amanda feel like a child again.

"Why are you doing this to yourself?"

"Doing what? Living my life?"

"Pulling yourself away from everyone who loves you?"

"Because of you," she said. "I'm going away because you badger me like this." She put the coffee down and fled upstairs, trying not to let her mother see her crying.

Her mother followed her and stood in the doorway.

"I'm sorry," she said in that contrite voice that drove Amanda crazy. "I'm sorry I'm interfering again."

Amanda sighed and took her mother's hand. Her mother hugged her.

"My baby girl," her mother said. "It's just that no matter how old you get, you'll always be my baby."

They packed the car together. It wasn't snowing as badly as her mother had said it would. In fact, it had almost stopped. She stuck her head out the window.

"I love you. I'll be alright mom. I promise, I promise, I promise."

The flakes thickened as Amanda drove route 9 through the Brookfields and west into Ware. Her plan was to drive to Amherst and stop for coffee and then head all the way up route 91 without stopping. She was a good driver and a careful driver, and she was used to driving in storms. It snowed almost every day in Vermont either on her way to work or on the way back.

It was a sticky kind of snow that whirled around the windshield making driving hard, disorienting. She put on a tape of the Grateful Dead, an old one she'd found in the loft and drove along, trying to concentrate. Music always helped her concentrate. She went into a few minor slides but, fortunately, there was little traffic on the road.

When she got to Amherst, she shivered and stretched her legs out in the cold air. The snow, the swish of the wiper, the hum of the heater had hypnotized her into a state where she'd almost missed the turn onto the common, but now she was here and feeling very tired and in need of a pit stop.

She sat down on a stool at a counter facing out the window watching snow swirl around people, buildings, cars. It seemed to be letting up a little. They would have sanded the highway when she got back on; she was leaving the blizzard behind.

She watched students going by and listened to rap music being piped in. A tall boy with ears red from the cold walked by blowing warmth into his gloveless hands, and a crowd of girls with either short hair or hair down to their butts wearing army jackets unbuttoned over thick sweaters laughed. A man walked by with his head shaved and a long braid down the back. He was older, probably a professor or someone who had been working on a degree for the last 20 years.

Sometimes she missed working at the University, that feeling of being connected to something. Even still, with all the loneliness, she wanted to be in Vermont—needed the isolation to serve her a while longer. Even there, she didn't have peace. It was hard to explain how something gnawed at her when she was up there and how severed she felt when she was away. The hallucinations or whatever they were seemed more real to her than anything else in her life right now. She was waiting for a time when she could go up to Vermont and feel none of the pull between past and present. She'd felt it always, even as a child, maybe even more then.

After a second cup of coffee, she hit the ladies room and walked out into the snow. It was colder, and flakes were still coming down sticking to her jacket and hair as she walked to the car. She turned on the engine and let the heat melt some of the snow. There was a snowball fight in progress on the common. She watched it for a while, and when everything melted on the windows, she headed towards route 91 in Northampton.

There were still a few hours of daylight as she traveled north, snow falling like a blanket on the road like a light summer gauze curtain around her car. It was getting heavy again. Further north, there was ice everywhere, but the snow had actually stopped. Jason's car was in the driveway when she pulled in. She remembered then she'd asked him to keep an eye on the loft.

When she walked in and smelled Jason's cooking, she realized how hungry and weary she was, and Jason grinned at her as she flopped down on the bed. He filled their plates, and they sat in front of the window eating silently. She in the rocking chair and he in the overstuffed chair. They sat and watched darkness fall around them.

"I wondered if you'd make it," he said, as she scraped the last of the gravy from her plate.

"The roads weren't that bad," she said.

"Now that you're here and fed, I have to go. Working second shift."

She nodded. "Thanks for the homecoming supper."

She walked Jason to the door and gave him a hug. He kissed her on the forehead, and he was gone.

So she would have her heart's desire—an empty loft with all the lights out and all the machines buzzing. For a while, she lost herself in the noise and darkness, but when it started snowing again, she unplugged the machines and went up to the window seat to watch the snow.

She looked again in the draw. Pulled out some books from behind the crayons, and she found a book her mother had given her for her twelfth or thirteenth birthday. It was a book of short biographies of woman in the 19th century. One was of a pioneer woman who had traveled through the mountains with her husband trying to set up house and having babies. It was startling at the end when she dies in childbirth and you find out she is only thirty-one. Amanda had been most inspired by the story of the young Maria Mitchell who stayed up all night with her father charting the skies and discovered a comet by the time she was thirty.

She closed the drawer and took up a new book, *Einstein in Love*, which her mother had given her for Christmas. Then she hopped into bed with the book still in her hand reading beautiful sentences about light and speed and the grace of the world being somehow masked.

Hmm? Why is the grace of the world weird? In religion, grace was usually something unearthly, bestowed upon someone for doing something good. In the catholic religion, it was almost like collateral for doing bad things, sins. What did it mean to be full of grace? Kind of like good karma but even more ethereal. A feeling of lightheadedness, forgiveness, relief or release, grace could also mean smooth movement.

Was the weird grace of the world the universe with planets and moons and the sun smoothly revolving and revolving in patterns with gravity pulling them closer than other forces pulling them away then gravity pulling them back again to keep them on track?

She half noticed the stove was going out and needed more oil. *I'll be freezing in the morning if I don't get my butt out of here and start up the stove,* she thought, but she was so comfortable, and she didn't want to completely lose her train of thought. How is the weird grace masked? A mask covers something. It's a deception sometimes, a masquerade, pretending to be something that it isn't. How could speed mask anything? Was it a diversion?

She put her head under the sheet and closed her eyes. The phone rang, and the lights came on, even though she had turned them off. She shivered in the heat although she thought the stove was very low. She lay flat and rigid, her head feeling as if it were falling back into the mattress. The light was too bright even with her eyes closed, even through the sheet. Like a million giant suns were right outside the loft window. She heard a crash and the beeping sound of the phone being knocked off the hook. The she heard a child's voice singing, "ABCDEFG." *Maybe there was a fire.* "HIJKLMNOP," but she didn't smell burning. "QRSTUV." Maybe you didn't, "WXYZ," just before flames consumed you.

She'd been reading that Einstein, especially when he was a student, sometimes would hardly eat and sleep when he was working out a theory. She peeked out from under the covers with one eye, but of course, she wasn't in the loft anymore. She was in Einstein's room when he was working so hard he dozed off and was almost overcome with fumes from a stove until a friend happened to stop by and check on him. She was sitting in one of those uncomfortable Victorian chairs; he lay on the couch going in and out of consciousness.

She wished she could do something to save him, but she couldn't move from the chair. He began to speak to her in a quiet voice.

"At least my job as a clerk allowed me to think, allowed my mind to wander. Such rote work can be good, though others find it boring. Now my teaching can get in the way. I work best in solitude. I'm still precise about my duties and finish them as quickly as possible giving me time to write down notes and theories"

He started coughing. She wished he would save his breath. Where was that person who was supposed to show up and save him?

Again, she tried to get up because the room was starting to

Sleepwalking Backwards

fill up with smoke. She had to do something, but she was stuck in the chair. She decided to see if she could talk. Maybe she could direct him to leave, let him know he was in danger. She found she could talk, but he refused to listen to her—it was like he heard but was too far gone to understand. So she started to talk about other things, if only just to keep him from talking and using up his oxygen.

"I'm from the future," she said.

He seemed quite interested in that and leaned forward. She searched her mind for things to say.

"You're going to live a long life, so I wish your friend would hurry up and get here to save you."

He looked at her inquisitively.

"You're going to live a long life, and when you get older, your hair is going to be all sticking out, kind of like mine. You're going to discover all kinds of breakthrough theories in physics, prove theories about the universe."

His eyes brightened as much as they could in the smoke.

"In case you're ever discouraged, it was all worth it." It was just a general heads up for him. She didn't want to tell him he would feel bad about some of the things mankind used his discoveries for. She decided to tell him good things he would not ever know in his lifetime.

"You discovered a way for people to be able to harness light and use the energy to develop laser beams. They're not used for war; they're used for medicine. People can go and have surgery now and not be cut up because of you. They're even used in supermarkets to scan things."

He smiled.

She wondered if he knew what a supermarket was. Where the hell was his friend? She tried to get out of the chair again but could not move.

Einstein sat back, coughing.

She pushed and pushed herself to get up until finally she

felt herself move just as the door opened and someone rushed through to save him.

Amanda used this opportunity to sneak by the friend, now that she knew Einstein would be saved, and look outside. She stood at the door watching a snowball fight under 19th century gas lamps, too enthralled in how romantic and quaint it was with glow of the lamps in the snow to notice a ball come hurling toward her. She opened her mouth to say no, getting ready for the impact, and heard her mother's voice—*Amanda, No*. The snowball picked up mass until it was a huge hurricane drifting around her, pulling her down.

Mommy, Amanda cried, when she could still speak, for the snow was falling into her mouth and her nose. Her chest heaving trying to breathe, she couldn't, couldn't, her mouth, her nose covered.

Mommy. She tried to lift up her arms to the voices and sounds of the panicked scraping above her, but her eyelids crushed with the deep cold would not let her see. Each time, she sensed a hole in the cavern of drifted snow and opened her mouth to breathe, each time she could sense an almost-rescue, it would quickly fill again, clogging her mouth like frosting on a cake. It covered her until she let it, let her body drift down into the clump of white.

Then she was freezing and rubbing her hands together, blowing on them. She told herself to throw off the blanket covering her face, but she didn't want to. She had to get up and find a flashlight or matches, fast. She had to pee badly. No light from the window, no moon, no stars. It was snowing. She made her way to the bathroom and felt around for something to hold onto. It was so dark, no heat, no light.

She rifled around beneath the sink and found a battery-powered lantern. Oh please, she thought as she switched it on. *Have batteries, please.* The light went on. It wasn't much, but it was something. It gave her enough light to find the gas heater and matches. She held the blanket around her, and slowly warmth filled the room. The glow of the heater made her sleepy, and she sat on the bed and must have fallen asleep. She awoke trembling in what seemed like a minute later. It was almost daylight, and Jason was there. She'd been sleeping for hours.

Jason switched on the light. The electricity worked again. It hurt her eyes; she covered her face with the blanket.

"Too much light," she said.

"What are you turning into a vampire here?"

She groaned. He was as bad as Peter.

He pulled the blanket from her face.

"I hate January" she said, as he handed her a cup of red zinger. "Especially in Vermont."

She got up and looked outside. A few more feet of snow had fallen overnight.

"You don't look too good," he said. "I'll make you an omelet."

What had happened through the night? Something changed. First, she thought she was burning to death then almost froze to death. She remembered a blizzard, snow pushed into her mouth like she was smothering. She didn't even know. She had that suffocation dream when she came up here last winter and talked of marriage. But it wasn't that. It was something sad, something beyond comprehension.

"Hope you don't have to work today."

"No," she said "not until tomorrow."

She turned around quickly from the window, compelled to move. Jason stared at her. He said her eyes looked haunted.

"Something's wrong," she said. "Something's wrong at home." She picked up the cell phone, but it wasn't working. "Damn." She ran down the stairs and began to pack. "I have to go down to Worcester."

Jason was upstairs cooking. "Some of the roads are closed,"

he said

"I don't care," she yelled.

"Okay," Jason said. "We can try to get through, but first, let's have an omelet; it might be a long ride down."

Amanda was holding onto one of the machines. Her arms stretched out, her head down. "Something's wrong," she cried. "Something is wrong!"

PART III

Somehow, You Heal

She remembers a time of snow and stars, a sudden absence,
a loss of balance. She remembers a smell, a word, a touch;
then, all around everything had shifted
Hydrus the water snake, Leo the lion
Lacerta, the lizard
Lyra, the harp
Leaena the lioness, Lepre the hair
Sagittarius, the archer
The bow stretcher, quiver
The arrow, the herdsman
The archer's knee
Pleides, the sisters, the seven sisters
The starry seven on the shoulder of the bull
Maia the firstborn, most beautiful sister
Electra the lost
Withdrew her light in sorrow
The Milky Way
Stream of the ocean
The river of heaven
Men call it milk

Chapter One

"The snow had begun in the gloaming—"
The first snowfall, Whittier

Amanda and Jason were just beginning to leave the driveway when Peter's car pulled in. Amanda rolled down her window. She'd been worried about him since the accident.

"What are you doing here?" She asked, relieved to see him. He didn't say anything. Jason backed up, and Amanda flew out of the car.

The three stood in the cold morning, Peter leaning against the car, Jason and Amanda crowding around him. Amanda studied him. He looked alright, just a little tired and pale. His gloved hands were in his pockets, his head down. He looked at her sideways, and she could see his breath as he spoke.

"Your dad's sick."

"What's wrong with him?" He never completely got over the flu he had over the holidays, but he seemed to be getting stronger when she left.

"Your mom knows more than I do," he said turning toward her. He put his arm on her shoulder then took her in his arms. He gave her a bear hug, his chin resting on the top of her head. It felt so warm, comforting, but still, she pulled away, searched his face.

"I'll bring you down," he said.

"Did he fall and have an accident or something?" Peter and Jason looked from one to the other. "I knew something had happened. We were just leaving to go down."

"Why don't you get your stuff and both come down with me?"

"What the hell, Peter," she said. "Just tell me what's going on."

"He has cancer," Peter said.

"How can he have cancer? What kind of cancer?"

"Colon cancer, I think. Your mother knows more. He's in surgery."

"When did this happen? Why didn't anyone call me?"

She ran to the car, got her bags, and the three of them got into Peter's car. He put his arm around her as he drove.

"It happened really suddenly early this morning. He got really sick, and his back started to hurt really badly. Your mom called me to take him to the hospital, but by the time I got there, she had called 911. She asked me to come up here and bring you down."

Amanda tried to listen to every word but found herself lost in the blue gray expanse above the snow-covered mountains. Plows and sanders were out everywhere with the sun gleaming off the steel blades as snow was pushed away, pushed aside. She imagined it ripping through the veil of gauze, the walls of a snow house that she had felt was falling around her when she drove up here yesterday.

Peter's voice had stopped. She didn't know how long he had been talking then not talking. The silence began to become unbearable when they crossed into Massachusetts. She sobbed quietly, and Peter pulled her closer, put his hand on her shoulder.

When they got to the hospital, they found her mother in the surgical waiting room. Her hair tied back in a kerchief, no makeup, her nails chipped and bitten. She stood, staring out a small window with her arms crossed, her shoulders drooped, not even noticing that they had come in. Amanda ran over to her and hugged her. Her mother pulled away a little.

She shook her head. "He never eats right. Never takes vitamins," she said, looking at Amanda but speaking to herself. "I told him to at least take vitamins."

Her body shook, but she did not cry. Amanda led her to a chair. Peter and Jason sat close by them.

"Is he still in surgery?"

Amanda's mother nodded.

"What are they doing? Why is it taking so long?" Amanda tried to control the quivering in her voice. She wanted information, but she also wanted to be strong for her mother.

Peter answered. "Colectomy."

"They have to take his colon out? What? Can't they just remove the cancer?" She felt panic rise, and she was almost yelling.

"No. It's a colostomy. They're not removing his colon. Let's go for a walk. Get something to eat," Jason said.

She looked at him like he was crazy; still, he pulled her to the door. "I'm not leaving here."

"No. I just mean in the cafeteria. Peter can sit with your mom. We can get something for her."

Peter nodded.

"What if the doctor comes? I want to be here. I have questions."

"Peter will come get us."

He nodded again.

She could hear her voice getting even louder and didn't want to upset her mother, so she followed Jason. "Your mom needs something to eat," he whispered, looking over in her direction. "She's been here a long time."

Jason led her to the cafeteria, made her sit, and brought her a cup of strong, black coffee and a muffin. He bought a salad and sparkling water for her mother.

"Why didn't they know?" she asked. "Don't they give tests now? Isn't there some kind of screening test they give to people our parent's age?"

Jason tried to get Amanda to take some of the muffin. She pushed his hand away.

"I've never seen my mother so quiet, so disheveled," Amanda said. "I have to get back before the doctor comes."

In the elevator, tears rolled down her face, and she was afraid that people would see them when the door opened, but no one was there, just a blank, white wall. Jason found a chair in the hallway and sat Amanda there until she was a little more composed. He knelt on the floor next to her as she sipped the coffee and took small pieces of the muffin as he handed them to her. Then she began to choke and cry.

"What if he doesn't make it?"

"He will."

Amanda sobbed.

"Take your time," Jason said. "We won't go back until you're ready."

She tried to compose herself, embarrassed to be emoting so openly. "I'm okay now," she said to Jason.

"Are you sure?"

"Yeah." Her voice broke a little. She looked sideways at Jason.

"He's going to be alright." Jason said. "He's going to be alright.

In the waiting room, Amanda gave her mother the offerings of salad and water. She didn't eat or drink, just held them for a few minutes, and then put them on a chair. *This is how Jason feels*, she thought, *when others don't accept his comfort*. She went to the window and watched the snow squalls that had started up again, looked through the glass, no distortions like the window in her office. Everything here was clean and clear, all the windows disinfected. *This is a hospital*, she thought, *where blood splattered and souls left their bodies*. She touched the glass with her hand. It was cold, not flexible. How did the souls get through?

When the doctor came in, she tried to read the expression on his face before words were spoken. He looked serious but not grim. She breathed deeply and walked over to the others, listening to the words, noticing that his hands still wore the rubber gloves.

Good thing he came in when he did. Not too much infection. They think they got it all. He seems strong and they will probably be able to reverse the colostomy in a few months if there are no post-surgical complications.

Her mother asked when they could see him. The doctor said he was still out, but they could come in and see him now. So Amanda took her mother by the arm and led her to the recovery room where her father lay on a stretcher hooked up to an IV and monitors.

"Daddy." She rushed to him and touched his arm and tried to put her head down on his chest, but she couldn't get close because there were too many tubes, and she was afraid of pulling something out, so she moved away. They had said something about infection. She might have a cold. When she stepped back, she nearly bumped into her mother who was taking a handful of herbs from her purse and swallowing them without water. She had said nothing directly to Amanda since they had come down. *Is she mad at me? Disappointed?* Amanda tried to figure out her changed mother and her ill father.

Vermont had always been the place where she didn't know what to expect; this had been the predictable place, the place she came for solace, her parent's home, her anchor.

Her father woke up before they left the hospital, his skin so pale and transparent she could see the veins in his wrists. He smiled at her and said he was going to be alright. She had been so preoccupied at Christmas time she hadn't noticed how much weight he had lost. He looked at her with watery eyes unfocused from drugs and pain and tried to assure her he would be alright. She hugged him as well as she could with all the tubes around, afraid to kiss him, afraid she might give him a slight cold. Wanting to touch, but afraid to, never wanting to let go.

That night Amanda stayed in her childhood room. Jason was downstairs in the basement on the couch, a room that held little comfort for Amanda since the machines were not there anymore. She knew she would not sleep. The storm was over. She sat on the bed with a pillow behind her and a pillow in front of her and stared out the window at the dark sky. She tried to sleep for a while, tried to read, thought about going down to make coffee.

Finally, she gave up and went to the window and looked down into the yard where she used to have her tea parties when she was little. Funny how her parents had stayed here all these years. When she was a toddler, they had left rainbow house and moved all over the place until they settled here. How could they change so much, so quickly, especially her mother who had once been willing to give up everything to be with her dad?

Her father would have stayed in Vermont. She was sure of that. He had wanted to stay at Rainbow House. She could tell by the way he used to talk about it, the excitement in his voice when he used to tell her stories. She knew he missed the machines even if he never played them anymore. She should have grown up there. Her father would have been happier. It was her mother who had needed all this stability. Now her father might be dying and had never lived the life he wanted.

It wasn't fair. She wanted to punch the window just to hear glass shatter, feel blood on her hands, and cry for what she had done, whatever it was, whatever had caused them to leave the Rainbow House. Maybe she sleepwalked there, even when she was a toddler. Her mother could have been afraid she would disappear into a mountain of snow, get hit by a snowplow. She went to the bed and punched the pillow over and over again. *Why did you do it? Why did you keep us from living up there? Why did you give up your dreams?* Was it her birth that had somehow changed their lives? She wrapped herself in a down comforter as if it were a magic cloak, walked to the window with her pillow, and fell asleep on the floor.

She woke up all mixed up about time. There was an old alarm clock in her room, but it wasn't plugged in. Was it still January? What day was it? Maybe she was supposed to be working today, she thought, in a panic. She couldn't remember the number to call for work and then remembered Jason was downstairs. He would know it. She went downstairs following the smell of coffee to the kitchen. It was so quiet in the house, but someone had brewed coffee. Where were Jason and her mom? They better not have gone to the hospital without her.

She looked downstairs and there they were sitting on the floor meditating, surrounded by crystals. In desperation, she almost felt like joining them, but instead, she closed the door, looked up the number to the hospital, and called to see how her father was feeling. He'd had a good night, still mostly sleeping.

"Tell him we'll be there in a little while," she said, then waited about twenty minutes before opening the door to the basement again. Now they were chanting. And she thought she had been going on some strange head-trips. *Why don't they just get their butts up and go to the hospital?* She wanted to shout at them, but even she was reluctant to break the spell.

"I'm going to the hospital," she yelled down, finally.

Her mother opened her eyes and looked up to the top of the stairs.

"Wait for us," Jason yelled. She walked down the stairs and sat down next to her mother, put her arm around her, and looked into her swollen eyes. The anger she had felt last night was fading.

Amanda spoke very softly. "I called. They said we could go any time since he's in ICU."

Her mother didn't say anything.

"I'll call Peter. I'm sure he'll want to come with us," she said a little louder.

Still, her mother said nothing.

She looked at Jason. He looked away. She was getting angry again. She sat up pleading for something.

"Yesterday they said we could go in anytime. They let you go in early when someone's in ICU. Are you going to just sit around with this stupid chanting and crystals all day?" Amanda asked loudly.

Who is being the practical one now? she thought, as she ran up the stairs. She woke up the dog that had been sleeping under the dining room table and almost tripped over him as she went for the phone and dialed Peter's number. He wasn't home. Where in the hell was he? Didn't he know she wanted to be with him today? She needed him? Where in the hell was he?

When she hung up the phone, Jason and her mother were in the kitchen.

"We were just getting ourselves ready, spiritually, to see him," Jason said. "You should do the same. He doesn't need any anger and negativity right now."

Amanda shook her head and drank another cup of coffee.

By the time they got to the hospital, Amanda was ready to go back to Vermont and take her father with her. Her mother was so annoying and even Jason. She still couldn't get in touch with Peter. She had wanted to take two cars, but her mother wouldn't hear of it, and her mother seemed so needy, she just gave in. She had wanted to stop by Peter's, but not with these two. She was relieved to see her father was awake and eating. He was still in the ICU surrounded by tubes and beeping monitors, but he smiled at them and put aside his vanilla pudding. Soon, he closed his eyes again.

Amanda stayed with her father while her mother and Jason searched for a nurse for information. Hospitals made her uncomfortable. She sat next to the bed, unable to say anything, just staring at the walls and watching the dripping and listening to the beeps. She closed her eyes trying to pretend these were only the beeps of video games, and the IV was filling her dad with energy dots to evade the mouth of the monster.

"You want some books?" she asked him finally, hoping he could hear through all those layers of medication "Do you want me to bring some movies?"

She felt hands on her shoulder, looked up, and saw Peter. *Thank God.* They kissed on the lips.

"They almost wouldn't let me in. Said he had too many visitors"

Amanda sighed. "Jason and mom are running around trying to track down information from a nurse or a doctor. They're making me crazy. They were downstairs chanting before we came. I was trying to call you so I wouldn't have to drive with them."

"I was at the University. I'm teaching an interim course. It starts next week. I wanted to get things organized."

"Oh." Amanda looked again at her father; nothing seemed to matter now. Peter pulled up a chair next to her, and she rested her head on his shoulder. The university. It seemed so long ago that she had taught there.

"They haven't found a replacement for you yet," he said.

Oh, please, Peter, she thought, *no pressure, not now*.

Her mom came back into the room. "They're going to move him to a regular room later today." She was beaming with an unworldly smile.

Oh man, Amanda thought. *She's losing it.*

"I wish he could come home." Her mother sighed. "I want him to get into a healthier zone than a hospital."

Jason came in right after her.

"It even smells terrible in here," he whispered to no one in particular. "Haven't they ever heard of aromatherapy?"

Chapter Two

It's funny how they treat her after the incident at the store. Suzanne is more guarded toward her, more attentive, but in a different kind of way than before. Gloria's outburst has actually given her power of some kind, and it is as if Suzanne, by not telling Thomas about it, is holding onto power of her own. She knows Suzanne hasn't told Thomas because he is acting as if she is heading toward normalcy and seems to be waiting for her to desire another field trip into the real world. The best thing is that Amanda seems much less guarded with her. That her mommy could go away and come back with ice cream and presents seems to have opened up a trust she has not felt with Amanda for a long time.

All through the next week, Gloria rises with a purpose. She plants her vegetable garden and flowerbeds at the edge of the woods. Thomas and Amanda come out with snacks and lemonade. When she gets tired, she goes to the bench. Sits, rests, and remembers good things. She remembers Amanda's birth and her infant suckling, her downy hair that Gloria would smell and kiss. Could this be postpartum depression when she remembers she loved motherhood? The weight of her baby's body on her lap when they bathed her and brought her to Gloria in the evening. That weight outside of her body instead of inside; she remembers the wonderful, new feeling as she pushed the blanket away from the baby's face, held the back of her head as she had been taught, and first put her finger into the baby's mouth to teach her to root for the nipple. She remembers it all, and it should have been good, but somehow it gave her an empty feeling. Why was it so painful to remember this love? She would make herself remember through the pain. Get to what had broken inside her. She needed to. She needed to for Amanda.

Determined to get to the bottom of what is going on with her, Gloria is reading some of Suzanne's books at night when everyone is asleep. She puzzles over what she thinks must be postpartum depression because she can't even remotely think that she would want to harm her baby. Thomas and Amanda go out for ice cream every day now inviting Gloria who just shakes her head so they always bring some back for her, and their new evening routine is ice cream sodas.

She sits on the bench and thinks of how she is losing her acute sense of hearing as she moves back into the region of everyday life. Identifying the birds is harder than it had been a few weeks ago, and she no longer has the sense of when the deer will pass through the back yard. Her time on the bench seems more haphazard. Her memory is opening up to the larger world, the world outside the deep emotions, but it comes in fits and starts like an eye blinking.

In her memory, she goes back further than before. She thinks of chalk and sour milk. Clues come and go like falling stars at the periphery of her conscious mind. She is trying to keep the images in her vision, but they disintegrate before she can grasp their meaning. Why does she feel an emptiness even about her childhood? A childhood she'd always considered happy. It must have been that she was remembering how the smell of her milk, leaking when she was not breastfeeding Amanda anymore, made her think of the small milk in cardboard containers they used to have at recess in first grade. It always smelled sour and not like the cold bottles her mother fetched from their doorstep every morning and placed immediately into the refrigerator. It had disappointed her that it was not cold, not like home. She had wanted something familiar. Her family had moved into a different house over the summer, not far from where they had lived before, but in a better section of town.

She remembers her parents were very happy because it was a nicer house, a nicer neighborhood. Her father's business was doing well. It had been a happy time for the family so she hadn't wanted to tell them she was lonely. She missed the old place, the place they had wanted to get away from. Even her sister who was three years older than her hung back from the kids at the new school. There was no help there. Had Suzanne been offish and socially awkward before this? Gloria didn't know. She had only just started school and had not had the opportunity to see if her sister had established any friendships beyond the narrow streets of the old neighborhood.

She knew there was one girl a few houses away whom Suzanne considered her best friend, and her parents had had to assure her that they were not moving so far away that they would not see each other at least on a weekly basis. She had seen them holding hands on the day the moving truck was there, swearing they would always be best friends, living for the day when they would be at the regional high school and see each other every day again.

Was that move the start of her parents nagging Suzanne about being too introverted, too bookish? Gloria couldn't remember, but she remembers that all through their childhood, they had pegged Suzanne as the studious one, the serious one, and Gloria as the airhead who liked to shop. Her father even then wanted Suzanne to take over his business, and her mother saw Gloria as the one who would be her little debutante.

She did not want to put any expectations on Amanda, did not want to control her life like that. What was she doing here, then, mute on this bench unable to articulate her overwhelming love for her daughter without a profound feeling of emptiness getting in the way? Why was she obsessing now on the smell of milk, the smell of her own body after having Amanda? Why did even the memory of the smell make her choke and feel a deep loneliness?

That year, she remembers, the first year they really had money, she could feel a change not only in the place they lived, but in the way they lived. Her mother took them downtown shopping more often and told them they would only be shopping in the better stores. There was also an anxiety that had never been there before about what she would wear and how she would decorate the house.

They shopped at Denholms, Eddies, Filenes. She remembers that as her mother became more secure in money, she became more nervous. She had to shop at the best stores, and even Suzanne and Gloria had to dress in a certain way and behave in a certain way. She was the wife of the president of a company now—even her stockings had to be a particular brand.

Gloria remembered trying to sit patiently as her mother pulled out one dress after another, looking herself over in a full-length mirror. The sales ladies always said they looked good, but she would try to solicit Suzanne's opinion who would hardly notice anything around her, her head in a book. Soon, Gloria remembered, with Suzanne's lack of interest, her mother began to turn to her instead asking how did a hat look or a dress fit, making Gloria a conspirator in this world of obligated spending. Her mother's attention had made Gloria feel grown up. The excitement about this new ability to purchase the best was already seeping into Gloria something that later made her feel guilty when Thomas spoke about people being too materialistic.

As much as she'd loved him, she'd still felt the sting of rejection, as if Thomas' family were better than hers for having less. It was the other side of the idealism that attracted her to him, the smugness. *If they could have had more money*, she thought, *his family would have jumped at the chance.*

What would the schools here be like for Amanda? She and Thomas had always planned on home-schooling. She looked up and saw a hawk perched in the oak at the edge of the woods.

Strange that she hadn't heard or seen it land. *Such large birds, so silent in their majesty.* It gives her a chill as she imagines its pointy beak, its glassy eyes scouring the landscape for prey. She shifts on the bench, and the bird unwraps its large wings plunging itself into the chaos of air with the reckless trust of instinct. If she could only measure up, accept chaos with such grace. She cringes reflexively as the shadow of wings pass over her, the soft underbelly of whitish brown pulled along with the currents. She licks her lips, her mouth suddenly very dry.

She pads over to the woods, the movement of her body a relief after hours of sitting. She picks up a feather, twirls it around in her fingers, and places it in the knot of a braid in her hair. She braids her hair every day now, one long braid on the side that falls to the front in a thick rope of auburn. Suzanne had been happy to see her fuss with her hair and says it shows she is getting better, taking an interest in her appearance. Thomas has never liked her taking so much time on such trivialities, but fixing her hair had always relaxed her. Brushing it out is a special comfort these days as she unwinds the knot of braid before going to bed and trying to sleep. Any routine helps, any repetitive movement that will ground her.

For lack of anything else to do, she sits down again and fidgets with the edge of her braid. The thick, uneven strands clump together in what could be a paintbrush, and she remembers as a child looking at paintings and sometimes wanting to be in them, wishing she could paint herself into some static scene of peaceful landscape or just walk into the frame, insert herself into an unchanging landscape. She wishes she could do that now.

The energy of the movement of life could be so draining, but she has to keep remembering. She cannot forget her daughter. Even when she had been in the middle of the fog, she thinks, she remembered one thing—holding Amanda in her arms. As all the forces of gravity pulled her deep into herself, she swirled her around. She could not let herself believe that she had been a total blank, a flopping rag doll without emotions. But, even that, she cannot remember.

She smiles, remembering her favorite doll. Her father had brought it home and given it to her right before they had moved—a doll she could dance with. Made of cloth and nearly her height, it had hands that were like round, cloth paws and feet that were soft black shoes with black straps attached to the bottom. She could strap the doll's feet onto her own, hold it out from her body in a waltz position, and glide around the kitchen floor. Or she could hold both its hand/paws, attach its feet to hers, and twirl around the kitchen in a wild polka. She had brought the doll to their new house but had not been allowed to dance in the kitchen there because she might break something or mar the chrome on the gleaming counters, and her shoes would ruin the finish on the floor. They had a housekeeper who came in and knew how to keep everything shiny.

Had she turned into that doll when she was in the gray? Her body a floppy mass that someone else controlled? From now on, she would always keep control of her own movements. She would speak in her own time and remember in her own time, too.

She remembers the smell of chalk from her first year at school and the squeak as the teacher wrote on the blackboard. Writing and reading were new and interesting. Her teacher wrote fast—click, click , click on the blackboard—with a nervous energy that moved from her head to her hand, to the movement of her fingers. Brisk, sharp letters— she wished she could write that fast. She had liked the repetition. It had never bored her to write the same sentence and short paragraph over and over again. That is how they taught in those days, grinding it into your head. It had its advantages.

By the holidays, her mother had decided that Worcester was just not big enough for shopping. She took them to Boston and

New York so their dresses and shoes would be different from everyone else's. They stayed in hotels. Her father had business meetings while the girls shopped. She remembers walking along Newbury Street holding her mother's hand and how they stopped at displays of mannequins enjoying Christmas in their static joy.

In New York, the Christmas windows had simply scared her. Life-size teddy bears with huge green bows posed at drum sets, on bicycles. Scenes of motion and life, yet static, like the pictures she had tried to imagine walking into, only these were not just landscapes. There was another dimension, an almost-life. Even her father joined them one day on a special family outing. She remembers now how her parents were the ones who stared with wonder, pointing as she stood very close to them, trying to show excitement instead of fear. Nodding her head, not saying a word, she would glance over at Suzanne who looked bored as usual, realizing that she was the one her parents were depending on to channel their childhood hopes. Even Santa Clause had scared her that year.

The store in New York was too big with a line winding all the way up the stairs to where Santa sat. She wanted to see Santa at Denholmsin Worcester, sit on his lap there. He had looked more tired that year, less cheery as he reached for small wrapped packages from under the tree beside his chair and handed one to each child after they whispered to him their yearly desires. Smile for the camera, and then she was abruptly picked up by a stranger and handed back to her parents. "Isn't that nice?" her parents said. "You even got a present before Christmas."

It was funny, Gloria thought, how she could remember this particular Christmas from so many years ago but could not remember last Christmas. Her first holiday with Amanda was like a black hole in her memory, like the black holes scientists had discovered out in the universe that seemed to be pouring everything into a vortex. *Then, it was gone. Where did it go?* How long would she have to sit, day after day, piecing her life together like a crazy quilt that had been ripped apart? She would have to be patient; that is all there was to it. She'd place all the squares out, puzzle them out until they fit into the right sequence, then take up the needle, and sew as she stitched all her parts back together.

She hears the front door slam; Thomas and Amanda finally come out to see her. Her heart rejoices, jumps inside her, always a chance that emotion might break through the wall. But she looks up and it is only Thomas. Where is their child? He holds a bouquet of wildflowers, presents it to her, sits next to her on the bench, and kisses her on the lips.

"Happy First Anniversary," he says.

She smiles at him, coyly, as she does not even remember getting married.

"Later we'll have champagne," he says

She kisses back, trying to make herself speak, trying to explain what a phony she is. She can't remember the wedding. He could tell her the story of their wedding, if he knew. Strange that when they went to the calendar today, Suzanne didn't remind her. *Was she at our wedding?*

Gloria wanted to reciprocate the attention from Thomas, but she sat pondering how this self-imposed silence, though necessary, was difficult. It kept her from getting help, from sharing love, but it bought her time, long stretches of time, to put her life together in her own way until she was ready for all the distractions of her own voice, spoken. Maybe it was selfish, but this time, she wouldn't give everyone what they wanted until she was ready. Parts of her remembered everything, but those parts of her were selfish and hoarding and afraid. So afraid that speaking the words would make it so.

In the evening, after a glass of champagne that makes her dizzy, she kisses Thomas with more feeling. Suzanne has taken

Amanda out so they can be alone. They are playful in their touching, and Thomas seems more relaxed. She does not feel the urgency of speech. As she falls asleep in his arms, he kisses her on the head, and says I love you in a determined but wistful way as if she weren't really there, as if it was a burden to love her, as if their love has suffered great loss.

Chapter Three

"THE SNOW HAD BEGUN IN THE GLOAMING AND BUSILY ALL THE NIGHT—" —WHITTIER

Amanda pulled into the driveway of the university and took a deep breath, the same old dirty snow in the parking lot of the same old building. She unlocked the door. It was freezing inside. Small icicles had formed even on the inside of the windows. She looked out at the large oak, its branches covered with ice sticking out every which way like Einstein's unruly, white hair. The building smelled musty. Probably nobody had used it since she was gone. At least she had kept her key.

She didn't want anyone, especially Peter, to know she had come here. Maybe she hadn't totally broken her connection with teaching. A sabbatical, they might still call it. She looked around her office. The old coffee maker, the mat on the floor—nothing had been moved, nothing touched. She looked out the window with the beveled glass, and the distortions made her mind drift. Maybe she could hole away here? Maybe this could be her new, quiet place to breathe—away from her mother, away from Peter, away from her father's illness.

She panicked at the thought that the university may want to get rid of this building; it might not even be worth heating if no one taught here. She could buy it, bring down her telescopes, her books, her video games. She'd have a skylight built into the roof, maybe even a dome. Just like Maria Mitchell, she'd have her own little school here.

She could teach Kepler's dream, and it wouldn't matter how many students showed up because she would be in charge. She stared out the window and tried to figure out a plan. She'd teach the spring semester and then approach the school over the summer about buying this building. They might sell it cheap, happy to get it off their hands. That way she could be near all the people she loved and have her own world.

Everyone was annoying her now except for her sick father. Seeing him just made her sad. Jason was the worst, buttering her mom up for some reason. He was even worse than Peter. He had taken a leave of absence in Vermont to nurse her dad. *Who does that?* She supposed he was good at caring for all of them. He made sure they were well fed, anyway. The smell of the soups and breads he made every day made them all feel more cared for, and she supposed her mother needed that right now. She certainly couldn't handle it. She could only sit with her dad, read to him, watch movies. She'd never been good at nursing.

She had called the hotel to say she would be out for a while, but she hadn't officially quit. Not yet. She didn't want to tell anyone, even Jason, that she was thinking of not going back up there to live because somehow she thought he would be disappointed. She'd always thought of the chalet as haunted and that Jason was the medium. Part of the game she played, sometimes she thought of him as not a real person or as someone with one foot in another world. His mother had died young, she knew, wasted away with cancer, and he'd cried when he'd told her about it. She was sick all the time even when they were children at Stellafane. He had told her sometimes he thought he still heard her voice. Is that why he stayed here to take care of her father? She didn't want to think about that right now. She needed to be here for her dad, too. She needed to be strong for him, and she needed to have some kind of routine—any boring routine. She would accept any mundane, boring lifestyle. *Just, please God, make my father well.*

She sat down on the mat and stared at the walls. "Daddy, I love you," she whispered.

She punched the mat with her fist, the release of anger

shooting through her gut and into her brain, making her too restless to sit. She got up and kicked the matt, paced the room, kicked the mat again, and kicked it again. Still, she wanted to punch something. What if she punched a hole in the window, the one with distorted glass? Would she see clearly then? Ripping her hand through the hard pane, would there be blood or would her arm flow through smoothly transporting her to another place, a place of understanding?

"Daddy," she sobbed, her voice getting louder with each word. "You have to get better. You can't leave me." She was almost shouting. "You can't go away."

She pounded her foot hard enough to feel the floorboards shake, and she almost felt the glass shatter. Then she collapsed onto the mat and lay there for what seemed like a very long time, but when she finally got up enough energy to walk to her car, it was barely noon. She'd never been good at keeping track of time.

She stopped at Dunkin Donuts for coffee and to wash her face before going home, not wanting anyone to know she'd been crying. She entered the door of her parent's house hesitantly, with a sick stomach. Now her days depended on how her dad was doing. This morning, before she left, he had been sleeping peacefully.

The smell of the bread Jason was cooking overpowered the antiseptic smell of the den where her father was staying since he'd come home from the hospital. Jason had him out of the hospital bed and propped up on a recliner. The TV was on, but his eyes were closed. Amanda sat down on the couch next to him and listened to him breathe; she glanced at Comedy Central on the TV. It was part of Jason's overall therapy plan, laughter therapy, really, he'd said. When she looked at him wearily, he said, "You can literally laugh yourself well." She got a three stooges tape, which she knew was one of her father's favorites, and put it into the VCR. He opened his eyes, and she sat with him on the edge of the recliner.

She knew the chemo made him weak, as well as the cancer, but she was glad Jason had not talked her mom and dad into refusing that treatment. He was really trying to butt in way too much now. They literally had to kick Jason out of the room when they made the decision, as her mother had been leaning towards alternatives. That was fine, Amanda thought, along with Chemo.

Her father opened his eyes.

"Hi dad." She leaned over and kissed him, and he must have seen the concern in her eyes.

"It's just the chemo, honey. It will get rid of the cancer."

Amanda nodded and watched Moe iron the side of Larry's head with a hot iron. "Ouch," she said.

Her dad laughed.

She sat down on the couch. "I went to the university today, to my old office."

"You think of trying to get your job back?"

"Maybe, if it's still available."

"I think Peter said it was."

"No. I don't know. I don't want him to know what my plans are right now." She laughed. "Especially since I don't have any. It was deserted except for a few offices in administration, but it was kind of nice to be there again." Amanda sighed.

Her dad had nodded off.

Jason poked his head in. Amanda looked at him. He looked at her dad and shook his head. She knew what he thought: chemo is poison. He came over and took her hand leading her into the kitchen. "Sit. Eat."

She looked out the sliding glass door to the trees bent down with ice as he waited on her. He brought a plate of bread, a bowl of soup, and even brought flowers for the table. He said nothing, just watched her eat. It was funny how Jason got himself into these roles of waiter, nurse, cook, healer. Jason was a wanna-be medicine man.

She put her spoon down, lowered her head, and tears dripped off her chin adding salt to her soup. Jason put his arm around her and brought her head to his shoulder.

"Thank you for taking care of my father" she whispered, grateful and resentful all at once. She knew she couldn't do it even if she wanted to, and her mother was just useless lately.

"I'm getting paid," he said. "This gig pays me much more than the hotel," but she knew it was a labor of love, Jason trying to save someone because he hadn't been able to save his mother.

"Still, you have to stay down here, away from your life in Vermont. I know you love it up there. I know you're uncomfortable being away for too long."

Jason pulled his arm away and went over to the sink. "Actually, I'm beginning to get a little sick of the winters up there."

He cleaned the dishes and cleared the counters in what he now seemed to consider his kitchen. That seemed to be fine with her mother, at least for now, remarkable enough, because everything else must have been so overwhelming that she didn't want to cook or bake or even clean her own kitchen. Amanda had not seen sunshine muffins on the counter since her father had gotten sick.

"Eat your soup," Jason said, as he left the kitchen. "I have to go. Your mother is showing houses all afternoon, and I won't be home until after dinner. Make sure your dad takes his pills around three, and try to get him to have some soup and bread when he wakes up."

"Yes, sir," Amanda said and saluted him. "Thanks, Jason, really," she said. "Thanks for everything."

Jason was seeing one of the nurses at the hospital where her father had been and she wondered if they were having dinner together. It didn't matter; she was glad he had a girlfriend.

Only now Peter realized he wasn't gay and was paranoid about him living here. She just wondered what was keeping him down here. Would he really quit his job? Vermont was the place that Jason had always said was better than anywhere else. It was purer, he said, more honest. The trees were bigger, the snow was higher, magical things happened in Vermont. When she and Jason had been together, it had been like their Oz. It's where her parent's had taken flight in the seventies, the rainbow house. Would it be left to a community of ghosts?

She needed to go up soon. Check on the chalet. She wanted to go up with Jason, but he was so busy and preoccupied. She could go with Peter but she wasn't sure if that was a good idea. Maybe it would be best if she went alone. A few days by herself to think about if she wanted her job back and if she wanted try again with Peter. It had been two weeks since her dad had been home from the hospital. Could she handle being that far away, even for one day?

The phone rang. She got it before the second ring. Peter. His voice sounded so far away.

"How's he doing today?"

"Okay, I guess, tired."

She brought the phone downstairs looking into the hallway mirror as she went by. She hadn't had time to get her haircut, and the spikes were growing out and down. She almost looked like a girl. She slumped down on the couch while Peter talked to her about the syllabus he was putting together for Spring Semester. How could he still have so much enthusiasm?

"What are you doing tonight?" he asked.

Amanda sat up taken by surprise. They hadn't had an actual date in a long time. Peter was coming over a lot, especially the first week her dad was home, but they hadn't talked about their relationship—that tricky question that lurked between them.

"Nothing, you want to come over?" She asked it quickly before she had to commit to an actual date.

"How about we go out to eat? The Struck or maybe Tatnuck Book Seller?"

"I don't know. My mom is out right now, and Jason is out tonight. I can't leave dad alone."

"I'll be over in a while then, and when your mom comes home, we'll go. See you in a while," he said and hung up.

That was it. Peter had made up his mind. They were going on a date.

Amanda went back up into the living room. Her dad was still sleeping, and the three stooges were still slapping each other around. She went to the couch, covered up, and fell asleep until the doorbell rang. She staggered, as a sleepwalker, to the door and opened it to a woman with what looked like a backpack and also a clipboard with several important papers. The visiting nurse—he still had one a day. She took his blood pressure, his temp, changed the bag while Amanda sat in the kitchen and put on some coffee. She looked at the time and realized she had forgotten his medicine. She was a terrible nurse to her father, such a terrible, forgetful daughter. She would give it to him when the nurse left.

The nurse wasn't long, and when she was done, she sat with Amanda for a few minutes in the kitchen asking her questions and reassuring her that her father was improving. She accepted a cup of coffee from Amanda while she filled out papers. After she left, Amanda brought her coffee into the living room.

"That smells so good," her father said.

Amanda smiled sheepishly. She knew he wasn't supposed to have coffee. It was strictly forbidden on Jason's care plan.

Please, he said with his eyes, as if he were trapped and she was the only other sane one in the house.

So she went and brought him a mug with lots of cream and one sugar, just the way he liked it, and hoped that her mother would not walk in soon. She was a terrible nurse. If he died, it would be her fault.

The Three Stooges had ended, an old Bette Davis movie was on TV now. *Whatever Happened to Baby Jane*—good campy fun, so she pulled a chair right next to where her father was sitting, rested her head on his shoulder just like when she was a little girl, and they watched the movie together in silence until her mother came home.

Peter came in right after her mother looking at their transformed living room. He hadn't seen the latest therapy. A circle of crystals dangled from the ceiling like some hideous mobile.

"Why didn't they just place the bed under a chandelier?" Peter asked as they walked into the kitchen and away from her mother.

"Dad isn't complaining about it. He says if it makes them feel better, what's the harm?"

"If they fall on his head and knock him out, he could be harmed."

Amanda looked at him and laughed.

He took her arm. "I have to get you out of this house tonight, skinny girl. You want to go to the Struck?"

"I think you need reservations there."

"The struck? I love that place," her mother said when she walked into the kitchen. "It was started in the seventies by some of our college friends. It was called the Struck of Loke then." She sat down at the table with them. "A couple of guys who baked wonderful breads were looking for a place to sell them besides just to college kids. The waiters used to serve you in whiteface like mimes, and there were life-size people made of papier-Mache placed here and there at different tables."

Amanda just watched amazed as her mother spoke so freely and unguardedly about her "pre-rainbow house" days. It seemed she was more accessible somehow, as if, with this new grief and worry, there was some letting go of the past.

"We were thinking of going there tonight," Peter said. "But I think we need reservations."

"I think you do," her mother said. "It's not very big. When you're dad's better, I think that will be the first place we will go."

Peter was right. She had to get out of the house. Her mother's new openness was kind of scary. She was gushing in that manic way that alarmed Amanda, that something in her mother's voice that she had never trusted. They decided to eat at Tatnuck Bookseller. She felt bad for her dad trapped here; her mother had already put in a tape of healing scenes and music for them both to watch for the evening. She was sure her father had had enough of waterfalls and sunsets. Amanda warmed up some soup for her dad and kissed him on the cheek. Then she and Peter left for dinner.

It was Friday night, so Tatnuck was crowded. They had time to browse before their name was called and their table was ready. There were lots of books on sale tables, books about the holidays and books about the millennium. All the gifty things were on sale now. There was a book about the origins of coffee boxed with Egyptian mugs on either side—mugs she would have liked, with nice thick handles. There was a book about Van Gogh boxed between candles with stars.

She strolled through the aisles like she was at the circus. She'd been alone so much in Vermont and then only focused on her father's illness since coming down that she was unaccustomed to the abundance of stimulation. So many people were in one place talking, bustling, examining merchandise, like old-fashioned scenes of just before Christmas. She closed her eyes, breathed deeply for a moment, and heard a distant bell weaving through the conversations around her. She heard a child laughing. Would she be thrown back into another century right here in the store? She opened her eyes to see some unattended kids playing with wind chimes that were dangling from shelves in the new age area. Then she almost tripped over a giant copy of *If You Give a Mouse a Cookie* that had fallen on the floor. Finally, she heard their name called and looked around for Peter. She waited at the cash register until she saw him coming. They were seated at the Star Trek table.

Their first real date in longer than Amanda could remember. There wasn't exactly privacy, but the atmosphere was good. A lot of professors from Worcester U ate lunch here. She expected Peter to order a beer, but he ordered ice tea. She drank wine, and after two glasses, she began to feel a little buzz. She ate slowly. Her favorite part was the salad and bread. Peter had a large plate of some kind of fish, probably salmon, but she had not been paying attention when he ordered. She managed to pick at a small dish of pasta. She hadn't realized how tired she was, and relaxed from the wine, she began to nod off. She could feel Peter staring at her.

"I'm not much company," she said.

"You probably haven't been sleeping much." He brought his chair toward hers.

"It seems like I do. It seems like that's all I do." That was part of the problem; she had nothing to do down here.

"You want some coffee?"

"Black and strong, very strong," she said.

"That could be why you haven't been sleeping."

Before she could get the 'you sound like my mother out,' he was on his way to the coffee bar and looking into the desert case.

She watched him behind half-closed eyes. There was this commitment thing again, staring her right in the face. How much of herself would he expect her to give up? Would she get sick of him, he of her? He had such a cute butt, and he was good to her, but he was older. Did he want to be her father or something? He wasn't that much older. She was afraid he would dominate her. He came back with two cups of coffee and made it a point to tell her he was drinking decaf. When the dessert tray came, she ordered something with lots of chocolate—real chocolate, not carob. The sugar should knock her out in a while, even if the coffee kept her awake.

"This was nice," she said as they drove out of the parking lot and onto Chandler Street. Peter had his arm on the back of the seat around Amanda.

"Want to go to the apartment? We could call your mom from there. Tell her where we are?"

She noticed he didn't say 'his' or 'our' just 'the' apartment. Amanda wanted to go, kind of, but she was afraid. Afraid of what, she wasn't sure. "I don't think so. My mom might be lonely. My dad falls asleep early."

She was afraid Peter would be angry, but he smiled at her.

"That's alright. I'll just take you home, and we can go parking in the driveway."

Peter stopped the car when they were almost to the top of her parent's long driveway. Amanda crawled into his lap on the driver's side, and they kissed. He was just putting his hand up the back of her sweater when headlights came from behind blinding them. Peter sat up and the horn honked, and one of Amanda's legs kicked a cup of coffee, spilling it onto the floor.

Jason came to the window. Peter rolled it down.

"You guys okay?"

"We were," Peter said.

Jason looked at Amanda who shrugged her shoulders and looked uncomfortable.

"I can just walk up to the house." Jason said." I'll leave my car at the bottom."

"That's alright. We were just going in."

Peter put the car into gear and drove the rest of the way too quickly. Jason followed, and they all walked into the house together as if they were best friends.

"The kids are home," Amanda's mother said in a voice too

chipper as if they were all twelve years old. Amanda was glad to see her father was at least still awake and had even moved into the kitchen. She could tell Jason was freaking out because her mother had moved him out of the chair. He was still too controlling about the whole nursing thing.

"Isn't it wonderful?" Her mother gushed, "He wanted to move around tonight, and we're looking at some old photo albums."

"It's a good sign," Jason said. "But I think he should go back into the living room now."

"I am getting tired," her dad said.

Jason gave her mom a look. "How many cups of tea did he drink?" Jason asked as they brought him into the living room. "I'm supposed to monitor his intake of fluids for the visiting nurse."

Peter sighed, groaned.

"Sure you don't want to go over and stay at the apartment?"

She wanted to say yes, but something she didn't understand was keeping her here. "I don't want to go out again. It's so cold, and it's late."

He pouted

"Why don't you stay here? You can sneak up to my room in the middle of the night, even more fun than parking in the driveway."

"Where will I sleep?"

"Downstairs, in the 'fun room.' Even better, I'll sneak down there."

"That's Jason's room."

"He's been sleeping on the couch in the living room in case dad needs something in the night."

The light went out in the living room. Jason and her mom came back in, arguing. "He needs to stay in there near the crystals. He can't be moved around this late at night."

Amanda got up and closed the kitchen door so her father

wouldn't hear.

"It's better for him to get up and move around." Fascinating, her mother's bossiness was finally taking over.

"You put me in charge of his care, so you have to trust me."

"Watch it, Jason." Her mother shouted, "I can fire you just as quickly." Then she put her head down on the table and began to cry uncontrollably. Amanda and Jason sat down on either side and hugged her. Peter stood over Amanda and stroked her hair.

"Shh,"Amanda said. "Let's go downstairs so we don't wake daddy."

So they all went down, Amanda and Jason still holding onto her mother. Amanda asked Peter to grab the photo albums and bring them down. As soon as they were downstairs, Peter sat on the couch and started looking through the albums. Amanda sat by her mom on a stool while Jason went to the fridge and took out milk and fruit. Amanda watched him take some St. John's wart from under the counter and mix everything together in the blender.

"I'll fix us all something to calm our nerves and bring back vitality," Jason said.

"Just a beer for me," Peter called from the couch putting the albums down on the floor.

Amanda went in back to the fridge and got two beers.

"You're not having my special drink?" He sounded disappointed. Apparently he hadn't heard Peter over the sound of the blender.

"We all have our happy drinks," she said. "But I'll take two of the glasses."

She brought them over to the couch and poured the beer. Jason handed a glass of his special drink to her mother.

"Here's to daddy's health" she said. They all clinked glasses and drank.

"He's getting better," Jason said. "This is good. We've got to send positive energy up to him. We have to try to keep everything as positive as we can. It's a major part of his care plan."

"I didn't mean to yell up there Jason." She drank down the happy drink real fast. "It's just that I haven't been sleeping well. Even with those new herbs you gave me. I can make it to work, but I just think about him all day."

"I'm trying to help you," Jason said "Trying to take care of him so you can get some rest. That's what you pay me for. I'm here to take care of you, too."

"Dr. Quack," Peter whispered into Amanda's ear.

"The St. John's should help you sleep, and I'll do some reflexology to help get rid of your headache."

Peter whispered again, "Graduate of Quackster University."

Amanda laughed and hit him on the arm. She got up to get them both another beer and kissed her mom on the cheek as she walked by, glad that Jason was here to keep her mom occupied, but she still thought it was strange her mom was giving up so much power in this situation. She had been kind of glad when her mom had that outburst at Jason earlier. It surprised her that she would be that relieved at the return of the old control freak.

From way behind the shelves, she pulled out a bag of pretzels she'd bought and hidden behind the healthy stuff. Then she went back to the couch and sat next to Peter. Her mother came over and sat on the opposite side of the couch and took her shoes off. Jason, sitting cross-legged on the floor, took one of her feet then the other and squeezed on the toes explaining that as he massaged the left foot, the right side of her sinuses would drain, and working on the left foot would drain her right side.

"I didn't need to know that," Peter whispered into Amanda's ear. Amanda kicked him.

"That's much better," her mother said.

Amanda looked at the photo album and saw the usual pictures of their summers in Vermont and times at Stellafane. Peter had never seen them and seemed only vaguely interested.

"Remember this summer, mom?" she asked, taking the albums from her lap and bringing it to her mother. "I think I was about ten, and dad and I collected all that weird stuff and tried to make a flying machine."

Her mother was only half listening, enjoying her draining sinuses.

After she got to the last picture, there was a smaller album inside the big one. She'd never seen it before. She looked in amazement at the pictures of her parents wedding in Vermont. It was labeled Tom and Gloria June 1977. It was the back yard of the chalet.

The first picture was just of an arbor covered with flowers and folding chairs set up everywhere. In the next picture, her parents stood in front of the arbor. He wore a white tux with sandals, his hair was down to his shoulders, and he had a daisy stuck above his left ear. Her mother wore a crinkly yellow dress and hair down to her waist with a chain of daisies like a halo in her hair. In the next picture, she saw a little girl—herself?—pulling at her mother's dress. But how could it have been her? The dates were wrong.

Why hadn't she seen these pictures before? Anger rose in her gut, the kind of anger that had made her want to punch pillows and put her fist through glass. She had been told there were no pictures when she was a baby. Her parents were too poor or didn't have a camera up there, or whatever her mother had said. In the next one, her mother looked pregnant. Yes, even with that dress, loose as it was, she could see her mother's big tummy. So her mother must have been pregnant with her when they got married, so who was this other little girl who was so desperately clutching her mother's arm? Did Aunt Suzanne have a daughter? Did she have a cousin she didn't know about?

"Mom, was I around before you were married?" Amanda looked at her, holding down her anger. There must be a reason she had never seen these before, even though she had asked so many times for pictures, something of her early childhood. Her mom saw the small album she was holding. She went pale.

"Mom, were you pregnant with me when you got married?"

Her mother started to gag, to tremble. Now she was going to act all needy. What was the big deal? She didn't care if she was born or conceived before her parents were married. Was that the big secret? She always thought it was special enough that she was conceived and born at the Rainbow House. Her mother got up and went for the downstairs bathroom. Jason watched her, alarmed. It was too bad that all this was coming out with Jason and Peter here, but her mother should have shown her these pictures years ago. Jason looked like he was mad at her; Peter only looked puzzled. Amanda shrugged.

"I've never seen these pictures of my parents' wedding before. My mother told me there were none." She could hear her mother crying in the bathroom. "Oh, for God sakes," Amanda said and pounded on the door. "Mom, it's okay. I promise I won't ask any more questions. I don't care about the circumstances of my birth. I just wondered why I'd never seen the pictures."

He mother finally came out and collapsed on the couch. She sat up gagging between sobs. She whispered, "You had a sister.... and...I killed her."

Amanda sat by her mother and held her. Peter and Jason just stared.

"Leave us alone," Amanda shouted and gave them her most unhinging stare. Peter bolted upstairs, but Jason stayed behind. *He's so annoying. Some things can't be fixed with crystals and ginseng.* "Get the hell out of here." She yelled, and he finally left.

She could feel her mother convulsing in her arms. She knew

it couldn't be true what her mother was saying. There were probably a lot of kids up at the Rainbow House, now that she thought about it; they were probably all making love, not war, and not using birth control. Maybe one of the children up there got sick. They probably didn't have access to good medical care, and it was a commune, so all the little kids would have been considered her brothers and sisters.

"Mom" Amanda said. "It's alright. Something bad must have happened up there. I understand now why you don't like to talk about it. I'm sure it wasn't your fault."

Her mother stopped crying for a few minutes and wiped her eyes. "Amanda, you have to listen to me." She pleaded, "You had a sister, and she died because of me." She broke down into sobs again.

"Mom, stop it. You're all upset about dad. You don't know what you're saying."

Her mother got a fierce look in her eyes, grabbed the album from the table, and opened to the wedding pictures. "There" she pointed to the little girl tugging on her dress. "April Rainbow." Her chin was set firm, daring anyone's denial. "My baby." Her voice broke again, and she clutched the album to her chest rocking back and forth saying, "My baby, my baby."

Amanda shook her head and looked into her mother's swollen eyes. "I don't believe you," she said. "You're hallucinating or something."

Her mother held onto her and cried again, "She died because of me; I wasn't watching."

"Stop it." Amanda pulled away. "You're not making sense."

"Please forgive me. I was so frightened when you began to sleepwalk—afraid you would wander into the woods, into the snow."

Her mother began to cry hard, deep grieving cries. "Wander into the trees," she keened. "Wander into the snow."

Jason opened the door and walked down the stairs

sheepishly. Amanda nodded, and he came over to the couch.

"She was our spring baby." Her mother almost smiled. "And you were our summer one." She pointed to the picture. "She helped me make the daisy chain for my hair. She was so much fun and so full of life."

Her mother looked through her, her face haunted.

"When you were born, she was my little helper. She'd fetch me clean diapers and the pail. She'd follow me around, watch me breast feed, coo at you, trying to make you smile. That winter was cold and bitter with snowstorm after snowstorm, blizzard after blizzard. Spring never comes early up there. It was late March, and we were still getting snow, and I was telling your father I might not want to spend another winter there. It was too isolating with little children. It wasn't like it had been in the early seventies. The people who came around were more troubling. Bikers came and took advantage of our hospitality, and the runaways who came were younger and younger. A few years earlier, I would have admired their insistence on freedom and adventure, but I was growing out of all that because I was a mother. Our open living had become a kind of nightmare. I had thought we could make it last in the beginning, but your father did not want to give up his ideals."

Her mother slammed the book shut her mouth resolute, her chin trembling, she stared at the wall.

"The people who turned up and stayed with us the summer before you were born were just freeloaders. They didn't contribute to the household at all. I worried that there may be dangerous people around for the first time. I worried because I had a child."

"You were a good mother," Amanda said, hugging her, feeling weird to be reassuring her mother. She didn't really believe what her mother was saying. It must be some flashbacks; her mother must be reliving some bad acid trip from back in the day.

"You were the most precious little thing. You and April were my angels."

Peter opened the door. Amanda thought he had gone home by now.

"You're dad's up," he said. "He wanted to go into the kitchen so I helped him"

Jason flew up the stairs. Amanda and her mom went up after him. He insisted he wanted to be in another room for a while so all Jason could do was make them all some tea.

"Coffee for me," Amanda said.

"Me too," her dad said.

Jason said coffee was not part of the care plan.

"For God Sakes" he said. "I'll get up and make it myself."

Jason gave Amanda a nasty look. She gave him back a 'What?' look.

Her father went on. "Is part of the care plan to have everyone yelling and screaming and crying downstairs?"

Amanda had never seen her father so angry. In fact, she barely ever remembered seeing him angry at all.

He looked at them all. "What the hell is going on?"

Her mother moved her chair closer to his. She took his hand. "She knows, Thomas; she knows about April." She was not crying, but she was obviously holding his hand in a vice grip, as it was turning white. He was probably on pain meds and hardly felt it. It was one-thirty in the morning.

"Good," is all he said? "Thank God."

Amanda's mother began to tremble again. Tears fell into her teacup. "I told her how I killed her."

"Gloria, you didn't kill her."

"Please forgive me."

"Gloria, you didn't kill her. She suffocated, in the snow."

"It was my fault."

"She was playing."

"I should have been with her."

"You watched her from the window. She was used to the snow. There was so much that winter. She was almost five."

"But I wasn't out there." Gloria turned her head away.

"These things, they happen so fast, even if you were....No one can see anything like that happening; no one can do anything to stop it. I thought it was *my* fault.

"*It was my fault,*" her mother insisted

"Is that what you were thinking, Gloria, all those weeks, months?"

Her mother nodded her head.

"All these years?"

Her mother nodded again.

Amanda was hearing these strange words, a secret language between her parents being deciphered. As they talked about the child they had lost, she forced herself to stay up and listen. Peter had fallen asleep on the couch downstairs. Jason was nodding off in a kitchen chair. Amanda sat, drinking coffee, watching their faces as they talked about the child they had lost over twenty years ago. Her mother taking comfort from her pale sick husband, their talk now seemed to hold little emotion as if they were sharing a dream, a nightmare. She wasn't sure if they were aware that she was in the room. She put her head down on the table and pretended sleep hoping they would speak more freely. Her father spoke slowly as if he were acting, giving an aside in a play.

"We ran out together. I dug furiously through the snow, but I didn't dig fast enough. I thought it was my fault that I didn't dig fast enough, and when I got to her, the tiny lips were blue."

"She loved the snow," her mother said. "That was the funny thing about it. We could never keep her indoors when it was snowing."

It was like they were talking to Amanda, and they were talking to each other, and they were talking to themselves all at the same time.

"We could never keep her in. I was so worried about it. I was so worried about the people who might show up in the summer, like I had some premonition that we had to get out of there that winter because I was worried that some weirdo, some sick dangerous person would take her away. I never thought it would be snow. The snow that was falling and falling around us…"

"She loved the snow so much," her father said. "Remember when we made that entire snow family, just her and I?"

"It was too cold for Amanda to be out, so we watched from the window, Amanda and I."

"Remember how she would dance around and catch snowflakes on her tongue?"

"We couldn't keep her in. She loved the snow."

"And I kept digging and digging and digging to try to find her. Hadn't I told her that snow forts were dangerous?" Her father's voice sounded angry for few minutes, and then the emotion left again. "But it was hardly a fort at all."

"And she didn't have as much as a cold that winter," her mother said in a voice filled with something like amazement. "Everyone was getting the flu and coughing and fevers, but she didn't have anything more than a few sniffles all winter. I thought the outdoors was good for her. She always had healthy red cheeks when she came in, and her eyes would be shining waiting for me to warm up hot cocoa."

"I kept digging and throwing the snow out of the way sure I would find my little girl. I have nightmares of digging and digging and digging and pushing snow away."

"They have better medical care now, don't they, Thomas? If it happened today, maybe they could have saved her. There was no 911, no cell phones, no machines to keep people breathing."

"I did CPR." Anger again, despondency.

"I know you did, honey. You did all you could, even more. It should have never happened in the first place. I should have been out there with her. I should have seen what was going to happen. When I looked out and didn't see her there, I just thought she was behind the mound or had walked to the back of the house. Of course you always get that feeling of panic, but then somehow I just knew she was under."

Silence for a few minutes and Amanda longed to look up, but she didn't want to interrupt their private reverie. Her mother spoke again.

"I don't know if I thought I saw a leg kicking or if I just saw the snow moving but I just knew she was under. It was a windy day. It could have been the wind causing a wisp of flakes to be scattering from the pile. But somehow, I knew it wasn't. I shouldn't have let it happen in the first place. But if there had only been life flights and cell phones. It wasn't your fault, Thomas."

"It wasn't yours either."

"And I've been waiting all these years," Amanda's mom said, "for you to tell me you forgive me."

Amanda opened one eye and looked at her parents. They were in each other's arms sobbing. Her father looked paler than ever. She got up silently and poured more coffee, her back to them. She nudged Jason.

"I need help getting dad into bed," she said. By the time Jason rallied and got up, her parents were wrapped in each other's arms fast asleep.

Jason looked at Amanda. "This could be tricky."

Chapter Four

Gloria has run out of steam for the garden and sits alone on the bench this morning. It was hard for her to fall asleep last night. She was anxious about where Suzanne had taken the baby. She would just be starting to relax and enjoy her time with Thomas and suddenly she would panic. Had someone kidnapped her baby? Where would Suzanne be keeping her so late? She had been afraid Suzanne had taken her to a hotel and they would be away all night. She didn't think she could handle waking up in the morning and finding Amanda wasn't there. But Amanda was there in the morning, and Gloria had stood by her bed watching her listening to her breathe as the sun rose. Aunt Suzanne had kept her out way too late.

Gloria feels like her mind and memory are going to open up today, unfold like a morning glory. She feels giddy. That's why she sits rather than working in the garden. It's not a setback; it's a choice. As she and Thomas were drinking champagne last night, he talked a little about their wedding, and pictures began to form in her mind. Pieces of their life up here began to drift around the edges of her consciousness. She remembers how it had been a parade, a festival every day. She had got caught up in it, but it was not like real life. Even though she and her family had had money, they had worked very hard. It was hard to let go, to celebrate life. Copies of the book *Be Here Now* were cherished like the bible. That philosophy kept getting thrown in her face. Everybody was on a journey, but why did they have to end up here?

She remembers resentment, fear that Thomas would take up with someone else. Everyone slept around. To own someone was uncool, and it was wrong to be jealous. She remembers when they first came up here to establish the community.

Thomas drove the first group in the Rainbow Bus looking so sexy with a bandana around his curls. Joints were passed around, even acid; it made Gloria nervous they would get pulled over. They thought they lived in some kind of Neverland where nothing bad could happen to them. Gloria had never thought that way. Thomas had told her not to be so uptight.

Everyone was singing Country Joe and the Fish, elated because the Vietnam War was ending. Even though that year had started with Nixon's swearing in by late January the draft had ended and by spring, the troops were coming home. It looked like Nixon was already on his way out, the Watergate scandal closing in on him.

One generation had finally triumphed in its wild dance of peace, tromping through the Woodstock mud to get close enough to hear the music of Jimi Hendrix with his electrified guitar chords vibrating our national anthem through the air. She wasn't there, but she remembers seeing the movie at the drive-in. Remembers how when he first began to play it, his head was down, his eyes reverential and downcast, no flashiness, just slowly picking out each vibrating note like he was creating an energy, stronger than a moment of silence, trying to unite the whole country, unite generations in honoring our county's overwhelming loss.

She remembers when he got to the part about the rocket's red glare how he looked up suddenly, his body a ballet of jerky movements, his face contorted, soulful, painfully deep in concentration, channeling the movement of dying soldiers, giving up the notes to the air, bringing peace and war together in a macabre dance of pride and death. Had we taken our parent's hawkishness and made it our own? Powerful, moving and confusing, she had watched that anthem, that dance, and she had felt it too. Felt that in that moment he had brought together those clashing forces of love and destruction. More powerful, less boring, blood and death were still there, but we had taken off its suit and tie.

You must sacrifice for freedom, we had been told, and Jimi Hendrix was our sacrificial lamb mirroring the cries of the soldiers dying for our freedom. Purple haze, a dual national anthem, a cop-out of our own, the fog of hallucinogens causing every movement to be intense, immediate, the flashes of light perception mimicking the fireworks of artillery fire and bombs. Jimi Hendrix carefully plucking out each note of the national anthem on his electric guitar, our parents probably thinking he had not earned the right.

The busload of high spirits had made her nervous. That much freedom had always made her nervous, knowing the other shoe would drop, knowing freedom had a price, but because she loved Thomas, she was literally going along for the ride. She wanted to feel the same high spirits that they did. She'd smoked dope occasionally, but she'd never liked the feeling of being too messed up. Sometimes she would pretend to be high—even then, she'd been a phony.

She had been glad of one thing that day. They had decided not to take the bus all the way across the country. She was glad they had a destination, one she was familiar with, one that was in her family. Suzanne had been more than happy for them to have a commune up here. She had wrestled it away from their parents, who had set it up as a trust for her when she turned 22, although their father had tried to fight that in court after she had 'turned on him'. But she wanted to live in California, so she was delighted when Thomas and Gloria had told her about their plans for the Rainbow House, delighted with an opportunity to stick it once again to their dad. She had always been so much more competitive, so much more driven than Gloria.

One thing that Gloria was glad of was that somehow her illness, her descent into the gray, had seemed to bring her family back together somewhat. She knew her parents had been up here when she first became aware of her surroundings again. She had heard Suzanne and her father arguing about her care, but she also heard them talking, just talking of everyday concerns. And even when they had argued about her, their voices had a certain treble of reconciliation, moving toward a common end unlike the shouting that had taken place coast to coast at the time of Suzanne's inheritance. Gloria had always thought it ironic that this place that represented peace and harmony to Thomas, and so many others had cut a deep rift within her own family.

She remembers the feeling when they arrived with that first group. They all stumbled off the bus and walked around the grounds. Some started to set up tents; some just threw down sleeping bags on the grass. This was their destination, their paradise. Some ran around yelling, overwhelmed with freedom. Some jumped in the pond in back. It was a hot day.

Others sat on the ground sharing joints and kisses. Gloria had gone inside with some of the other girls. She knew where everything was, so she helped make huge pitchers of lemonade. She kind of remembers trying to feel as joyous as everyone, trying not to feel jealous because this was her family's home, her sisters. Nobody owned anything, she had to tell herself. It all belonged to the community. She remembers Thomas coming up behind her, lifting her up, carrying her up the stairs, and putting her down on the window seat in front of the huge picture window.

"This is it," he said

They'd gazed together out the window at the joyous energy. People played music, couples tumbled on the grass, and two girls emerged from the woods, daisy chains in their hair, more wildflowers trailing from their hands. Gloria remembers Thomas holding her, how he smelled of sweat and pot, and when they kissed, his lips were salty. He'd playfully rubbed his head across her stomach.

"This is it," he said.

She smiles now thinking about how she had been selfishly glad that they had the top of the loft to themselves and they would be sleeping inside, here in the bed, next to the bathroom.

More busloads of kids came up over the years but never with the same joy of that first time. The ones who came to the Rainbow House after that came out of their buses or cars looking confused, disoriented, excited, but more apprehensive, dropped off in the middle of an established community, seeking to find a niche.

That first time, freedom burst like a napalm bomb, opening like orange and lime green flower, petals dripping from the sky like Dali's distorted clocks elongating time, and no one really had a place, except maybe her and Thomas as overseers. Thomas had said everyone was equal, but everyone knew he was actually the leader, and she had more power because it was her family's property.

Suddenly Gloria feels cold even though it is hot out. She puts her knees on the bench and hangs onto them with her hands. She feels herself tremble as tears roll down onto her thighs. She shakes with frustration trying to remember if there's something from that time she is missing, something personal with her and Thomas.

Had he been unfaithful? Had she come across him on the lawn or even in their own bed and staggered away, helpless, unable to confront him? Had he betrayed her and he didn't even know she knew? Had the burden of internalizing, pretending everything was fine, even though their wedding, even through the birth of Amanda—had it broken her, pushed her into the gray, a place where she could only keep the people she loved at the periphery, at the edges of her vision for fear of another betrayal? Could that possibly be what had scorched her spirit so deeply, not one big staggering event, but the small day-to-day betrayals of living with a lie? She just couldn't or wouldn't remember, and he couldn't tell because until she could speak and ask, he didn't even know the question.

Thomas had talked about their wedding last night not knowing that she could not remember, not knowing how painful it was to remember. She had been pregnant with Amanda, really big. How could she forget that? Even as she cries and her body shakes, she thinks that she has some flashes of remembrance. Her big belly, the heat, children tugging at her dress, an arbor they stood under, but, maybe she was just making it up. She had wanted to speak last night so badly, wanted details, who had been there, what had they served, what had made them decide to finally marry? Even simple words—Who was there? Who was at our wedding? They were somehow too much as if emptiness had burst into their lives as they walked through the arch instead of the fulfillment that marriage was supposed to bring. It had cursed them to get married after all that time.

Gloria tries to pull herself together quickly because she can hear Amanda's little voice calling out to her as the door slams. Thomas and she come for a visit.

"Tell mommy what you did last night?" Thomas says as Amanda runs into Gloria's arms. "Tell her where Auntie took you."

Gloria gives her daughter a crushing hug, hoping that she thinks mommy is crying because she is so glad to see her; partly, she is. Thomas is trying to make them talk—she and Amanda both, trying to force her to converse out loud with her daughter. *I can't,* she wants to yell. *Not yet.* But she doesn't want to have an outburst now while she holds Amanda.

Thomas coaches the baby.

""Mama, ta," Amanda says, her chubby hand pointing to the sky. She looks at Gloria full of earnest enthusiasm. She looks at Thomas who whispers to her. She looks at Gloria and points. "Fane, tas."

Aunt Suzanne must have taken her to Stellafane last night, the star party they'd discovered in Vermont a few years ago. She remembers being there with Thomas, riding along, looking for a place to camp, wanting to get away from paradise and have privacy for a few days. Even Thomas had tired of it sometimes, tired of the crowds in paradise. She is so delighted with a memory so close. She whispers the word "stars" and points to the sky with Amanda. "At night," she whispers. Thomas hears but does not react. Relief flows through her bones as the memory becomes clearer. She can whisper to her daughter but has no words for the others, not yet.

The memory of their escape to Stellafane brings her some relief along with emptiness, an anchor she clings to, but a rusty one. One string of taut memory could split her spirit like a surgeon, cutting through flesh but could also be her hope of salvation. Whatever this was, this inability to communicate, it was deeper than her love for Thomas. She couldn't let him pull her out of it yet, though now she realized she needed to be hauled in. *Have patience with me,* her weary smile said to Thomas. *Unravel the rope slowly so I can float for a while longer in this anesthesia of forgetfulness before I reach for the heavy braided twine that will lift me from this dark place.*

At the thought of it, her heart aches, but aches with what? At what she would be leaving behind, the silt that would fall through her toes as she is being lifted from the underworld? The layer of sanity she would have to push through, the ones she already had? Maybe there had been a brain injury and it was only a matter of her brain taking its time, the swelling going down a little more each day, the synapses of the brain weaving together again in the correct formation. She hopes it was something physical; she could cope with that.

Amanda climbs down and toddles to Thomas.

"Let's go for a walk," he says

He pulls Gloria from the bench, and she feels the warmth of

his strong hand in hers, pulling her up to the surface. She thinks, *I'm almost ready.* They each take one of Amanda's hands and play one, two, three, whee with her down by the pond and down the long driveway. She wants Thomas to talk to her about Stellafane, but he talks only to Amanda. Why would he after so many weeks or months of her not answering back? *Try now*, she wants to tell him. *I might be able to give you a nod of recognition.* How could he know, how could he know she only remembers glimpses of the place, longs trails to walk, tents and telescopes set up everywhere.

Amanda is getting tired and throws herself on the ground, so they turn around. Thomas carries Amanda into the house but turns around and looks toward Gloria before closing the door. What did he want? What was he expecting? She hangs back, goes to the bench, and sits down, tries to process it all. The memory of Stellafane, the walk, the joy, and sadness of the pull toward family. Re-entry. It's always a dicey time, fraught with danger.

That evening, they are all just hanging out downstairs. Thomas works on metric tables, Suzanne organizes for a yoga class, and Gloria sits with Amanda helping her make puzzles, build with blocks. Suddenly, she takes Amanda's hand and brings her up the stairs. Gloria is aware that Suzanne is aware of the movement but does not step in; she only looks up, briefly, and goes on with her business again. Gloria knows that this means she is getting better. Once up the stairs, she picks Amanda up and lifts her onto the window seat, securing Amanda with her arm.

"Tas," Amanda says, pointing to the sky, putting her face right into Gloria's close enough for Gloria to smell her baby breath "Tas," she repeats, earnestly.

"Stars," Gloria whispers to her. "Look at all the stars."

Amanda looks at her, touches her mouth, and pulls on her lips where the words have come from.

"Ta?"
Gloria points up and nods her head.

Chapter Five

> THE SNOW HAD BEGUN IN THE GLOAMING
> AND BUSILY ALL THE NIGHT
> HAD BEEN HEAPING FIELD AND HIGHWAY
> WITH A SILENCE DEEP AND WHITE —JAMES RUSSELL LOWELL

It had been over a week since Amanda had learned about her sister, and now, gazing out the window of her childhood room, she felt betrayed. At first, she'd been relieved to know the truth, happy her parents seemed close again, but it was like her whole childhood had been a lie. She wanted to escape back up to Vermont, but it was like now all that was ruined forever. It was a place of grief and emptiness now, no longer a place of solitude. The knowledge of what had drawn her there all this time was too much to bear. It was better filled with shadows. Amanda wept for the sister she didn't remember—a sister who might have played with her, brought her a rattle, showed her how to use it. After all these years, her mother should have kept the damn secret to herself.

She would only stay around here now to be close to her dad. If it weren't for that, she' be out of here. She could be at Peter's right now or try going back up to Vermont. She could even get a place of her own around here except for that little problem of no income. She sat on the bed, threw her pillow against the wall, and decided go to her old office at the University to think. It was barely six-thirty, but she knew she couldn't fall back asleep. She longed for a tea party, some silent perspective, but now that was all weird because of what had happened there. She wanted to go up but could not imagine being there alone. She remembered the paths her mother had shoveled at Thanksgiving and all through her childhood. Paths to nowhere that, as a child, she thought her mother was shoveling for her.

At least her father was getting better. They were optimistic enough to set up surgery to reverse the colostomy in a few months. The combination of chemo and Jason's care plan seemed to be working. They had a routine now of watching old movies all afternoon while her mother worked and Jason was out grocery shopping or whatever he did in his spare time.

She'd asked her dad why hadn't they sold the chalet in Vermont after it happened and why did they go up there every summer? He told her he wanted to sell it, but it was her mother who couldn't. "I guess she thought it would be like abandoning April, though she never told me that. She did say once she couldn't bear to have someone else live there," he had said.

Amanda had always wondered why they kept it even when they didn't go up anymore. Until she'd moved up this winter, they had to pay someone to check on it all the time. Funny how she'd always thought it was her mother who'd wanted it sold.

She went to the closet and looked at all the swishy skirts, silky blouses, and bulky sweaters. Teacher clothes. Most of her comfortable stuff was still up in Vermont since they'd left so quickly. She found an old pair of jeans and put them on along with a Stellafane tee shirt and a huge flannel shirt that probably belonged to Peter. She tip-toed down stairs because everyone was still sleeping, and, not wanting to wake up her father, she decided to go to Dunkin Donuts for coffee and a bagel. She ran to the car because it was so cold.

It was barely seven, and the moon was still visible, a waning crescent. In a few days, it would be a new moon and perfect for observing if it stayed this cold and clear. But where could she go to observe here? The hill was socked in with snow. She shook her head. She'd have to go back to Vermont at least one more time before making any decisions here. She'd be alone. She could observe. She could dream and think.

It must have been earlier than she thought because the

security guard was still at the gates with the bar down when she entered the college. She rolled down the window. He must have seen the faculty sticker on her car. He lifted the bar.

"Students will be back soon," he said.

She smiled and nodded and waved to him as she drove through and around to the old part of the campus.

Walking past the pillars and rubbing her hands together for warmth, she unlocked the heavy door and rushed up the stairs to the office for some reason thinking it would be warmer there. It wasn't. She plugged in a space heater and sat in front of it until her toes and hands were toasty, but her back was still freezing. What the hell was she doing here? She wondered if they had held any classes here this winter. Peter kept saying they still didn't have anyone to replace her.

At least they kept the heat at 62 so the pipes wouldn't burst. Probably one of the art teachers would take students out here during the winter to sketch the interesting icicle formations on the windows. She tried turning the thermostat up to seventy and looked out the beveled window. Bright morning sun hit the ice on the trees. She wouldn't mind living here, if it were heated. Maybe the University would rent it to her? She'd do upkeep and pay heat. Probably they'd be all kinds of complicated insurance things involved.

She sat down on the matt and thought about Peter. Would they get back together? It seemed like he wanted to. If she moved back down here and got her job back, if she *could* get it, would she be happy? Six months ago, she felt like she was being pulled into something so overwhelming she didn't know what to do and backed away. She had felt so happy the day they were up in Vermont last winter and Peter had hinted at marriage, but then, that night, she'd dreamed she was being smothered with a pillow. It was a scary dream, a vivid dream, and at the time, she thought it must have been Peter in her dream, but, now, she didn't know. Maybe in the dream she was being smothered by a sister she'd barely known—a voice, a smell, the ghost sister. Maybe that's who was cutting off her oxygen every time she went up there alone and making her have those weird visions.

What kind of early trauma would she have had as an infant picking up on her parent's grief? And then they had buried it, had buried everything with their baby, even the joy she had brought them. The thought came to her putting her in a sudden panic. Could she ever get married? Ever risk having a child? Ever risk losing one?

She got up and paced, sat at her desk, and looked through her drawers. She hadn't cleared anything out when she left. All the notes on the course on Kepler's Dream that so few had signed up for last summer. She was an okay teacher. She did well at her job here. Maybe she should see if she could get it back. Not the worst gig in the world.

She liked the idea of being a teacher if, like Maria Mitchel, she could teach for the sake of knowledge and not grades. She was reading Mitchell's biography: the soul of an astronomer. Not only had she discovered a comet when she was barely thirty, she had felt it was her mission, her duty to teach. When she was still a teenager, she started her own school for girls in her parent's home. Amanda was fascinated when she read how, in a house with ten brothers and sisters, she was given her own closet-sized study. When she was twelve years old, she observed an eclipse with her father and wrote down "the exact second when the shadow of the moon touched the rim of the sun." When she came to the part about Maria trying to make sense of her baby sister dying at three, Amanda put the book down.

The radiator hissed; the sun was starting to warm her up through the windows. She plugged in the microwave she'd left and warmed up some instant coffee and drank with her mittens on. All she needed was to move the games down here and she'd be happy. How would she approach the administration about that one? Maybe she would offer to teach a course, for free, on the history of the seventies and eighties. She would present it to the administration as an interactive course where part of the curriculum was to experience the beginnings of computer systems for home use and they might let her bring the games down here.

She was getting hungry; eating breakfast in the morning only kept her feeling hungrier all day long. There were a few muffins Jason had made in her bag. She pulled them out now convinced his cooking was making her gain weight.

She looked at them, smelled them. *What are they?* She took a bite. *Interesting.* Some kind of weird spice and nuts, definitely nuts, but she couldn't figure out what kind. She took another bite, slowly, savoring little bits at a time. They were tastier than they looked. A storm had come up when she wasn't paying attention. The wind shook the windows, and the rain lashed against them. Maybe she should go lower. She could no longer see anything out the window but flashes of light. The distorted window seemed to be beaconing all the electromagnetic energy into her direction. The wind shook the pane of glass almost to the breaking point. She grabbed her coat and hurried downstairs. *Everything will be fine*, she said to herself, as she flew down the stairs, reciting the names of the seven sisters. *Maia: first born, most beautiful, Electra: the lost one, withdrew her light in sorrow; Merope: mortal, enveloped in a nebulous haze.*

As she walked downstairs, it was warmer, strange. She opened the door to the classroom and smelled burning, and just as she was ready to slam the door and run for the front door, she heard a voice.

"Come in," a young woman's voice said. "Sit by the stove."

She walked in hesitantly. There was a fire alright, but it was in a potbellied stove in the middle of the room. It still looked like a schoolroom but one from about 100 years ago.

Amanda smoothed her hair down and walked in slowly. The young Maria Mitchell, probably only about eighteen, sat by the stove with a book opened in her lap.

"Don't be afraid. Sit here." She pointed to another chair by the stove. "You're welcome to sit in on our lessons."

She's younger than I am, Amanda thought, *at least five years younger and she probably thinks I'm about twelve and a boy. She thinks I'm an orphan, maybe, some kid who hangs around the docks and tries to get on ships.* The strange thing was she didn't seem to be too surprised at Amanda's presence. She went on with her teaching as if Amanda weren't there. The children didn't react to her; she didn't think they could see her. But then, in the middle of a lesson, Maria came right up to Amanda and began to speak to her.

"I love to teach like my father did. We're not very good at making money, but we get by."

Amanda was just wondering if she should say something back to her, but Maria turned around and went back to teaching. She came over to Amanda and knelt down by the side of her chair. The pupils didn't seem to notice.

"One of my father's favorite motto's was 'an undevout Astronomer is mad.' He would say, 'How could you raise your eyes to the stars and not be filled with awe?'"

Maria turned to one of the students and instructed her to get more wood for the fire. She went outside, and Maria adjusted the load in the stove. When the girl came back, she added a few logs so there was a good burn. The other pupils talked and laughed quietly, not bothered at all by Amanda.

"I have doubts about my religious faith," Maria went on. "I like dressing plain and living simple like the other Quakers, but they have too many rules." Obviously she didn't think Amanda was a boy from the docks or she wouldn't be talking to her like this. "I want independence of thought; they seem to discourage questioning of any kind."

Amanda tried to speak, but she couldn't. What did she look like? Who did Maria think she was?

"If the others can't see you, I know there is something strange. You are a spirit, an omen. You look like a boy from the waterfront, but I see the future in your eyes. You must be he seventh son of a seventh son."

Amanda blinked, looked away.

"No please." Maria said. "Speak to me with your eyes. You know my life. You know at age 25 I will stop going to meeting."

Maria began to tremble in spite of the fire's heat. She trembled, and Amanda took her hand.

"The fire," Amanda whispered, angry at herself for saying the word. Just the blink had made her see a terrible fire.

"Yes, the fire will be nearly the worst night of my life. We'll lose the Athenaeum, the rooftop observatory, and we will watch helplessly as the blazing fire burns Nantucket into a volcano of red smoldering ash. We'll hold each other and cry once the flames are out."

Amanda closed her eyes, and suddenly they were outside. Bells clanged loudly. Someone was filling buckets of water and handing them to people. Buckets of water handed from person to person. Flames went through the buildings. People screamed and cried, keening for the loss but still working. Amanda was suddenly aware that Maria was standing next to her. She sobbed "It is the worst night of my life. We lose the Athenaeum, the rooftop observatory, we lose everything."

Amanda opened her eyes again and there was Maria sitting in front of her, fine.

"I need water," Maria said and got up and poured herself a glass from a pitcher on a table in the corner. She breathed deeply before sitting down again.

"But really the fire was a kind of new beginning. They rebuilt the athenaeum, and I got my job back, but it wasn't the same. Nothing in Nantucket was the same, especially me."

She laughed. Amanda was surprised at how her face lit up when she laughed.

"Quiet down girls," she said to her giggling students.

"They don't expect girls around here to have any real education," she complained to Amanda. "They hardly expect them to be taught the basics. I intend to change all that."

She knelt down beside Amanda's chair.

"After they rebuilt the Athenaeum, I was still restless. I felt I needed purpose."

""Even beyond looking at the skies?" Amanda whispered.

"Even beyond my passion for observing."

"Then there will be the night." Maria smiled again.

"The comet," Amanda whispered.

"Yes, the comet."

Amanda closed her eyes and was in a room full of people. It was a small, cozy gathering. She sat by the fire, next to Maria. Everyone was talking. There was a table with a cake half eaten and a punch bowl. She felt like she could stay forever just listening and watching. Next to her, Maria muttered.

"I wonder when I can escape. I have to go up top. Why is it every night there is one of these parties? It's the clearest night for observing."

She got up and walked to a man pouring punch. Amanda got up and followed her not knowing what else to do.

"I have to go up, papa." She whispered loudly, "Can I go now?"

The man nodded, and Amanda followed Maria out the door and up some drafty stairs to the rooftop. It was still clear, and just as Amanda thought she would die from the cold, she felt warmth again. She opened her eyes, and Maria still knelt in front of her as if she didn't realize Amanda's comings and goings.

"I knew there was something out there for me that night,"

she said "waiting to be found. Someday I'll tell my students we especially need imagination in science. It is not all mathematics nor all logic, but it is somewhat beauty and poetry. Someday that is what I'll say. I see it in your eyes."

"I have to go now," Amanda whispered. "Can I go now?"

Maria nodded.

And Maria disappeared, but there was a small girl, a waif standing in the corner. She looked at Amanda scared, mistrustful.

Amanda cocked her head, put her arms out toward the child. The child walked to her and took her hands. Amanda felt no weight, no touch. She pulled her hands away, frightened.

Why are you here?

Why did you summon me?

You belong in Vermont.

Why did you resurrect me?

The child did not look sad or scared or mistrustful anymore, only curious as she waited for answers.

"I guess I always had these feelings I didn't know what to do with."

"Love?" The child cocked her head.

"Love, I guess," Amanda said. "A sister."

The child smiled

Amanda reached her hands out, palms up. The child took her hands, but Amanda still felt nothing. She squeezed only air, her hands making two fists. "Love like a burden, love I didn't know what to do with, my mother's sorrow." She loosened the fists and watched the child's hands slip away. "I wonder if maybe you have been alive all this time, in an alternate universe."

"Amanda." Peter was yelling, shaking her.

She looked at him, startled.

"Are you alright?" He was shouting like she was deaf. "What happened?"

"I don't know... I guess I... I don't know. Maybe I fell asleep."

"You seemed more like you were passed out." She was sitting in one of the student desks. He helped her up. She did feel a little dizzy.

"I'm hungry" she said.

"That's why I came. We were supposed to meet for lunch. You never showed."

"What time is it?"

"After one, I thought maybe you went home. There've been so many brownouts from the storm, the computers are all screwed up. They cancelled the class I was teaching today." Peter followed her up the stairs. She was actually glad, she felt a little shaky.

She gathered her books and papers into a satchel-like backpack and glanced over at Peter who was lying on the mattress under the window making eyes at her.

"I'd love to," she said, "but believe it or not, I am so damn hungry, I wish we could call out for pizza delivery."

"I have my cell," Peter said.

"Yea, like that would ever work here, and they'd never find this building anyway."

Peter made a sad face.

"Let's pick up Pizza and go home," she said.

The rain snow mix was letting up. They walked down the stairs together and before they went out, Amanda opened the door to the classroom and peeked in. Everything was normal. No Maria, no students, no burning Nantucket. She took a deep breath and followed Peter out the door.

Chapter Six

Last night, after Amanda was asleep, Thomas got the idea that it would be good to move her bench so she could look at the flowers she had planted on the other side of the house as they grew. He said they needed a new perspective. They, as a family, could sit on the bench when they finished watering the garden every morning. Gloria had followed him out of the house and nearly clawed at his hand as he tried to move it. She tried to say no. *It needs to be here,* she wanted to say, but she choked on the words because her mind wanted to say something nonsensical like, *There is one side for the living and one side for the dead.* But if she said that, she knew he would stop trusting her sanity.

Sitting here today, she feels that anger rise in her again, how she felt when Thomas tried to move the bench. The other side of the house, the place that she had planted flowers was for the living, and this side, in its deep, hushed silence belongs to the dead. Tears fall and her body shakes. Reaching for nonsense again, she tries to fathom her own loss. Why does she feel there was another baby, another head she smelled and kissed? Was there a twin that had died? No, it was something else. Something went wrong. Miscarriage? What was it?

She throws herself down on the bench and sobs, relieved at the thought that no one would come to comfort her. Suzanne and Thomas don't stare at her through the window anymore. This side of the house is now beyond comfort—this side of the house that has pulled her into the gray. She could dig at the earth on the other side of the house and find something, but here, here she will find nothing. This side has stolen her voice. She cries for a long time, sobbing loudly, listening to the noise of her vocal chords.

"Bastards, you bastards," she screams, surprised at the sound of her own voice loosened, hoarse from weeks, months of disuse. She pounds her fists into the wood, frightened at her rage.

Who is she speaking to?

You will say the words. They can't steal your voice any longer. She looks up at the large picture window of the loft, and she sees herself looking down at herself. That's who is speaking, the *other* her. Her self in the window isn't paying attention to her grieving—she is looking at something else. Then Gloria, with all the energy she has, steps into the vision of the woman at the window that is her but is not her... and she sees a child playing in the snow, and then the child is gone.

The Gloria on the bench sees the woman in the window's face cringe, hears her shout, "No" in a long, wailing trail of a voice, the one syllable elongated as if it were a runaway train, the sound extending through walls, through time.

"No!"

She is the woman in the window, extending her hand as if its flesh and muscle have the strength to break through the window and pull back the child disappearing beneath a blanket of snow. The Gloria on the bench runs to the mounds digging through the invisible snow. The Gloria at the window screams at the cruel glass, the thick walls that come between her and her child's life, but the Gloria on the bench cannot save her.

"No" she screams, digging at the grass, which she thinks is snow.

She will no longer let the glass, thicker and colder than the membrane that had separated the beating hearts of her and her first child, separate them. But because the Gloria at the window holds another child in her arms, she will bring her voice back into the air in a tempered swoon, so as not to frighten the child she holds, and it will filter like a dirge through the window. *My April, my darling, my baby, don't go.*

Then she is gone. The woman in the window is gone, and Suzanne is lifting Gloria's arm and leading her to the house. Thomas is putting Amanda into the car. Gloria tries to run to them, but Suzanne has her in some kind of restraint, and she finds she has little energy left to fight, but her voice is back, and she yells.

"No, No. Don't take my baby away. You bastard. Don't take my baby away."

It is a relief and a betrayal to speak again in their presence, anger the only words for grief. Rage the only comfort. Her mother self knew it was right. They need to take Amanda away until she can hold her in her arms and only whisper a dirge. *My April, my darling, my dying baby, snow angel, my soul, my wandering star.*

Suzanne gives her a sedative, which surprises Gloria knowing it is against all her principles, and it is somehow a victory for Gloria that she has made her sister go against her beliefs. She wants to be drugged, but Suzanne has not given her quite enough. She lies on the bed subdued but not asleep staring out the window, trying not to be the woman who looked out at the snow-covered child. She gazes out the window thinking about not feeling the horror, only emptiness, the lack of feeling. She thinks of the tire swing that she thought had been for all the other children that were here when it was a commune, when they tried to change the world. She sees her daughter, April Rainbow, spinning wildly, unwinding like the bobbin of an unmade dress, whose thread disappeared when it had barely reached the needle that would bind the cloth together. Gloria sits up in bed and watches her daughter spin off with no fear, her little girl smile.

"Look at me, mommy. Watch me swing."

Spinning away until she disappears, Gloria thinks what a relief it would be to crash through the glass and enter the shadow world to search for her lost child. Like Wendy who'd flown through a window and never come back, her child would be a child forever. She wanted to follow April Rainbow until she reached the end of breath, the end of a heartbeat, and pull her back to the Earth, pull her back again into her own womb, give her life again.

She contemplates it, crashing through the glass hoping to find in her flight through the air the gentle, soft baby arms of her daughter. She contemplates it deeply but cannot do it—cannot leave another child motherless.

Chapter Seven

THE MILKY WAY

Amanda spent the night with Peter at what he was now calling their apartment. In the morning, as Peter was shaving, she went into the guest room where there was a closet with some of her teacher clothes in it, an emergency stash with everything when they used to go back and forth between apartments. She walked into the room slowly looking around for subtle evidence of anyone else's stuff being left behind. Nothing seemed changed at all. Some blouses and skirts hung in the closet. There was an open duffle bag packed with casual clothes on the floor. When she pushed the skirts aside, she saw a shelf with a Tampax, a hair dryer, and gel. Above that was another shelf with a box that contained her wedding dress. It smelled a little musty. She took it out and hung it on its satin-covered hangar.

This was her room. This was where they had moved most of the furniture she wanted to keep from her apartment, her bed, her bureau, and her rocking chair. She was glad there wasn't evidence of other women in this room. She didn't doubt that Mrs. Hyper TA had stayed overnight with Peter at least a few times, but at least she had not been in here. Amanda dressed like a teacher, and she and Peter had coffee together. She was going to inquire about her job there.

"Why don't we both go in my car?" Peter asked.

"I'd rather take both. You'll probably be there longer, and I want to spend the afternoon with my dad."

It felt strange going to the administration building. She'd hardly given a notice when she left. She tried not to skulk around; she was going for apologetic but not pitiful. Peter told her she should go to the head of the math department, but she had always felt inferior there, more comfortable with science. The secretary stopped her and asked who she was here to see—that's how often she had been in this building. She didn't know what to say. *I'm a professor here, I used to be a professor here, I'm going to be again. I'm the weirdo with the office in the old buildings.* She said what Peter had told her to say—she'd been on sabbatical and was coming back.

"Oh." Still unsure where to send her, what category she fit into, Amanda tried to help the secretary.

"I'm not sure if I'm teaching this semester. I've been away." *Far, far away,* she wanted to add.

"Oh."

"Medical leave." Remembering more of what Peter had told her to say.

The secretary gave her an even more suspicious look.

"Not for me," she said. "My father's very sick." She was getting annoyed knowing she was giving out way too much information to the wrong person.

The secretary seemed to be looking for files in her drawer for her name and the words sabbatical or medical leave. She found her name in a file and finally smiled a little.

"Oh, you're the one with the office in the back. I didn't even know you were away." She looked at Amanda a little less oddly.

Amanda was feeling less intimidated, but suddenly she couldn't remember the name of the head of the department. She never payed attention to those things. Peter was probably right; she should schmooze just a little. Now she wanted to ask if so and so was in, but she couldn't think of his name.

"Nobody's really here yet." The secretary finally said. "They've been coming in around ten."

Amanda sighed and wondered if there was any coffee in the teacher's lounge.

There were a few people in the lounge already. Hyer's TA

made coffee, and someone had brought in Dunkin Donuts. She sat down and opened her briefcase pretending to do something. She opened a book and daydreamed, stared out the window, listened to the coffee brewing, smelled it, breathed it in. She tried not to make eye contact with anyone, especially the TA, but she came over anyway with the box of donuts and offered one to Amanda. Amanda took a chocolate covered donut and put it down on a napkin.

"Thanks," she said.

"You're coming back?" *Is she worried about her boyfriend or her job or both?*

'Probably," she said "Maybe not until next semester."

Amanda smiled at her. *The TA isn't bad*, she thought. She wished she could remember her name.

She went off, and Amanda watched for a while. She was a schmoozer and a flirt. She could see how Peter had been attracted to her. It would never have lasted. She'd have been outdoing Peter at his own game.

Amanda got up and poured another cup of coffee. It was almost ten, time for her to go up and embarrass herself again. Maybe she wouldn't do it today. Maybe she would just go to the office in the back and hide away.

As she was walking out, she ran into Peter.

"Well," he said.

"Nobody comes in until ten during break. I'm on my way up there now."

They kissed, and she had no choice now but to head back upstairs.

Fortunately, as she headed through the door the head of the department was just getting into his office. She definitely knew him by sight. It was still a problem that she couldn't remember his name, but the secretary helped her there.

"This lady is here to talk to you, Carl" she said as Amanda walked through the door.

He turned around and smiled at her.

"Amanda, you're back. Peter said you might be in this week." He opened the door and waited for her to step in first. "Sorry to hear about your father," he said. "How is he?"

"Better," Amanda said.

She sat down in a chair, and he sat down behind an immaculately clean desk. He was very skinny and had a nervous habit of rubbing his palms together as she spoke. He wasn't very good at socializing, possibly worse than Amanda. She knew he was a brilliant man.

"You're probably all set for the semester," Amanda said.

"We are," he said, "but we only hired a temporary because you did apply for the sabbatical." She was confused; Peter must have filled out the papers and forged her name. "We do have a temporary replacement in your courses for the spring semester, but I made a couple of calls, and the science department could use you to teach an enrichment course in Astronomy for eight weeks in March and April if you're interested."

"I'm interested," Amanda said.

"Great," he said. "Talk to Healy in Science, and he'll get you the details."

"Thanks so much," she said, shaking Carl's hand.

"Good to have you back," he said. "You definitely on for the fall?"

Amanda nodded.

"Good," he said and walked her to the doorway.

Amanda was ecstatic. She was hardly thinking about Vermont and all the things she's felt she was giving into, all the compromises she had felt she made for other people. She was so happy they wanted her to teach an enrichment course in Astronomy. She felt relief, grounding, sort of.

When she got to her parent's house, it was after lunch. Her mother was working, and Jason was getting ready to leave. Her father was sleeping on the couch.

"He did real well on the weekend," Jason said, beaming. "But he's tired."

Jason insisted on heating up some herbed vegetables he had made for their lunch before going out the door. She sat at the table and let him take care of her. She was dying to tell Jason she had decided to stay down here, but somehow she thought that it would be disloyal to Peter not to tell him first. Jason sat with her drinking a smoothie and watching her eat the vegetables and a slab of homemade bread. Outside of the kitchen, on the deck, the dog wagged his tail and pushed his nose against the glass hoping to be let in. Amanda ignored him; he was too rambunctious for her to handle right now.

They sat in silence for a few minutes

"I don't think I'm going back," she said.

"To the college?"

""To Vermont," she said, looking out at the hyper dog.

"Oh." Jason looked at her, laughed. "I don't think I am either."

"What? Your life is in Vermont." She was surprised at her own passion at Jason's decision. "Dad's going to be better. Then what will you do here?"

"Kayla wants me to go to school in Boston under some chef or something."

"Wow." Maybe Jason had found someone who understood him.

"They gave me my job back," she said, in spite of herself, suddenly babbling on almost like her mother did. *Scary*. She was happy for Jason, but she wasn't sure if she wanted him to be gone from Vermont, too. "And I'm teaching a course in Astronomy this semester. Just like a nightlife course." She shrugged.

If Jason stayed down here, too, it would be just like this lonely deserted chalet up there haunted by the ghost of April Rainbow. "It doesn't start until March so I'm hoping by then, most of the snow will be gone so I can take them on field trips to the hill to observe," she said. *Still babbling.*

Hadn't all these years been haunted anyway? Haunted by her sister that she didn't know? Jason was staring at her intensely. Hadn't April Rainbow's spirit been ruling their lives for years because her mother had buried it? Buried, buried a secret like little April Rainbow buried in the snow?

Amanda couldn't stop talking. "They said in the fall I could have my full course load back. And Peter and I will probably get married." She looked at Jason wildly and began to blubber. Then she began to cry.

He took her hand and brought her onto his lap. She cried into his tee shirt.

"I'm getting you all soaked," she said.

"It's okay," he said. "That's what I'm here for."

"Part of dad's care plan, right? That you take care of all of us, body, and soul."

Jason nodded. "What is it?" Jason asked. "Is it that you don't want to get married? Don't want to teach? Don't want to leave Vermont?"

"Don't know," she said, shaking her head. "Just don't know, maybe all three. I'm just so confused. I'm weird, right?"

"Unique," he said. "Don't beat yourself up. Your father has cancer. You just found out about a sister you never knew you had who died when you were a baby. You're processing. It's healthy." He put his face right down by hers. "Give yourself a little time. I think you're on the right track."

Amanda put her head on his shoulder and sighed. "I guess."

What she couldn't tell him was that she *knew* she wanted to be down here, married to Peter, but she wanted him, Jason, to be up there. She knew he was falling in love with this new woman, but she was hoping they would live in Vermont. It's like if Jason wasn't there either, this whole part of her life was blown away. She didn't like change—at least not this much.

Something had to stay the same. She had to grab onto something. If Jason wasn't there, she had to grab onto April Rainbow who would never leave Vermont—a voice she almost remembered hearing, like an echo in the snow.

Although Amanda's course didn't start until March, she went to her office at the college every morning. She read, drank coffee, and wrote notes out for the course. She stared out the window, wrote in a journal, and met Peter for lunch every day in the cafeteria, usually relieved to hear the buzz of people around her and so many conversations at once after the solitude of her office. Maybe she was morphing into a more social being. She had moved back in with Peter. They made plans for a wedding in the summer.

"You're dad's getting better all the time," he said to her when she fretted about him not being up for the wedding. He was right. There was actually a date set for a reversal of the colostomy in early May.

"Maybe we should elope," she said almost every other day as they ate supper at the apartment. He would look at her, exasperated, and then, one day, he seemed to change his mind.

"Maybe we should. We could do that right now. Just go ourselves and have a big party afterwards," he said surprising her. "Isn't that what you want?"

She panicked. How did he know what she wanted?

"No!" she said, ignoring Peter's exasperated look. "I think my dad wants to walk me down the aisle. We'll have to wait until he's recuperated."

"What about August?"

She didn't want to tell him, but first, she wanted to check what weekend Stellafane was in the summer.

"Maybe August," she said.

By early March, when Amanda had started teaching her class, they announced the date to her parents, the third Sunday in August. Her mother took it from there, but Amanda found she didn't mind. She was happy teaching the nightlife course working with students who were older and actually wanted to learn. Peter couldn't complain about her observing when she could be with him because it was part of her class. Now that they had actually set a date, he seemed less nervous about the time she spent away from him.

She was in her office alone in the morning, drinking coffee, working on notes, and looking over journals she had her students write. The March sun finally warmed the windows, and she put her reading down and stared out her favorite beveled window. Restless, she walked downstairs to the empty classroom and walked around touching every desk. She looked at the window in the back where last year Peter had written I love you. By next fall, they'd be here again—her math students only in it for the grades. Suddenly she felt like she was going to faint, the air was stale or too close. She held onto a desk. *Stress,* she thought. Worry about her father. Maybe eating would make her feel better. She didn't have her watch, but it was probably time for lunch. Coffee, at least, would help her mood. She used to be able to get through the morning eating almost nothing. It wasn't as warm as it seemed from the sun shining through the windows so she went upstairs to get her jacket before heading to the cafeteria to meet Peter.

She couldn't find him then remembered he had meetings all day. She decided to visit her dad, but before going there, she stopped and got her hair cut and spiked. It felt good. She'd been ignoring it growing over her ears, and it was driving her crazy. She picked up some movies from the video store and went mid-afternoon to her parent's house. No one was home—not even her father. Sometimes Jason took him out shopping now, or somewhere, just to get him out of the house. He worked from home sometimes now, his computer set up in the living room. Maybe her mother had taken him out for a late lunch.

She went downstairs and rested on the couch. Her energy level was low; maybe she was fighting off a virus. Still, she didn't want to take all the supplements her mother kept pushing on her. She had taken some black coffee down, and that did her just fine. She missed having the afternoon alone with her dad and was just about to doze off when she heard someone come in. It was her parents. Her mother opened the door to the basement and called her name, and the dog came bounding down on top of her. Amanda barely had the energy to push him off. Her mother came down next, shooing the dog away. Amanda had forgotten about her haircut until her mother looked at her and frowned.

"Amanda, you chopped all your hair off."

"You don't like it, do you?"

"I just thought you might want to look like a girl for your wedding."

"Mom, that's not until August. It will grow back by then." Amanda smiled. "This is my summer haircut."

"It's not summer, yet."

"Okay, my spring haircut."

Her mother shook her head.

"Okay, this is the way I like to wear my hair." If her mother didn't mind her own business, she might get a tattoo of a teardrop on one of her cheeks before the wedding and a big ole' star on her forehead. She hoped her mother wasn't planning on burning incense as they walked down the aisle. She was sure that would make her sick to her stomach. It occurred to her that she should probably pay at least some attention to what her mother was planning.

Her mother took papaya juice out of the fridge; just watching her drink it made Amanda gag.

"Why don't you invite Peter over here for dinner? I need to talk to you about the menu."

Amanda rolled her eyes. Every time she had a free evening,

her mother wanted to talk to her about the wedding.

"Don't give me that look like a fifteen-year-old. It's less than six months away; you have no idea what goes into planning a wedding."

"It's basically going to be a party, mom. We just want a fun party." She was waiting for her mother to say, 'There is nothing fun about a wedding.' "You act like it's some kind of serious business."

"A lifetime commitment isn't serious business?"

Amanda sighed.

When she kissed her mom and dad goodbye after supper, she could tell they would be okay. Her mom and dad were almost like a new couple, alone in the house, getting to know each other. For so many years since Amanda had been a little girl, her father had spent so many months out of the year on business trips. Now he was home all the time. It must be different for both of them. Maybe not bad as he got better. Something to adjust to, wondering how things would be when he got well again.

Later, Peter had his arm around her in bed as they watched the late news. "Maybe we should elope," he said. "Don't you resent your mother taking over?"

"It makes her happy, I guess," she said. "Keeps her busy." She put the light out, and they held each other. "Let's go up to Vermont just to get away this weekend," Amanda said.

She couldn't see his face well, but she perceived in the way his body moved away slightly that Peter was uncomfortable with that. Was he still afraid that the loft would have some strange effect on her?

"Just for the weekend, to get away from my mom."

"I guess that would be okay," Peter said.

She sat up. "If you've already made other plans, just tell me"

Peter stroked her back. "No. It sounds good."

"I'm not going to want to live up there, Peter. I promise. You won't have to drag me away."

He pulled her back to him. "It's a good idea," he said. "Like an anniversary. It was just about a year ago we were up there, and it was the first time we talked about getting married." He put her head on his chest, put his hands through her short spiky hair, and brushed her face with his fingertips. "Don't you feel strange now, though, knowing what happened?"

Amanda touched his arm and sat up. "It's weird. It's like I'm kind of sad, but relieved. Like there was always a big secret, and I found out what it was, like maybe I was always searching for something, and now I'm not."

All she'd really found was a box, a book, a few poems, and some dried flowers. He pulled her down to him again, and they fell asleep clinging to each other.

They drove up to Vermont on the weekend. The late March weather had turned sunny and warm after the terrible storms that pushed the cold air away. There were still patches of snow, especially as they drove further north, but it was mostly mud, mud everywhere. Amanda had packed up the telescope and all the eyepieces. They had taken one car. Peter seemed intense and quiet as they drove up 91. She asked him to get off at the Stellafane exit. She was feeling a little car sick and also wanted to stop at the Vermont Country Store. When they got out of the car, she felt a little better.

It wasn't very crowded like in the summer. She took crackers from a barrel and tried all the cheeses they were offering. They bought candy and strange muffin mixes to bring back to her mom and dad. They were like little kids roaming around the store with no particular direction. Amanda tried on masks and hats while Peter used the bathroom. They looked at cards together and showed funny ones to each other but didn't buy any.

"Feeling better?"

Amanda nodded

They decided not to get on the highway again but go the long and winding way and stop wherever they wanted. There were some good places to eat in Chester. It was after four by the time they made it to the chalet. Amanda felt good but tired and hungry again. Peter took a beer and offered her one.

"No thanks," she said. It would only give her heartburn, and she knew she was drinking for two. She wondered how he'd feel about it. She studied his face as he gulped down a beer and read the newspaper. He didn't seem to notice that stare. Should she tell him now or wait until he was a little zonked? It would ruin the wedding plans.

Her mother would freak. Of course, she got married with a big belly, so who was she to judge? Amanda thought her belly might not get that big. She'd be about eight months along in August. Oh, it would be so hot. She hadn't thought about that before. Still, she was glad she would be having it in fall when the apples blossomed and not the spring flowers, when the apples fell and the smell of cider and donuts filled the orchards. She never wanted a spring baby, never. It was better that she was pregnant now. If it had happened right after they got married, she would have had an April child.

She plugged in the machines and played Ms. Packman for a while. Peter came up behind her and kissed her hair. They went upstairs and lay together for a while, and then Peter fell asleep as the sun went down. She rested her head on his shoulder thinking how this would affect her job in the fall. She had just told them she would be teaching her courses again, but lots of teachers worked while they were pregnant. What about childcare? Her mother? Her mother could watch the baby. But her mother would be mad at her for ruining the wedding. Maybe they could have it earlier, like in May? She wondered if she would fit into the dress even then. She had tried it on last night and could still zip it up. Maybe if they got married in April, or maybe next week.

What about observing? She might be a little tired, but she could sleep during the day instead of going to the office in the morning. It had worked out for the best that she hadn't got her full-time job back yet. She might not be able to make it to the hill, but Peter had already started clearing his tools out of the observatory in the back yard. She would teach her baby while it was still inside of her. She would recite the names of stars like a lullaby. She would start with the names of birds in the stars. *Apus: the curious sparrow, Aquila: the eagle, Columba Naoe: Noah's dove, bearer of good news.* She would sing to her belly of all things in the sky with wings. *Carvis: the raven, Cygnus: the swan, Grus: the crane, Pegusus: the winged horse.* She would whisper like a prayer of all things that move. *Eridinus: a river of stars that flows like a stream across the sky, Sagitta: the arrow always aimed at the scorpoin's heart.* In the spring, she would take the baby with her in one of those little snuggly things that people use to hold their babies in front and hold it close to her heartbeat as she aimed her telescope like a wandering ship through the skies.

Amanda went over to the window listening to Peter's low whistles and snores. She looked back at his face. Who will the baby look like? What parts of my baby will look like him? She sat by the window and stared out as stars appeared hoping Peter would wake up soon. If not, she would wake him up before midnight. What should she say? How would she tell him? She touched her warm stomach and looked out again. Stars were appearing. The planets Jupiter and Saturn appeared. Through the window with binoculars, she spotted Mars faint and quite low in the sky.

Peter slept through the night, but she woke up an hour or so before dawn. She touched the window glass. How would she tell her mother? She would call her later today, she decided, after she told Peter. She couldn't tell her she was pregnant over the phone but she would leave a cryptic message, tell her it was time to re-decorate the fun room.

She looked up as the Milky Way Galaxy appeared like shark's teeth or like the wing of a huge white bird fluttering across the sky.

Epilogue

Gloria speaking

On Amanda's first birthday, they have a party outside, two picnic tables set up on the good side of the house, the side where Gloria has dug and buried and planted. The phlox and the pansies hail her; tomatoes and green peppers grow abundant on the vine. She buries her scoop into the ice cream and watches Amanda, surrounded by playgroup friends. The cone hat cutting into the soft flesh under her chin, she pulls out the candle, grabbing it fast before anyone else and licks the frosting off the bottom. Thomas snaps a picture, and Gloria turns around with a puzzled look, her thoughts interrupted, stricken, diverted to the other side of the house, the side of loss.

Thomas comes up behind her, puts his arm around her waist. She knows he is wondering, with man guilt, if they will be together in the evening, if she will be able to come to him with the pain beyond words and affirm their love. He would say it doesn't matter, but she knows, she knows it does.

"Tonight she'll be exhausted," Gloria whispers into his ear. "I'll put her down early."

Nine years since the moon landing. Every year since they'd met, she and Thomas had made love on that day—except last year, when Amanda was born. They'd been convinced April Rainbow was conceived on this day in 1973 and laughed at the coincidence of Amanda being born on the day.

In the last few weeks, Gloria had continued to dig and plant, avoiding the other area of the yard, avoiding the memory bench, not speaking to the others of loss, speaking only of concerns of the living. What should we have for dinner? Should we go out for ice cream? Who would bring Amanda to play group? Her voice rose against the pain, words thrown into the air, words alone enough affirmation of life for all of them.

They did not force her to speak of it. Even her shrink sister didn't try to make her talk about what happened; they knew better or maybe were afraid. It was just as well. She didn't want to reveal herself to them, reveal the depth of her emptiness. It was something she didn't want to speak of. As she got up each morning and stood by the window, greedy for silence, she never stood long, not long enough for them to notice— not long enough for them to see that each morning, for a brief time, she became the woman at the window. Each morning, she decided again and again if she would let herself leap, the mass of her, crashing through the glass, the solid membrane, between the living and the dead, she could search out the spinning child.

Last year, as she had been birthing Amanda, April had pushed her way into the room, unwilling to wait outside, upset by her mother's screams. She watched patiently as Amanda was washed and placed into Gloria's arms. Then April had placed her chubby hand on Amanda's infant body. She stroked the downy hair, looked up at Gloria, and smiled. This would always be a day of celebration, for the sake of Amanda's birth, for the sake of April's smile.

Gloria wouldn't speak of sadness or loss, ever. She would keep her memories an abstraction to protect Amanda against the loss beyond sharing. This other child, held her here, gravitated her, kept her tethered to the present, while the Earth spun out away, every which way, into the galaxy.

Made in the USA
Lexington, KY
04 June 2017